Shadows of Chivalry

Not every knight is what he seems

Dana,
I'm so glad we got
meet! Can't wait to
see what your future
holds! Rachel

RACHEL MILLER

Published by Author Academy Elite
PO Box 43, Powell, OH 43065
www.AuthorAcademyElite.com

Identifiers:
LCCN: 2020918749
ISBN: 978-1-64746-530-8 (Paperback)
ISBN: 978-1-64746-531-5 (Hardback)
ISBN: 978-1-64746-532-2 (Ebook)

Scripture quotations from The Authorized (King James) Version. Rights in the Authorized Version in the United Kingdom are vested in the Crown. Reproduced by permission of the Crown's patentee, Cambridge University Press.

CHIVALRY

A Code of Conduct
rooted in the expected characteristics of a knight;

A Life Built Around
compassion, courage, and commitment to doing what is right,
walking in honor, justice, and courteousness;

Preparedness
to come to the aid of the weak, to defend the helpless,
vulnerable, and afflicted;

Devotion
to Christ, His people, and the work He has put before us.

DEDICATED

To Christ
who set the example of chivalry
and calls us to live it out day by day.

To all those who have risen to the challenge,
taken risks, and walked chivalrously
in my life and in the lives of those around me.
Especially to those "heroes"
who know the significance of Bus #123. *Spasibo!*
(Thank you.)

To Grant and Reese
As you step into these new chapters of your lives, go with courage,
seek to do right, defend the weak, live with honor, walk in love, fight
the good fight, find and finish your course, keep the faith—and never
be afraid to be the men God has created you to be.

ACKNOWLEDGMENTS

To each of you who has given your time to beta read, counsel,
correct, push, encourage, and keep me on track—
Thank you!

Anna, Mary, Jessica, Marta, Sarah,
Sherri, Candace, and the entire AAE team!

PROLOGUE

*Is the world completely devoid of knights in shining armor?
What has happened to chivalry, to valor, to strength in the face
of adversity?*

Kelly stopped typing. She stared at the screen, wondering if she
dared send her questions out into the world. With one click, she
could express the ache in her heart. But would she, in the same
moment, be condemning others? They had tried to help. In fact,
in their minds, they had done all they could. But it wasn't enough.
There had been no daring rescue, no fight to the end, no battle to
the death — not that she wanted anyone to die. That was what had
gotten them into this mess in the first place.

No, she didn't want anyone to die. She just wanted someone to
commit: to follow their pledge, to make their vow and see it through —
even if it meant personal sacrifice, even if it meant inconvenience
and hurt. She wanted one man to step up and stand. Just one.

CHAPTER 1

Kelly Vance shivered at the dark bus stop. Winter would never end, not this time around. She was sure of it. She was accustomed to snow, used to cold and wind, but enough was enough. She'd taken the bus four different times because her car wouldn't start in the cold. Next paycheck, she'd be getting that block heater her friends were always telling her she needed. That couldn't come soon enough.

A gust of wind dusted her face with a spray of icy snow. She sighed, wiping the moisture away and then tucking a lock of brown hair further under her white snow hat. She glanced up the street, taking in the mounds of plowed snow that tapered into the deep drifts blanketing her world. She sighed again. What difference would a block heater make? The snow was too deep, and the side streets had yet to be plowed. Her little car would never make it through.

A set of headlights appeared around the corner, and she squinted in their direction. Relief settled over her. Finally, bus #123 lumbered toward her.

"Good morning," a cheerful voice broke into Kelly's gloom.

She turned to see a smiling, blue-eyed man with a glow of cold in his cheeks.

"Bit nippy this morning, isn't it?" he continued, shoving his hands into his pockets and stamping his feet.

"A bit?" Kelly gasped. "It's fifteen below!"

The man laughed. "It could be twenty below. Then we'd really have something to complain about."

"I suppose you're right there."

"You don't usually take this bus, do you?" The man shivered as he stepped closer to Kelly and the curb.

"No. Just when my car won't start."

"Oh, so it's been one of those mornings, has it?"

"Unfortunately."

The man shrugged, and the leather computer bag at his side bounced up and down with the movement. "Maybe not unfortunately. My mom always used to tell me things like that could be God keeping us safe from something worse. It's His mercy, I suppose."

Kelly studied the stranger for a moment. He wasn't a big man, slightly under six feet, she guessed, and of slender build. He seemed sincere and full of energy. His eyes danced with kindness.

A smile slid across Kelly's face, lighting her dark eyes. "In every thing give thanks?"

"Exactly. Well, here she is," the man said as the bus slid to a stop. "Hope you have a pleasant day."

Kelly watched him climb aboard the bus, swipe his pass, and push his way to a back seat. *What an unusual man*, she thought. She couldn't help but wonder if he was always so cheerful, always searching for ways to cheer others.

"Are you getting on, or not?" The bus driver's bellow, so opposite the kindness she had just experienced, rattled her out of her trance.

"Yes, yes. I'm sorry. But I don't have a pass." She hurried up the steps, reaching into her pocket for the change she'd counted out before leaving home. "I'll have to buy one." She glanced over her shoulder and smiled. The kind man had seated himself beside an elderly woman. He was well on his way to brightening her weary face with his contagious grin.

❈ ❈ ❈

Kelly stepped through her office door. She peeled off the extra layers she had put on to keep warm, and then, realizing the heating system was down again, began putting the layers back on.

2

"Hope you have a pleasant day!" she mumbled, wishing the man's happiness could have preceded her and warmed her office. She groaned. "Make the best of it, Kelly. He was right. It could be much worse. Just make the best of it."

Contentment settled over her as she glanced around her small office. For six years, this had been more than her job. It had been her passion. The pay was minimal, especially for the number of hours she poured into it, but lives were being changed. That made it worth it. Not a day went by without her thoughts returning to the afternoon her best friend had invited her to the ChaiNook, sat her down, and altered the course of her life.

"I have a proposition for you," her friend had said. "It isn't the job you've always dreamed of, but it might advance that writing career you're always talking about starting."

Kelly chuckled at the thought of her beaming friend. She'd been so excited, so full of vision and hope.

"I've been promoted," she'd announced. "You're looking at the new Assistant Director of the Trevor Street Crisis Center! My first job is to hire someone to help us better connect with the community through blogging and social media. I want it to be you, Kelly. Please say yes!"

The rest was history. Kelly left her job managing the office of a small, stagnant thrift store and had spent the last six years telling the stories of the men, women, and children who found help, peace, and hope at the center. Now, joy climbed in Kelly's eyes at the thought. It was worth it. It was even worth the long wait for the bus in the freezing weather, followed by a long day in a freezing office.

A knock at the door pulled her thoughts to the present. She glanced up and saw her best friend, Kali Shepherd, through the tall, narrow window beside the door. As she waited, Kali cast a furtive glance around the main office. With each second, anxiety built in the lines of her face.

"What's gotten into her this morning?" Kelly wondered to herself. "Come in."

Kali hurried through the door, locking it behind her. She turned to face Kelly, eyes wide and face pale. For a moment, she stared at Kelly, shock apparent in every line of her slender frame. Then, somehow, the pretty blonde blurted out, "Sam's dead."

"What!"

"Shh. Keep your voice down. I don't want the others to hear—not yet."

But Kelly was too shocked to register her friend's concern for their officemates. "What are you talking about? Sam? Our Sam? Mr. Thompson? What do you mean he's dead? How can that even be possible?"

"His brother just called me."

"Micah?"

Kali nodded. "Sam wasn't at church, and he missed a family get-together with their cousins yesterday afternoon. So, Micah went over to check on him after the evening service. He found him—"

"Found him? What do you mean found him? Like he committed suicide found him or what?"

"No, no! It was an accident. They think he was cleaning the snow off his roof and slipped." Kali paused, her emotions beginning the swing from shock to sorrow. Tears crept into her eyes. "His house is so tall on that one side. Oh, Kelly, I hope he didn't suffer. I hope he didn't lay there crying out for help."

Kelly stared at her friend, still stunned by the news. How could this be happening? There must be some mistake. A noise in the office drew her eyes to the interior window. Her officemates were setting their day in motion, completely unaware their lives were about to change forever, unaware Mr. Thompson was gone.

Mr. Thompson. It was what they called him in the office as if he were very much their elder. But Sam was young, barely over forty. He was older than Kelly, yes, but he'd just been finishing college as she'd arrived. He'd given his entire life to making the center run, to changing lives. Sam had changed her life and taught her to hope when things seemed hopeless. That's what he'd want them to do now. But how could they? How could they carry on without him?

"What are we going to do?" she could hear the panic in her own whispered words.

"I don't know." Kali sank down into a chair near the door. "I don't even know how to tell the others. They're going to have so many questions. Questions for which I have no answers."

"Does the board know?"

"Not yet. Micah said he thought it would be best if I talked to them, but he wanted to come by and share a little more detail with us first. He's on his way over. He'll probably be here anytime." She paused considering her earlier conversation with Micah. "I think he was up all night. I wish he had called us and not handled it alone. It sounds like he has his hands full. He has the funeral to plan, but he has to wait until the autopsy is finished before he'll know when they can schedule it."

"Autopsy?"

"The police have to investigate. They have to rule out foul play."

"But who would want to hurt Sam? He's never hurt a soul in his entire life."

"I don't think they'll find anything. I'm sure it was an accident, but the police have to do their job. When Micah gets here, I'll need you to meet with us. You'll need to write the press release. Micah also mentioned he'd like your help with the obituary. I'm sorry, Kelly. I know that won't be easy."

Kelly's heart sat like a rock in her chest. She couldn't feel it beating. Maybe that was why she couldn't cry or feel the pain she would have expected in such a moment. Maybe her heart had stopped, died right along with Sam. But, no, she knew that wasn't true. It was still alive. She was still alive, and she would have to do this. She would have to bear the news to the world outside their walls: Sam—Mr. Thompson—was dead.

CHAPTER 2

"Thanks for meeting with us, Kelly. I can't begin to tell you how glad I am to see both of you and how grateful I am for your help." Micah Thompson pulled out the chair at the end of the long conference table and motioned for the two women to sit. "I still can't believe this is happening. I keep thinking I'm going to wake up from some bad dream." He paused to blow on his cold, red hands. He rubbed his hands together, then shoved them into his coat pockets. "Heat out again?"

Kelly nodded. The lump in her throat prevented her from speaking. Her heart broke at the sight before her. Normally, Micah was an effervescent, outgoing, incredibly diligent man. He was tall, muscular, and ready for just about any task you set before him — but today, he appeared broken. His face was pale. His eyes were red-rimmed and dull, void of their usual light and constantly on the verge of filling with tears. The dark circles beneath them confirmed Kali's earlier suspicions that he'd had no sleep the previous night.

As they'd walked through the main office to the conference room, he'd avoided eye contact with the others in the office. That wasn't like him. Like his brother, Micah generally sought out the people around him, asking about their lives and families, even their interests and hobbies if he knew the person well enough. This morning, however, he'd barely managed to stumble through small talk as the two of them had waited for Kali to finish a phone call with an area vendor.

"I want you to know that Sam—You both meant the world to him. I don't know how many times I'd be over at his house watching a football game, and he'd be telling me about things around here. He always talked through football for the sheer fact it wasn't baseball. Anyway, he'd always say, 'I don't know what I'd do without Kelly and Kali.' He always liked the way that sounded. 'Kelly and Kali,' like it was a trademarked brand or something."

The two women managed tight, nervous laughs. It was true. From the day they'd met, Sam had teased them about their names. He often said they'd become best friends just so people would get their names confused. "Kelly and Kali, Kali and Kelly," he would sing as he wandered through the building in search of them. Now, the very thought hurt.

"I'm not sure how much we should say to anyone as long as the police are still investigating," Micah continued, "but I don't want the staff here to find out via social media or the press or some other grapevine. They meant too much to Sam. They're as much family as I—was. I also don't want to leave you to share the news alone. That wouldn't be fair to you. Is everyone here today?"

"All of our core staff," Kali answered. "Well, except for Mac. He's in Florida visiting his daughter."

Micah nodded his understanding. "I think we should talk to them as soon as we're done here."

"Before we've talked to the board?" incredulity slipped into Kali's question before she could stop it.

"You haven't talked to them yet?"

Kali hesitated. She glanced at Kelly then back at her exhausted friend. "No...I thought you... I wanted to talk with you face to face first. I thought that's what you wanted, but maybe I misunderstood. They'll have a lot of questions. I'm not sure how to answer those questions, Micah."

"I'm sorry. I did tell you I wanted to talk to you first, didn't I?" He groaned and ran his hands through his dark hair. "I'm sorry. I'm having trouble keeping my mind focused. Everything is just...I don't know. I can't keep my mind on what's going on around me." In truth, Micah's mind kept racing back to the sight of his brother sprawled lifeless in the snow. The memory of the other man's cold skin beneath his touch as he checked for a pulse still radiated up his arm.

He forced his thoughts back to the present. Kali was right. There would be a lot of questions, a lot of decisions, a lot of changes. New grief drove a sharp pain through his heart. What would become of the center, of its staff—his best friends? He pushed the anguish back and sighed.

"Why don't we notify the board together before we talk to the rest of the staff? I wish I could tell you I plan to step into Sam's shoes and keep this place running, but I can't. My mom...she's taking it very hard." Again, he paused, drawing in a deep, steadying breath. "She wants Sam to be buried in Washington. Wants him closer to home. Dad wants me to come home and help for a while. I think he's overwhelmed by Mom's response.

"I put in for a six-month leave of absence at work before I came over here. My boss is checking for openings in their Seattle office that I might be able to transfer into, but I'm not holding my breath. I'm not sure I want to move back to Seattle anyway." Micah stopped, realizing he'd wandered into his own maze of decisions. "I'm sorry. We need to get back to things here. Kali, I know Sam would want you to take over, at least temporarily; and I'm pretty sure he'd want Kelly to step into your shoes. Do you think you can do that, Kelly, and still maintain the other position?"

Kelly nodded, still fighting tears. She didn't know if she could do it all, but she would do her best. For Sam and Micah and Kali, she would do her best.

"Do you mind writing the press release?"

"No. I don't mind. I'll come up with something and email it to you before I send it out. It shouldn't take me long. I'll keep it short."

Micah nodded then grimaced, "I kind of offered my parents your services in writing the obituary as well. I can find someone else to help if you're not comfortable with that."

"I would be honored, Micah. Your brother did so much for me. I'd like to do this one last thing for him."

A light of appreciation dared to glimmer in Micah's eyes. "Thank you," he whispered, "I'll help you."

"Has all of your family been notified, Micah? We don't want them finding out when the statement is released." Without realizing it, Kali was already stepping up, already showing the leadership Micah had known she would offer the organization.

"Yes. I did that early this morning. The only one who doesn't know is my cousin who's deployed in the Middle East. His wife already had a video call scheduled for tonight. She thought it would be best if she told him then. I think she's even going to try to get some advanced warning to his commander. Nick and Sam were pretty tight. I think it will hit him hard." He choked out the last sentence, wishing he could deliver the message in person, heart breaking over the knowledge that his cousin would have no one to share in his grief.

Kelly saw Kali take gentle hold of their friend's forearm. Micah looked up at Kali, a little surprised by the action.

"You're going to make it through this, Micah, you will. I know it doesn't feel like it right now, but you will."

The man's tears finally escaped. He wiped at them in embarrassment. "I know Sam's with the Lord, girls, but I'm just…I'm not ready for him to be gone."

Kali said something more, something soft and comforting. But Kelly didn't hear it. She was too busy wiping her own eyes and trying to contain the sobs that threatened. Kali had always been better at this sort of thing. As Kelly watched, however, she realized Kali was better at this for another reason. Something in her friend's eyes went far beyond friendship, and Micah's eyes returned it. Surprise flitted through Kelly's mind. The three of them were together nearly every day. How had she never seen that before?

"We should call the board members," Kali was saying. "We need to get moving before people start finding out through the grapevine as you put it, Micah. I think if we call Mr. Marsh, he can get the word out to the others."

Micah and Kelly nodded their agreement, but neither could speak. As they attempted to regain their composure, Kali placed her cellphone in the center of the table. She dialed the number and set the phone to speaker. They went through the line of receptionists and assistants at Marsh and Line Clothiers until, at last, Mr. Marsh's assistant had directed the call to the man himself.

"McKinsey Marsh speaking."

"Hello, Mr. Marsh, this is Kali Shepherd from the Trevor Street Crisis Center."

"Well, Kali! Hello! How are you this cold morning?"

"I'm... I'm okay, Mr. Marsh. How are you?"

"Couldn't be better. How can I help you?"

Kali hesitated. She glanced at Micah, but he nodded for her to proceed.

"I'm, um, well, I'm here with Kelly Vance and Micah Thompson. I'm... I'm afraid we have some bad news."

"Okay. I'm listening."

"Sam was doing some work on his house this weekend and fell."

"Is he all right?"

Kali hesitated again. She swallowed hard. "He's gone, sir."

The silence on the other end of the line was deafening. The trio in the conference room waited what seemed a very long time.

"Gone?" Marsh gasped at last. "Just like that?"

Micah leaned in toward the phone. "We're not really sure what happened, Mr. Marsh, but it appeared to me that he either fell from the roof or the ladder went out from under him as he was getting up on the roof."

"So, you were there?"

"No, sir. He wasn't answering any of my texts or calls, so I decided I should go to the house and see what was going on. That's...that's when —"

"I'm so sorry, Micah. I can't imagine how difficult that must be for you. I'm just...I'm so sorry. Can I do anything to help?"

"Well, Mr. Marsh," Kali stepped back in, seeing Micah was struggling to control his emotions, "we were hoping you might be able to contact the rest of the board members for us. At this point, we haven't made any other calls. We haven't even talked to our staff yet."

"Well, when you talk to them, tell them not to worry. I'll talk to the rest of the board. We'll stand behind you." Marsh hesitated but then pressed on with the confidence of a man who had faced more than one crisis. "I hate to ask this, but I know the other men will ask: Do you have any idea what you're going to do there at the center for the time being?"

Micah saw Kali begin to speak and reached out, taking her hand and stopping her. "Mr. Marsh, my brother trusted these two women sitting right here more than anyone else in this ministry."

"You're absolutely right there, Micah. I've never heard him say anything but good about either of them."

"I think, if he could choose, he would leave them in charge. So, I've asked Kali to step into the director's position and Kelly to step into the assistant director's position for the time being. Maybe that wasn't my place. I don't know. But I think it's what Sam would want. Down the road, I'm sure things will have to be revisited, and whether they stay in those positions or not will be up to them and the board. But for now, I think it's the wisest move. They know the staff and all of the programs. I know they will do very well."

"I agree. I know you girls are probably pretty overwhelmed at the moment, but Sam trusted you, Micah trusts you, and I trust you. I know you'll do fine. If there's anything I can do to help—anything— please call me. I'll even drive a shuttle car if you need me to."

The last statement brought an involuntary chuckle from Kali. The thought of the kind, fatherly man driving single moms and their children around town wasn't far-fetched, but when you considered he was one of the foremost businessmen in the city it changed the picture a bit.

"Thank you, Mr. Marsh," she said.

"You bet. And, Micah, again, I am so sorry. I'll be praying for your entire family."

"Thank you, sir."

"Kali, I'll get back with you as soon as I've notified everyone else. Talk to you soon."

As the call ended, Kali looked up from her phone to the others. She glanced toward the main office and back to her friends, her stomach knotting. "Now, for the really hard one. Are we ready for this?"

Kelly ran her fingers under her eyes, checking to make sure any trace of tears had been wiped from her face. "I don't think we'll ever be ready, but it has to be done. I'll go call everyone in."

CHAPTER 3

Even with the generous help of their board members and partners, the Trevor Street Crisis Center was generally understaffed and underfunded. Its conference room was a conglomeration of used furniture, discarded throw rugs, and donated coffee mugs, none of which matched. Its staffers were mostly volunteers or part-time employees. Some were there because they wanted to feel they had a purpose or were doing something good, but most were there out of passionate love for God and the people they served. They carried out their work with every ounce of life in them. Now, four of those staffers sat around the conference table, huddled deep in their coats, staring expectantly at Kali, Kelly, and Micah.

"I'm sorry, everyone," Kelly began. "We'll start in just a minute. Sarah is still on a call. We want to wait for her."

"I'm here!" Sarah, a pretty redhead, all but ran into the room, her cheeks decidedly rosy with embarrassment. She was new to the organization but not unfamiliar with it. More than once, Sam and the crisis center had come to her rescue. "I'm sorry. Oh! Micah! I didn't know you were here. You look exhausted…and a little stressed. I'm sorry I kept you waiting."

Micah smiled. "It's nice to see you, Sarah. You're not late. You were just doing your job."

Sarah blushed once again as she sank into a chair. Micah always seemed to excel in the area of people skills. He was always gregarious, always trying to make sure others felt comfortable and never ill at ease because of him.

Once the girl had found her seat, Kali glanced at Kelly and then at Micah. She took a deep breath and turned to face the others. "I'm not really sure how to start this. …Mr. Thompson…Sam…Sam was in an accident over the weekend. He was working on his house, and something went wrong."

"Is he all right?" Brandon, a stylish but somewhat awkward college student, leaned forward in his seat as he spoke. His eyes fixed on Kali. "What happened? Was he hurt?"

Kali held up a hand to forestall the questions she knew were coming. Tears rose in her eyes. For the first time since Micah had arrived, she felt she might lose her composure. She bit her lip and then in little more than a whisper managed, "Mr. Thompson passed away."

Five sets of shocked, horrified eyes stared back at the threesome at the head of the table.

"Passed away? But how? *How* did this happen?" Brenda fired the questions at Micah indignantly, almost as if he had perpetrated the act. The sharp words were uncharacteristic of the kind, middle-aged woman and caught Micah off guard.

"I-I'm not sure," he faltered. "Sam fell. I'm not sure how it happened. …He just fell."

Brandon was out of his seat now and pacing behind the empty chair at the foot of the table. "What's going to happen to the center?"

"We're going to do our best to keep going," Kali replied. "That's what Sam would want us to do."

"For now," Micah began, "I've asked Kali to take Sam's place as director. Kelly will step into Kali's position as best she can with her other responsibilities. Eventually, I'm sure the board will meet to determine if that's a suitable solution. They may want to bring in someone else to run things. You never know."

"But who could ever run this place besides Sam?" Brenda was on the verge of breaking. It was evident in every movement, every word. "He *was* this place. He built it from a little ministry out of his car to what it is today. No one will ever be able to do what he did."

13

Micah blinked back tears. The woman's admiration for his brother touched him deeply. He understood her initial outburst. He'd felt it too, still did in fact. He swallowed back the pain rising in his chest and throat.

"You're right, Brenda, no one will ever replace Sam. No one will ever do things like he did them, including Kali, but he would want the center to keep going. He wouldn't want everything to stop just because he's gone. It would've grieved him if that happened."

"Brenda," Kali said, "we're going to face a lot of questions, a lot of unknowns, but God will lead us through them, just as He always has. Everything else may change, but He will not."

Tears streamed down Brenda's face. She nodded but could not speak.

Sharon, Brenda's desk mate, reached for her friend's hand then pulled back, unsure and paralyzed by the other woman's raw emotions. She said nothing.

The room fell silent. Kelly watched as her friends processed the news of their loss. She saw pain, regret, sorrow, and a myriad of other emotions creep into their eyes. Shoulders stooped. Long, deep breaths were taken and let out slowly. Tears were wiped away.

"What do you want us to do today?" Gil, the ever-practical, ever-dependable accountant broke the silence.

"Um," Kali hesitated, running a hand through her thick, curly blonde hair, "for now, just work on whatever you were working on… if you can. I understand if you just need to step out for a while—for the whole day if necessary. Kelly is going to be working with Micah on the press release and obituary. Once the press release is out, it's possible we may have some calls to field. Sarah, don't worry, I won't leave that to you. Just forward them to me. I wouldn't expect too much activity though until tomorrow. By then, the community will have begun to hear the news. I'm sure a few people Mr. Thompson worked closely with will want to know more, will want to help the family or send flowers. We may be swamped tomorrow."

Brandon moved toward the head of the table, his ordinarily bright eyes shadowed with emotion. "When is the funeral?"

Micah swiveled in his chair to better face the younger man. "We're not sure yet, but it will probably be in Washington. When we're done, I'm going to talk to Pastor Hanson and Pastor Meeks about having a memorial service here in town. This is where Sam's life was. We need to do something here. He had very few friends, and even less family, left back home — just my parents and my other brother's family. But I think my mom needs him to be close. She's pretty devastated."

"I'd be willing to put together a memory video if you want." A glimmer had returned to Brandon's eyes. This was his part at the center. It was something he was good at, and, like Kelly, he felt it was his last chance to do something for the man who had done so much for him.

"That would be wonderful, Brandon. I'll have my sister-in-law go by my folks' house and see if we can't get some pre- Trevor Street pics to you."

Brandon nodded with enthusiasm. "I'll start pulling images together. You guys just let me know how long to make it and what music you want me to use."

"Can we do anything to help your family, Micah?"

"We'll let you know, Sarah. I'm not sure what's going to happen. Thank you for being willing to help. I just, I honestly don't know. It's like there's this big empty question mark in front of us."

The room fell silent again at those words. Micah never talked like that. He was always positive, always saw the possibilities in a situation. For the first time, the five staffers saw the personal toll their friend's grief was beginning to take on him.

"Micah," Brenda said, "swing by here this evening. I'll go back to the kitchen this afternoon and make something for your dinner. I'll make extra in case you have other family members or even friends to feed."

"Thank you, Brenda. That would be an enormous blessing. I'll call in later and find out how it's going. I'll let you know how many people if it's more than just me. I want to keep a couple of my cousins close right now. They're pretty torn up."

"Sounds good. I'll be waiting for your call."

Micah turned his attention back to the group. "I know we all need to get busy, but there's one thing I want to say before we go. ...I want you all to know how much you meant to my brother. I can't fully express it. I'm not even sure he could do that. But, this…this right here was his life, and it wasn't this building or this ministry or the people whose lives you touch every day—it was you. Each and every one of you.

"We'd get together on the weekends or in the evenings, and he'd be talking about you, concerned for your welfare, praying for needs you had shared with him." He paused, his mind wandering back to college days. "A long time ago, before he started the center, it used to bother me the way he cared so much about other people. He seemed so focused on meeting other people's needs…like he was obsessed. At times, I thought he was so wrapped up with others that he would lose his love for us, his family. But little by little, I realized he hadn't forgotten us. He'd just added everyone else to our family. He truly loved each and every one of you. …You made a difference in his life. …You…"

Micah's voice trailed off. His gaze dropped to the table. Kelly saw Kali slip her hand over his.

"It's okay, Micah," Kali whispered. "Thank you."

Tears slid down every cheek in the room.

Sharon jumped to her feet, sending her chair rolling back toward the wall. "I think we should get back to work." The thin, middle-aged woman spun away from the table and fled the room.

Brenda rose slowly. "I'll check on her. Micah, I'm so sorry for your loss." She went to Micah's side, wrapped her arms around him, and held him tight.

The man barely contained the emotion that threatened to rush out of him at her embrace. But somehow, he kept it in check.

"We love you, Micah," she whispered, and then she was gone.

Micah rose as the other staffers followed Brenda's example, Brandon with a quick hug, Sarah with a tight, desperate squeeze that he might have expected from someone who had lost their own father. Finally, Gil stood before him, big, sloppy, and above all else faithful.

If Micah stood 6'4," Gil easily came in at 6'7." He slouched, as was his usual stance. Tears streamed freely down his face, and his lips quivered. The big man felt Kelly and Kali's uneasiness as they watched. His pinched face muscles ached with the effort of finding words in the storm of his emotions, but there were none. Neither a single word nor a thousand words combined could express the tangle in his heart.

He stepped forward, pulling his friend into a massive bear hug, and thumping him heartily on the back as if to express the comfort he seemed unable to speak. Then he stepped back and, with one massive hand still on his friend's shoulder, whispered, "We're in this together…all the way. Where we can't carry each other, God is already carrying us."

He ran his sleeve across his streaming eyes and stepped through the office door, leaving the three friends alone again.

CHAPTER 4

Kelly sat quietly in her seat, her mind absorbed by the events of the day. The bus rocked back and forth as it lumbered through one intersection after another, but she didn't notice the motion. Her thoughts still whirled with the news they'd received. She couldn't believe it was true. It couldn't be. But it was. *Why? Why would God take one of His most faithful men—and especially so young?* Kelly sighed, wiping away the tears that trickled down her cheeks. She felt someone slide into the seat beside her but didn't turn to greet them. Instead, she turned her face to the frosty window, hoping they wouldn't notice her tears.

"Something tells me your day never got any better."

Kelly spun around at the voice. To her surprise, the cheerful man who had greeted her at the bus stop that morning sat beside her. This time, however, his blue eyes weren't smiling. Instead, they swam with concern.

"Are you all right?"

"No. No, I can honestly say I am not all right."

"Want to talk about it?"

Kelly studied the man for a moment. His features were kind. He had been kind to her that morning and seemed honest and trustworthy, but she knew nothing about him.

"It's okay if you don't want to talk. I can pray without knowing details."

"You would do that?"

The man shrugged. "Why not?"

"But you've never met me before. You don't know anything about me."

"Sure, I've met you before. I met you this morning."

Despite Kelly's confusion and grief, the man's words pulled a short laugh out of her. "You know what I mean."

"See," he teased, "you're smiling already."

Kelly wiped at her damp cheeks. She bit her lip then started to speak, but the very thought of forming the words one more time brought tears again.

The man's eyes shadowed. "You're really upset. What happened?"

Kelly hesitated. "My—" she started to say boss, but Sam had been more than that to all of them. "My friend had an accident over the weekend. He died. He was so young, barely over forty. I just don't understand it. I just..." her stomach tightened. "It takes my breath away and hurts so bad. I can't even describe it."

The man sat motionless, stunned at her news. He said nothing, but his eyes told her to go on.

"I helped his brother write the obituary. I've written a lot of things, but that was the hardest thing I've ever written. His brother stepped out of the room at one point. We'd been talking about their childhood." Tears cut her words short. She fiddled with the strap of her red, leather purse. "I could hear him in the bathroom—sobbing."

Kelly's voice trailed off, but her seatmate only waited, somehow knowing she had more to say.

"You know how people say, 'He'd give you the shirt off his back'?"

"Yes."

"I saw him do it once."

"What?"

"We were delivering Thanksgiving baskets to families in a low-income neighborhood. At one house, the teenage son was headed out to work, but his mother felt he was underdressed for the weather. We were at the door with the father and could hear them arguing in the kitchen. Finally, we heard the boy say, 'Mom, I don't have a warmer sweater. This is all I've got.' That's when my friend called the boy out, looked him over, and said, 'I think this'll fit.'

"He took off his coat and scarf, pulled his sweater off, and handed it to the boy. Just like that. Later, when I mentioned it, he just shrugged it off and said, 'I have so many sweaters at home. I can't even get them in my drawers. There wasn't anything special about giving him that sweater.' I couldn't believe it."

"Wow." The man shook his head in amazement. "I'm so sorry for your loss. I wish I'd had a chance to meet your friend. He sounds like a good man."

"He was." The words left a bad taste in Kelly's mouth and an absolute repulsion in her heart. "How is it that one minute we *are* and the next minute we *were*? Just like that our entire life is in the past tense as if already in the process of being forgotten."

"You won't forget, and neither will his family. That boy will never forget. You can bet on it."

Kelly nodded, once more wiping her eyes. "You're right. I know you are."

"Here's our stop."

"What?"

"Are you getting off where you got on this morning?"

"Yes."

"Then this is our stop. Can I carry something for you?"

"No, no. I've got it."

The man stood and stepped back, letting her pass and then following her off of the bus. They stood silently on the icy sidewalk as the bus grumbled away.

"Thank you for listening," Kelly managed when the world had quieted around them. "You didn't have to do that, but you did. Thank you."

"We all need a listening ear from time to time. Who are you going home to? I'd hate for you to be alone tonight. You're more than welcome to have supper with my father and me."

"Thank you, but I'm exhausted. I just want to go home, have a nice warm bowl of soup, and crawl under the blankets until morning."

"Are you sure?"

Kelly nodded.

"Okay. But the offer stands."

"How do you know we'll ever see each other again?"

He shrugged, his blue eyes twinkling. "I have a feeling about these kinds of things. Go home. Get some rest. Spend some time with God."

"You know nothing about me. What makes you think I would spend time with God?"

"Your response this morning. '*In every thing give thanks.*' It's straight from the Bible."

Kelly blushed and bit the corner of her mouth. He was right; she *had* said that. "Somehow that answer doesn't seem so easy tonight," she admitted.

"No, I'm sure it doesn't, but it still applies—as heartless as that may sound. I'll be praying for you. When is the funeral?"

"The funeral won't be here, but there will be a memorial service Wednesday."

"That's quick."

"His brother needs to get to Washington so he can help his parents plan the funeral."

"I see. Well, if you ever need to talk," he pointed at the bus stop sign over their heads. "I'm pretty easy to find."

"Thank you. I'll remember that." She offered the man a faint but grateful wave and then disappeared down the dark sidewalk that led home, daring to hope they'd meet again.

CHAPTER 5

Matt stepped through the front door of his father's house. He flipped on the entry light and tossed his leather bag onto a shelf near the door.

"Dad? Are you home?" He waited, but no answer came. "Guess it's just me tonight. ...Time for some supper. What to eat?" The man removed his coat and scarf and hung them on the coat rack opposite the shelf where his bag had taken up residence. The action sent his mind wandering back to the bus. He thought of the sweater the woman's friend had given away. *That* was love. The kind of love he only wished was in his own life.

He left the entryway and wandered through the dark house to the kitchen. He switched on the light and let his gaze sweep around the large, empty room. On nights like this, the sense of his mother's absence was sharp.

"Mom," he said as though the woman were at the stove, "I'd like some of your beef stew for dinner. Yep, that's what I want. Don't have any? Well, this stuff in the can will have to do then."

"Talking to yourself again?"

Matt spun around, can of soup in hand. "Dad! I didn't hear you come in." He felt his cheeks redden at the thought he'd been caught talking to the empty room. Then he grinned, knowing his father was prone to do the same. "I was just telling Mom I'd like some of her beef stew."

"Mm. Me too. But I see you're settling for exactly what I had in mind. Got enough for two there?"

"For sure." Matt set the large can of soup down on the counter and went in search of the can opener.

"So," his father began in an exaggerated tone, "was today your bus day?"

Matt grinned. "Yes, today was a bus day."

"And?"

"You should come with me someday."

"Ah, I can't move as fast as you. You're cut out for these adventures. I'm too old."

"You'd do fine."

The younger man went about his cooking, dumping the soup into a pot and locating a ladle with which to stir it, almost as if he'd forgotten his father's question. His father, on the other hand, had forgotten nothing. He watched Matt for a moment. He could see an uncommon heaviness about his son.

"What's bothering you?" he asked at last.

"What?"

"Was your 'spying' a bad experience today? Bad day at the office?"

"No. Work was fine. ...I met this girl on the bus this morning. At the stop, actually. I've never seen her before. Her car had broken down, so she rode. Anyway, she was pleasant but seemed a little stressed."

"Well, what did you do about it?"

Matt laughed. His father never gave him the option of sitting still when a need was at hand, especially when it involved women and children.

"I told her what Mom always used to say about delays and difficulties being God's mercies."

"And?"

"She said, '*In every thing give thanks.*' Then the bus came, and we got separated."

The older man waited, certain there would be more to the story, but Matt said nothing. "Seems like a good answer to me. Seems like a normal conversation, so why has it stuck with you?"

23

"Because she was on the bus tonight as well. …She was crying."

The white-haired man slid onto one of the tall bar stools surrounding the island in the center of the kitchen, his gaze growing serious. "Why was she crying?"

"She lost a friend. She was so broken. He sounded like a good man. She told me about how he literally gave someone the shirt off his back. …I hated to send her home alone. I offered her supper with us, but she said she just wanted to go home. I can't blame her. She doesn't know us. I would have said no in her place too. …I think I'll be riding the bus a bit more in the next few weeks. Just in case she needs a friend."

"What was her name?"

"I don't know. We didn't really talk about her. Just about him and how senseless it seemed that someone so kind would be gone so young."

"So, he was young?"

"Yes. Sounded like he was just a couple years older than me. … Why do you ask?"

"Was it unexpected, an accident?"

"I think so. Why?"

"Because I think I know who she was talking about."

Matt's ladle clanked against the side of the soup pot as he let go to spin toward his father.

"What? How could you know?" But as soon as he saw the mist over his father's blue eyes, he understood. The other man's words only confirmed it.

"It's all over the local news this evening. I suppose since you rode the bus you didn't hear it."

Matt stared at his father, his thoughts racing and breath catching in his chest. "You knew him, didn't you?"

The older man nodded. "I knew him."

CHAPTER 6

"How in the world does this program work?" Kelly stared at the computer screen, muttering in frustration.

It had been a week. The "few" people Kali had expected to call or drop by had turned out in droves. The newspaper and local TV stations had called for interviews. Even the Christian radio station had come by to do a story on Sam and the legacy he left behind in the form of the crisis center. In short, life had been chaotic and greatly lacking the one person who normally would have calmed the storm.

The memorial service had gone well with over four hundred people in attendance. Everyone was grateful for Brandon's suggestion to record the service. The day had turned into a celebration. Yes, there was weeping, but one person after another told stories of how Mr. Thompson had let God work through him to change their life.

"This will be good for my mom to see," Micah had said as he packed the DVD into his bag before leaving the church. "I want her to see how many lives Sam touched. I want her to know that, even though it was shorter than we wanted, his life wasn't wasted. In fact, I'd say he made better use of his forty years than most men make of seventy."

Micah had already been in Washington for four days. The funeral was over. He'd emailed that it had gone well. The church he'd grown up in had rallied around the family. The formalities were over, but the pain had not left.

The week at the crisis center had been overwhelming: Phones ringing off the hook while community members, former staffers, current and past clients stopped by to offer their condolences. Several clients had begged them not to close the center. The needs in the community didn't stop just because they were grieving.

An expectant mother had come in with no place to live. She sobbed at the thought that she would lose her baby to the state if she didn't have a place to take him when he came into the world.

A veteran had limped in, almost by accident. He was new in town and looking for Job Services. The bits and pieces of his story further shattered their hearts. His tale of lost friends and broken family ties hit them all hard. When they'd told him their director had just passed away, he'd stared in horror. Tears rolled down his cheeks.

"I'm so sorry," he whispered, "I know your pain." He'd stood and laid a strong hand on Kelly's shoulder. "I won't trouble you any further today. I'll be back in a week or two. When you've had a little more time. Thank you for still being here for the rest of us when you're hurting, but don't forget to take care of yourselves." Then he limped out, leaving them in tears.

The remainder of the week had been increasingly difficult. Everyone was exhausted and emotional. They'd been on the verge of arguing several times. Finally, Kali had sent everyone home Saturday afternoon. Most of the staff had chosen to take today, Monday, off as well. In fact, everyone was gone but Kelly and Kali.

"How's it going?" Kali asked as she stepped into Kelly's office.

"How do you use this program? I can't figure anything out. I'd like to throw the whole computer out the window."

"Then just wait until Gil gets here tomorrow. I couldn't figure it out either."

"But don't we need to know where we are financially? The board members have been calling all morning. I think I've talked to every single one of them."

"Yes, but if we can't figure it out today, we—and they—will just have to wait."

Kelly groaned in defeat. "Well, what else should I be working on then?"

"That's an enormous question?" Kali dropped into the chair beside the door and heaved a tremendous sigh. "I don't know where to begin. I need to go through Sam's desk, make sure we haven't missed any urgent tasks, but I'm so tired. I can't even pull my thoughts together."

Kelly studied her friend for a moment, concern building in her heart. "How are you really, Kali? I mean, Sam and I were friends for as long as you were, but you worked with him so closely for so many years. I know you were close—"

"Oh, Kelly. You and Sam were just as close. He had such respect for you. Not just respect—love. You were family to him. Just like Micah said."

"But that's the thing."

"What?"

"I think you and Micah are pretty close too."

Kali blushed and let her gaze drop to her lap. "So, you did notice."

"You're my best friend! Of course, I noticed...but not until he was here, and we were talking about Sam."

"We've been seeing one another for a while now. We haven't said much to anyone other than our parents because we didn't want the pressure. Neither of us is as young as we once were. The teasing didn't appeal to us, but we were serious."

"Were?"

Kali squirmed in her seat. "I don't know what's going to happen any more than he does. His mom is so broken, Kelly. I talked with her for a while on the phone last night. She just sobbed. ...I don't know. I couldn't help her. Micah told me she isn't really functioning at all. Just completely in a fog. His dad is so heartbroken both by the loss and by watching his wife grieve."

"Maybe you should go out there?"

Kali shook her head. "No. I need to be here. I can't leave you with everything."

"I wouldn't be alone. The others are here. We'd be okay. Maybe they need you more than we do, Kali."

But Kali shook her head even more emphatically than before. "No. We talked about it last night and agreed this is best. Micah is hoping to be back in a couple of weeks for a few days. We're going to decide then what we should do. That will give us a better picture of how things are playing out on both ends."

"Are you sure?"

"I'm sure."

Kelly considered her determined friend for a moment. She loved Kali like the sister she'd never had. She had known her since college and knew every line of her face. Today, those lines told her that, while her friend would pull out a valiant effort to fight through her pain, inside she was falling apart and completely exhausted.

"Kali, I know your apartment is just as empty as mine. Do you want to come stay with me for a couple days?"

The blond woman grew thoughtful. She considered the prospect with pursed lips, weighing the comforts of her friend's companionship against the discomforts of a night on an unfamiliar bed. "Maybe. But not tonight. Tonight, I just want to go home and go to bed."

"I know. Me too. ...Did Sam know? About you and Micah?"

Kali chuckled. "Sam knew before Micah and I knew. We were going to tell you that week, but when Micah had to leave, we decided not to say anything to anyone."

"I figured it was something like that. I wish he weren't so far away."

The conversation lulled for a moment. Kelly didn't want to add to Kali's load, but she felt she must tell her what she'd been seeing. She cleared her throat and fiddled with a small pile of paper clips that had spilled out onto her desk. Glancing up at Kali and then back to the paper clips, she said, "I think we're going to lose Sarah."

"What? What makes you think that?"

Kelly shrugged. "Sam brought her here. He invested a lot in her. He's the one who convinced her to stay in school with the promise he'd give her a job when she was done. He always made sure she got to her school activities. He made sure she got to church. He even made sure she enrolled in college this year.

"I think she's feeling like a ship adrift without him. I've caught her several times just staring at his office door. ...Not that I haven't done the same a time or two myself. ...But she's starting to distance herself from the rest of us...especially Brandon. She won't even talk to him unless she has to. I'm not sure she's going to stick it out."

"We can't let her go," Kali said, leaning forward in her seat with an urgency that betrayed her love for the girl. "If we let her go, she'll go back to her old friends. They'll drag her down, right back where she was when we met her. We can't let that happen."

"I know. That's what worries me the most. It's one thing to lose Sarah's help around the center. It's another thing to lose Sarah."

Kali stood and began pacing, anxiously pulling at the hem of her shirt. "Do you think I should call her? Maybe we need to talk."

"I'll do it. If you don't mind handling things here alone. I'll take her to the ChaiNook. I'm pretty sure that's her favorite tea place. I don't think she's a coffee drinker."

Kali stopped her pacing. She stared at her friend and then burst into laughter. "*You're* not a coffee drinker. That's why you don't want to go for coffee."

"See," Kelly rebutted, "Sarah and I are the perfect match! Who needs coffee! ...So, do you mind?"

"I don't mind at all. She's far more important than all the other stuff going on here today."

"Okay. But, Kali, please lock the doors."

"What? Why?"

"Sam always said if we were here alone, we needed to lock the doors."

"But what if someone needs help. It's not like it's after dark or something."

Kelly looked up from the text she was sending Sarah and cast a disapproving glance in her friend's direction. She switched off her computer, stood, and moved to the coat rack. "Just do it, Kali. Don't let anyone in you don't know. Trevor Street isn't exactly the suburbs, and you know it."

"Fine. I'll lock the doors."

"Okay. I'll go get Sarah and be back in about an hour and a half."

"Your car is running?"

Kelly stopped her planned exit and stared at her friend. "I forgot that little detail. Well, I'll see if she wants to meet me at a bus stop."

"Take my car. I'll go get the keys. ...What did they say about your car anyway?"

"Ugh. It's going to be a while before it runs again. Our guys said they could repair it, but I'm fourth in line after the center's vehicles and a couple of our single moms. Not to mention the cost of the parts. If my dad were around, he could fix it. But since he's all toasty warm in Arizona, I'm stuck."

Kali laughed. "I'm sorry. I know it's not funny that you have to take the bus everywhere, especially with as cold as it's been the last couple of weeks… but the way you said it! Knowing your dad, he's enjoying that sunshine." She giggled once more. "I'm sorry. I'll go get my keys."

❄ ❄ ❄

Kelly waited at a table near the front of the ChaiNook. She played with the edge of the napkin that lay under her cup as she glanced out the window. It was snowing—again. She groaned. She liked snow. She really did. Just not this much snow. Her eyes scanned the parking lot for some sign of Sarah. The girl had just finished a class and was waiting for her brother to pick her up when Kelly had called her. She'd texted a few minutes later to say her brother would drop her off at the ChaiNook while he ran a couple of errands. Now, Kelly waited. She'd been waiting for about twenty minutes. She wondered if Sarah's brother had decided his tasks were more important. Maybe he'd decided not to bring Sarah after all. It wouldn't be unlike him.

"There you are."

Kelly turned toward the voice. "Sarah! How did I miss you coming in? I was watching for you. Have you already ordered?"

"No. I saw you and came right over."

"Well, let's go get you something. What would you like?"

"What are you having?"

"A London Fog."

"Ew. I'm not much of an Earl Grey fan. I think I'll have that one with the caramel in it. What's it called? You know, the one with the caramel and pecan flavoring?"

"Oh, I know what you're talking about. I wish I had thought of that before I ordered. I love a good London Fog, but that—whatever it's called—is heavenly. Here, have a seat. I'll order for you."

"Are you sure? I don't mind getting it myself."

"Nope. I invited you, so it's my treat."

Sarah seated herself. While she waited, she glanced around at the other customers. The shop was quiet, which she guessed was typical for a Monday afternoon. Three women sat in low armchairs in the far corner of the room, their Bibles and study books spread out on a coffee table between them. A businessman and his newspaper, behind which he seemed to be hiding, warmed themselves in the corner where a TV silently broadcast the weekend's sports results. She squinted to read the subtitles on the screen.

"What are you looking at?"

Only as she turned to answer Kelly did Sarah realize she was on the verge of tears. Her lip trembled, and she swallowed hard before saying, "They're talking about the upcoming baseball season. Mr. Thompson would have been over there as soon as he realized what they're talking about." She wiped her eyes and looked away.

"You're right. He would've been. That was the only sport he ever talked about with real passion. I think Micah wrangled him into watching football, but Sam was a baseball man."

"Sometimes I wondered why he didn't quit his job at the center and become a reporter or something so he could be at all the games."

Kelly chuckled as she set Sarah's cup down on the table. She took a sip of her own drink and then sat down. "How are you doing, Sarah?"

The girl let her gaze drop, ashamed at the answer she knew to be true.

"I know you're hurting, Sarah, just like the rest of us. I wanted to make sure you had someone to talk to if you needed to talk."

"Thanks. I'm okay, just shocked. I don't understand the whole thing. Mr. Thompson was the best man I have ever known. Why would God take him? We needed him. We still need him."

"I know. I don't understand it either. I really don't think we're meant to understand why. I mean, I think God might give us some glimpses down the road, but only He knows the real reasons. We can't see from start to finish, only He can."

"I know." Sarah wiped the tears from her face and began digging through her backpack for a Kleenex.

"Here, I'll grab some napkins." Kelly jumped up and went to the condiment station in the middle of the shop, where she grabbed a handful of napkins. Her hurried trip across the room caught the attention of several other customers, but she didn't care. Her friend needed napkins. She rushed back and handed the wad of rumpled tissue to Sarah.

"Thank you. I'm sorry. I'm such a mess."

"*Oh*, Sarah. Don't apologize. We're all a mess!"

"Not you and Kali. I haven't seen either of you lose it like this. I don't know how you do it. You just keep going, doing everything you used to do plus everything Mr. Thompson used to do, plus everything new. I can't even sit at my desk without feeling like everything inside of me is going to fall apart and ooze out where everyone can see it."

She paused to blow her nose but found the napkins were never meant for that.

"They're waxy, aren't they?" Kelly asked apologetically, sliding to the edge of her chair as she did so. "I could grab some toilet paper if you want."

Sarah burst into laughter. "No! That's okay. I'll be fine with my waxy napkins."

"Just thought I'd offer." Kelly shrugged off her friend's response with a grin. Even she had to admit the idea of traipsing across the room with a handful of toilet paper streaming out behind her was a bit embarrassing. She cleared her throat and settled back in her seat. "How are things at home, Sarah?"

Sarah shrugged. She pulled the lid off her latte and blew on the frothy liquid. Tears slipped down her cheeks again.

"They don't understand. 'He was just your boss,' they say. 'Why does it bother you so much?' They don't know what he did for me. And they don't care. I tried to explain it to both my mom and my brother, but they think I'm ungrateful to them."

"In what way?"

"Well, they're the ones who put a roof over my head, who keep food on the table. I contribute, but they contribute more. They think I don't appreciate it."

"Do you?"

"Of course I do. I do, Kelly."

"But?"

"But they do those things because they feel they have to not because they love me. They've just always felt it was their duty. They didn't care if I went to school. When I was little, they didn't even get me up in the morning. I had to do it myself. They didn't make sure I made it to the bus, I did. They didn't come to my band performances or Christmas programs—but Mr. Thompson did. He actually cared what happened. He made sure I got to church. He made sure I finished my school assignments. I always acted like it bugged me when he asked if I had my homework done, but secretly, it made me feel loved—like someone actually cared. He did so many things no one else ever did for me. …Did you know he bought the dress I wore to my graduation?"

"No. I didn't know that."

"Yes, and not just mine. He bought Anthony's suit and Michael's shoes. He must have helped at least six or seven of us, just from my school. I don't know about the other schools. Michael never would have won the science fair if it hadn't been for Mr. Thompson. Michael had the idea, and all the research was done, but he didn't have the money to buy the supplies for his display. So, Mr. Thompson got him help through the center's education fund."

"Education fund?"

"Yes. That's what Michael told me. He said the center has access to an education fund, and Mr. Thompson was able to get the funds for the project. I'm sure that's where my scholarship came from too. …But that's the thing, Mr. Thompson always went out of the way for us. He actually cared."

A deep, painful longing filled Kelly's heart. She'd never met anyone who cared for others the way Sam had, no one. "He cared about a lot of people," she whispered.

"It didn't matter who you were," Sarah added. "He loved you like you were his brother or sister or best friend."

"I know. I've never met anyone like him. I doubt I ever will."

"I'm *sure* I won't. I don't know what I'm going to do."

"What do you mean?"

"Mr. Thompson was the only one who ever believed in me. My family doesn't care if I finish college or not. They want me to drop out and get a real job."

"A real job?"

"They said working at the center is a waste of time. John says there's no room for advancement, so I should just go find something else."

"But Sarah, what you're learning at the center could prepare you for so many other jobs. You're the best administrative assistant we've had since I've been there, and that's a long time. Honestly, you've taken on so much, I almost feel like we should change your title."

"That's what Brenda told me too."

"Well, she's right. We need you, Sarah, and it sounds to me like you need us. Please, don't give up."

"I don't want to quit. I'm afraid if I quit working at the center, I'll quit everything else too."

"Then don't quit. Stay with us. You have my number. Call me anytime you need me. Even if you just need someone to talk to."

"Can you pick me up for church on Sunday?"

"Of course — Well, maybe not. My car is still broken. But I'll bet Kali can. I drove her car here. I'll let her know you need a ride and have her give you a call."

"Okay. ...Thank you, Kelly. I needed this." Sarah's phone buzzed. She took a moment to read the incoming text. "I need to go," she said with disappointment. "My brother is waiting. I told him we'd probably only be a half hour. I should have told him an hour, but I was afraid he would say no."

"That's okay. I'm just glad we had the time we had. See you tomorrow, right?"

"I'll be there."

The two women hugged. Kelly watched her friend hurry out, and then cleaned up the mess of napkins she'd left behind on the table. As she crossed the room to a trash can, she had the strange feeling someone was watching her, but when she looked around everyone seemed preoccupied with their own business. She shrugged off the feeling, grabbed her coat and purse from the table, and headed out into the cold.

CHAPTER 7

Matt leaned over his desk, forehead resting in his hands, eyes fixed on the sheet of paper before him with intense concentration.

"Hey, boss."

The man's gaze came up to his assistant, but the shadows in his eyes betrayed his distraction.

"Everything okay, boss?"

"Yeah. Why do you ask?"

The tall, slender woman shrugged. "You look a little stressed."

"Oh. I'm fine. Just thinking…sometimes that is a little stressful." He grinned at his own joke and tossed his pen down on the desk. "How can I help you, Mel?"

"I just wondered if you needed anything else before I head home."

"Is it that time already?"

"Actually, it's almost seven."

"Seven! How did that happen?"

"Pretty much the same way it happens every day. Those hands just keep marching around the clock."

"It's no wonder I'm having trouble thinking. My brain needs a break."

"So, I can go?"

"Yes, please. I am sorry to keep you so late."

"Oh, you didn't keep me. I have my own stack of stuff to deal with."

"All right, well, have a good evening."

"Thanks. Don't stay too long."

"I won't. Good night, Mel."

Matt watched the young woman slip out the door and past the glass walls separating his office from the rest of the accounting department. She gathered a few items from around her desk, shoved them into her purse, and then, catching his eye before stepping onto the elevator, waved goodnight and was gone. He returned the gesture with a grin. She'd always puzzled him a bit. Her eclectic sense of style and nonchalant approach to life seemed out of place in this crazy, high-strung corporate world, but he'd never had a better assistant—anywhere. He was grateful for her, blue heels, orange skirts, lavender vintage blouses, and all.

Many of the lights had already been switched off, leaving the modern, brightly painted suite of offices as forlorn and empty as if the interior had been designed and left to itself three decades ago. *Yellow,* he mused, *why did they paint the whole department that horrid shade of yellow.* He glanced down at the spreadsheet he'd been studying a moment before and sighed.

"No sense fussing over this tonight. It'll still be here in the morning."

Within five minutes, he had the entire department put to bed and was stepping out onto the sidewalk that ran in front of the building. It was a cold night, but he'd expected as much. It had been cold all day. His feet turned toward the bus stop, and he started the brisk ten-minute walk. Hope grew within him as he drew near, but as he rounded the last corner he saw the bench at the stop was empty. He'd have no traveling companion tonight. No new friend. No fellow passengers to chat with while he waited.

He was always a little disappointed to end up at the stop alone, but over the last week he'd especially felt it. He'd been concerned for the girl who'd lost her friend, but she hadn't ridden the bus since that day, not once. At least, not once that had coincided with his own daily journey. Tonight would be no different.

Maybe her car had been fixed. If that were the case, then riding alone wasn't such a bad thing. But he was pretty sure that wasn't the situation. He met many people only once on these buses. Often, he watched for them to ride again and never saw them, but this time was different. He felt somehow as if he'd abandoned her when she needed someone. He wanted to make sure she was all right. She seemed strong, but everyone needs a friend to lean on from time to time. Even the strongest people need someone they can trust.

He knew she'd been that person for her friend today. He'd seen them at the ChaiNook. He'd observed from behind his newspaper as she bravely listened to the other girl's heartache. All along, and for the remainder of the day, he couldn't shake the question: Who was there for *her*? Anyone?

The bus pulled to a stop, and Matt realized he'd been so deep in thought he didn't even remember boarding it. He jumped out of his seat, grabbed his computer bag, and rushed to the front of the bus.

"Thought you'd gone to sleep on me back there, Matt," the driver said as Matt neared the doors.

"No. Just distracted tonight. Thanks for the ride, Gordon."

"Heh, it's my job, man."

"I know, but you do it well. Not like some guys who practically throw you to the floor every time they brake or accelerate. ...Hey, I don't want to hold you up, but do you remember that girl I got off with last week? The one who had been crying?"

"The dark-haired girl? Sure, I remember her."

"Has she ridden since then?"

"Sure. Every day. Well, I haven't seen her yet today, but I get the feeling she's been working pretty late these days. She usually gets on the stop after yours."

Matt nodded, processing the information. "Does she seem okay?"

"Okay?"

"Well, it's just that — Never mind. Thanks for the ride, Gordy."

"You bet. Have a good one, Matt."

Matt trudged home. He didn't like the feeling he had about this situation. More than that, he didn't like that he was usually right when he had this feeling. He had just started up the driveway when car lights swung in behind him. He turned to see his father's car and stepped out of the way. The garage door groaned open, and the car pulled forward. As Matt reached the front steps, the door groaned shut once more. He'd barely had a chance to toss his computer bag down on the shelf in the entryway when the door from the garage swung open, and his father stepped inside.

"Hello, son. I brought Chinese."

"Wow! Your timing is perfect! How did you know I'd just be getting home and haven't eaten for hours?"

"It's Monday, isn't it?"

Matt laughed and took the bag of Chinese carryout from his father while the older man removed his hat and coat.

"So, how was the bus today?"

"Quiet. I was the only one on it most of the way."

"Did you talk to anyone?"

"Just the driver."

"Well, perhaps another day."

"How was your day, Dad?"

"Oh, it was all right. My assistant is out sick. Poor thing, she's been sick since Thursday. No one can find anything without her."

"Sounds about right." Matt said with a grin.

"How about you? How was your day?"

Matt shrugged and led the way into the kitchen. "It was all right." He paused to set the bag of food on the counter, reaching into the sack and pulling out one of several boxes of food. "I saw that girl today."

"What girl?"

"The one I met on the bus whose friend had passed away."

Matt saw a shadow pass over his father's blue eyes. He dropped his own gaze, pretending to concentrate on sorting the packages of sauce that had come with their meal. His father hadn't said much about the man who'd died, but Matt could tell that, whoever he was, he had made an enormous impact on his life.

"Did you speak to her?"

Matt's gaze shot up from the pile of sauces. "No," he replied, surprised to hear his father resume the conversation. "She was with someone, and I didn't want to interrupt. The other girl was crying. I mean *crying*. Snot and tears running everywhere."

"Do you think it was because of what happened last week?"

"I'm sure of it. I only heard parts of their conversation, but I'm sure that was what they were talking about. And..." Matt hesitated, not sure he should go any further.

"And what?"

"I think they both worked with the man who passed away."

"With Sam Thompson."

"Yes. Mr. Thompson. That's the name the girl used."

"What makes you think they worked with him?"

"Just sounded like it to me. The crying girl was very young, probably just out of high school. The girl I met on the bus seemed to be there to listen and comfort...and get extra napkins to cry into. She seems like a strong woman, and she seemed like she was trying especially hard to be strong for her friend."

"Isn't that a good thing?"

"Yes. Of course it is, but...but she appeared very tired. I remember how it was for us after Mom died. Do you remember how exhausted we both were for no apparent reason at all?"

The older man nodded slowly. "I remember well. Sometimes, I still feel that way."

"I know you do. I can see it in you, just like I saw it in her today. She's standing strong, but I think she's under amazing pressure. I think she was trying to convince the other girl not to quit."

Matt's father sat down on one of the stools at the island. He sighed. "I was afraid that would start happening. Where there is no leader, people begin to falter and fall away."

"No leader? You think he was their boss? Even if he was, it seems a bit early to start giving up, don't you think?"

The older man shrugged. "You said she was young. This is a big one to overcome when you're fresh out of high school."

Matt dumped the food out of the cardboard containers and into various bowls. His thoughts turned to the bits and pieces of the conversation he'd overheard.

"Everything I have heard about Mr. Thompson makes me think he was a rare kind of man."

"He was. You've heard of the Trevor Street Crisis Center, right?"

"Yes. I don't know much about it, but I've heard of it. It's one of the larger charities in town, isn't it?"

"It's more than just a charity, believe me. Sam Thompson founded it."

"What?"

The older man nodded. "Yes. I truly believe he could have been the top real estate developer in the city—maybe in the region—but he *chose* a life among the broken and struggling instead. I always came away from conversations with Sam feeling humbled. He wasn't a bragger, wasn't the kind of man that goes around telling you what he's doing. It was the suggestions he made, the ideas he came up with. Sometimes, I'd think, 'That'll never work.' But then he'd go on to give an example of how it had already been done. By the time the conversation was over, you realized *he'd* done it, had weeded out the problems, and had a plan to go forward. He wasn't scared of sacrifice, wasn't afraid to fight for others. …The world is lacking such men."

Matt handed a plate to his father and started dishing out food. "I wish I'd had a chance to meet him."

"I wish I'd thought to introduce the two of you. I think you would've had a lot in common. …So, what do you plan to do?"

"What do you mean?"

"Well, you're obviously still concerned for this girl. What do you plan to do?"

"I don't know. I don't know that I can do anything more than pray for her. Gordy said she's been working late, so I thought I'd try—"

"Working later than us? That's not good. Especially not for a woman coming home alone on a bus."

Matt chuckled, his eyes twinkling. "You'd think she was your own daughter! But you're right. It isn't really safe. Like I was saying, I thought maybe I'd try coming home a little later. Maybe we'll meet up that way. If so, I'll try to encourage her not to overdo it and to get some rest." Matt drummed his fingers on the counter thoughtfully and then huffed. "Enough about my day. Did you conquer any kingdoms today?"

"Ha! I was lucky to get into my email!"

CHAPTER 8

Micah stood in the living room of his parents' home, hands on hips, eyes taking in the disarray around him. In all his growing up years, he'd never seen the living room and kitchen so cluttered. Several days' worth of mail scattered itself across the round kitchen table. A half-folded basket of laundry rested on its side near his mother's recliner. Beside the recliner, wads of napkins, Kleenex, and toilet paper littered an end table along with a cluster of coffee cups, drinking glasses, sandwich plates, and forks.

His mother, who hadn't gone to bed with a messy kitchen for the first 43 years of her marriage, hadn't touched the dishes in three days. They filled the counter and both sides of the sink. He'd tried to keep up with the housework, but he'd left the dishes on purpose, hoping the sight of them would spur his mother to action, but they hadn't. Things were out of control, far out of control, and he had no idea how to bring them back. One thing was for sure, he'd have to take care of the dishes before he could start supper.

He cleared the mess from the end table and stepped from the carpeted living room onto the laminate flooring in the kitchen. His dad had just put the new laminate down two weeks before Sam's accident. Sam had never seen it, would never see it. Micah pushed the thought away as he dropped the dishes into the already mounding sink and turned on the water. He glanced at the clock. 4:30. The workday was nearly done in most offices. He was pretty sure his day had hours and hours left to go.

He'd just emptied the sink of its piles and was sloshing dish soap into suds under a stream of hot water when he heard his phone ringing on the table behind him.

"Of course," he muttered. "Silent all day, but now that I've got my hands all wet you start ringing." He grabbed a towel in a frenzied attempt to dry his hands and rushed to the phone. "Hello?"

"Hey, Micah, this is Carla at Affinity."

"Oh! Hi, Carla. Good to hear from you." Hope climbed in Micah's eyes as he headed back toward the sink to turn off the water.

"Well, I hope you still feel that way when I tell you why I've called."

"Why do you say that?"

"Micah, we've been searching everywhere. I've personally called every software development company in the area. I've even looked into private consulting companies. But I've come up empty-handed. I've talked to them about small jobs that you might be able to freelance and special projects where they might be able to bring you in temporarily. I've practically begged them to make something up just for you. But I've got nothing for you. Everyone either sees your resume and says, 'Lang Computing is going to do everything they can to keep this guy when his leave is up.' Or they have nothing available. Or they want a two-year commitment, and I know you're not ready for that. I'm sorry, Micah. I really have tried. I've been at it for a week. I don't know why this has to be so difficult. I don't think I've ever come up with so many dead ends as I have for you. I really am sorry."

"That's okay, Carla. I know you've put everything into it you can. Something will work out. I have a meeting with Lang later this week. I'm hoping for some small projects out of the Seattle office, but there's also a possibility of some remote work from some of their other locations. There's no guarantee anything will come of it, but I'm going to keep trying. At least they're still holding my other position."

"For how long?"

"My boss gave me six months, but the corporate office was pushing for four to five with an occasional visit. I'm just..." he paused, surveying the mess around him. "I don't know how I'll be able to drop everything here, make the twelve-hour trip to spend a day or two in the office, and then make the twelve-hour trip back, especially with so little income."

"But you do have a little?"

"Income? Yeah, but it's just rent off of a couple of houses. Most of it goes back into the properties. The little bit that's left barely covers my bills. It's bad enough I'm eating my parents' groceries, but I'm also bumming rides with them just about everywhere we go. They don't mind, but I do."

"I'm sorry, Micah. I can tell you're frustrated. Don't give up. I'll keep looking. Would you be interested in a temporary office management position?"

Micah hesitated. He'd always felt if a man needed work badly enough, he would take just about anything. For the first time in his life, he realized that in some moments, that prospect only served to increase the stress levels of every aspect of life. "Maybe," he said at last. "What kind of office?"

"Well, I don't actually have anything right now. But I know one of my partners has been talking to the owner of a small chain of women's dress stores. Their office manager is going on maternity leave soon, and, well—"

"You're kidding me, right? Do you know how much I know about women's clothing? Zero. Every time I buy something for my mom, she either exchanges it or wears it for housework."

Carla broke into laughter. "It can't be that bad!"

"Oh! Yes, it can. ...Let's just hold off until after my meeting with Lang. Keep an ear out. Maybe one of the companies you've already talked with will come up with something in the meantime. For the moment, I've got my hands full here at the house anyway."

"You're sure?"

"Yeah. There's enough stress at home without me trying to learn a whole new industry just to survive the next four to six months."

"Okay. Well, I'll keep your name on our board, and you keep me in the loop. How's that sound?"

"Sounds perfect. Thank you for all you've done, Carla, and thanks for calling."

"No problem, and I hope things start smoothing out for you a little. Have a good evening."

"You too."

Micah laid the phone down on the table and shuffled back to the sink. He didn't hold out much hope for the meeting with Lang Computing. He'd worked there since the summer between his freshman and sophomore years in college, more years than he cared to count. But even with the seniority he'd earned—or maybe because of it—he knew they would push for him to be back in his office as soon as possible. The more comfortable he was with odd jobs or small projects, the less impetus to get back home. He knew that would be their approach. He'd seen it on more than one occasion. It made sense in a way, but it also made life more complicated.

He picked up a stack of plates and set them down into the warm, sudsy water. He dripped his way to the dishwasher and pulled it open. Then he groaned. It was full, and the dishes were dirty.

"How did we miss turning this on? And how in the world do we have any dishes left to eat off of?" He opened the cabinet above the dishwasher and peered inside. "We don't. That's how."

He'd just reached into the cabinet under the sink for dishwasher detergent when he heard his phone ringing once more. He groaned again and reached for the phone.

"Hey, Dad, what's up?"

"I'm just leaving the office. Well, I'm attempting to. As long as no one stops me on the way out, I should be out of here in the next five minutes. Thought I'd call and check in before I head your way. How are things going?"

"It's pretty quiet here. I cleaned up Sam's old stuff that mom hauled out in the family room. I tried to put it into some kind of order. Hope that was the right move. She wasn't thrilled with me.

"I'm just starting the dishes, so I have someplace to cook supper. The dishwasher didn't get started last night, so I'll have to hand-wash everything on the counters. Probably won't start supper for another hour, maybe more. I'm not even sure what to fix. We're just about out of everything. ...I'm sorry. I guess things are kind of a mess."

Andy Thompson didn't respond immediately. He knew his son well. Up to this point, Micah had done his best to make every conversation positive, upbeat, and encouraging. Something wasn't right.

"How's your mom?" he ventured at last.

"I haven't seen her for hours. I'm not sure where she is or what she's doing. Might be taking a nap. I don't know."

"Micah, what's going on? You're not telling me something."

Micah groaned, running a hand across the back of his neck. "Everything's fine. I'm just...I don't know. We can talk when you get home."

"Did you hear back from Affinity yet?"

"Yeah."

When Micah said nothing more, the picture of his day came into full focus for his father.

"Okay, listen, I'll order a pizza. As long as the traffic isn't too bad, I should beat dinner there. You and I can finish up the dishes together and be ready to settle in for the evening by the time the food arrives. How's that sound?"

"Are you sure?"

"I'm positive."

"I'm not going to argue. I'll be ready."

Two hours later, the pizza was gone, the kitchen was nearly clean, and Gloria Thompson had found a seat in her recliner. She said nothing as the men finished straightening the kitchen. Instead, she burrowed in with laptop perched on her knees and finger scrolling through page after page of social media content.

Micah glanced in her direction and sighed. Then he felt a heavy hand on his shoulder.

"I think you need a break," Andy whispered as Micah turned to meet his father's gaze. "Let's get out of here."

"But what about Mom?" Micah whispered in return.

"She'll be all right." The tall, heavyset Andy Thompson stepped away and into the living room. "Gloria, I've been wanting to take Micah to my new favorite coffee shop around the corner. Do you mind if we go?"

Gloria glanced up from the computer. "No, dear. That's fine. I'll — " She cut herself off, leaning forward and studying the computer screen with an expression of dissatisfaction deepening the lines of her face.

"Is something wrong?"

"Kelly Vance used to post for the crisis center every day. I haven't seen a new post in days, maybe weeks. Those girls had better get it together, or that place is going to fall apart."

"Mom! How can you say that?" Micah stared at his mother in disbelief. She'd been on him all day over just about everything, but this was going too far. "Those girls are working like nobody's business to keep that center going. Every time I've talked with Kali, she's been completely exhausted. I can hear it in her voice. I can't believe you'd say that."

"Well, how is anyone going to know they're still there if they don't see any online activity? You need to get on them about it, Micah. Your brother didn't put his whole life into that place to have them run it into the ground in a matter of weeks."

Tears, pain, and grief clutched at Micah's chest. He couldn't speak. The angry knot in his throat wouldn't allow it. He tossed the towel he'd been folding onto the counter and went to the closet for his jacket. He donned the jacket and headed for the back door. "I'll be waiting in the car, Dad."

"I'll be out in just a second."

Andy waited until his son had gone and the door had firmly clicked into place. Then he turned back to his wife.

"That was uncalled for, and you know it. You know those girls as well as you know your own sons. You know they're fighting for all they're worth. And, you know how much they meant to Sam, and how much they mean to Micah, both of them. That boy has put his entire life on hold for us. The least you could do is show him a little compassion and gratitude in return."

Gloria stared back at her husband, unaccustomed to such stern reproach from the kind man. He'd always been firm in his leadership of their home, but this was beyond firm. She saw anger, grief, and great disappointment deep in his eyes. She turned away, ashamed. "I'm sorry. Please tell him I'm sorry."

"*You* can tell him when we get back. ...Do you want me to bring you anything?"

"No. ...I'm sorry, Andy. I wasn't thinking. I forgot about him and Kali seeing one another, and I know he's always been good friends with Kelly too."

"Micah dating Kali has nothing to do with this. It's your attitude toward them that's so out of place. Those girls love you. If they heard you talk that way, they'd be devastated."

"You're right. I'm sorry. I'm so sorry." Tears trickled down her cheeks. She hated who she'd become in the days since Sam's death, but she couldn't find a way out of the darkness. "Forgive me, Andy, please."

"I forgive you, but it's your son you need to talk to."

"I will. I promise."

"Good. We'll be home in a couple of hours." And with that, he left her to her tears.

❊ ❊ ❊

Andy fiddled with the corrugated cup sleeve around his steaming drink. He glanced up at his son, who'd said almost nothing since leaving the house. Sam and Micah had always been good friends growing up, but since college they'd been inseparable. They depended on one another, encouraged one another, challenged one another. They'd helped one another through major decisions and deep valleys. They were always pushing one another to do the next thing. They'd built a family around the crisis center. And then suddenly, it was all gone for Micah. Everything. He'd not only lost his brother but in coming home, he'd lost the rest of his life as well. Andy choked back tears as he sipped at his coffee and then set it back on the table.

"I take it from your lack of enthusiasm on the phone earlier that Affinity hasn't found anything for you."

Micah shook his head. "Not a thing, and I know they've been hard at it all week."

"How tight are you?"

Micah shrugged, turning his tall cup of coffee in a small circle on the table. "I've got money in savings, but that's for—" He cut himself off. He'd never told anyone what he was saving for, now he felt a little embarrassed about it.

"For starting a new life with Kali?"

"How did you know?"

"Micah, your brother, Sam, has had you two paired up in my mind since you were in college."

"Since college?"

"Yes. That Christmas when Zack got engaged, I asked Sam if anyone was in the picture for him. He said no, but he had hopes for you. He thought the two of you would be a great match but figured it would be years before either of you realized it. He was sure right about that!"

Micah managed a lopsided grin. "I knew he'd been hopeful for a while, but I didn't know it was that long."

"So, how tight are you?"

"If I dip into my savings, I can probably go without any additional income for about a year. Maybe. …If I leave my savings alone, I'll be in trouble once my house insurances and taxes come due in the spring. But that's with you guys paying for groceries and gas. I don't want to keep doing that, Dad."

"It's all right, Micah. I appreciate so much what you're doing. If I didn't know you were at home, I wouldn't be able to go to work myself. I've got to finish out this year before I can retire. I *need* you here. But I do think you need to get out of the house more often. The church has a men's Bible study on Thursday nights. Maybe you should go."

Micah shrugged, his eyes darting away from his father's gaze. He didn't want to pursue new activities and friendships. He just wanted life to be normal again.

"You don't want to go?"

Again, the younger man shrugged.

"Son?"

Micah looked up but then leaned forward, resting his elbows on the table and hiding his face behind his hands.

"What is it, Micah?"

"I just want life to go back to the way it used to be, Dad. I know it can't, but I just want it to go back to normal. I want Sam to walk through the front door and light up the whole room with that laugh of his. I want it to go back to that."

"I know. I do too. For everyone's sake. ...We're going to get through this, Micah. By God's grace, we'll get through this. But we're going to have to keep our eyes on the Lord and do our best to point your mom in that direction. She'll get through this too. It's just going to take time."

At the mention of his mother, Micah broke. He let his arms fall crossed on the table and rested his forehead against them. Sobs of the most embarrassing kind shook his body. He felt his dad's hands clasp over his heaving shoulders. He tried to force back the emotion that had overwhelmed him, but it was too late. He'd been pushing it back for two weeks only to find now that it had been amassing strength against him.

Andy was glad the coffee shop was nearly empty. The baristas knew him well and knew the story of what had happened. They cast a sympathetic eye in the direction of his table and nodded their understanding as he met their gazes. Tears streamed down his own cheeks as he leaned toward his son. He rested his cheek just above Micah's ear and whispered, "God isn't going to leave us, son. Everything's going to be all right. It's okay. Just let it out. Just let it all out."

CHAPTER 9

K ali reached for her cellphone, not bothering to check who was calling in the midst of her morning routine.

"This is Kali," she said as she dug through her makeup bag in search of her mascara.

"Miss Shepherd, hello! This is McKinsey Marsh."

"Oh. Mr. Marsh, good morning. How are you?"

"I'm doing well. Listen, I've been talking with the members of the board, and we felt like maybe it was time to meet with you. You know, to hear some of your thoughts on the future now that it's been a couple weeks." The man's grimace was evident in his voice. "I'm sorry, Miss Shepherd, I know a couple weeks is nothing when you've gone through the kind of loss you all have faced."

"It's all right, Mr. Marsh. You don't have to apologize. I knew this day was coming and probably sooner than later. When would you like to meet?

"Well, we were thinking around ten."

Kali hesitated. She wanted to blurt out, "Today! Ten o'clock today!" but instead, she managed to say, "At your office?"

"No, we reserved the conference room at the ChaiNook. Everyone needs a chance to get out of their offices from time to time."

"Oh, that will be nice. Should I prepare anything in particular for the meeting?"

"Well, I had one of my clerks pull the last financial report Sam gave us, so I'll bring copies of that along. Can you bring a list of all of the programs and projects the center has going?"

"Sure. That shouldn't be a problem."

"That should cover everything then. We mostly just want to be sure we know where we are and what direction we're heading."

"All right. Well then, I guess I'll see you at ten."

"Sounds great. Talk to you then."

Kali hung up and stared at her pale reflection in the mirror. "Well, Kali, here goes," she said as she pulled out her blush with the hope of making some improvement in her appearance. "Now you can take your papers in there and tell them you have absolutely no plan at all."

She glanced down at her phone. 7:30. She had a few minutes, just enough time. She quickly dialed and waited.

"Hello," came a groggy voice.

"Did I wake you? I'm sorry. I forgot about the time difference."

"Kali?"

"Sorry, Micah. I just… I wanted to talk."

"That's okay. You talk. I'll wake up."

Kali laughed. "Oh, I miss you."

"I miss you too. So, what's up?"

"I just got a call from Mr. Marsh. The board wants to meet and hear about our plans for the future."

"When?"

"This morning."

"This morning! They sure didn't give you much warning, did they?"

"That's okay. I've known this was coming, but that doesn't change the fact that I don't have a plan."

"That's not true."

"What do you mean?"

"Every time I've talked to you, you've had a plan."

"What?"

"Every time I've talked to you, you've said the same thing: 'I guess we just trust the Lord to show us what to do.' That's what you've said."

"But, Micah, they want something concrete, and you know it."

"What is more concrete than a God who never fails, never changes, and never leaves us?"

Kali was silent.

"Well?"

"Nothing."

"Exactly. You have nothing to worry about, Kali. You are doing a tremendous job, and I know you'll continue to. Don't second-guess yourself. You go in there, tell them how it is, and how you plan to continue—one step at a time with God's help. They're good men. All of them have had moments when they've had no one but God to rely on. They'll understand."

"Are you sure?"

"Yes! Of course, I'm sure. If I weren't, I wouldn't be telling you this."

"But what if I mess it up?"

"You won't."

Kali was silent again. She fiddled with her blush compact, trying to pull her thoughts together. She looked up, meeting her own gaze in the mirror and wishing with everything in her that Micah was standing there instead.

"I wish you were here."

"I know. So do I."

"How are things going there?"

Micah hesitated, embarrassment crept over him at the memory of the previous evening's events. He had gathered his composure and found himself at peace by the time he and his father arrived home. But he'd also willingly allowed his dad to serve as the buffer between him and his mom. She'd apologized, and he'd accepted it. But then, he'd gone straight to his room. Now, after extra time with the Lord and a good night's sleep, he was feeling more like himself.

"Yesterday was rough, but we're surviving."

"How's your mom?"

"She's all right, pretty emotionally unpredictable. Some days she seems fine, and then she's down again. I think that's just normal for where we are. ...I need to get back there, but I don't know when that's going to happen. I wish I could say it would be in a week or so.

I need to start going through Sam's things so we can work toward settling the estate."

Again, Kali was quiet.

"Are you there, Kal?"

"Yes. I'm sorry."

"What's bothering you?"

Tears slipped down the young woman's face, ruining the makeup she'd just applied. "I miss him so much, Micah. I just never realized how much he did around here, not just at the center but all over the community. I keep finding bits and pieces of him and his influence at every turn. I feel like I'm walking through his days and seeing what he was actually doing and...I just miss him so much."

"And I'm faced with the opposite. It's been so long since Sam was in Seattle. It's like every life but ours goes on, and all without a trace of Sam. ...I just want to go sit in his living room and watch a game. I think I could just sit there for days." Micah sighed. "Hopefully, I'll be home soon. I'm going to try. I don't know the dates yet, but I'll be there as soon as I can."

"I'll help you when you get here. You shouldn't do that job alone."

"Thanks. ...Oh, the dog wants out, and everyone else is still asleep. She's going to rip right through the door. I better go. Call me before you go to the meeting. We'll pray together."

"Okay. Thank you."

"You bet."

Kali disconnected the call, dried her cheeks, and patted away the mascara that had gathered around her eyes. She screwed up her face at her reflection. "Guess I'd better start over."

❄ ❄ ❄

Kali stepped out of her blue Corsica and slipped her phone into her pocket. She grabbed her laptop and a folder of printouts then locked the car. She took a deep breath and turned toward the front of the ChaiNook.

"Lord," she whispered, "thank you for Micah. Please, help me through this."

She traipsed across the frozen parking lot and through the front door of the glass building. She was surprised to find that only one of the board members had beaten her to the meeting room. Mr. Truman, a tall, fair-haired man, was seated at the conference table, leaning over his own set of papers and fingering the warm cup of coffee he'd already ordered.

"Good morning," she greeted, her voice trembling slightly.

"Ah, Miss Shepherd, so good to see you."

"Please, call me Kali."

"Very well, Kali, have you ordered anything yet?"

"No, I thought I'd get situated first and then order."

"Well, allow me to do it for you. What would you like?"

"Oh, thank you. I think I'd be up for something strong today. How about the Morning Zinger with a shot of caramel?"

"Cream?"

"No. Not today."

"All right. I'll be right back."

And he was. It seemed Kali had barely had the time to set up her laptop and lay out a packet for each member of the board before the man had returned and set the cup down beside the computer.

"Wow. That was fast."

"I got there just before the rest of the line." The man smiled, but something was missing. Something told her the kind gesture had been out of guilt.

"Kali, I got here early because I need to talk with you."

"Okay. How can I help?"

"Well, I don't know how much you know about each of us on the board."

"A little, but not a lot."

"I joined the board at Sam's invitation. We were friends from church, and he asked me to be here for counsel. After I joined, I would go back to my office and tell my coworkers about what a fine job the center was doing. About a year later, my boss decided he wanted to support the center with monthly donations."

"Well, you must be a good ambassador," Kali teased, sensing the man was feeling more and more guilt by the moment and wanting to relieve the growing tension.

Truman shook his head. "Not as good as I should be. You see, try as I might, I haven't been able to convince him to continue supporting the center now that Sam is gone. He feels Sam was the backbone of the place, and no one will be able to take it over and lead it the way Sam did. He's right, of course—about Sam. No one will replace Sam."

The man paused to settle the emotion rising within him. He'd known Sam for a long time. Sam had been the one to get him out of the pews and into action. His life had forever changed because of Sam—for the better. He knew his boss was right about the impact Sam had on the crisis center, its staff, and ministries; but he also knew the center could still carry out the work Sam had begun. He leaned forward, resting his forearms against the conference table and turning his coffee cup in his fingers.

"It'll never be exactly the same," he said, "but that doesn't mean it won't still do a world of good. ...Anyway, he's decided to pull his funding until the center has a new director who has proven they'll lead in the right direction. I'm sorry. I wish I had better news. I wish I could tell you he was going to stand behind you all the way, but I can't. I'm just really, really sorry."

"It's all right, Mr. Truman. We all knew this could happen with any of our partners. Thank you for being so gracious in the way you handled it. Please tell your employer we are very grateful for his past support, and we understand completely. ...And thank *you* for the tea."

The man nodded. An anemic smile touched the corners of his mouth as he turned his attention to the file Kali had laid on top of his other papers. "I plan to stay on the board as long as I'm welcome, Miss Shepherd. Sam was a good friend, and the center is doing good work." The man wiped at a tear before continuing. "If you ever need anything, just let me know."

"Thank you, Mr. Truman. I'll remember that."

※ ※ ※

Gil leaned around Kelly and pounded on the delete key. "Why won't it delete?" he mumbled, aggravation clear in his voice. "It should work. It always works."

"I smell garlic," Kelly interjected. "What did you have for lunch, Gil?"

"Sorry. I spilled Chicken Alfredo on my shirt."

"Oh, that sounds yummy. I think I have a box mix at home. Maybe that's what I'll have for supper."

"No. I should just bring you some leftovers. My wife makes the best Alfredo sauce. I'll bring some with me the next time I'm here."

"Really! Thanks! I'll be looking forward to it."

A vibration at Kelly's hip caught the young woman off guard. She reached into her pocket and pulled out the phone. Concern passed over her face. "It's a text from Kali. She's done. Should we call her?"

Gil stepped back and straightened to his full six feet seven inches. "Might as well. We'll need something to do while we restart your computer."

"Ugh. I was afraid it was coming to that. It's always something with these machines, isn't it?"

Gil lumbered around the desk and seated himself across from her. "Just be glad we have them. It would be a lot harder to run this place without them." As he spoke, he hit the speaker button on Kelly's desk phone and dialed Kali's number.

"You're right. I'll shut it down and stop my complaining."

The phone was ringing now. It rang several times, in fact.

"Hello?"

"Hey, Kali. Gil and I were just sitting here working on my computer, so we thought we'd give you a call. How'd it go?"

Kali didn't respond. They heard the slam of the car door and the dinging seatbelt indicator. Still, she said nothing.

Kelly bit her lip and shot a suspicious glance in Gil's direction. "Kali, is everything okay?"

"Sorry, guys. I was just trying to get in the car. I don't want to broadcast everything all over the ChaiNook parking lot. I don't want to spread anything that shouldn't be spread."

Kelly glanced at Gil again. His frown mirrored her fears that whatever news Kali had wasn't going to be good. "So...How'd it go?" Kelly persisted.

"Well, I'd say the meeting went pretty well. Micah was right. They were all content to let the Lord lead one step at a time, although they do want to know how we plan to go about finding a new director. They asked if I would be willing to take the position permanently."

"And?" Kelly was always hopeful on this point. She didn't feel ready for some new face to take Sam's place. They'd been handed enough change. She wasn't prepared for the remainder of their world to be yanked out from under them.

"*And* I told them exactly what I've told all of you. I'm willing to do this for a while, but I don't sense the Lord leading me into it permanently."

Kelly's shoulders sagged.

Gil shrugged as if to say, "You already knew that, Kelly."

"We agreed that we'll try to finish out the month as we are. No changes. But next month, we'll begin taking applications and allow some candidates to help out on projects so we can see how they work and what their philosophies are. Once we've got a good feel for things, we'll either recommend them to the board or tell them to catch the next bus...in Mr. Oberlander's words."

"Well, that sounds like a plan. What else did you talk about?"

"We went over all of the programs and projects. One of the Hope House projects needs some adjustment, Kelly, so we'll need to talk about that. Otherwise, they agreed to leave everything as it is. All the programs will stay in place. We'll continue to take on new clients as we see fit within the scope of those programs—nothing new—just what we've got going already."

"I don't think we could handle anything new anyway," Gil said.

"It's good they've given us that freedom, though, right? They could've said nothing new, not even clients, until we have things back in order."

"Yeah." Kali's voice was hollow as if the good news meant nothing.

"Kali, what is it? You seem discouraged."

"Mr. Truman came early to talk with me. He wants to remain on the board because he cares about the center, but apparently, his employer who has been a long-time partner, has decided to withdraw his support."

Gil's face blanched. The color left it so fast that, for a moment, Kelly thought he was on the verge of being ill.

"Kali...Gil has a terrible look on his face. What are you trying to tell us?"

"I glanced over the spreadsheet during the meeting. I'm not positive who his employer is, but...the only company I see that gives monthly, other than Marsh and Line, is Wymont Steel. After everyone left, I started doing some math. I'd say they give at least a third of our annual income."

"What!"

But Gil was shaking his head. "It's closer to forty-five percent. And since they give monthly, it's not like there's any reserve from a big annual donation."

Kelly stared at the man across from her. He was completely open and honest, always. He would be hiding nothing, exaggerating nothing.

"Are their donations given to support specific projects?" she asked.

Gil shook his head but then realized Kali couldn't see him. "No. They give to the general fund. So, on the good side, it doesn't mean any one program will take the brunt of the loss. On the other hand, everything will feel it."

"Well," Kali said resolutely, "I guess we know what we'll be doing the rest of the day and probably most of tomorrow—finding ways to cut back with the least damage to our clients. ...Traffic around here is moving slow. I'll be back to the office as quick as I can, but it's going to be a while. Get your calculator ready, Gil."

CHAPTER 10

Bus #123 had come and gone four times, but Matt wasn't waiting on the bus. He was waiting for the girl. After seeing her in the ChaiNook with her friend and hearing Gordy's report of her late nights, he decided it was time to be more intentional in his spying. Once more, the bus rumbled to a stop in front of him, and the doors slid open.

"Hey, are you holding out for a better-looking driver or what?"

Matt chuckled and leaned forward in his seat on the bench. "Hey, Gordy."

"Man, this is the fifth time I've passed you up. What are you doing?"

"Waiting for someone."

"That girl?"

"What?"

"The one you asked me about, I'll bet. This is her stop, *not* yours. You two got something going?"

"No, it's nothing like that."

"But it *is* her."

"I'm worried about her."

"You confuse me, man. You seem like a perfectly normal guy, but then you go around talking to strangers and waiting for—how long?—not even knowing if they're coming. Are you some kind of stalker? I never took you for a stalker."

"Stalker!" Matt guffawed. "No. I'm not a stalker. I just want to help people. My dad calls me his 'community spy.' I watch for people who need an encouraging word or help of some kind and then we do what we can. That's all."

Gordy stared for a moment then, remembering the passengers on his bus, he said, "Well, if it's any help, she's been riding the 8:20 all week. So, I'll see you next time around."

Matt waved, "See you in a few."

The bus had barely made its way around the corner when Matt heard light footsteps approaching from the other direction. He turned and saw the slender figure of "the girl" approaching. He smiled. His wait in the horrid cold had not been in vain.

"Well, hello there," he said as she approached the stop. "Haven't seen you for a while."

Kelly's cheeks colored, but the night hid her blushing. "Are you always this friendly with people you don't know? Never mind. I'm pretty sure I know the answer. *Why* are you always so friendly with people you don't know?"

"You're the second person to ask me that in the last three minutes. ...You just missed the bus. ...So, the car still isn't running, I take it?"

"No. I'm not sure it will ever run again. At least not until my dad comes for a visit."

"Your parents don't live around here?"

"No. My dad started having some health problems a few years ago, and his doctors recommended he move to a warmer climate. So, they're in Arizona, but they come back in the summers for a little while."

"Do you have other family in the area?"

Kelly started to answer but then stopped. These were the sort of questions that could lead to a man finding out just how vulnerable a woman was.

"Why do you want to know?"

"I'm sorry. I didn't mean to pry. I just wondered if you had family in the area. I'm sure the last couple of weeks have been rough. ...I've been praying by the way."

Kelly smiled and dared to sit down next to him. He seemed kind enough, the street was well lit, and she was tired.

"Thanks," she replied. "We need it."

"We?"

"Oh, I guess I didn't explain that part the other day. My friend was also my boss. I work at the Trevor Street Crisis Center."

"You work at the Crisis Center? So...that means your friend was Sam Thompson."

Kelly straightened in her seat and faced the man, eyes wide and hopeful. "You knew him?"

"No. My father knew him a little. I'm not really sure how well they knew one another, but Dad was visibly moved by the news. The little you both have told me has given me the impression Mr. Thompson was a good man."

Tears crept into the woman's eyes, but she forced them back. "He was."

"So...how are things at the center?"

She set her large, red purse down between her feet and fiddled with the leather strap. "Everything's different. We're all trying so hard to keep things together, but I think most of us just want to fall apart."

"He was the director, right?"

"Yes."

"Who's doing that now?"

"My best friend, Kali Shepherd, has taken over temporarily. She was the Assistant Director. But it doesn't really matter who has what title because we're all just trying to survive."

"Have you been able to keep all of the outreach programs up and running? I know that center does a lot for this community."

"So far, we haven't had to turn anyone away. One man found out what was going on and left because he didn't want to cause us any more grief. I think he'll be back. It broke my heart." She paused, remembering the veteran whose story had touched them all so deeply. The events of the day and Kali's conversation with Mr. Truman crept through her mind and ached in the pit of her stomach. "But things could start changing."

"What do you mean?"

Kelly shrugged and dropped the strap down onto the bag. "I don't know how much I should say."

"Do you think you might have to step back on your programs?"

"We found out today that, after this month, our committed donations—the ones that have been promised as long term, regular donations—will be cut. By a lot. We only lost one partner, but their giving was significant. We've spent all afternoon and this evening working on finding ways to cut expenses without hurting our clients."

"Did you find enough cuts?"

"I don't know. Our accountant is still working on things. He's a volunteer though, so he won't be back in until Saturday."

"I work in accounting. Maybe I could go over it for you."

"Really?"

"Sure, well, I mean, I'd have to do it after work, but I'm supposed to get off early tomorrow anyway. I could just give you my email address, and you guys could send me whatever you felt was pertinent."

"Hmm." Kelly shivered and shoved her hands into her pockets. "I suppose we could. I'll have to check with Kali. She may not want to share that kind of information without knowing you."

"I understand. Here," the man pulled a pen and notebook out of his coat pocket and began to write. "Here is my email address. If she's open to it, go ahead and send me the info. If not, no worries. I'll just keep praying for you."

He tore the page out of the notebook and handed it to Kelly with a smile.

"Thanks," she said, folding the paper and slipping it into the outside pocket of her purse.

"So, how are *you*?" he asked. "You look tired."

"Wow! Thanks! Just what a girl wants to hear!"

Matt laughed. "I know. My mother always told me I need to work on tact and charm."

"I'm okay. But you're right, I am tired—a lot. Even when the day isn't really stressful, I still feel exhausted."

"That's pretty normal when you're grieving."

"You speak from experience?"

He nodded.

"Your mother?"

Matt turned sharply toward her, his eyes shooting questions.

But Kelly remained calm. "You always talk about what she *used* to say, not what she says."

He nodded again, this time letting his gaze drop away from hers.

"So...someone caught you in your own game?" she teased.

"Ha! I guess you're right. You did."

"Has it been long?"

"About three years. Doesn't seem long though. ...Things will get better for you, for all of you, but it will take time. ...Oh, here comes the bus."

The bus eased toward the curb, its brakes chirping as it slid to a stop on the ice. Matt helped his new friend gather her things. He followed her onto the bus, not missing Gordy's wink as they passed him.

⁂ ⁂ ⁂

Matt shuffled through the dark house and dropped onto the sofa: hat, boots, coat, and computer bag all still intact.

"You're home late," his father noted from his armchair. "Were the buses off schedule?"

"No. I was waiting, hoping to meet up with that girl from the bus. She was working late again."

"Did you meet up with her?"

Matt nodded and stretched his legs out. He leaned his head against the spine of the sofa and yawned.

"How was she?"

"Seemed okay, but no more than okay."

The older man considered his son. He had the appearance of a man thoroughly spent. Chances were it had been a long, busy day at the office, followed by a long wait in that bitter, strength-sapping cold, and a conversation that had laid an enormous burden on his shoulders.

"There's spaghetti in the kitchen," he offered. "I'll bring you some if you'd like."

"Naw. I'm not hungry."

"Did you eat already?"

"No. Just not hungry."

"What's the matter?"

Matt met his father's gaze, confused.

"The only time you're not hungry is when something is bothering you."

"I'm just tired."

"No, something is bothering you."

"You're persistent, aren't you?" Matt laughed.

The white-haired man grinned. "You're right. I am. So, what did you talk about with this girl?"

"Actually, we talked about the center. ...She said they've run into a bit of a mystery."

"Oh?"

"Remember, I told you I had seen her talking with another one of their staff at the ChaiNook?"

"Yes."

"Well, I overheard them talking about an education fund that day. Tonight, after we got on the bus, 'the girl' told me they have no idea what education fund this girl is talking about. They've gone over all their financial information and can't find that they've ever had an education fund. I suggested maybe it was something Sam was doing on his own."

"Wait. So not only were you talking about the center, but you've also made the connection to Sam? She knows you know who her friend was? Did you tell her you overheard them at the ChaiNook?"

"Absolutely not. There was no way I was going to tell her that. But, yes, we did make the connection to Sam. I also told her you knew him."

"How did she respond?"

Matt shrugged. "If anything, I think it was a bit of a comfort to know we had some kind of connection to Sam, no matter how small. ...Anyway, I suggested maybe the education fund was something Sam was doing on his own, but at the same time I thought maybe you knew something about it."

"Me!" The man shook his head. "No, Sam and I never talked about anything like that. Maybe it was something he was doing with someone in his church or one of the members of the board, or one of the other service providers in town. I had nothing to do with it. Why would you think I would have something to do with it?"

"Because I never know what you're up to."

The man chuckled. "Your old man keeps you hopping, doesn't he?"

"Yes. Yes, you do."

"It's good for you. ...So, was that it? Did you talk about anything else?"

"Yeah," Matt replied, a heavy sigh falling over the word. "We did."

"Oh. We've found it."

"Found what?"

"Whatever's bothering you."

"I suppose you're right. I'm not sure how much I should say. She was pretty guarded. Let's just say, I offered my professional help."

"Hmm. Was she open to your help?"

"Hesitantly. She said she'd have to check with her boss. I gave her my 'spy' email address." He grinned, knowing his father's love for their community spying. It was their secret. One that had brought them more joy than anything else in the years since Matt's mom had passed away. Now, his father didn't disappoint. A smile slid across the older man's face and up into his blue eyes.

"Well, that's a start," he said. "I told you that email address would come in handy. ...So, how far are you willing to take this?"

"What do you mean?"

"You're gathering information like you always do, helping where you can, but you're getting a lot closer than you normally do."

"In what way?"

"It's keeping you from eating. That's not normal. Most of the time, you just take it in stride. You're on the verge of sinking your whole heart right into this thing."

"There's nothing to sink into. I might be able to help them figure out some stuff, but their problems are way bigger than me. All I can do is pray."

The older man raised an eyebrow. "Are you sure? I think this situation has stirred something in you, and you're not sure what to do with it."

Matt hesitated, but he knew his dad wouldn't let it go. "It's Sam."

"What do you mean? You never met Sam."

"I know. That's what's bugging me. I feel cheated. I feel like I need to know more about him. Something in his life is missing in mine."

"What do you think it is?"

"I don't know. I mean, *love* is the easy answer, but I think there's more to it than that."

Matt's father leaned back in his soft seat, folding his hands out in front of him in a thoughtful manner. "Yes, Sam was full of love, but you're right. It went beyond the emotion and into the action. I guess you call that charity."

"But, Dad, I think it goes beyond even that. I just can't put my finger on it."

"Well, pray about it. But be careful. You're on the verge of blowing your cover."

"Yeah. I know. I think Gordy wasn't sure whether to turn me in as a stalker or give me dating advice."

""Dating advice!" The older man burst out, his eyes twinkling. "Only people who date need that. You haven't been on a date since high school."

"I have better things to do than sit around messing with some poor girl's emotions."

"Just make sure you don't do that unintentionally with this girl."

Matt's brow furrowed. He stared at his father for a moment, dumbfounded. "You think I'm at risk of hurting her? That's the last thing I want to do."

"It's easier done than we realize, Matt. We traipse through life like an elephant dancing through a jungle and never realize we've captured the attention of a young woman and dashed all her hopes in the blink of an eye. Just be careful. If you're going to keep any distance in this, you're probably going to have to make sure she doesn't know your little meetings are anything more than accidental."

"But what if somewhere down the line she finds out they've been intentional and thinks I've been lying to her?"

"Now you see how difficult this could be to manage. You need to pray about where God wants you in this one. I want you to do as much good as you can in this situation. But you've got to decide whether it's more important for you to help her outright or to be able to continue helping others. Or, maybe, there's some way you can accomplish both. The closer you get, the greater the chance of both her and others finding out who you are and what you've been up to. If you want to remain anonymous, you're going to have to be very careful."

"Ugh." Matt groaned, closing his eyes and pulling at his hair. "Now, I'll never get to sleep."

"Just give it to the Lord, Matt. He'll lead you. I'll be praying about it too. ...And, maybe the Lord will have me take a bigger part in this one than I ever have before. Let's just pray about it. God will provide an answer."

CHAPTER 11

Kali puzzled over the number coming up on her Caller ID. She didn't recognize it, and she didn't have time for a sales call. She glanced toward the main office. Sarah was away from her desk, Brandon was on another line, and neither Gil nor Brenda were scheduled to work today. Kali's mouth twisted to one side as she reached for the receiver. She sighed and then forced a smile onto her face.

"Trevor Street Crisis Center. This is Kali. ...Hello?"

"Miss Shepherd?"

"Yes."

"Hi. This is McKinsey Marsh."

"Oh. Mr. Marsh. I'm sorry. Your name didn't come up on the caller ID."

The man on the other end of the line chuckled. "That's probably because I'm hiding in a break room."

"What? Why?"

"It's a long story that has a lot to do with a frozen pipe."

"Oh, my. I don't think I even want to know."

"No. It's better you don't." The man laughed again and then drew a deep breath. "Hey, listen, I won't keep you long. I just wanted to touch base and find out your impression of yesterday's meeting."

"I thought it went well. Everyone seemed to be open to where we are. I was a bit nervous someone would insist on a more definite plan than I could offer."

"No. Most of us have gone through something similar, and we know these situations take time. Did you have any questions, or has anything come to mind that you need help with?"

Kali played with the cord connecting her keyboard to her computer tower, wondering how much she should say.

"Miss Shepherd?"

"I'm sorry. I was just thinking. Something happened before the meeting. I didn't want to bring it up in the meeting because I wasn't sure of the ramifications, but I'm surprised Mr. Truman didn't say anything."

"Oh? What was that?"

"Mr. Truman came early because he wanted to talk. His employer doesn't feel they can continue to give until we have a new director."

Even over the phone, Kali heard Marsh gasp and swallow hard. "Truman's employer? Isn't that Wymont Steel?"

"Yes, sir."

"But that's...that's—"

"Forty-five percent of our income."

"Oh, Miss Shepherd. I am so sorry. Why didn't he say anything? That will affect every single thing we talked about in that meeting. Everything."

"I know. I think he was embarrassed by the situation, and I wasn't sure who his employer was until Gil confirmed it for me. Gil, Kelly, and I have been going over our accounts, but I'm just not sure how we're going to be able to keep all of these programs going. Even if we cut our salaries down to bare bones, I just don't know how we're going to do it."

"Okay. Don't panic. The Lord has a plan. ...Why don't you send what you guys have come up with to me, and I will have the head of my accounting department look at it. He's good with issues like this, and he has a heart for people. He'll be very conscientious about it."

"You would do that?"

"No!" Marsh laughed. "He will!"

"Oh, Mr. Marsh, thank you! Gil will be gone until Saturday. That's too long to go without a plan in this situation. Thank you so much."

"You're welcome. ...Now, I received a call from a local pastor today. He gave me the name of a man who might be interested in working with you, possibly even in taking over the directorship. I have his information if you're interested."

Kali hesitated. She wasn't sure any of them were ready for that step, not yet. "I thought we agreed to wait until the end of the month."

"Yes, we did. So, I thought perhaps you could check the calendar for an event next month where he could help. If you want. I'm not telling you what to do. I don't know the man. I've never even heard of him. ...So, if he turns out to be a bum, don't blame me."

"That's not very reassuring." Kali said with a hint of teasing in her voice.

"I know. I'm sorry. I'll email you the information this afternoon, and you guys can talk it over and do whatever you want."

"Sounds like a good plan. I'm so nervous about this part of it, Mr. Marsh. Sam isn't going to be easy to replace."

"No one will be like him, Kali, no one. But you want the right person to take his place. Don't rush. Just let God lead you. I'm praying for you daily, all of you."

"Thank you."

"I'll be watching for that email with your financial plan. You have a good day."

"Thank you, Mr. Marsh. I'll get right on it."

❖ ❖ ❖

Matt stepped out of the elevator and onto the dimly lit floor that housed the accounting department of Marsh and Line Clothiers. "Hey, Mel. ...Haven't you gone to lunch yet?" he asked, starting to pass his assistant and then stopping to wait for her answer.

"No, I had a guest after you left."

"A guest?"

"Yes. The upstairs kind."

"Oh, really?" Matt leaned back on one heel and crossed his arms over his chest, his eyes lighting up with curiosity.

"Yes. Mr. Marsh came down and left a packet for you. He wants you to handle it personally, no one else. He was firm on that point."

Matt's eyes widened. "I don't think that's ever happened before."

"It's on your desk."

"Did he give a time-frame or any other specifics?"

"He said the cover sheet will tell you all you need to know."

"Well, I guess I'd better check it out. Go get your lunch. I can handle the phones for a while."

"Thanks, boss. I'm starving."

Matt grinned then twirled on his heel and stepped light-heartedly into his office. He closed the door behind him and strode to the desk, eager to learn more of his new assignment. The blue file glowed atop the spray of papers on his desk. That, he knew, was a sign it was of utmost importance. Blue always meant high priority in their office. He picked up the file and flipped open the front cover. A broad smile slid across his face as he read the cover page: "Financial Plan for the Trevor Street Crisis Center."

He couldn't stop the chuckle rising up from deep within him. "Well, Lord," he said softly, "You worked it out so I can help—and no one will ever know it was me."

CHAPTER 12

Sarah gathered several scraps of paper from her desk and slipped them into a file. She dropped the folder into a large stack of similar files and turned back to the rest of the work before her. She sighed and leaned forward on the desk, resting her chin in her hand. Her eyes drifted across the room, momentarily resting on each of her coworkers and finally falling on the door of the director's office. Tears climbed in her eyes. The intercom on her desk rang, and she wiped the moisture from her eyelashes as she reached for the receiver.

"Yes?"

"Sarah, this is Kali. Can you bring me the application file for the director's position? It's in the top drawer of the big cabinet. Please."

"Sure. I'll be right there."

The young woman hung up the phone, pushed back her red hair, and braced herself. Strange how a simple act like pulling a file could be so heart-wrenching. She stood slowly and went to the cabinet. The folder, still quite thin, was difficult to find in the sea of neatly labeled files. When at last she reached it, she hesitated, glancing toward Sam's office once more.

"This wasn't my idea," she whispered. "And I don't think it was Kali's idea either. No one will replace you."

She pulled the file from the drawer and tromped to Kali's office. "Here you are," she said, crossing the room and handing the file to her friend.

"Thank you. ...Sarah, shut the door and sit for a minute."

Sarah obeyed, seating herself with eyes firmly cast on the floor and waiting for Kali to continue.

Kali watched the girl for a moment. She appeared broken, like a child whose hope has been snatched away. "Sarah, how are you doing?"

The young woman shrugged.

"How are things at home?"

"Okay."

"Really?"

Sarah started to nod, then stopped. She shook her head, tears slipping down her cheeks.

"My mom told me last night that I have to start putting out job applications, not just looking. She says after this semester, the center will drop my sponsorship, and I will have to drop out of school. So, I might as well just drop out now. I don't want to quit, Kali. I love college. I love everything about it. And I love working here, even though..."

Kali waited, but the girl did not seem inclined to continue. "Even though what?"

"Why did he ever go up on that roof by himself? Didn't he know he could get hurt? Why didn't he think about what would happen to us if something happened to him? Didn't he know we needed him?" The words tumbled out in an unstoppable torrent. Sarah bit down hard on her lip, trying to keep a similar flood of tears from escaping. Her voice dropped to a choked whisper. "Why did he do it, Kali? We need him."

The same angry questions had run through Kali's mind more than once. She knew it was part of the process they were all passing through, but for Sarah, it could mean destruction. Kali stood and made her way around the desk to the chair next to where the girl sat. She pulled Sarah into her arms and held her tight.

"I know, Sarah. I know," she whispered. "Mr. Thompson didn't mean for any of this to happen. He, like all of us, was just trying to scrape by. His roof leaked if he didn't keep the snow cleaned off. He'd done it a dozen times. This time, he just slipped."

The sobs escaped. Sarah's entire body shook with the pain that tore at her heart. "Kali, I'm not ready for a new director."

"I know. Neither am I. Oh, Sarah, I wish I could just make everything better. For you. For everyone. Just remember, even though Mr. Thompson is gone, God has not left us. He will not leave us. He promised that, and He never goes back on His promises.

"We'll do our best to help you stay in school next year. I can't guarantee we'll be able to do as much as what Mr. Thompson had arranged. I don't even know how he arranged it. But we will do the best we can. All right? Please, don't give up."

Slowly, the girl's tears began to subside. Kali held her until her breathing had calmed, and she seemed more at rest. Then she sat back. "Why don't you slip out to the ladies' room and get cleaned up a bit. We'll go to lunch together. I just need to make one call."

Sarah wiped at her nose. "Okay. Kali, thank you."

"We love you, Sarah. All of us. We don't want anything to happen to you. We're going to do our best to protect you."

Sarah slipped out of the room, shutting the door with only a whisper as it glided across the carpet. Kali went back to her desk, file still in hand. She took a deep breath to regain her composure, picked up her phone, and dialed the number Mr. Marsh had sent.

A gruff voice answered, sending a shiver dancing down her spine. She was tempted to hang up. That voice could never replace Sam's kind, happy voice. She couldn't go through with it—she had to.

"Hello, is this Wallace Kerry?"

"Yes."

"Hi, Mr. Kerry. This is Kali Shepherd at the Trevor Street Crisis Center. I received your information, sort of through the grapevine, from Mr. Marsh at Marsh and Line Clothiers. He said you're interested in working with us."

"Yes. Thank you for calling."

"I wondered if you might be able to bring in your resume and sit down to chat with the acting Assistant Director and me sometime later this week."

"I would love to. What time works for you?"

"Well, I was thinking perhaps Friday morning around eleven. I seem to have an opening then. We're getting ready for our Spring

Clothing Exchange. Mr. Marsh thought you might like to join us to get an idea of how things operate around here."

"That does sound like a good idea. Now, when is this exchange?"

"It won't be until next month, but we'll have lots to do to get ready. ...For now, let's focus on getting acquainted, and then we can fill you in on the details."

"Sounds like a good starting point. I'll see you on Friday at eleven then."

"Wonderful. Have a good afternoon, Mr. Kerry."

Before Kali had even had a chance to anticipate his goodbye, the receiver clicked with no parting salutation from the man. He seemed in a hurry to get away from her. His voice had softened as they spoke, and his words had all been kind, but something still didn't sit right. Maybe that same dread Sarah was feeling was steering her own heart. She'd never be ready for another director. No one could replace Sam.

Her computer dinged. She sat down and pulled up the email program. *Five new messages.* She glanced over the subjects and senders. All of them would require time, time she didn't have right now. They'd have to wait until she got back from lunch. But, before she could move away from the desk, she noticed the program was receiving something else. It was slow coming, which made her think it was something substantial. The computer dinged again, and the message popped into the queue. "Financial Plan," read the subject line. She glanced at the sender. Marsh and Line Clothiers. She shot a look out into the main office. Seeing Sarah had not returned, Kali clicked on the email and began to read.

Dear Miss Shepherd,

Mr. Marsh asked me to go over the files you sent in light of your recently lost partner. I've tried to find the best uses for your current funds. It's hard to make truly wise decisions because I am not fully aware of the scope and needs of each program.

My initial proposal is to cut salaries by no less than 10%, 15-20% would be better. I have made significant changes to the

*program funding as well, but I tried not to lose more than 5-10%
from any one place.*

*This is just a proposal. There is still time and room to
reconfigure before the end of the month. Would you be able to
send more information on the following programs:...*

A long list followed. Kali skipped to the end of the email.

*I wish to express how deeply sorry I was to hear of the loss of
your director. From all accounts, he was a good and godly man. I
too am a Christian, but as I hear his testimony, I am humbled.
I will be praying for you and your staff and look forward to
receiving the above information from you as soon as possible.*

Regards,

M.M.

"M. M.?" Kali said with more than a hint of confusion in her voice.

"M&Ms? I'll take some."

Kali looked up to see Kelly standing in the doorway. "Be quiet,
you." She laughed and started gathering her things for lunch. "I just
got the financial proposal back from Marsh and Line."

"And?"

"It's tough. I haven't read the full proposal, but he's recommending
huge salary cuts."

"We expected that, didn't we?"

"Yes. It's just the thought of having to tell Sarah and Brenda
and Mac. ...Speaking of Sarah, we were just getting ready to go to
lunch. Would you care to join us?"

"I'd love to! Let me get my bag." Kelly started out the door, then
stopped and glanced over her shoulder at her friend. "It'll work out,
Kali. We'll go over it when we get back. Maybe it won't be as bad
as we're afraid it is. It'll work out. ...Save me some M&Ms."

CHAPTER 13

Matt sank deeper into the sofa than he'd been all day. He pulled his feet up under him and tugged at the blanket around his shoulders. He flipped the top page in the stack of papers he'd been reading and began going over its back:

"The shuttle program started several years ago when we realized many of the single moms in the area surrounding the center often struggled to find transportation to and from important appointments such as medical appointments, job interviews or training, CPS visits, etc. We felt this was a simple, basic need that could be met easily as long as we had the right equipment and qualified volunteer drivers.

"Over the last five years, we have transported scores of women and their children more than 50,000 miles. Each trip allows us to learn more about the family's needs, to share counsel, and to demonstrate the love of Christ. We currently have two volunteer mechanics and ten drivers operating four vehicles."

"Wow," Matt whispered to himself. "Who would have thought of such a simple but effective outreach? —Sam Thompson, that's who."

"Matt! Are you here?"

Matt turned in his seat and looked back through the house toward the front door. "I'm in the den, Dad."

No response came, but Matt could hear his father's steps echoing off the wood floors until the man was standing in the doorway.

"Are you sick?"

"No, just had some stuff that needed extra attention, so I brought it home at lunchtime. Fewer distractions here."

"It's cold in here. Didn't you reset the thermostat when you came in?"

"Nah. I've had a fire going most of the time. I just let it burn down because I know the heat will be coming on in a few minutes. In fact," he paused, listening, "there it goes now. I can hear the furnace starting up."

"You are your mother's son. She never did like that hot air blowing around, always preferred a fire."

"Yep. So why are you home early?"

"I was worried about you."

"Worried about me? Why?"

"I had a meeting cancel, so I stopped by your office, thinking you might want to grab an early supper. But they told me you'd gone home at lunch and hadn't been answering any calls or text messages. I thought maybe you'd gone home sick. I even picked up a whole case of chicken noodle soup on my way home."

"A whole case!" Matt nearly choked with laughter. "Well, I guess we'll be eating chicken and noodles for a while."

The older man shrugged, managing to smile at his own folly, "I can think of worse things to have around. ...So, what are you working on?"

Matt picked up the stack of papers that rested in his lap and waved them through the air haphazardly, "I've had this for two days now and barely had a chance to touch it, so I thought I'd better get on it."

"What is it?"

"Well, you know I've been working on the financial plan for the Trevor Street Crisis Center?"

"Yes." The man chuckled. "The Lord really worked that one out, didn't He?"

Matt's eyes lit up at that, and he couldn't help the grin that slid across his face. "Yes, He did. So, when I sent my first proposal, I asked

Miss Shepherd to send me more detailed information about each program, how it works, and specifics on its financial requirements. At first, she sent a generic PDF, which they send out to potential partners. It gives a brief overview of each program.

"Later, however, she sent a file their volunteer accountant pulled together last fall. It goes into intricate detail of what resources each program needs to operate. It also gives far more detailed descriptions of the goals and procedures of each program."

"Really?" Curiosity drew the older man into the room and over to the enormous, leather armchair where he sank down on the seat's edge. "What do you think so far?"

"I'm not finding much waste, that's for sure. I'm overwhelmed by all they've been doing. They only had six employees with Sam, the rest are volunteers. Even their accountant is a volunteer—and he has no small task on his hands. I'm just...my head is swimming with it all."

The older man studied his son for a moment. Once again, he could see a deepening passion for the situation at the center, but he decided to say nothing for now. "So, have you decided on any recommendations?"

"How? How can I ask them to cut anything? I mean, which would you rather cut: a program helping single moms get their kids to the doctor or a program mentoring at-risk kids or a life-skills program for those same kids? How do you choose between those? And *all* of the choices are along those lines."

"Well, I'll be praying for you."

Matt rolled his eyes and grunted. "Thanks. I don't suppose you'd want to look over it with me."

"Maybe. But not tonight. Tonight, I'm going to eat chicken and noodle soup, read a few pages in a book, and go to sleep. I'm beat. Want some soup?"

Matt slid to the edge of his seat. "It sounds like we'd better get started on it, or we'll still be eating it this time next year."

CHAPTER 14

"Excuse me, Miss?"

Sarah popped up from behind her desk, her face red both with embarrassment and with the warmth of practically standing on her head in search of her pen. She blinked dumbly at the man before her. The stranger was average height with a large belly and thick glasses, which perched on the tip of a thin, pointed nose.

"I'm sorry," she stammered, "I dropped something, and I can't seem to find where it went. How can I help you?"

"I'm here to see Miss Shepherd."

"Is she expecting you?"

The man pushed his glasses up and wiped the back of his hand across his mouth. "Yes. We have an appointment at eleven. My name is Wallace Kerry."

"Oh, Mr. Kerry. Yes, she is expecting you. Let me see if she's ready."

Sarah hurried around her desk, across the main office, and into Kali's office. She knocked on the doorframe but went straight to the desk without stopping.

"Mr. Kerry's here."

"All right. Just send him in. Have Kelly come in here, please."

"He's nothing like what I expected," Sarah whispered, glancing over her shoulder at the man who still waited at her desk.

"Is that good or bad?" Kali whispered in return.

Sarah's mouth twisted to one side, her eyes darting in the opposite direction, then she grinned at Kali. "You'll just have to see for yourself." She spun around, stepped out of the office and said, "Miss Shepherd will see you now, Mr. Kerry."

Kali watched the man seated across from her. In the last five minutes, he had wiped his nose with his fingers more times than she could count. She was destined to get sick. There was no way around it. She'd have to disinfect his chair once he'd gone—and anything else he'd touched for that matter. She glanced at Kelly, who sat quietly in the corner, watching and listening. The raised eyebrow she saw from her friend told her Kelly hadn't missed the man's action either. Kali's gaze went back to the man just in time to see him wipe his nose once more. She couldn't help the smile that twitched at the corner of her mouth.

"I'm surprised we've never met before," he was saying. "I've been involved in various ministries at most of the churches in the area for many years."

Kali shrugged. "Sometimes this town is just big enough that people you think you ought to know, you don't. So, tell me about why you're interested in working with us, Mr. Kerry."

"Sure." The man pulled his suit jacket a little tighter and rearranged himself in his chair as he gathered his thoughts. "Well, I met Sam Thompson at a garage sale a few years ago."

"At a garage sale?" Kelly couldn't help her voice cracking with surprise at that beginning.

"Yes. We just happened to end up at the same sale. There he was, piling up all the children's clothing he could, armloads of it, and then offering to take the whole lot at some ridiculously low price. I couldn't believe what I was seeing, so I asked him, 'Do you have a dozen kids, or do you run a children's home?' I was joking, but he came back completely serious. He told me who he was, what the center was all about, and how he intended to use the clothes. He smiled the whole time he was telling me about it. I could tell he absolutely loved what he was doing. The more I listened, the more I realized this was something I could get behind.

"But you know how life goes. I had other ministries I was involved in, and it just never seemed to work out for me to come down here. Well, a couple weeks before Sam passed, I ran into him again. We were talking about the center, and he suggested I come down here for a couple days and learn how things work. We'd actually set it up for the week after his accident.

"At about the same time, several doors of opportunity that had seemed pretty wide open for my own ministry just shut with no apparent reason. When I heard about Sam, I started praying about what would happen here, and finally let Pastor Hanson know I was interested in helping. He's probably the one who gave you my information."

"So then," Kelly put in, "I take it you have a résumé and references?"

Kali glanced in her friend's direction, sensing impatience in her voice. Her own eyebrow went up this time, sending a warning to the other woman. But neither Kelly nor Mr. Kerry seemed to notice.

"Yes. Here you are." The man reached down into the computer bag he had positioned on the floor next to his chair. He pulled out a neat packet and handed it to Kali. Then he leaned back, pushing his glasses up once more.

"So, have you had any experience running a ministry like this in the past?" Kali asked as she took the packet.

"Not a ministry with so many different facets, however, I have run individual ministries similar to the programs you have going now."

"I see." Kali's eyes swept over the résumé for a few moments, but to her grief-weary mind it seemed like nothing more than random bits of information. She would have to study it later when she could read it out loud and think it through. "How many years of experience do you have in these types of ministries?"

"Oh, at least fifteen. Like I said, I've worked with most of the churches in town at some point or another."

"How long was your longest time in one ministry?"

The man grew thoughtful. He wiped his mouth, leaving a grimy white trail on his fingers. "Well," he said as he ran his sticky fingers across his shirt and pulled his jacket tight again, "some of them I've worked simultaneously, but I'd say the longest was probably, oh, about three and a half, maybe four years."

Kali nodded, somehow feeling his answer fit the man's personality. "Well," she said at last, "I'd like to read over your information a bit, and I thought I'd give you some info about our upcoming clothing exchange so you can see if you'd be interested in helping. We'll have to do a background check before we can allow you to do any work, volunteer or otherwise, with the center. We thought the prep-week coming up might be a good place for you to get a flavor for how we work around here."

"Sure," the man's eyes took on a new light as he spoke. He grew animated, leaning forward in his seat and pushing his glasses up with his knuckles. "That sounds like a great idea. When should I be here?"

"Well, we start prepping on Monday, but I won't have the results of the background check by then. I'll give you a call when I get it."

"Sounds perfect."

"Good. Then I will call you as soon as we get the background check. Then you can come in whenever you are available next week to help us sort clothing and eventually set up the exchange."

"Wonderful! I'll be waiting for your call." The man stood, stepped up to Kali's desk, and thrust out his hand.

Kali cringed. She forced a smile and shook the man's hand, sensing at the same time that Kelly was smirking at her on the other side of the room.

"Thanks for coming in, Mr. Kerry," Kelly said, shoving her hands into her pockets as she came to her friend's rescue, "I hope you have a wonderful afternoon."

"Thank you, ma'am." The man nodded in Kelly's direction, and then he was gone, almost quicker than Kali could reach for her hand sanitizer—almost.

CHAPTER 15

Kelly stared at the blinking cursor on the screen. She'd caught up on everything else, or maybe she'd just run out of ways to delay the inevitable. She needed to work on a new blog post for the website, but every time she tried, her mind went blank and her heart felt empty. How could she write to encourage others when she had so little to offer?

"Kelly, how many tables do we need to set up at the community center for the clothing exchange?"

"Mac!" Kelly greeted their lovable maintenance man with an enormous smile as he came through her office door. "How are you?" She said, leaving her seat and rushing to give the man a hug.

"I'm good, Miss Kelly. How are you?"

"I'm fine. How was your trip to see your daughter?"

"It was good, but when I heard what was going on here, I wanted to come back to be with all of you. I'm sorry I couldn't come sooner. It was too expensive to change the tickets."

"Oh, Mac, we understand. We missed you too. I'm so glad you're back."

"I know you missed me! This place is a mess!"

Kelly laughed heartily, the weight from the previous moment disappearing from her thoughts. "Believe it or not, we really did try to keep up with things. It's just been so busy."

"No problem! I'll have this place back in good shape in no time. Now, how many tables should I have ready to load into the trailer for the clothing exchange?"

"Let's start with twenty-five. Do you need help?"

"I'll help." Brandon, who sat at Gil's desk just outside Kelly's office, had been listening to the conversation and now rose from his seat.

"Aren't you working on information packets for the exchange?" Kelly said.

"Yes, but I could use a break, and Mac needs the help."

"Why are you at Gil's desk anyway?"

"Oh, I was just looking up some information for one of the brochures. He forgot to give it to me before he left last night."

"All right. If you help Mac, don't get so distracted that those packets don't get done."

"No worries. They'll get done. Let's go, Mac." The two men walked off, smiling and catching up on all the news from Mac's trip.

Kelly watched them go and then returned to her desk. Brandon had been a bright spot in all of this. Sarah still seemed to keep her distance, but she seemed to be doing that with everyone from time to time.

Brandon had been moved by Sam's death, just as they all had been, but he had also stepped up in a way they had never expected. He'd been one step ahead of them on several occasions, filling in where Mac normally would have been working, helping Gil with projects he couldn't keep up with, helping Brenda clean and reorganize the kitchen for a health department inspection, even dropping a note of encouragement on Sharon's desk a time or two.

The young college student had gone far beyond anyone's expectations. Brandon came in, day after day, even on days when he wasn't scheduled to be there. Sometimes he just stopped by to say hello. Other days, he offered help on projects Sam typically would have overseen. All the while, his own responsibilities were never left unfinished. It was good to have a dependable soul on their ship.

"Kelly."

"Hmm?" Kelly looked up from the still flashing cursor, surprised she hadn't noticed Kali stepping through her doorway.

"You okay?"

"Yes. I was just thinking how nice it is to have Mac back, and what a blessing Brandon has been."

Kali's blue eyes lit up. "Mac does bring life back to this place. He's a good man."

Kelly returned her friend's smile, but then a quizzical expression climbed in her eyes. "What are you up to?"

"Oh, I just wanted to go over some details for the clothing exchange. Do you have a few minutes?"

"For you? Always."

Kali took up her usual seat near the door. She pushed the door shut before shuffling through the stack of papers she'd brought with her. "We've done this so many times now. It's old hat—but with a major twist."

"There's no Sam to lead it?"

"Exactly."

Did you ask Micah if he'd be willing to come help?"

"No. I couldn't. Things are not going well out there. He wanted to be back here to start going through Sam's house weeks ago, but… His mom is still really struggling. I would say she's battling depression, but I think Micah and his dad are the only ones battling it."

"Have they talked to anyone who might be able to help her? A counselor or pastor?"

"I don't know. I think Micah is about to break. He doesn't want to leave his dad with everything, but he's under so much pressure. He hasn't found any work out there. If he didn't have a couple of rental properties here in town, he'd be in big trouble. His position here is still being held for him. In fact, the company wants him to make a trip soon so he can give some counsel on a couple of projects. They just want him to come for a day or two, but he's not sure about leaving his parents. I think he's torn, just completely torn."

"What about his brother, Zach?"

"He's just far enough out of town and working fifty hours a week. It's hard for him to get away to come help."

"Maybe Mrs. Thompson could go spend some time with Zach's family. I'm sure it would do her good to see her grandkids for a few days."

Kali shrugged, and Kelly could see the idea held little promise.

"So," Kelly continued, "if Micah hasn't found any work, does that mean he doesn't have the money to come back here?"

Tears welled in Kali's eyes. "Yes," she whispered.

"Would he come if he had the money?"

"I don't know. I haven't asked him. But where would we get the money?"

"I don't think that's our job. I think that's a job for Mr. Marsh."

"But, Kelly, don't you think that's a bit forward?"

"No. I think it's a bit necessary. For all of us. We have no one but you and me to take the lead on this thing, and we're already swamped with our usual work."

"Well…actually…that's what I wanted to talk to you about. … There is Mr. Kerry."

"Mr. Kerry! The guy who wipes his nose all the time?"

"Kelly!"

"What? It's true."

"Well, of course it's true, but that doesn't mean you should describe him that way to others."

Kelly started to make a smart retort but realized it would only bring them to the brink of an argument. She had little regard for Wallace Kerry, but she knew Kali was hopeful. She had so much resting on her shoulders. She needed a break, and she was hoping the strange man might somehow prove to be as worthy of their respect as he and his résumé claimed he was.

"I'm sorry. You're right," Kelly conceded. "I'll tell you what, let me call Mr. Marsh and discuss it with him. If we can get Micah out here for the rest of this week and a few days following the exchange so he can go through some of Sam's things and spend a couple days at work, then let's do it. If not…well…then we'll let Mr. Kerry give it a shot."

Kali pursed her lips in contemplation. "Well…all right. But tell me something first, aside from the nose wiping, what is it you don't like about Mr. Kerry?"

Kelly leaned back in her chair and tugged at her sweater, drawing it tight around her and wishing, not for the first time, that the zipper hadn't broken. She took a deep breath and let it out slowly, trying to find the words she needed and coming up short. "I don't know. There is something—a gruffness, an arrogance, a harshness—something seems to lie under the surface. …I keep expecting it to come out in full bloom, but so far it hasn't."

"Maybe that's just a perception. He seems to behave in a kind manner most of the time."

"I know. I'm just…I don't trust him. Not fully. Not yet."

"Maybe this week will alleviate some of that."

"I hope so. …Okay," Kelly decisively pulled the phone toward her as she spoke, "you go do whatever it was you were going to do, and I'll call Mr. Marsh."

"I was going to talk to you, remember? But you kind of hijacked the conversation."

"Oh, yeah." Kelly's cheeks reddened as she spoke. "Sorry about that. What else did you want to talk about?"

"We need to get our shuttle drivers up to speed on their responsibilities for the days of the exchange, and make sure we don't have any conflicts with regular shuttle clients already having appointments scheduled that we're not aware of. We also need to find out how Brenda is doing on the food preparation. She may need additional help. We need to start letting churches and volunteers know the volunteer schedule." Kali returned to the list in her hands, making sure she was still on track. "Oh, yes. We need to be sure Sharon has enough help with staging all of the clothing. That will be the biggest job. I know she's fairly well organized, but I also know what happens between the storage room and the community center. Oh, and then there's all of the stuff that has nothing to do with the clothing exchange."

"Stop," Kelly said, holding up both hands and waving back the next long recitation of upcoming tasks. "You go talk to Brenda and Sharon. I'm calling Mr. Marsh. We need Micah. In fact, we may need a whole army of Micahs."

Kelly had already picked up the phone and was dialing before Kali even had a chance to get out her "But—"

Kelly waved her off and shooed her out the door as she heard a clicking sound on the other end of the line.

"Marsh and Line Clothiers. How may I direct your call?"

"Mr. McKinsey Marsh, please."

"Just one moment. I'll transfer you to his assistant."

"Thank you."

Kelly leaned back in her chair, at perfect peace that she was doing the right thing. She listened to the soft music that played as she waited. It was pleasant, very much like Mr. Marsh himself had always seemed in their phone conversations. She'd never met him in person, but the few times they'd spoken on the phone she'd liked him. She often wondered about the "Line" portion of the company. She'd never had any acquaintance with that side of the business.

"McKinsey Marsh."

"Oh. Uh. Mr. Marsh?"

"Yes, this is McKinsey Marsh."

"Oh, hello. I thought I was being transferred to your assistant, but this is better. You're the one I actually want to talk to. This is Kelly Vance from the Trevor Street Crisis Center."

"Well, hello there. How can I help you?"

The man's voice was kind and welcoming. Still, Kelly couldn't help feeling a little awkward about her call barging straight onto his desk. "I'm sorry to bother you so unexpectedly, Mr. Marsh, it's just that…well, we need a little extra help, and we're not sure how to go about getting it here."

"Getting it here? What do you mean?"

"Well, we have our Spring Clothing Exchange coming up this weekend. We'll be preparing all week. It requires an enormous amount of oversight, oversight which Sam usually would have given. Kali and I are both swamped with everything else. I mean, we have to keep everything else moving smoothly at the same time as we're pulling the exchange together. Kali is getting overwhelmed, and to be honest, I've already been overwhelmed for a couple of days.

"So, we were wondering…actually, I was wondering…if you might be able to talk to the board about helping us find a way to get Micah Thompson back here for about two weeks. He's helped us with this project in the past and knows it inside and out. He also needs to get back here for a while to take care of some business regarding Sam's house and his own job. He doesn't know I'm calling by the way. I just… I don't know. I thought perhaps we could present the need to the board and see if anyone has any ideas or ways to make it happen. I know it's short notice. We're just finding it to be a bit much."

Marsh grunted a thoughtful sort of grunt. Kelly was sure she could hear him drumming his fingers on the desk. "What about that man Kerry?" he said. "I thought Miss Shepherd had brought him in and interviewed him and was planning to use his help this week."

"That is a possibility..."

"But?"

"But I think we'd be better off with someone we know better, and who has a better understanding of the goals, purposes, and modes of operations the center has held to all these years. I'm sure he's a good man, Mr. Marsh, we're...I mean...I'm just not very comfortable with him yet."

The man was silent for a moment. Then he cleared his throat and said in a fatherly tone, "That was very courageous of you."

"What do you mean?"

"Admitting you have qualms and that they are yours instead of hiding behind the others, but I wonder... Do the others share your concerns?"

"I'm not sure. Some do, I think."

"Well, let me see what I can do. When do you need Micah here?"

"No later than Thursday, I'd say. Wednesday would be better."

"All right. I'm sure, at this point, some of it may depend on the airlines, but we'll see what we can do. ...Do me a favor. Send all of the information for the flights, Micah's contact information, and for the exchange itself to Mel Zimmerman. She's the assistant in the accounting department and usually handles all of our travel arrangements as well. Do you have her email address?"

"I don't, but I think Kali does."

"Well, if she doesn't, just give Mel a call and let her know you talked with me. You get the details to her, and I'll get on the phone with the other board members. We'll see what we can do. Maybe someone will have some extra miles they aren't going to use. ...Miss Vance, how are Sam's parents doing?"

Kelly hesitated. She knew what Kali had shared earlier had come from her friends' private conversations. She didn't want to betray their trust. At the same time, she wanted to paint an accurate picture for the man. She let out a deep breath, laced with frustration.

"Not very well from what I hear. Kali thinks his mom is really dealing with depression, and his dad is just plain worn out. Micah's been stretched pretty thin trying to help them."

Again, a thoughtful silence met her explanation. Finally, Marsh responded. "Miss Vance, do you have their contact information?"

"Yes. Of course."

"Can you include that in the information you send to Miss Zimmerman? I think I'd like to try to do something for them."

"Of course. I'll be sure to."

"Wonderful."

"Thank you, Mr. Marsh. Thank you so much."

"You're welcome. I'm glad to help. ...Miss Vance, how are *you*? You girls have carried on over there, taking care of everyone who walks through those doors, but you have been through tremendous loss. How are *you* holding up?"

Kelly choked at the sincere compassion in the man's voice. No one ever asked that question. They were just expected to press on, to do as they always had done, and be who they'd always been. She blinked back tears and somehow managed to whisper, "I'm okay, Mr. Marsh. Thank you for asking."

The man knew from her pinched voice that his suspicions had been right. His two hero women were feeling frail.

"Kelly—I hope you don't mind me calling you Kelly—I want you to know I pray for you every morning. *Every* morning. I can't be there day in and day out, but I am there in prayer, fighting with you. Don't give up. We may have a long battle ahead of us, but you and Miss Shepherd and the others are not in it alone. We're here, and we're praying."

Kelly could not speak. She was too overwhelmed by the emotion his kindness had brought.

The man took her silence in stride. He knew he'd said enough and had no desire to push her any closer to the emotional precipice she was nearing. "Well, I'll let you get back to your work," he said. "If you ever need anything, please don't hesitate to call. That's why we're here."

"Thank you, Mr. Marsh. Thank you so much."

"Anytime."

The line clicked, and the call ended. Kelly set the receiver in its cradle, rose mechanically, crossed the room, and closed her office door. She needed a moment to pull herself together. She took a deep breath and let it out as she leaned back against the door. As he had spoken, the man's kindness had been like tearing away a bandage on a wound, but now it was like a warm blanket, wrapping around her in that cold office. Better still was the thought that Micah could be getting on a plane any day now. And, at least for a few days, they might just have that one precious comfort of normalcy and friendship.

CHAPTER 16

Sharon drew in a deep breath and let it out in loud frustration. She set down a stack of clothes and let her hands come to rest on her hips as she surveyed the large hall. The stress levels at the crisis center were growing. She'd felt the pressure not only of her regular resource development duties but also of the increased load of preparing for the clothing exchange. She'd set up for the exchange three years in a row, but on the previous occasions she'd had quite a few volunteers helping her. This year, in the wake of Mr. Thompson's death, volunteers were scarce.

People seemed to have forgotten they existed as if the center had died with Mr. Thompson. Sometimes, Sharon wondered if it had. Maybe they were all doing this, all fighting to keep something alive that had no hope of survival. What was the point? Why go through all the stress and the frustration and the fatigue? Why push the hurt of losing Mr. Thompson to a deeper level? Why delay the inevitable pain of dealing with the loss?

"Do you need help, Sharon?"

Sharon jumped, spinning around at the sound of the voice and meeting Brandon's gaze with wide, frightened eyes.

"I'm sorry. I didn't mean to startle you." The dark-haired young man smiled a smooth, bewitching smile.

Sharon had always thought he'd make a handsome husband for one of her girls. If only her girls were interested in good men.

"Can I help you with anything?"

"Brandon, you don't know how glad I am to see you."

The smile broadened into a grin. "That tells me you have work for me."

"I most certainly do. See that section of tables at the far end of the room?"

"The empty ones?"

"Yes. Those are meant to be the boys' sizes 7-14 shirts, shorts, pants, whatever it might be. If it goes into that size group, it needs to be on those tables. Everything needs to be sorted by size, item type, and preferably by style—dress versus play versus casual. Most of the work is already done, but there's always a chance something has gotten mixed up between the crisis center and here. The clothes should all be in the boxes under the tables."

Brandon nodded, but the grimace on his face told Sharon he had no idea how he would manage the request.

"Come on. I'll show you."

The pair walked across the large hall of the community center, neither speaking. Brandon was content to survey the transformation the room had already undergone since they'd set up the tables the previous day. Sharon, on the other hand, had her ears tuned to the conversations around her. That, she had learned, was a good way to avoid mistakes made by volunteers who didn't quite know what they were doing.

"You all have done a good job putting this together." She heard one man saying.

"Well," came the response from a second man, "I've really had little part in it, but when I do have a chance, we'll do things differently. I think we could have been a bit more organized."

Sharon turned in the direction of the conversation, her eyes taking on the piercing gaze of a hawk as she hunted the room for the speakers.

"Seems very organized to me," came the first voice again.

"Well, just think how quickly this would all go up if some of this sorting was already done."

"It's mostly sorted, just a few things out of place. It's more about arrangement than sorting, I'd say."

"I'm not sure this is a beneficial endeavor anyway." The second man's voice had taken on a superior tone, the sort of tone generally associated with an elevated nose. "I mean, what does it really do for anyone? Sure, a few women find clothes for their kids, but their kids will grow, the clothes will tear. What is it doing in the long run? It's not like it's teaching them job skills or helping them advance or sharing the gospel with them."

As the last three words were spoken, Sharon rounded the corner of a tall rack of dresses, her eyes landing on the speaker. Wallace Kerry. That strange man who dared to think he could take Mr. Thompson's place. Kali had sent him over to help and get acquainted with the way the exchange worked. He'd spent all of three hours here, and now he seemed to know everything—and then some.

"I don't know," continued the other man, whom Sharon recognized as Jordan Penny, a longtime volunteer and one of Sam's college friends. "First of all, they include a lot of good literature in the packets they hand out. A lot. Secondly, people in this neighborhood know this is a Christian organization. They know the exchange is being done out of love for God *and* for them. Thirdly, the center has other programs that meet those long-term goals you were talking about. I've been in the place of needing a quick answer to needs like this, and I'm eternally grateful to the people who helped me in those moments. They carried me through until I was able to go on to the next step."

Kerry shrugged. "Maybe. But if there was a need to cut spending, this is where I would start."

Horror flashed through Sharon's eyes. She turned away so the men would not see it. Sharon had lived a hard life. She rarely let anyone see emotion, rarely allowed herself to feel it, but this center— this program—meant the world to her. This program had kept her kids in clothes while she struggled to recover from the devastation that resulted from her husband's murder. Mr. Thompson's insistence that she come to the very first exchange to see if she could find school clothes for her girls had led her not just to the center but also to church and then to Christ. She was appalled at Kerry's behavior. The man's arrogance! The presumption! How could he say such things? Tears rolled down her cheeks. She hurried toward the exit, not wanting anyone to see her devastated heart.

"Sharon? Where are you going?" Brandon called after her.

But all she could do was wave his question away and rush through the exit of the large hall.

CHAPTER 17

Micah sat on a park bench overlooking Puget Sound, coffee in one hand, New Testament in the other. He did not read. He did not sip the hot, caffeine and sugar-laced liquid. Instead, he stared. He stared into the dull, morning sky and prayed.

"Lord, I need to go home. I need to see Kali. I need to spend a few days at work and start working on Sam's house. I didn't even get his refrigerator cleaned out. It must be awful by now. We'll probably just have to take it to the dump."

He moaned, his gaze dropping to the stones beneath his feet.

"Lord, I need a break. I can't do this anymore. I need to get away. …We need help, Lord. We need some serious help. Someone who's gone through this before. Someone who knows what we can expect. …How long am I going to feel like my guts have been torn out? How long is Mom going to be completely beside herself? Please, Lord, we need You."

He gazed out across the water once more. Behind him, the city was beginning to awake, but the Sound was still. A light fog danced across its surface, obscuring the most distant points of the water and catching the colors of the sunrise behind him. He could get used to this one thing about Seattle. The rest? The rest he could live without. He was already tired of the traffic, the noise, the mud, and the rain. He loved his parents and his brother and sister-in-law and their children, but this wasn't home. Not anymore. It wasn't home because this wasn't where his life was, it wasn't where Sam would have been, and it wasn't home because Kali wasn't with him. Without her, no place would ever be home.

"Lord, I miss her." He set his coffee aside and ran his hand through his dark hair.

The tiny sound coming from his pocket was so soft he nearly missed it. Had it not been for the vibration, he never would have realized someone was calling. Making a mental note to change the ringtone, he set his New Testament on the bench and began digging in his jeans' pocket. He managed to free the phone and was answering it before he even had it to his ear.

"Micah Thompson."

"Mr. Thompson, good morning. I hope I'm not calling too early."

"No, not at all."

"Oh, good. This is Melanie Zimmerman from Marsh and Line Clothiers. Mr. Marsh asked me to contact you about some travel arrangements."

"Marsh and Line? Travel arrangements? Is this some kind of joke?"

"No. Not at all. You see, Mr. Marsh is on the Board of Directors for the Trevor Street Crisis Center."

"Yes, I'm aware of that."

"Well, the center is still in need of a director, and they are about to have their Spring Clothing Exchange. Mr. Marsh is also aware you have some business to tend to here in town. So, after a bit of searching, we've been able to find a ticket for you to return for two weeks to help out and get some of your other work taken care of. I just need a few bits of information from you."

Micah stared, his mouth hanging open and his free hand resting on his hip.

"Mr. Thompson?"

"I don't understand. He's just sending me a ticket? How did he know I had business to tend to there?"

"Well, he's not just sending you a ticket. It'll all be electronic, you know. You'll need to check in online before your departure. As to how he knew you had things to tend to — I'm not really sure on that one. It's just what he told me. So, I will need your date of birth —"

"Wait. No. This isn't happening. I mean…I need to talk to my parents. I can't just up and leave them for two weeks."

"Mr. Marsh has already spoken with your father."

"What?"

"Yes. He spoke with him last night, very late apparently, and he has made arrangements for your parents to get away at the same time."

"Get away?"

"Yes. There's a retreat center for families who have recently lost a loved one. It's about sixty miles from your parents' home. They are under-booked right now, and Mr. Marsh was able to get your parents a cabin in a more secluded part of the resort. They will be close enough to everything to still participate in any events they wish to participate in, or they can just spend their time tucked away in the woods and walking the trails."

Micah shook his head in disbelief, trying desperately to grasp what the woman was telling him. "This can't be happening."

"I'm sorry?"

"You don't understand. I was just sitting here, praying God would open the doors for me to go back and at the same time praying about how to help my parents while I was gone. I…I just don't know what to say."

"Just say your birthdate. That would be a good place to start."

Micah laughed. He tossed his head back and sucked in a deep breath of the sea air, forcing the threatening tears to stay in his eyes. "Thank you. Thank you so much. Please, tell Mr. Marsh I said thank you, and the rest of the board too if they had any part in this."

"I will. Now, when were you born, Mr. Thompson?"

❈ ❈ ❈

"Kali! He's coming!" Kelly raced into her friend's office and slammed the door behind her, rattling the thin wall that separated them from the main office.

"What's going on? What are you talking about?"

"Micah, of course. Micah is coming!"

Kali's eyes widened, and she leaned forward, grabbing the edge of her desk. "Are you sure?"

"Yes! I just got an email from Mel Zimmerman. Everything is set. He will be coming in on Thursday and will be picking up a rental car at the airport, so no one has to meet him there. He'll be able to come straight to the Community Center! Isn't that wonderful!"

Kali was too overwhelmed to speak. Her heart soared. Micah was coming home! What a wonderful thought.

"I wish he were coming tomorrow," Kelly bubbled on with enthusiasm, "but I'm sure it was hard to find tickets on such short notice. Oh, Kali, aren't you excited?"

Kali nodded, blinking back tears and wiping her eyes. "Thank you, Kelly. Thank you."

CHAPTER 18

Kali could hear the phone at the reception desk ringing. She glanced out to the main office and saw that Brenda, Gil, and Brandon were all on the phone. Sharon and Sarah, she knew, were at the community center with Mac, and Kelly was in a meeting with the shuttle drivers. She picked up the receiver of her desk phone, and pushed the flashing line.

"Trevor Street Crisis Center. Kali speaking."

"Hi...I...uh...Is this the place that does the clothes thing?"

"The clothing exchange?"

"Yeah. ...When is it? I heard about it from a friend, but she didn't know when it was."

"It's on Friday and Saturday. All day both days, from nine until seven."

"And it's free?"

"Entrance is free, yes."

"But the clothes, are the clothes free?"

"It's an exchange. We ask that you bring at least three — clean — pieces of clothing. They should be in good repair as well, no stains or holes. That's all."

"So, we have to bring three?"

"Well, you can bring more if you like."

"Oh, okay. Well, thanks."

"You bet. Have a nice afternoon."

101

Kali turned back to the computer, trying to remember where she had been in the process of matching new students with available tutors, which were few and far between. She had just reached for her mouse when the desk phone buzzed. She groaned and tapped the speaker button.

"Yes?"

"Kali," came Gil's voice, "the rescue mission just called. They're wondering if we have any space at Hope House for a mom, two toddlers, and an infant."

"What!"

"Their house burned last night. The mission is full. They have no relatives in town. They'd only lived here about a month, so no real connection to the community at all. They lost everything. If ever there was a crisis—"

"No kidding. Okay, um, Kelly is handling Hope House right now. I'll go see if they're about done in that meeting. Thanks, Gil."

"Yep."

Kali lifted the receiver and dropped it back into place, ending the call. She saved her work and then headed for the conference room. Her knock was answered by several cheerful voices.

"Hey, guys," she said as she entered.

The ten volunteer drivers smiled back at her, some waved, others nodded.

"I'm sorry to interrupt. Are you making good progress?"

"We sure are," Kelly said. "These guys are awesome."

Kali's eyes brightened. Just being in the room with this group of men and women lifted her spirits. "I know they are," she beamed. "Best team we have. …Hey, Kelly, something has come up. How soon do you think you'll be available?"

"Five minutes?"

"Sounds great. I'll be in my office…as long as nothing else comes up. Oh! Since you don't have a car, maybe someone here could volunteer to help you this afternoon. Someone with child seats."

❊ ❊ ❊

Kelly stepped out of the warm car and onto the icy street. "I'll be quick, Abby."

"No problem. Take your time. My mom said I could be here as long as you need me."

"Thank you. And thank your mom for me too."

"I will."

Kelly pulled open the heavy front door and stomped her way into the lobby of the mission, leaving a trail of snow behind her. The large, poorly lit room was empty.

"Hello?" she called. "Anybody here?"

"I'll be out in just a second," came a panicked voice from a room somewhere down a narrow hall. "I'll be right there!"

Kelly chuckled to herself. "Boy, can I relate," she whispered.

"Did you say something?"

Kelly turned to see a tall, young man covered in flour emerging from the hallway.

"Just talking to myself."

"Oh, you know what they say about that."

"That it's a sign of insanity or that it's the only way to ensure a decent conversation?"

"Ha-ha! I'm inclined to believe the first, but I embrace the second. How can I help you?"

"I'm Kelly Vance from the crisis center. I'm supposed to pick someone up for the Hope House."

"Oh, yes. I heard you were coming. I'll go see if I can find her. She was in the dining room with her kids a little bit ago. I'll be right back."

Kelly waited patiently, wandering around the room and looking at the posters and pictures hung about the walls to advertise or celebrate various events. She noticed one man was in the pictures frequently. He seemed to change from one event to another, first appearing gruff and unkempt, and, little by little, taking on a softer, kinder appearance—jolly even. She smiled, wishing she could meet the man and learn his story.

"Miss Vance?" The tall man had returned and now searched the room for her. "Oh, there you are. She'll be right here. She was changing the little one's diaper." The man's eyes widened and lips curled, indicating the diaper had been a rather unpleasant one.

Kelly chuckled, but then she pointed to one of the posters. "Who is this man?" she asked.

"Let's see." The man stepped closer and leaned in to get a better view of the picture. "Oh, that's Frank."

"Does he live here?"

"Used to. Now he works here."

"Really?"

"Yeah. He's my boss actually."

"Your boss?"

"Yup. He's an amazing cook. Me, on the other hand, I'm good at making messes. I used to run the kitchen, but when Frank came along, I gladly surrendered my post."

Again, Kelly was laughing. "How did he go from here," she said, pointing to the first picture, "to being your boss?"

"Well, more importantly for you, how did he come to the mission in the first place? Frank came to us through Sam Thompson. They met on a street corner near the Market Square shopping development. Sam heard his story, got him medical help through the VA, and lined him up with us. Little by little, he's just turned into a whole new person. He reconnected with his children last summer, found out he has six grandchildren. It's a pretty awesome story."

"Did Sam know how well he was doing?"

The man shrugged. "I'm not sure. I hope so, but if he didn't before, he does now."

Tears climbed in Kelly's eyes at that thought. "You're right. He does." She reached to wipe her eyes as a young blonde woman walked into the room, infant in her arms and two little boys toddling beside her.

"Ah, here we go," the man said, turning away from the photos and moving toward the young woman. "Miss Vance, this is Brianna. Brianna, this is Kelly Vance from the Trevor Street Crisis Center. She's going to take you to the Hope House. Do you have everything?"

"Yes. This is it."

Kelly's eyes widened. The woman before her wore an old sweater over a thin t-shirt and well-loved pajama bottoms. Her two boys were also in their pajamas, no shoes, no coats or hats, just their footy pajamas.

"It's only ten degrees outside. Do you have any coats or shoes for the boys?"

Brianna shook her head. "Nope. This is us. This is all we have."

"Okay. Well, we need to take care of that. Let's head back to the center first and then we'll go from there. I have a car outside. Let me carry one of the boys for you, so their feet don't get wet."

"I'll get the other one," the tall man said.

Brianna nodded her thanks and directed one of the boys toward Kelly. "Come on, Evan. This is Miss Vance. She's going to carry you out to the car. It's okay. She's a nice lady. There you go."

Kelly picked up the tense, frightened little boy. She looked deep into his big, blue eyes. "So," she said, "you're Evan, huh? I'm Kelly. Did you know I have a little nephew about your size? His name is Nicholas. I think we'll get along just fine, kiddo."

The boy glanced at his mother, who smiled and brushed her finger across his cheek. Kelly felt him relax. He looked back at her, grinned sheepishly, and then nuzzled down against her neck.

"The boys are so tired," Brianna said. "I had just put them to bed when I discovered the hot water heater had caught fire. I had to rip them out of bed and get us all outside. We've been up ever since."

"You've been up ever since?"

Brianna nodded.

"Oh, let's get out of here. We need to get you guys settled."

❊ ❊ ❊

Kelly led Brianna into the main office of the crisis center and then stopped dead in her tracks. "*What* is going on?" she whispered, taking a wide-eyed survey of the room. She had never seen so many people rushing around the office, answering phones, making calls, gathering boxes and bags and trash cans and any other receptacle they could find.

Brandon rushed by them, a fistful of garbage sacks dangling from one hand and a stack of small storage bins under the other arm.

"Brandon, what on earth is going on?"

Brandon looked in her direction, still on the move, and groaned. "You need to talk to Kali. We're in a mess. A big one."

Kelly's shoulders stooped. "Great. Okay, Brianna, do you see that open door there on the other side of the office? That's the conference room. Why don't you guys go in there and make yourselves comfortable. I'll be right there."

"Kelly, I'm so sorry. We're just adding to your stress."

"No. Not at all. Please, don't think that, Brianna. I don't know what's going on here, but you and your babies are my number one priority. You guys get settled, and I'll be right back."

Kelly hurried to her friend's office, but Kali wasn't there. She turned and saw Gil coming out of a storage room, his arms full of plastic containers.

"Gil, where's Kali?"

"I think she's in the garage."

"The garage?"

"No, no. I'm here."

Kali rushed toward them from the hall that led to the back entrance, panting and wiping oil from her hands.

"Kali, what have you been doing? You're covered in oil!"

"I know. I'm pretty sure my favorite shirt is ruined."

"What happened?"

"I stretched too far trying to reach a storage bin and knocked over a can of oil."

Kelly scrunched up her face. "Sorry. I'm sure that was rather unpleasant. ...What's going on here? What's with all the storage bins and containers?"

"You're not going to believe it. I'm so glad you're back. We need *all* the help we can get. While everyone was at lunch, something triggered the sprinkler system in the community center. By the time everyone got back, the hall was flooded, and everything was soaked. All of the boxes are ruined. So, now, not only do we have to find a way to dry everything and boxes to put it all in, but we also have to find a new venue."

Kelly stared. Then she blinked repeatedly. "Kali, how are we ever going to find a new place *and* get everything set up in the next day and a half? We've already been at this for three days."

"I know. That's why I'm so glad to see you. I need your help."

"But, Kali, I can't help."

"What do you mean you can't help?"

"I mean, I can't help. I have an exhausted mom with three babies that have no clothes, no coats, no hats, no shoes, no home. I just came back here to get the paperwork filled out and then planned to take them over to the exchange for some clothes. That part obviously won't work, but I've got to get them settled. They've been up all night."

Kali ran her hands through her thick, blond curls and turned away for a moment. When she turned back, Kelly could see she was on the verge of tears. "Come into my office, please."

The two stepped into the room, and Kali shut the door, closing out the chaos of the other room.

"Kelly, I can't do this. I can't do this alone. I *need* you. Micah won't be here until late tomorrow afternoon. Everyone is in a panic. I've got all this and all the other usual stuff, and no one to help keep everything running smoothly. I can't do this." Kali took a deep breath, trying desperately to control her emotions. "Please, Kelly. I need you."

"Let's think this through," Kelly said, pacing the floor as she spoke. "You definitely need help. I definitely need to help Brianna. I can skip the paperwork and take it to them on a break Friday or Saturday. I can take her and get her situated at Hope House. Actually..." Kelly tapped a slender finger to her lips. "Amanda is still there. She's always asking what she can do to help the other women in the home. I'll let her get Brianna and her kids fed, bathed, and settled. Then I can come back and line up a new venue. You should focus on the other stuff you have going. But where does that leave us with the logistics of getting everything torn down, dried, moved, and set back up?"

"That's the hard part. I don't think Sharon can handle it all. Something has been bothering her all week. I don't know what it is, but she has seemed on edge. Maybe it's just the stress of it all. ...I tried to call Jordan. He helped out the other day. But all I got was his voicemail."

"Jordan's been pretty distant and distracted since Sam died. I mean, he was at the community center the other day, but he's not his usual self. I think it hit him harder than he wants to admit."

Kali nodded. "I noticed that too. But if he and the kids could help us transport stuff, it would be huge. It would probably be good for him too."

"What about Brandon and Gil, can't they go over and help?"

"No. They have to completely redo the maps and all of the other media-based stuff once we know our new location. They'll be just as swamped as everyone else. …Which reminds me, once we know where we're going to be, you'll need to put out a press release so we can hopefully redirect as many people as possible to the right place."

Kelly stopped pacing. She nodded her understanding of the need for the press release and chewed the corner of her mouth as she mulled over the situation. At last, she sighed. "I guess that leaves us with just one person."

"Who?"

"Mr. Kerry."

"Mr. Kerry?" Kali stared at her friend, knowing how uncomfortable she was around the man. "Do you think he can handle it?"

"Well, he thinks he can, or he wouldn't have applied for the position, right? I guess this is the chance for him to prove it. He said he wouldn't be available this morning, but if we needed him this afternoon to give him a call."

"I guess you're right. All he would have to do is get things packed up and to a laundromat—or four. That's a lot of clothes for just one place. Maybe by the time they get to that point, one of us will be free to help. I'll give him a call and see if he's willing to do it."

"Okay. Keep me posted." Kelly paused. She could see her friend was almost as frayed as the woman waiting for her in the conference room. She returned to where Kali stood and embraced her. "I love you, Kali. You're my best friend. I'm not going to abandon you. We just have to work through the details as they come. We'll make it. I'm sure we will."

CHAPTER 19

Micah stood in line at the QuickRide Car Rental service desk, realizing, not for the first time, that this particular company did *not* live up to their name. He reached into his pocket and pulled out his phone.

"*One missed call and voicemail,*" read the notification on the face of the phone.

"Huh, must have come through while I was waiting on my bags," he said to himself, sliding his finger across the screen and waiting for his voicemail to pop up. It was from Kali. He smiled as he lifted the device to his ear. Just a little longer and they'd be together again.

"Hi, Micah," came the sweetly familiar voice. "I know you're probably boarding, or maybe even already in the air. I just wanted to let you know we've moved the Clothing Exchange to yet another location. Things fell through at the hotel, so now we're in the gymnasium at Shallow Brook Christian School. I'm finishing up at the office, and Kelly is busy transporting clothing from one place to another. But we'll both be headed over there for the evening about the time you get in. We'll just plan on meeting you there. Can't wait to see you! Text me when you get here!"

Micah's smile widened. It was good to hear her voice, even if it did sound a bit frazzled. He accessed his text messages and began typing: "*Standing in line at SlowMotors Rental Company. See you soon!*"

* * *

Kelly walked into the gymnasium of Shallow Brook Christian School, arms full of shirts that had spilled out of their container in the back of the center's minivan. Her eyes swept across the enormous gym and came to rest on her longtime friend Jordan Penny, who worked quietly at a nearby table.

"Hey, Jordy," she said as she stepped up to the table. "Where's Sharon?"

"Um…I think she's over by the stage. Mr. Kerry's giving everyone a pep talk of sorts."

"A pep talk? We don't have time for pep talks. We have less than eighteen hours to get this place in shape, and we don't even have half the clothes on the tables."

Jordan shrugged and flashed a knowing smile in her direction. "Why do you think I'm not over there? And why do you think I just sent my girls for another load? I don't know where you guys found him, but I don't think he's a good fit for this place."

"He seems to think he is," Kelly said. "I'll go see if I can get everyone moving."

"Is there more to carry in?"

"A ton. …Thanks for coming on such short notice. You guys have been a huge help. I know how busy you are, Jordan. It means a lot that you would step away from everything to help us."

A grin spread across Jordan's face and up into the dancing blue eyes that all but hid under his tangle of gelled, blonde curls. The curls bounced as he leaned forward and playfully slapped his friend's shoulder. "That's what friends are for, Kelly. …Man, I've got to get a haircut tomorrow."

Kelly burst out laughing. "I was thinking the same thing. Thank you, Jordy. You always brighten a place up."

"It's my pleasure."

Kelly smiled at him once more and then returned to the task at hand. She spotted an empty table not far from where she stood, deposited her armload of shirts, and made her way toward the front of the gymnasium. As she approached, she could see Wallace Kerry standing near the stage, his arms spread open wide—except when he was wiping his nose. His voice was soft. Before him stood several of their regular volunteers, listening with brows furrowed and arms crossed. Confusion, and in some cases anger, filled their faces.

"See, this is the problem these days," Kerry was saying. "People get themselves tangled up in organizations that don't have enough leadership or guidance, and they get sidetracked and pulled away. Now, this, this is where this event should have been held in the first place. Right here in the gymnasium of a Christian school. Not in some city-owned community center. We need a leader here that will stand on God's principles and not get caught up in all the other things—things that water us down as Christians. All this doing, doing, doing. We've got to *be* who God wants us to be before we can do what God wants us to do."

Kelly's mouth gaped. She couldn't believe what she was hearing. How could he stand there, in the midst of one of their longest standing events, an event that had brought more women and children into local churches than she could count, and say such things? How could he imply Sam, of all people, had been tangled up in worldly things? Sam who'd died because he put so little emphasis on his own comfort. Sam, who sought God day after day, moment by moment. How could he imply Sam wasn't who God wanted him to be?

"If we can get this ministry refocused, then we'll really be heading in the right direction." The man wiped his nose on the back of his hand. "I've got some great plans. I know every pastor in town, so, as director, I'll be making contact with all these men. We'll get this place turned around."

Kelly felt her chest tighten. Her hands clenched into fists at her sides. How dare he! How dare he say these things right here in the midst of their own event to volunteers who had given countless hours—days—to do nothing more than simply help others and serve God. How dare he!

Sharon stood on the far side of the little knot of volunteers. She could see Kelly, could see her face turning red and the hurt rising in her eyes. She saw the young woman tense and draw in a deep breath to brace herself. Knowing all too well the pain Kelly was feeling in such a moment of betrayal and realizing her friend was about to do something she would regret, Sharon pulled out her cellphone and dialed Kelly's number. Just as Kelly stepped forward to address the man, the sweet ringtone that so fit her personality filled the air.

The red of Kelly's anger deepened with embarrassment. She pulled her phone from her pocket and began a quick exodus to the corridor.

"Hello? Hello?"

"It's me, Kelly."

Kelly spun around to see Sharon following her out of the gymnasium.

"Are you all right?" the older woman asked.

"No. I'm not all right. How dare he? How can he stand there and make those kinds of statements, and accuse Sam—without actually saying it mind you—of all those things? Sam was a good man. He did what he believed God was leading him to do. Who is Mr. Kerry to question what he was never around to see? He knows nothing about this ministry and nothing about Sam. How dare he!"

"Kelly. Calm down."

"No! I will not calm down! How can he presume to stand in Sam's shoes and act like that? Doesn't he have a conscience? How can he defame Sam like that?"

"Kelly. It's okay. Calm down."

"It's not okay! There's nothing OK about it—nothing! Where is Gil? I thought someone said he was here. Or, Jordan. Jordy can help."

"Gil is helping Brenda set up the kitchen."

"I'm going to find him. I'm going to find one of them. We need to get that man out of here! He's done. I don't care if this whole event falls apart. That man has to go."

Sharon laid a gentle, but firm hand on Kelly's arm. She looked Kelly in the eyes with a gaze that melted the younger woman clean to the soul.

"Kelly," she whispered, "we know who Mr. Thompson was, and that is all that matters."

"But how can he say those things, Sharon, how?" Kelly dissolved into sobs and fell against Sharon, her heart broken anew. She felt Sharon's arms come up around her, and for the first time in weeks she felt loved.

"It's okay, Kelly. We're all still here, and we're not going to forget who Mr. Thompson was. I think you should take a break. Go get some fresh air. I'll find Gil. We'll take care of Mr. Kerry."

"But I can't leave you to handle all of this alone, Sharon. It's so much."

"God has brought us an abundance of volunteers this afternoon, far more than we expected. Just go, Kelly. Don't let anyone stop you. You just march right out those doors and don't come back until you're ready. We'll be all right."

Still crying, the young woman stepped back. She wiped at her tears to no avail. "I'm sorry, Sharon."

"No need to apologize. You've been strong for all of us. It's our turn to be strong for you. Now go, before people figure out you're here. Go."

❊ ❊ ❊

Micah pulled into the driveway of the Shallow Brook Christian School and glanced in his rearview mirror.

"Well, what do you know!" His eyes brightened with the broad grin that shot across his face. "A little blue Corsica right behind me. What are the odds?"

He pulled into a space and got out of the car, waiting as the Corsica pulled in beside him. The driver did not check to see who was beside her. Instead, she got out of the car and turned to walk toward the building.

"What? No hello?"

At the familiar voice, Kali spun around. "Micah! You're home!" She rushed around the rental car to where he was waiting and threw her arms around his neck, bouncing up and down with glee. "Oh, Micah! I have missed you so much! I'm so glad to see you."

He returned her hug, laughing and feeling the pressure of happy tears against his eyelids. Then he stepped away and studied her face in the dim evening light. "I have missed you so much, Kali. It's so good to see you. …You look tired. Are you okay?"

"Now that you're here, I'm wonderful."

113

He smiled at the comment. "And before I got here? I'm serious. Are you okay?"

"I'm fine. I'm just running on very little sleep and lots of caffeine. How was your flight?"

"Great. No problems. All of my luggage made it, and we even arrived on time. ...Shall we go inside? It's cold out here."

"Ha!" she laughed, nudging him toward the front of the building. "That warm Seattle weather has spoiled you! Yes, we can go inside. Kelly will be excited to see you. I know everyone else will be too, but Kel—"

As Micah reached to open the front door, it flew open, and, to their surprise, none other than Kelly rushed past them, tears streaming down her face.

"Kelly?" Kali said, her voice full of confusion.

But Kelly had not noticed whom she was passing. She did not hear her friend. She was set in whatever direction her distraught mind had chosen, and there was no deterring her.

Kali's confusion changed to concern. "This can't be good. We'd better get in there." She motioned for Micah to go inside.

"Should we go after her?" Despite Kali's urging, Micah stood motionless, staring after Kelly, who had disappeared around the corner of the building.

"No. I'll give her a couple minutes to calm down and then come back to find her. Let's go find out what happened."

The pair entered the building and let their eyes adjust to the strange light of the poorly lit corridor. Sharon stood at the main door leading into the gym, wringing her hands nervously.

"Sharon, is everything all right?"

"Kali. Micah! Oh, I'm so glad to see you both. No, things are not all right. I don't know where Mr. Kerry came from, but he needs to go. He has Kelly in tears. He just keeps going on and on about how things should be done and how the only way to do it is his way and how everything we've ever done here has been wrong because it isn't all connected to a church."

"But," Kali retorted, "most of the volunteers in there came from churches he claims to work with."

Micah put a steadying hand on Kali's shoulder. She turned and looked up into his serious eyes. Determination met her gaze.

"You stay here," he said, "I'll take care of this. Sharon, lead the way."

Without hesitation, Sharon stepped through the doorway and led Micah straight up to the stage where Kerry's diatribe continued.

"Mr. Kerry," she said brusquely, boldly interrupting his speech, "this is Micah Thompson, Sam's brother. Have you two met?"

The man stammered, pushing his glasses further up his nose. "No. No, I don't believe we have met. Mr. Thompson, very pleased —"

"Hello, Mr. Kerry," Micah interrupted, not bothering to take the offered hand, "I hear you've been helping the past couple of days."

"Yes. That's right."

"Thank you for that. I wasn't able to get here any sooner. If you don't mind, I'll be taking the lead from here. I believe we have a lot to accomplish between now and nine o'clock tomorrow morning. Miss Shepherd has a carload of stuff to unload. Would you mind going to see about that? Maybe a couple of others could head out that way too. Thank you all for being here. Let's get back to work."

Kerry never had a chance to get a word in edgewise. The fire in Micah's eyes told him not to take the directive as a suggestion. He pressed his lips together in a submissive smile, nodded, and walked away, tail dragging.

Sharon's eyes flashed her gratitude. "Thank you, Micah. Thank you."

CHAPTER 20

Matt stood at the window of the bus, watching the buildings and the streetlights and the billboards skate by as if part of some other world. He wondered about the crisis center. From what he'd heard, they should all be setting up at the community center and getting excited about the weekend ahead of them. Part of him wished he were there, but he knew he didn't dare. Someone would recognize him, and his secret would be out. Sometimes, he was learning, being the community spy had its drawbacks.

The bus slowed as they approached one of the many stops along the route. The doors slid open and revealed the lone bench and its sole, broken occupant. Something about the figure seemed familiar. It wasn't the stooped shoulders or the face buried in gloved hands or the coat. No, it was — it was the bag that sat between the woman's feet. It was her!

Matt sprang into action, barely managing to squeeze between the doors before they slammed shut. He slipped as he stepped out on the icy sidewalk. His arms and legs flailed in all directions until, at last, the motion stopped, and once more he studied the figure on the bench.

"This isn't your normal stop," he panted. "What are you doing here?"

The woman looked up. At first, he saw only sorrow in her face, but then it changed to surprise.

"What are *you* doing here?" she tilted her head to one side with curiosity.

"I was on my way home, but when the bus stopped I saw you. I almost didn't recognize you." He paused, noticing the tracks of fresh tears glistening in the streetlight. "You're crying. What happened?"

She shrugged and reached for the strap of the bag between her feet. She wrapped the leather around her fingers, first one way and then the other. He watched for a moment, then, with decision in his step, crossed the sidewalk and sat down beside her.

"Must have been pretty bad."

Again, she shrugged. "How could anyone…whatever happened to not speaking ill of the dead? How could anyone…"

Matt's brow furrowed and an intensity came up in his eyes. "I don't like the direction this is going. Did someone say something about Sam?"

"It was awful! Right there at the clothing exchange. The very man who was supposed to be helping us did nothing more than tear down the entire ministry with his wayward tongue. How could someone do that?"

She was sobbing again, and Matt knew this was far more than the pain the unnamed man had caused her. The flood of grief that had been pent up for weeks was now forced out by the ugliness of betrayal. He cautiously scooted closer and laid an arm across her trembling shoulders. At the same time, he searched his pockets for a tissue or napkin.

"I'm so sorry," he soothed. "No one ever should have done that. Especially not someone you trusted to help you. I'm so sorry. Shh… Don't let him win. Don't be angry. Sam wouldn't have wanted that. It's going to be all right."

This had never been Matt's strong suit, but somehow on this night, on this dark street with this girl who was so broken, he lost all the discomfort he'd felt in times past. Suddenly, he realized the embrace his uncle had given him three years earlier, the one that had carried him through all their grief and sadness, had been for this night. It had been to comfort this girl, to share the comfort he had received just as God had taught him to do.

"Shh…" he whispered, "it's going to be all right."

He let her cry until, finally, completely exhausted, Kelly quieted. She straightened in her seat and wiped her face. She studied her nameless friend, embarrassed, grateful, and overwhelmed. "Thank you," she whispered.

His usual embarrassment rushed back as they both became more aware of their awkward position.

"Are you okay?" he managed.

She nodded and dropped her gaze to her lap. "I'm sorry."

"No, please, don't apologize. ...Who did this?"

Kelly shook her head. "I think he's generally a good man, just a little short on discernment. I don't want to say anything that would cause him problems down the road. He just...he isn't the right one for the job, and now we know that."

Matt studied her once more, admiration swelling within him. That was no easy decision, and he knew it. The easy choice, the natural choice, would be to let it all out with no concern for the man or what consequences might befall him. But she had made the better choice.

"Sam, I think, would be proud of you for that. ...I am."

The woman turned away, blushing under the darkness that surrounded them.

"Have you had supper yet?" he asked.

Kelly shook her head. "No, but I should get back to the exchange."

Matt looked around them, confused. None of the buses she could catch at this stop would take her to the community center. "Weren't you headed home?"

"I don't know where I was headed." She said, laughing nervously at what her own state had been just a few moments before. "I was going toward home, but when the bus came, I knew I couldn't do it. I had to go back. But I was afraid to face him. I wanted to go home and just hide from the world, but I *need* to go back. I've sat here through four buses. The drivers probably think I'm nuts. I need to go back. Kali and the others need my help. We have so much left to do."

"Really?"

"This week has been one disaster after another."

Concern filled Matt's eyes. "I'm sorry to hear that. Can I at least walk you back? It's a long way. I mean, isn't that usually at the community center?"

"Usually. And it was supposed to be this year, but we've had to move. We're at Shallow Brook Christian's gym now."

"Oh. Well, that's not as far. There's a coffee shop between here and there. Can I get you some coffee and a pastry or something? I just don't want you walking back there by yourself this time of day."

"Thank you. I'd love something warm to drink. It's freezing out here."

"Yeah, I heard we're supposed to get more snow. So much for spring." The man stood and offered her his hand, which she received gratefully.

They walked in silence until they reached the coffee shop.

"What would you like to drink?" Matt asked as he heaved open the shop's heavy door.

"I don't come here very often. I'm not really sure what they have. But, not coffee. I don't drink coffee."

"What! You're kidding me, right?"

Kelly blushed. "No. I'm serious. I know it seems strange, but it's true. I'm a tea girl, through and through."

"Well, they have a pretty amazing caramel and coconut latte. You could have them make it into a tea latte instead. Do you like coconut?"

"Mm. I love coconut."

"Great! How about a sandwich or something?"

"No. That's okay. We'll have food there."

"Cookie? I'd happily split one of their massive, chocolate chunk cookies with you. *Happily.*"

Kelly chuckled. "Well then, I guess we'll have to have a cookie."

The duo placed their order, gathered napkins, and made their way out onto the street, each with a cup of warmth in their hands.

"How are things working out financially at the center?" Matt asked as they walked.

"Oh, I never emailed you, did I?"

"That's okay. I'm sure you've been very busy."

"One of our board members called the very next day, found out what was going on, and offered to have his accounting department take a look at our situation."

"Oh! That's great! Did they come up with a good plan?"

"As good as can be expected with such a huge cut."

"Were you able to save all of the programs?"

"So far."

"Did they mostly cut operational costs?"

Kelly hesitated. "You could say that."

Matt was quiet for a moment, wondering how far he should push. He decided to keep going. "They cut salaries, didn't they?"

She nodded.

"A lot?"

"We didn't follow their recommended cuts. Some of our staff just couldn't make it on the recommendations. They have families, and we wanted to make sure we weren't putting them into one of the crises we're helping others out of."

"Makes sense. So, will that adjustment endanger other programs?"

"No, I don't think so."

She wasn't telling him something. He knew it from the tone in her voice and the way she looked away each time she answered. He wanted to be sure the recommendations he'd made hadn't hurt them. Still, he determined not to press. He would get himself in trouble if he did that. He sighed inwardly and changed the subject.

"So, how did the clothing exchange end up at the school?"

"*That* is a story. The fire sprinklers at the community center malfunctioned. They flooded the hall and soaked everything. Kali, Sharon, and I spent all of last night at the laundromat drying, folding, and sorting clothes. We started setting up at the convention center at the hotel this morning, only to discover they had overbooked, and we were the later booking. So, we tore down, and Kali managed to get a hold of the school. We've been transporting and setting up over there since about three o'clock."

"Wow, you guys have had a week!"

"To say the least."

Matt grew thoughtful. After a long moment of silence, he said, "Can I ask you something?"

"Ha! You've never asked for permission before."

"True. I just...I was wondering about this man. What did he say?"

Kelly hesitated, not wanting to remember it, let alone repeat it. At the same time, the sincerity in her new friend's voice told her the conversation would be safe. "He basically said we've been going about everything the wrong way. He said we're tangled up with the city government instead of working with churches, just because we hold the clothing exchange at the community center."

"But I hear people at my church talking about volunteering at the center all the time."

"We work with churches all the time. I don't know where he's coming from on this. Sometimes we go out of our way to give them every opportunity to be involved. Sam always wanted the churches to be our primary source of support and staffing. He always said he wanted to walk *with* them, not against them." She stopped, her thoughts wandering away from the conversation to situations she had seen Sam navigate with the greatest of care.

"But?" Matt urged.

"We try, but it doesn't always work out that way."

"Hmm. Does that cause conflict?"

Kelly shrugged. "Sometimes. I think Sam went out of his way to make it work as often as possible. I don't know. He was good about not letting problems past his office door. Anyway... We were giving this man a chance to see how we work because he was interested in working with us, possibly even applying for the director's position. He'd already turned in a resume and everything. But he was bragging to everyone what he would change and how he would change it, and why it was all wrong."

"I'm sorry, so sorry. There's no call for that. I'd say he saw an opportunity to advance himself and tried to take it. His concern isn't about the center."

"No. It's not. It's all about him."

Matt sighed. "I've never understood people like that. I think...I think they're insecure in their own abilities, or maybe it's just pride."

"Maybe."

They said nothing as they walked across the parking lot toward the gymnasium. When they reached the door, Kelly started to enter, but Matt stopped. She met his gaze, eyes full of questions.

"Why don't you come in for a while? You can meet the rest of the staff. Sam's brother should be here by now."

"I can't. My dad will be wondering what has happened to me. A while back, I left the office early and took work home with me. When he stopped by the office and found out I wasn't there and wasn't answering my phone, he thought I was sick. He bought a whole case of chicken noodle soup. A whole case! Not to mention the four boxes of Kleenex I found later. ...I don't want him to worry."

"You could call him."

But Matt shook his head. "No. No, I should go."

"Okay. Well, if you have time, stop by tomorrow...or Saturday. We'll be here Saturday too."

"Maybe I will. Have a good night. I hope you can get some rest."

"Thanks, you too. ...And thank you for getting off that bus."

Matt smiled. "I'm glad I was there."

Kelly watched him walk away and then slipped inside the busy school building, glancing around as she did so.

"Kelly!" Kali called from across the lobby. "Where have you been? We've been looking for you. Why didn't you answer your phone?"

"Kali, slow down. She can't answer everything at once."

"Micah!" At the sight of her friend, Kelly rushed across the room and threw her arms around him, nearly starting to cry all over again. "It's so good to see you. I'm so glad you're here."

"Kelly, what happened?" Kali persisted. "Where have you been?"

Kelly stepped away from Micah and met her best friend's gaze, speaking in a hushed, nervous tone. "I'm sorry, Kali. I never intended to abandon you. I just...the things he said...I don't know—"

"Sharon told us what he said," Micah interrupted, "you had every reason to be upset."

"Is he still here?"

"No," Kali replied with an unmistakable tone of disgust. "We had him help Gil unload all the cars and then told him he was free to go—for good. Kelly, where were you?"

"I started home. I got all the way to the bus stop, but when the bus came, I knew I couldn't go. I knew I needed to come back here. It just took me a while to be ready to come back."

"Oh, Kelly. I'm so sorry all this happened," Kali said.

"It's my own fault. I'm the one who had the bright idea of having him help."

"Kelly, no! You had no idea he would do this. You can't blame yourself." Kali took her friend into her arms and held her tight. "I love you, friend. Please, don't hold this over yourself. You had no idea this would happen. Oh, I'm so sorry."

Kelly pushed away and wiped her eyes, not wanting to set the fountain to flowing again. "Thank you, Kali. I'm okay."

Kali smiled at her friend and pushed a tendril of hair away from Kelly's face, convinced the other woman would be all right. But then her expression changed to one of confusion. She stepped around Kelly and looked back at the door through which her friend had just come. "Kelly, who was that guy you were talking to before you came in?"

"Guy?" Micah said with enormous curiosity. "What guy?"

"Before she came in, she was talking to some guy. He had a cup from the same coffee shop as your cup. Kelly, what aren't you telling us?"

Kelly blushed. "He's...well, I guess you could say he's a friend. I met him on a bus a while back, and he just keeps showing up. He didn't want me to walk back here alone. I invited him to come in for a while, but he said he needed to get home."

"He keeps showing up?" Kali questioned suspiciously.

"Yeah. We ride the same bus. He must live near me."

"What's his name?" Micah asked.

"Honestly, I don't know."

"You don't know!" Kali gasped, shocked her friend would carry on such a friendship. "How long have you known this guy?"

"I met him the morning we found out about Sam. Then he was on the bus that night. It seems like he just pops up exactly when I need a friend. He's a very kind, Christian man."

"Does he know *your* name?" Micah's eyes glinted with teasing.

"Stop it. No. He doesn't. Is there any food around here? All I've had since lunch is half a monster cookie. I'm starving."

Micah laughed, his eyes twinkling. "Now this is a mystery I'm eager to solve."

CHAPTER 21

Kali pulled her car to a stop in front of the ramshackle house. She looked through the passenger's window toward the front door, taking in the house before her. This stop had become a regular part of her Sunday routine, but somehow today, with most of the snow having melted off, things appeared different, bleak. White paint peeled back from ancient siding. Trim drooped around cracked windows. The iron railing leading up the steps to the door leaned dangerously toward the yard. ...The yard! What a mess. Kali wondered if it had ever been properly tended. Couldn't they afford it? Was it a matter of insufficient time? Did they not know how to care for the lawn? Or was it simple laziness?

Light flashed off the panes of the storm door, and, though she couldn't see who, Kali knew someone was there. A moment more, and Sarah stepped out on the porch. She wore a long, soft pink skirt that fluttered in the breeze and a white, spring sweater. She smiled as she turned toward the car, but Kali could see something wasn't right. She watched as the girl walked down the path through the yard to the car and popped the door open.

"Good morning!" Kali said, her eyes beaming with kindness.

"Hi. Sorry, I'm running behind."

"No, no. You're not late. I just pulled up. If anyone's late, it's me." Sarah sighed. "I'm just glad I made it out the door."

Kali, feeling a knot form in her stomach, put the car in gear and pulled away from the curb. "Rough morning? Everything okay?"

"I don't know. My brother is acting strange."

"What kind of strange?"

"He told me he didn't want me to go this morning. Said it was a waste of time. That I should be pursuing other stuff."

"But he let you come."

"He said, 'I can't stop you. Do what you're going to do.' And then he stomped out and slammed the door. I don't know. It's the same old thing. Ever since Mr. Thompson died, they've wanted me out of church, out of college, and out of the crisis center."

The knot in Kali's stomach tightened. This was a touchy one, and it seemed to be getting more so by the day. She didn't want to encourage Sarah to rebel against her mother and brother's wishes in any way. At the same time, she knew the destructive nature of the path they would encourage her to take.

"Well," she began, drawing the word out, "why do you think they feel that way?"

"I don't know. They always seemed to like Mr. Thompson. I think it's because we don't have a director. I think they think everything is going to fall apart and take my life with it."

Kali squelched the urge to express the same fear. She knew God would provide a new director, but after the events surrounding the clothing exchange she couldn't help wondering if everything would fall apart before that day came. But as that emotion crossed her heart, her brain realized where it stemmed from. As they crossed a narrow street, she glanced at her young friend. "Maybe they aren't so much angry at you as they are scared for you. Do you think that's possible?"

"Maybe."

"The unknown is always scary, Sarah. Especially if we don't know the One who knows the future. Do you think it would help if I talked with your mom?"

"I don't know. Not right now. I don't think she would talk. She hasn't been doing too good lately."

"What do you mean?"

"She's been gambling again."

"Oh. And I'm sure that's adding to your brother's frustration and fear. He's probably afraid he'll end up with the weight of all the expenses and her gambling debt."

"And his own habits."

Kali turned toward her friend, shocked. "What habits?"

"Nothing illegal, but a huge waste of time and money."

"Like?"

"Mostly barhopping and gaming. He doesn't sleep much."

"I guess not. Well, how can we help? Would it help if I talked to your brother?"

"No."

"That was a pretty definite answer."

"He's so angry over it all. I don't know, Kali. I don't know if he'll let me keep working at the center much longer."

"Well, I'll be praying." Kali pulled to a stop at an intersection and then cast a smile in Sarah's direction. "We sure need you."

"I know."

Kali had made her last comment in a lighthearted manner, hoping to lighten the mood, but the tone of Sarah's answer revealed the statement had merely uncovered another layer of Sarah's struggle. Her smile disappeared as she pulled through the intersection.

"I want to be there so much," the girl continued. "Mr. Thompson did so much for me, but it wasn't just him. It was all of you. All of you have done so much. I just…I want to do the same, Kali. I want to help others."

"Well, Sarah, then that is exactly what we're going to pray God will allow you to do." Kali slowed the car, turning into the church parking lot and beginning the search for a parking space. "The Lord has a perfect place for you—for all of you—and this is a pretty good place to start looking for it."

※ ※ ※

As hard as she tried, Kali found it difficult to focus on the morning message or anything else going on around her. By the time the service was over, her mind was utterly preoccupied with the conversation they'd had on the way to church. Things at Sarah's house seemed to be getting worse and worse. If ever she needed to talk with Sam, this was it. But he was gone. Micah was back in Seattle. She had decided that, for now, she would simply pray, but as she stepped out of the auditorium and into the church atrium, another thought struck her. She pulled out her phone. Kelly should be done with her children's class by now.

"Hey, do you have lunch plans?" she texted.

"There you are!"

Kali turned to see Sarah moving toward her from across the atrium. "Hey! There *you* are. Where did you go?"

"Oh, I was just talking with one of the girls from the youth group. I haven't seen her much since I graduated."

"Oh? Who was it?"

"Jen."

"I know Jen. How is she?"

"Good. At least, I think she's doing well. We didn't talk long."

Kali's phone vibrated. She glanced down and silently read Kelly's reply.

"Have a meal in the crockpot. Want to join me?"

"Sarah, would you like to have lunch with Kelly and me?"

"I would love to, but I promised my mom I would be home this afternoon to help her with some work around the house. Sorry."

"That's okay. I don't want to cause any more problems by pressing the issue. Maybe we can do something later this week."

Gratitude lifted the corners of Sarah's lips into a pretty smile. "Thanks for understanding."

Kali put her arm around her young friend's shoulders. "That's what friends do, girl! Let's get going."

❃ ❃ ❃

A half-hour later, Kali slipped into Kelly's small apartment. "Wow!" she said with excitement. "What smells so good?"

"Hey!" Kelly peeked around the corner of the wall that separated her kitchen from her living room and the apartment door. "You got here sooner than I expected. I just put some garlic bread in the oven. It'll be ready in just a minute."

"That sounds yummy, but that isn't what I smell. What's in the crockpot?" Kali crossed the kitchen to the counter where the crockpot stood. She lifted the lid and peered through the rising steam into its interior, breathing in the delicious aroma. "Mm. That's wonderful."

"It's a new Italian sausage, Pepperoni, pasta thing."

"Sounds fantastic. ...How was your children's class today?"

"It was great! I love those kids. They get so excited about things we should *all* get excited about, but us 'grown-ups' have our priorities all set—usually in the wrong direction—and don't let things move us. How was your time with Sarah?"

"Well, that's kind of why I wanted to get together."

"Uh-oh. What happened?"

"Nothing happened. It's just what's going on at her house. I think we need to be able to give her family some kind of assurance that we're going to stick with Sarah and not let her go."

"But what have we done to make them think we're going to let her go? We've never even considered it. In fact, we'd do just about anything to hold onto her."

"I know. And she knows that too. But she thinks they're concerned the center will fall apart without a director."

"Huh," Kelly grunted. "Sometimes I wonder about that too."

"Yes, I know, but we know we're not giving up. They don't know that."

"So, do you have any ideas?"

"No. I asked if it would help if I talked to her mom and brother, and she was pretty sure it wouldn't be a good idea. I'm just not sure what we can do."

Kelly pulled the garlic bread out of the oven and set it on the stove. She set a salad out on the table in the little dining area and came back to the kitchen for the crockpot. "What if we talk to Mr. Marsh?"

"Why? What could he do?"

"Well, it's probably a long shot, but I know we aren't the only non-profit he and his company work with. Maybe he knows of another organization that the education fund might have come from. If we could figure out how that was established and can get her set up for next year, maybe that would give them the confidence that we're not going to quit on her."

Kali considered the idea. "I suppose it's worth a try."

"Even if he can't help with that, he might have some other advice."

"True." Kali chewed on her lip as she dumped the garlic bread from its tray to a basket. "Maybe I'll give him a call in the morning."

"You should. Now, let's taste this stuff. I've been looking forward to it all week."

* * *

Monday lived up to its name. As soon as Kali stepped through the front door of the crisis center, she wanted to turn around and go back. The phones were ringing, Brandon was clearly missing, and Gil started flagging her down as soon as he saw her. She flashed a grin in his direction and went straight to his desk.

"Why do I get the feeling this isn't going to be good?" she teased as she stepped up beside him.

The big man chuckled. "Because when I'm flagging you down, it almost always means we owe someone money."

"And who is it this time?"

"It's our city taxes. Somehow, we didn't get them into the spring plan."

Kali groaned and sat down on the edge of his desk. "I don't even want to know how much that is going to cost us."

"It's about twelve hundred dollars."

"I told you I didn't want to know. Ugh. I have a phone call to make, and then we can—Wait. Is this something we should have Mr. Marsh's accountant go over?"

"Um, actually, that might be a good idea. I'm going to have to go back home."

"What? Why?"

"Beth was sick all weekend. She thought she was feeling better this morning, but she called right after I got here and asked me to come back home to watch the kids. That's not like her, so I know she really isn't feeling well. I told her I needed to talk to you about this and then I would be home. So, if he is available to help, that would be wonderful."

"Oh, I'm so sorry. It's no fun to be that sick. Tell her I'll be praying she feels better."

"I will."

Kali glanced around the main office. "Have you seen Brandon?"

"No. Maybe he's sick too. Lots of stuff going around right now."

"I know. Sometimes I feel absolutely *doomed* to get sick!" Kali laughed, then stood up, realizing the day was getting away from them. "Okay. So, when you're ready, bring everything in so I know what to tell Mr. Marsh, and then I'll give him a call."

Gil nodded and straightened the papers on the desk in front of him. "I'll have it as organized as I can. I'm really sorry about this Kali. I know having both Brandon and I gone on the same day puts a lot more pressure on everyone else."

"It's okay, Gil. Your family is what's important. Just go home and be a daddy and a husband. That's where you need to be today—but next time you're here, we're giving you double the work."

Gil grunted. "I have no doubt about that."

CHAPTER 22

Matt sat at his desk, reviewing staff schedules and upcoming deadlines. He hated this one thing about Mondays. He rarely felt that weekend fog and fatigue many of his coworkers complained about. He usually came in encouraged from a weekend of spying and church services. But this, his least favorite of all tasks, always greeted him. He groaned and let the ringing phone in the main office divert his attention. He listened as Mel absentmindedly clicked on the speakerphone.

"Accounting. This is Mel. How may I help you?"

"Hi, Mel. This is Kali Shepherd from the Trevor Street Crisis Center."

Matt gasped at the sound of the woman's voice. He turned toward the glass wall that separated his office from the rest of the accounting department and gawked in the direction of his assistant.

"Oh, hello, Miss Shepherd," Mel was saying, "How are you?"

"I'm doing well, and you?"

"Just peachy. How can I help you?"

"I was trying to get a hold of Mr. Marsh, but the receptionist said he's out of town. So, I was wondering if it would be possible to speak with the man who has been helping us with our accounting. He might be able to answer our questions. I don't know his name. He just signs his emails *M.M.* Maybe you know who it is."

"Just a minute. Let me check on that." Mel turned toward Matt's office only to see him waving frantically.

"NO," he mouthed. "No. EMAIL." He jabbed his finger at the computer, repeating the word over and over. "EMAIL."

"Um... Miss Shepherd, I'm sorry. He's... in the middle of something. But he said if you send him an email, he'll get back to you as soon as possible. I think he's working on scheduling. He's always a little grumpy when he's doing that."

Matt's jaw dropped once more, and Mel grinned at him, eyes laughing.

"All right. I'll do that," Miss Shepherd was saying. "Thanks so much for your help, Mel."

"No problem. Have a good day."

Mel disconnected the call and raised her eyebrows at her boss. "What was that all about?" she asked.

He motioned for her to come into his office and waited as she strutted across the room and through the door.

"What has gotten into you today?" she asked.

"Nothing. I'm fine. And I'm not grumpy either. If they ever call again, either take a message or have them email me."

"Why? You never do business that way. 'Be personal,' that's what you always tell me."

"I know, Mel, but that's just the way it has to be."

"This whole thing has been weird. Ever since Mr. Marsh brought that folder down here."

Matt could see his assistant's wheels turning. He knew her well enough to know that would take her places it should never go.

"It's complicated," he blurted out, hoping to derail whatever story her mind was cooking up. "There aren't any problems. This is just the way it needs to be handled. Someday, I'll fill you in. Maybe. But not today. Now, could you pull their file for me? I'm sure Miss Shepherd won't be slow in getting that email sent."

Mel raised an eyebrow. "And there he goes with the diversion tactics. Someday will come, boss. Someday *will* come."

"Ha! With you around, I'm sure it will. Probably sooner than later."

※ ※ ※

Kali checked her email for the fifth time in thirty minutes. It wasn't imperative she hear back from Mr. Marsh's accountant before leaving for the day, but it would be nice. She skimmed over the list of new emails. Nothing. She sighed. "Oh, well," she whispered.

"What's wrong?"

"Oh, hey, Kelly. I didn't see you come in."

"Is something wrong?"

"No, I was just hoping good ol' M&Ms would email before the day was done, but it hasn't come yet."

Kelly couldn't help the amusement that twitched at the corners of her mouth. Poor M.M., whoever he was, had unwittingly found his way into their hearts and would forever be known as M&Ms at the crisis center. "Well, it's not like you can pay the taxes tonight anyway," she said at last.

"No, but I was hoping to find out about the education fund for Sarah."

"Hmm." Kelly sat down in the chair across from Kali's desk, considering her friend's disappointment. "Well," she said, "you know what Sam would've said."

A quizzical expression crossed Kali's face. Her eyebrows scrunched together. Then her blue eyes lit up for a brief second, only to have the excitement replaced by a scowl. "Patience is a virtue. …Whoever came up with that phrase anyway? Don't they know no one wants to be reminded of that?"

"But Sam sure drove it into our heads."

"Yes, he did. And I know he was right. …Would you like a ride home?"

"No. It's a nice evening. One of the first warm evenings we've had for a long time. I think I'll enjoy the walk tonight."

"Okay." Kali found herself impressed with her best friend. She'd gone all these weeks without a car and rarely complained. But as Kali considered her friend, she also saw hints of stress in her face. They weren't the stress of a long day kind of hints. These were going home to more stress kind of hints.

"Kelly," she began cautiously, "are you doing okay with everything since we… you know?"

"Cut our own pay?" Kelly laughed. "So far, I'm fine, but I'm getting a little nervous. With the cold weather hanging around for so long, I'm not sure what my electric bill is going to look like— baseboard heaters aren't the most cost-effective means of heating. How about you?"

"I'm making it. My lease will be up soon. I'm not sure what I'm going to do when it's time to renew."

"Are you thinking about finding a cheaper place?"

"Maybe." Kali shrugged and then yawned. She wiped moisture from her eyes and tried to shake off the sleepiness that had overcome her. "I've got to get out of here. I'm beat."

"Be careful driving home."

"I will. I'm not that far gone. Let's see, I'll just shut this down, and then I'll be ready to go." Kali reached for her computer mouse. The email program dinged, and she pulled her hand back, startled. She gasped. "Could it be! Oh, I hope it's from him. That would be the perfect end to the day. ...It is!"

"What's it say?" Kelly asked, jumping up out of her chair and rushing around the desk.

Kali read aloud:

"Miss Shepherd,

"I hope I'm not getting this information to you too late. Thank you for enclosing the updated financial information in your email. That was very helpful. In the attached document, you'll find my suggestions for making the tax payment with the least impact to other areas. I don't recommend cutting any further into your salaries, especially not the two that took the biggest hit with the last round of cuts. That sort of stress makes concentrating on the work at hand all the more difficult. So, I have found a few ways to cut back in the weeks ahead to sufficiently cover the twelve hundred.

"That was the easy one. As to the other matter, I cannot give you an answer. Mr. Marsh is out of town at present. I am not fully aware of the scope of projects and programs associated with the various charities Marsh and Line supports. I will have to do a

bit of homework in that department. I can't promise I'll have the information for you by tomorrow, but I will try to have it for you by the end of the week.

"I hope you have a lovely evening,

"M.M."

"Mr. Marsh was right," Kelly said, almost in a whisper.

"About what?"

"About M&Ms. He does have a heart for people."

"What makes you say that?"

"What he said about the salaries. I think that's his way of saying, 'I see what you did, and I can't stop you from doing it, but I'm going to try to protect you from taking it any further.' His wife is one lucky lady."

Kali twisted in her chair and shot a look of disbelief in her friend's direction. "How do you know he has a wife?"

Kelly laughed at herself. "I don't. I just assumed. I mean, he's an accountant—head of accounting—at one of the largest and most successful businesses in town. He's...*an accountant*. Gil has a wife. It just sort of rounds out the whole accountant image."

"You've been here too long. Go home and get to bed. Where do you come up with these things?"

"He's probably at least 50. That's my guess."

"Kelly! You're awful. What if he's straight out of college?"

"He has too much experience for that. No, he's got to be at least 50. Probably has three grown children, maybe even a couple of grandkids."

Kali rolled her eyes. "Go home."

Kelly laughed once more. "Good night, Kal. Love you, friend. See you in the morning."

❋ ❋ ❋

Matt trudged toward the bus stop, his computer bag heavy with the extra files he'd loaded into it. He grunted under the bag's weight. Today would have been a good day to drive rather than to ride the bus, but he hadn't known that in the morning. The air was nice enough. Even though winter still clung to the breeze, hints of spring were beginning to make their way out of the shadows.

"I am so ready for summer," he said to himself. He glanced behind him to see the bus approaching and groaned. He would have to run. He wondered if Gordy would take pity on him and wait. But then, what if Gordy wasn't driving? That thought put his feet in motion. He hoisted the heavy bag up on his shoulder and tried not to notice that its swinging nearly knocked him into the street with every step. He rounded the corner just up the road from the bus stop and froze.

She was there. His bus friend was at the stop! He couldn't ride with her tonight. He had too many questions in his mind. He would slip up. He would say something he shouldn't. He had no choice. She had seen him. She was waving and smiling with pleasure. A half-smile managed to creep up one side of his face as he waved back.

"Lord," he whispered, "please put Your hand over my mouth."

The bus coughed around the corner. Matt started running again until the smiling face in the driver's seat let him know he'd be okay.

"Hi!" He panted as he reached the stop. "Fancy...meeting you here."

"Really?" she teased. "Isn't this where we usually meet?"

"Very funny. Let's go. Gordy's waiting."

"You know the driver's name?"

"I know lots of people."

The pair climbed aboard the bus, swiped their passes, and then melded into the mass of tired commuters.

"There's a definite advantage to working late," Matt said. "The bus is never this crowded at seven or eight. I think it's going to be a while before we have a seat."

"Very true. So, how are you?"

Matt tilted his head at the directness of her manner. A determination he'd never seen before had come up in her eyes. She was up to something.

"I'm fine," he said, his voice warbling with caution. "And you?"

"Better than the last time I saw you. ...I want to thank you for that."

"No. Please, you don't need to say any—"

"No. Let me finish. I got to thinking about it later. Something could have happened to me. There I was, sitting on that bench in the dark with no one around most of the time, completely oblivious to my surroundings — I was the perfect target. When I got back to the gymnasium, Kali was furious with me. It really scared her that I had been gone so long. I was so upset I never gave it a second thought. So…thank you for being there."

He shrugged. "You're welcome, but I'd say God had more to do with it than I did. Like I said then, I almost went right by you. But I'm glad I was there." He paused and set his bag down on the floor between his feet, groaning as he did so.

"That looks heavy."

"It is. I've got extra homework tonight."

"Homework? Are you a student?"

Amusement lifted the corners of his mouth. She was trying to figure him out and not hiding it very well. "No. I haven't been a student for a long time. No, this is work homework."

"Wow. Do you take that much home with you often?"

"No, no. This is a special project. I've already decided that when I take all of this back, it will be in a car."

"Might save you some pain."

His blue eyes twinkled. "Especially if I have to run for any more buses!"

Their laughter dissolved into silence. Matt's mind swarmed with a million questions. Why had they cut their salaries so far? Was she okay? Why was it so important to find out about the education fund? But he could ask none of those questions. Instead, he defaulted to a safe zone. "Have you heard from your folks lately?"

"No. Well, not this week. But, I guess it's only Monday, right?"

"How's the center?"

"Busy, but I guess that's the way we want it, right? No room to get bored that way."

He studied her thoughtfully for a moment. She was smiling now, but he could see the day had taken its toll on her. "Sometimes, busyness just creates more stress and makes its own problems. I'd say it's better to be doing things well than to be doing so much that you never actually complete anything — especially when you're dealing with people. I'd also say busyness is a good way to wear yourself out, especially after everything you guys have been through this year."

Kelly bit her lip. She managed a smile, but tears glinted in her eyes.

"I'm sorry. I was too forward."

But Kelly was already shaking her head. "No. You're right. Busyness is also a good way to avoid the heavy stuff. ...You ...You really care about people, don't you? That's why you talk to strangers all the time because you actually care."

"It's my parent's fault," Matt teased. "My mom taught me to always be aware of the needs around me. My dad taught me to do something about them. I can't always help, but I always want to."

"So, you do what you can?"

"Yeah. I mean, that's all I can really do anyway, right?"

"I suppose you're right." Kelly glanced toward the front of the bus. "Oh, here's our stop already."

"Really?"

"Yep. Almost there."

"That's too bad. I have to go an extra stop tonight. I need to get something for supper."

Kelly frowned. She'd kind of hoped they could walk a little ways together. Maybe next time. She turned to leave the bus then stopped, looking back at him with kindness in her eyes.

"I hope your homework doesn't take you too long. Have a good night."

He waved after her, wishing he could get off the bus, but knowing he would say too much. His stomach growled. That Chinese restaurant couldn't come soon enough.

CHAPTER 23

Matt buried his chopsticks in a pile of rice, brushed crumbs from his hands, and flipped the page in the thick file on the table before him. He glanced around the room, noticing that, unlike his regular visits to the ChaiNook, he was the only one working. Happy families, laughing friends, smiling, ancient-looking couples, and one sad and lonely old man occupied the other tables. Only the old man seemed to have brought his cares with him. The others had left theirs at the door. He wondered about the man for a moment and then forced his thoughts back to the task at hand.

This, he decided, wasn't a care. Not really. It was a mission. He had to find the link between Sam Thompson and the education fund. But what if there wasn't one? What if Sam Thompson had worked with some other organization with which Marsh and Line had no connection? All of his searching would produce nothing.

"If God has given you an assignment, it will never end in nothing," he whispered to himself, his eyes misting at the thought of his mother. How many times had she said that? Far more times than he could count. She had said it when he'd been ready to give up on law school. She'd said it as he was completing his business degree. She had been right. Though both of those assignments had been full of difficulty, they had prepared him for where he was today. He never could have managed both the legal and accounting departments of Marsh and Line without that background.

Matt shook himself, realizing he had distracted himself again. He scooped up another mouthful of rice and chicken and went back to his work.

The file before him pertained to an organization which assisted homeless and runaway teens. Beyond the check he approved each quarter, he had heard very little about the organization in the past. Now, the more he read, the more impressed he was with the quality and magnitude of their work.

"I don't know why I'm so surprised," he said to himself. "Marsh and Line wouldn't be supporting anything that wasn't top notch. Still, this is pretty amazing. …Hmm…They help with GED prep, but it doesn't seem to go beyond that. …No scholarships that I can see."

He was about to close the file when a photo of a young girl caught his attention. She seemed familiar, but he couldn't place where he'd seen her before. The photo was clipped to a form that had been processed by hand four years earlier.

"Emma Johnson," he read aloud. "The name isn't familiar, but the face sure is." He ran his finger over the scribbled words on the page, his lips forming them with only the occasional hushed sound escaping:

"Emma's father was killed in a work-related accident three years ago. He was never much a part of the family, but his death has left Emma very volatile. At home, she has only her mother and older brother. Both are negligent and, at times, abusive. Emma does not want to drop out of school, but they seem to want her to quit so she can work. She has barely passed the minimum legal age for employment.

"Emma ran away two weeks ago after a fight with her brother. He had been drinking, and she was afraid he was going to become violent. So, she left. Since then, she has been staying with a friend or in a basement stairwell. She is asking for a place to stay until she feels it is safe to go home.

"Referred by Sam Thompson."

"Sam!" Matt's voice rose in surprise. He blushed as he realized several of the other customers in the restaurant had noticed his outburst. "Sorry," he said with a pathetic smile twisting its way across his face and wishing he could slip beneath the table.

He slouched further into the booth and, with cheeks still burning, turned his attention back to the file, back to the girl. He studied the picture again. He had definitely seen her before. The question was, where? He flipped the page and continued reading. The next document was a little newer, and he realized he was reading a case study that had been presented to Marsh and Line to illustrate the work the organization was doing and the lives they came in touch with every day.

He read the detailed report of the girl's behavior in the shelter house with care. For the most part, she was quiet, a good student, and helpful. But at times, she would flare, causing arguments, reacting to others, bursting into angry, defiant tirades and then melting into tears.

"She was hurt and afraid," he thought out loud. "She was alone."

The more he read, the more he wished he could help her. She was in and out of the shelter house for two years, then there was a gap. She reappeared at seventeen. The tone of the notes had changed some.

"Enrolled in GED prep program. Escorted weekly with three other students by Sam Thompson. Home life has improved some. She has grown and matured. Is faithful to her church. Is an excellent student."

The next entry surprised him. It didn't say she had gone on to complete her GED. Instead, it said, *"Went back to school."* That, he was sure, was Sam's doing. He would have wanted her not just to have the facts memorized so she could take a test but also to have the lessons and assignments to give her experience and practice before jumping out into life.

"So, where does that leave me?" He scooped more rice into his mouth and rolled it around with his tongue. "If she didn't get her GED there, then she probably didn't go on to college from there — assuming she even went to college. But maybe they would be able to tell me more anyway. Maybe they've kept up with her, or maybe they knew what plans Sam was pulling together for her future education—*if* he has been doing something like that." He shook his head, doubt rising in his eyes. It was a long shot. "This isn't much to go on, Lord. I need a little more."

The next file was labeled "New Mother's Hope." Immediately his heart filled with dread. "Please," he whispered, "don't let that girl be in this file."

The file was mostly filled with donor receipts and updates, but at the very bottom of the pile was a ragged set of pages held together with a large, red paper clip. Just under the clip, a yellow sticky note had curled its edges up around the message it contained. Matt smoothed the wrinkled paper and read the inscription.

> *"Mr. Marsh, attached is the information you requested. We are so grateful for your help in these matters. Jane."*

Matt removed the sticky note and began a perusal of the information in front of him. Each page was the handwritten story of how New Mother's Hope had assisted a young mother with nowhere else to turn. Stories of abuse, of homelessness, of sorrow, of empty loneliness, and of rejection sprawled across the pages. At times, he found himself wiping his eyes as the women testified of the peace and shelter they had found not only for themselves but also for their newborn babies. They had made connections to several other organizations for help with various needs. Some had found help getting their GEDs, and Matt carefully wrote down the names of the organizations that had helped them in that area. More than anything, one particular similarity stood out to him. Of the ten stories contained in the file, Sam Thompson had referred six to the organization. The last story especially captured his attention:

> *"If it hadn't been for Mr. Thompson, I never would have come to New Mother's Hope. My friends told me to have an abortion, but I told them that wasn't necessary because when my dad found out, he would beat the baby out of me. It was my friend Sarah who took me to meet Mr. Thompson. She said he had helped her, and he would know what to do. She made the arrangements, and*

he met us at the library. He didn't condemn me like I knew my father would. Even though I know this isn't my fault.

"Mr. Thompson asked me questions and listened to the answers. When he found out why I couldn't go home, he promised me he would make sure I didn't have to. But he wanted a promise from me in return. He said, 'Meg, you and your baby were both created by God in His image. You are precious in His sight. That makes you precious in my sight as well. When we love someone, and when we're committed to something, we need to be willing to stand up and fight for it, for them...even if it kills us. I'm going to fight for you, but I need you to promise me you will fight for that baby.' I remember his words as if it had just happened yesterday. I've been fighting ever since."

Matt wiped his eyes once more. This was getting ridiculous. He glanced around to see whether any of the other customers had noticed, but all of the other tables were empty. He pulled out his phone. Nine o'clock! How had it gotten so late?

"Excuse me."

He turned to see a cautious, kind-faced Asian man approaching. "I'm sorry, Matt, but we're ready to close. Will you be much longer?"

"No, I'm sorry. I got so absorbed in what I was reading that I lost track of where I was and what time it was." He grabbed his cup and swallowed the last of his tea. "I'll gather everything up and be on my way. Thank you so much for your kind patience."

"Take your time. We still have a few things to do. Just let me know when you are ready to go. The doors are already locked."

Matt shoved the bulky stack of files down into his bag. "I'm ready now."

The man smiled at his haste. "This way then."

Matt drew in a deep breath as he stepped out onto the street. The cold spring air was sweet and refreshing. As he turned toward home, his thoughts went back to his research. Marsh and Line gave regularly to ten charities. He was familiar with the crisis center and the shelter house. The rest were an entirely new world for him, and he was almost certain he was falling in love with that world. What must it be for one's life to be wholly devoted to serving God by serving others? Sam Thompson had known that joy.

Matt hiked the computer bag up a little further on his shoulder and shoved his hands deep into his jacket's pockets. Part of him wanted to simply stroll and enjoy the evening air. The rest of him wanted to get home and read more.

❈ ❈ ❈

Matt sat behind his large desk, staring through the glass wall that separated him from the rest of the accounting department. The morning had gotten away from him. The legal department had erupted at the news that a customer was suing Marsh and Line for five million dollars in damages after her son rolled a shopping cart out of an outlet store's parking lot and into a busy street, causing a six-car pile-up. The woman claimed the store was at fault for not having the proper curbing, even though surveillance footage showed the boy had deliberately pushed the cart through the parking lot entrance and into the street.

"No case," he muttered. "She has no case at all. Why do people do these things? In the end, she'll end up with less money and more debt instead of the millions she hopes to gain. There has to be some way to help her see how crooked that lawyer of hers is. ...Need my own spy for this one." He gasped. "Spy! I have other work to do."

He rose and rushed to the corner where he'd dropped his bag that morning. He pulled out the stack of charity files and toted it over to his desk where he plopped it down loudly. He fell into his chair and began flipping through the pile.

"Now this is work I can get into," he said. In the five feet across the room and back, Matt's bearing had altered completely. The light had returned to his eyes, and a smile spread across his face. He picked up his phone and dialed the number he had just located in the file.

"Shelter House," came a voice on the other end of the line. "How may I help you?"

"May I speak with your director, please?"

"May I tell her who's calling?"

"Yes, of course, this is—that is, I'm calling from Marsh and Line Clothiers on behalf of the Trevor Street Crisis Center."

"Just one minute, please."

Matt waited patiently, listening to the soft music that played over the line.

"Hello, Mr. Marsh, how are you today?" the voice was friendly, cheerful even.

"Hello, but this isn't Mr. Marsh. He's actually out of town. I'm the head of his legal and accounting departments. Recently, he's had me working on some projects for the Trevor Street Crisis Center. They had a request that has led me to you."

Oh. Okay. Well, I hope I can be of some help."

"Kali Shepherd asked me to do some digging to see if I can find out anything about an education fund. I'm not really sure what information they need except that Mr. Thompson had apparently helped someone through an education fund of some sort, and none of us can seem to find any trace of it."

"Okay. And how did that lead you to us?"

"Well, they asked me to check with other local organizations to see if we could get any kind of clue as to where the fund originated. As I was going through your file last night, I came across information on a girl Sam Thompson referred to your organization. I noticed you helped her with GED prep, and then she went back to school. I know that probably means that, if she even went on to college, you didn't have anything to do with the process; but I wondered if perhaps you had kept track of her and knew anything. I guess I thought maybe Sam would have helped her in the same way he helped whomever they're trying to help now, and maybe you would be aware of what he'd done."

"Well, Mr. …I'm sorry, I didn't catch your name."

"I apologize. I think I got ahead of myself and didn't give it. I'm Matt from the accounting department at Marsh and Line."

"Matt, I have to be very careful about what information I divulge regarding those we care for. I'm not sure I'll be able to say anything that will help you, but I will do my best. What was the girl's name?"

"Emma Johnson. She came to you about six years ago and was there off and on for about four years." Silence met his statement. He waited, but there was nothing. "Hello?"

"I'm sorry, Matt, but I don't understand. You say the Trevor Street Crisis Center had you checking into this?"

"Yes."

"I don't understand how I can be of any more help to you than Kali Shepherd."

"What do you mean?"

"Emma Johnson was the name we used on the case file we sent to Mr. Marsh. The girl is Sarah Wright. Why doesn't Kali just talk to Sarah herself?"

Matt hesitated. A shadow passed over his gaze. "I don't understand," he said at last.

"Sarah Wright works at the Crisis Center. She's their receptionist or office manager. I'm not sure which title Sam gave her. Why haven't you talked to her about this?"

The pieces finally fell together in Matt's mind. Now he knew where he had seen the girl in the photo. She was the same girl he'd seen his friend from the bus talking with at the ChaiNook—the very same girl he had overheard talking about the education fund.

"Matt, are you still there?"

"Yes. I'm sorry. I was just processing all of this. I don't think Sarah knows anything about the education fund. I'm sorry. I haven't spent much time at the center—well, none actually. Mr. Marsh usually handles these things, but with everything they've been through this year, he's asked me to give a little extra assistance. I've never actually met Sarah. I hadn't put two and two together."

"That's all right. I'm not sure I can help you much, though. I do know Sam had been talking about getting help for Sarah. He didn't want her to end up back at home without some outside goals and purpose. I know he had promised her that job if she would finish high school, which she did. He mentioned talking with Mitch Oberlander about it. He is a member of the Trevor Street board if I remember correctly. I think he should be your next call. Do you have his number?"

"If he is on the board, I'm sure the number will be in the Trevor Street file, just like your number was on file. I'll check. I'm sorry. I never asked your name either."

"My name is Joyce. If there's anything I can do to help in the future, please let me know. My heart just breaks for those girls over there. This whole thing with Sam Thompson has made us do some serious thinking about how we operate here. Sam was always very organized. I have a feeling he left them in pretty good shape. We, on the other hand, have a long way to go. If anything happened to any of our staff, we would be in a world of hurt. ...Maybe you should come work for us next."

Matt couldn't help but chuckle along with the woman's laughter. "I think my staff would be upset with me if I took on anything else."

"Yes. I saw the news this morning."

Matt swallowed hard, realizing his next call should be to PR for damage control instructions. "Aw, so you've heard."

"I think everyone in town has heard. I overheard people talking about it when I stopped by the ChaiNook earlier."

Matt sighed. "Well, people will talk. Probably doesn't matter what the outcome of the case, people will continue to talk. So, I guess we're just providing a little entertainment."

Joyce chuckled. "At least you can keep a sense of humor about it."

"Well, I'm not sure I was smiling when the paperwork appeared on my desk this morning, but I know the Lord will work it all out. I don't even really expect it to go to trial. Anyway, thank you for your help, Joyce."

"You bet. Matt, if you do find out about an education fund, can you let me know? We often have young people who could greatly benefit from something like that."

"I certainly will. Thank you very much, Joyce. I'll be in touch. Have a nice afternoon."

"You too."

Matt let the receiver click into place. "Mr. Oberlander," he mused aloud. "What would the postmaster have to do with an education fund?"

He pulled out the Trevor Street file, found the sheet of paper that contained the names and contact information of its board members, and dialed the number given for Mitch Oberlander. He wasn't surprised when the phone went immediately to voicemail.

"Hello, Mr. Oberlander," he began when the recording had finished. "I'm calling from Marsh and Line Clothiers on behalf of the Trevor Street Crisis Center. I wondered if I might speak with you regarding a matter that concerns the center. If you could give me a call back at this number, I should be in the office for the rest of the day. If I have to step out for any reason, I'll make sure my assistant knows how to reach me. I hope you have a wonderful day, and I look forward to hearing from you."

Matt dropped the phone back into its cradle and stared across the room, wondering where all of this would end up.

"You seem deep in thought."

Matt's eyes swung toward the door to see Mel standing there. "I was. Listen, I'm expecting a call from a man named Mitch Oberlander."

"The postmaster?"

"Yes. If he calls and I'm not here, please give him my cell number. In fact, you can even give him my home number."

"Wow. Must be important. You never give out that number."

"Well, he probably has it anyway. Somehow, I have a feeling he and my dad know one another."

"Why do you say that?"

"It turns out they're both fans of the same charitable organizations. I can't imagine they've never crossed paths. In fact, if I know my father, they've probably done some plotting together."

Mel giggled. "You and your father have the most interesting relationship of any father and son I've ever met. Honestly, I wish I had that kind of relationship with my dad."

"It wasn't always that way, Mel, believe me... but I'm glad for what God has given us now. ...Have you seen anything from PR about how they're handling the damage control for this lawsuit?"

"Actually, that's why I came in here. I just got off of the phone with Tanya. You were on the other line. She wants you to write up a statement for a press release, preferably one that minimizes the expected damage to the company from the case."

"Hmm," Matt said, realizing how easily his name appearing in press statements could lead to the staff at the crisis center discovering him. "I think I'll have Raska do that. Should be easy. I doubt we'll even go to trial. The parking lot is up to code. The carts were all properly stored. The camera footage shows her son taking the cart from the back of her car to the street and shoving it out into traffic while she stood there texting. Somebody ought to smack that lawyer of hers."

Mel stared back at her boss, a very pronounced frown tugging down at the corners of her mouth.

"What?" Matt said in a defensive tone.

"Somehow, I don't think Amanda will approve that last line."

"I'm sorry, Mel, but it bugs me when people step up in the name of justice but are, in fact, working their own greater injustices in the background."

"You think that's what's happening?"

"I know that's what's happening. That poor woman is probably going to be taken for every penny she has…and a few she doesn't have."

"What are you going to do about it?"

"I don't know. I—" Matt's mouth clapped shut. A light came into his eyes, and he burst out laughing. "You sound just like my dad!"

CHAPTER 24

K elly tapped lightly at Kali's office door and opened it enough to peek her head around its corner.

"May I come in?"

"Sure. Just let me finish this thought."

Kelly waited as Kali's fingers drummed out the last few lines of an email. She watched her friend glance over the text, hit send, and then spin around in her chair with a smile, her mind free to concentrate on the conversation.

"What's up?" Kali asked cheerfully.

"I just..." Kelly paused to push the office door shut and seated herself in the soft chair across the desk from Kali. "I wondered if you'd heard anything from M&Ms. I'm getting more and more concerned about Sarah. She's been very quiet this week. She seems discouraged."

"I know. I've noticed that too. I haven't heard anything, but, Kelly, we can't put too much pressure on him. I mean he's the head of both the legal and accounting departments at Marsh and Line. I heard they were hit with a huge lawsuit this week. He's probably up to his ears in that, and, as you pointed out, he probably has a family to care for as well. He's doing us a favor. He said he probably wouldn't have anything until the end of the week. It's only Thursday. He's always pulled through in the past. This one might take him a little longer than he thought, but I have faith he'll follow through."

"I know. I just wish he'd send us an update or something. I'm getting nervous."

"Well, you know what the answer for that is."

"I know. Prayer. Stop quoting Sam."

"What? You're the one always quoting Sam, Miss Patience-Is-A-Virtue. One, I might add, which you're not practicing at the moment."

"I know. I know."

"Was there anything else you wanted to talk about?"

Kelly's gaze dropped to her lap, her cheeks coloring.

"Kelly? What's wrong?"

The woman looked up with tears glistening in her brown eyes. "I don't know how I'm going to pay my rent, Kali. We've got to find a new director and get back on the right path. If you and I have to find additional work, this place will sink."

The light in Kali's face disappeared. She let out a heavy sigh. "About getting a director," she began, "I received an email from a man who used to volunteer here several years ago. His name is Chet Owens. Do you remember him?"

"A little."

"His email said he's been praying for us and that, after seeking the Lord for all these weeks, he would like to apply for the position."

Kelly drew in a sharp breath. "Really?"

"Yes."

"What do you think?"

"I don't know what to think," Kali said, twisting a cap back onto a pen and setting it aside. "It's been a while since I've seen him. I don't know much about his background. He included a résumé, but I haven't had a chance to read over it yet." As Kali spoke, a strange expression came over her friend's face. "What?"

"Is he still living in the area?"

"Yes. As far as I can tell, he's never moved."

"Then where has he been all of these years?"

"What do you mean?"

"If he's been in town all this time and has such regard and concern for this ministry, why hasn't he been here?"

"Kelly, don't you think you're jumping ahead of the game a little?"

"No. I don't. Look what we got into with Mr. Kerry. I don't want to go there again — ever."

Kali studied her friend for a moment, concern etching lines around her eyes. "Kelly, I don't want to hurt you, but I have to ask, are you sure this isn't because you're afraid of...well, of trying to replace Sam?"

"Absolutely not. I know we'll never replace Sam. Sam was one in a million. What I'm afraid of is getting an opportunist on board who has no real concern for what we do here.

"Kali, when you invited me to work here, I knew a lot about what you and Sam and the others did. But in reality, I knew nothing about this place. Nothing. I knew Sam's heart. We'd been friends for more than a decade. But all I saw about this place was the activity. Over the last six years, as I've written story after story, I've learned how Sam's heart was woven into this place until it became the heart of the ministry. If we don't find a man who has that heart, the Trevor Street Crisis Center will die."

"You're right. I agree. At the same time, we can't dismiss every candidate that comes along."

"I know that. This one, however, makes me nervous. Just be careful. That's all I'm asking."

"I will. I promise. ...How far short are you on your rent?"

"A hundred dollars. I might be able to come up with it."

"How?"

Kelly shrugged. "I don't know. Maybe I'll sell something. ...If I sell my car for five hundred and just use a hundred a month for rent that would make up the extra for the next five months."

"But your car isn't even running."

"Well, that's why I said five hundred. Running, it's worth about three thousand, but we're not there yet."

"How much will it cost to repair it?"

"Four or five hundred — minimum. That's why I was waiting for my Dad to come up this summer."

"Don't do anything drastic just yet. Let's pray about it and see what the Lord does. Okay?"

"Okay. ...Kali, are you swamped this afternoon?"

"Not really, why?"

"I'm just..." Kelly's voice trailed off. She wasn't sure she should voice what she was feeling. Kali's load was every bit as heavy as her own.

"You're having a rough day, aren't you?"

Tears of heartbreak and gratitude pressed hard against Kelly's eyelids. She wiped them away with the back of her hand. "I'm having trouble being *here* today. I just...I want things to go back to the way they were, and I know they never can. I want to fix everything, but I'm so exhausted and tired of everything that I want nothing to do with any of it. ...How can you feel so passionate about something and so exhausted by it at the same time?"

Kali chuckled. She had wondered the same from time to time. "Sometimes just walking in the door in the morning is exhausting, isn't it?"

"Yes. As soon as I see his office, I feel worn out. Sometimes I think it will be better when we have a new director, but then I change my mind. I realized one day that when we have a new director, instead of being sad that Sam isn't in his office, I'll just be sad because someone else is in his office. It'll be the final stamp. He's not coming back. Not that I ever thought he was, but it's like my brain is still expecting him to come back. Even all these weeks later."

"I know what you mean. I've had those exact same thoughts. I'll tell you what, I need to answer Mr. Owens' email, but then let's call it a day. We'll go spend the rest of the afternoon at the ChaiNook. Sarah and Brenda can hold the fort and call us if they need anything."

Gratitude climbed in Kelly's eyes. "Thank you," she whispered.

"Don't thank me. I'm being selfish. I'm having a hard day too. I don't want to be here any more than you do. Honestly, I think days like today when it's slow and quiet around here are the worst."

"What are you going to say to Chet Owens?"

"I'm going to let him know that I'll look over the information he sent, talk with my staff, and get back with him the first part of next week. How does that sound?"

Relief swept across Kelly's face. "Sounds very wise to me. I'll leave you to your work. I'm almost finished with the first draft of a new blog, so I'll just be working on that. Whenever you're ready to go, let me know."

CHAPTER 25

Matt sat down across from the middle-aged Mitch Oberlander, who had already made it halfway through his strong coffee while waiting for Matt to arrive and order.

"Sorry, I'm a little late." Matt extended his hand to the other man, but the postmaster only laughed.

"What is it with you young guys and these fancy coffees and teas? Whatever happened to black coffee and pekoe cut tea?"

Matt chuckled, his bright eyes dancing with pleasure at the ease with which Oberlander had begun the conversation.

"Those were never staple items at our house when I was growing up, Mr. Oberlander. My mom loved her specialty teas, and my dad was always trying some new coffee blend. He'd almost always make it stronger than he could stand it and then douse it with half a gallon of milk."

"So, where do you fall in this little game?"

"Oh, I'd say I'm a happy medium."

"In other words, you'll drink just about anything."

Again, Matt was laughing. "I guess so. My biggest struggle is always the sweetener. I never know which sweetener to use. The specialty drinks solve that problem. They could double as dessert."

Oberlander chuckled, his plump middle bouncing with delight. "Sounds like the perfect solution. So, your message said you needed to talk about the crisis center. What's going on?"

Matt glanced around the teahouse. Ever since the day he'd seen the girl from the bus here, he'd been nervous they'd meet up again at the wrong moment, and then his game would be up. From where he sat, he saw no one who could link him back to the center, to Marsh and Line, or to the community spying he did. A short wall stood behind their table, blocking his view of the main entrance. This bothered him a little, but there was nothing he could do about it. He cleared his throat.

"Well, I've been doing a little work with them, mostly helping with some of their finances and a few other things along those lines. They've asked me to try to help them find information on an education fund, which Sam Thompson used to help someone. No one seems to know anything about it."

Oberlander coughed. His cup banged against the table as he set his steaming coffee aside, intensity growing in his gaze. "That's because no one was supposed to know anything about it. How did you know to come to me?"

Matt cringed at the obvious affront his inquiry had been. "I didn't really. Someone at the Shelter House suggested I talk with you, but other than that I had nothing leading me to you."

"Oh." The man nodded almost apologetically and picked up his coffee once more. He sipped the dark liquid and then set it back down, this time with less energy. "I can see why they might have given that suggestion. Sam and I both communicated with them about it. The girl Sam helped was in their GED program, but I told Sam if I was going to help her, she needed to go back to school and finish strong. I didn't want to fund someone's college education if they weren't going to put their part into it."

"Wait." Matt interrupted. "You *were* the education fund? But—"

"How could I possibly do that on a postmaster's salary?"

"Exactly."

"I didn't. I grew up in a very wealthy family, Matt. But my father was a wise man. When he passed away, he set up an unusual arrangement. The funds he left are not in my control. They are set up so that they're still generating fairly hefty dividends and profits and are managed by one of the best financial firms in the nation, but I'm not allowed to touch them for personal use unless I spend an

155

equal amount on others first. The truth of the matter is that, over the years, it has rendered my wife and me so much joy to be able to give to others that we're actually quite behind in the usage of personal funds. It's a wonderful thing.

"So, when Sam came to me about Sarah, I knew exactly what I had to do. He was completely unaware of my situation. He just came to bounce ideas off of me, but I knew God wanted me to help that girl. ...If I were to venture a guess, I'd say Kali Shepherd is trying to find information because Sarah is probably wondering what's going to happen to her next year."

"You know, they haven't told me exactly why they need the information, but from everything I've learned on my little quest that would make perfect sense."

"Well, I'll tell you what. I don't want to give my identity away. Can you ask them, first of all, if that's what they're seeking, and secondly for confirmation that Sarah will be pursuing the same course of study? If that's the case, then you can assure them I will continue to cover her until she graduates."

Matt's face lit up. "Thank you, Mr. Oberlander. I can hardly wait! From Miss Shepherd's email, I think she's very concerned. I'll be glad to put one worry to bed for them."

"Just don't give it away."

"I won't. Believe me, I'm getting really good at keeping these kinds of secrets...although sometimes, I wonder if I'm just making my life more difficult. ...There is one thing, though."

"What's that?"

"Well, Joyce at the Shelter House wanted me to get back with her when I found something out. I think they have some young people who would benefit from something like what you've done for Sarah."

"Hmm. I see where you're going with this. I can't do any more than I already am. I have an annual cap, which I've nearly reached with my current commitments. But I know others who might be interested in getting involved in something like that. Give me a month. I'll see what I can pull together. Whatever we do, I think it would be quite appropriate to make it a program of the Trevor Street Crisis Center and to call it the Sam Thompson Education Fund. Don't you?"

The thought gripped Matt's heart in a way he had not expected. He found he could barely speak. "Yes. I think that would be perfect."

Oberlander shifted in his seat, obviously preparing to move the conversation in a new direction. "So, how are the finances at the center? I've heard rumors that they've lost some pretty major financial support since the board meeting we had right after Sam died."

Matt scrunched up his mouth, his upper lip curling slightly. "They've taken some huge hits. They're compensating for it by cutting salaries. I think Miss Shepherd and Miss Vance didn't want to hurt their other staff, so they took the bulk of it. To be honest, I don't know how they're going to make it on what they're getting paid. I'm very concerned about that."

"As well you should be. Without them, there would be no center. I'd like to do something to encourage them. Even if it's just to send them a card. Would you be able to get their home addresses for me? Here, my email address is on my business card."

The man reached into his coat pocket and pulled out a card, but it wasn't from the post office.

"You're an editor?"

Oberlander grinned. "That's what I do at night when I can't sleep. Usually takes me a while to get the post office out of my system. That gives me something to do. Just see what you can find out and then shoot me an email. Deal?"

"Deal."

The two men talked a while longer before Oberlander left. Matt settled down to enjoy another warm, comforting London Fog and a few minutes of quiet planning. With his first sip of the hot drink, however, he realized something wasn't quite right. It shouldn't need sweetener, but it certainly did. He stood and crossed the room to the station where the sweeteners were kept. As usual, he hesitated. Why were there so many different ways to sweeten a drink? The sound of a bell rattled into his decision-making, and he looked up to see who had opened the front door. A blonde woman stepped inside followed by — his friend from the bus! His mouth dropped open and then snapped shut again.

Matt grabbed a stir stick and whatever sweetener was closest to hand, and darted across the room to his seat, all but diving behind the wall. He watched the two women walk past him to the counter, barely daring to breathe lest they hear him. When their backs were to him, Matt tossed his sweetener on the table and made his way to the men's room. He could hide there until they had seated themselves. Then he would figure out how to make his escape.

It never occurred to Matt that there was no reason to fear seeing his friend here. Oberlander was gone. He could tuck his notes from their conversation away in the notebook he'd brought along and be perfectly safe so long as he maintained his composure. He had never seen the other woman before, so there was no danger of being recognized from that quarter. Still, Matt's mind spun with the fear he'd give something away. He waited just inside the bathroom door for a few minutes and then dared to peek out. The two women still stood near the cash register, waiting for someone to bring out their drinks. He was about to step back from the doorway when he heard someone say,

"We're having trouble with some of our equipment today. Why don't you find a seat, and we'll bring it out to you as soon as it's ready?"

Through the narrow crack, Matt saw the two women nod and smile. They turned and picked a seat directly behind the low wall and the seat where he'd been seated. This new situation gave Matt pause. He could slip out of the bathroom, grab his computer bag and tea, and sneak out the side door without ever being seen; or he could take advantage of their choice seats. They would never know he was on the other side of that wall. This could be his perfect opportunity to do a little spying.

He waited until they had received their drinks and then slipped across the room and slid into his seat behind them. At first, there was no conversation. They contentedly blew upon and sipped their hot drinks. It occurred to him as they tested their beverages that he should have waited until he was sure they weren't going to sweeten their drinks. But neither of them got up, and his hiding place remained a secret.

"I hope things are okay for Sarah at home," the girl from the bus began. "That brother of hers makes me nervous."

"Yeah," her friend replied. "I think he's okay as long as he stays sober, but I'm not sure that's happening these days."

"If she needs a safe place, we do have some space at the Hope House."

They were quiet for a moment, but then the other woman spoke. "I hope we hear back about the education fund soon. If we know her tuition is going to be covered, I'd like to see what we can do about getting her into a dorm, or even an apartment of her own. "

"Do you think her brother would let her do that?"

"I don't know. He's pretty controlling, but I'd still like to try."

The conversation lulled, and Matt took the opportunity to jot down what he'd heard.

"I don't know what we'd do without Mac and Brandon and Gil."

Once again, his bus friend had begun the conversation. Matt knew Gil was their volunteer accountant, and he remembered seeing Mac's name in the financial information. Brandon was new to him, but he didn't have long to consider that.

"I think it's getting to be a bit much for Mac," she continued. "You know, I saw Sam helping him shovel a few times last winter, and earlier this winter too, but I think he was doing it more often than I realized. Mac isn't as young as he once was."

"Maybe we need to find someone who'd be willing to help him."

"We can't hire anyone else."

"No, but maybe someone would volunteer."

"I guess. I don't know. Except for some of our diehards, we've been running shorter and shorter on volunteers of late. ...Why do you think that is?"

Matt's bus friend paused, and Matt sensed she was about to share something that had been nagging at her.

"Do you think it's because I haven't been able to keep up with the blogs and social media as well as I used to?"

"Could be."

"I'm sorry about that. It just seems like by the time I've taken care of everything going on at the office, Hope House, and the shuttle schedules...I sit down to the computer, and I've got nothing left. I don't know what to say. I don't have any heart to say it with even if I *could* figure out what to say."

"It's okay. Really. I know I wouldn't be able to do it. You've done a great job with the blogs you've managed to post. Don't beat yourself up about it. Maybe Brandon could pick some of that up for you. He's on social media all the time, might as well put it to good work."

"Now there's an idea. I hate to give up that job. I might never get it back. Not that I would miss the social media part of it, but the blogging..."

"We'll get a director eventually, and then you can blog your heart out."

"That's just the thing, Kali. I have to get my heart *back* if I intend to blog it out."

They were silent again, and Matt wondered if it was to fight back tears. *He* was undoubtedly on the verge.

"My lease is up next month. How much longer on yours?" the blonde woman asked.

"Six months."

"Oh."

"Why?"

"Because you're not the only one coming up short on rent."

"Kali, why didn't you say anything?"

"I was going to, but I figured you were in the same boat, and I didn't want to burden you."

"Oh. I'm sorry I didn't show you the same courtesy."

"Stop. I don't want to hear any apologies from you. You've been a rock. You had to listen to that awful speech Mr. Kerry delivered at the clothing exchange, and you never brought it up again. You've never complained about the extra work you've inherited. You're always trying to keep the peace between all of us when we're stressed out and ready to snap at one another. If I can't handle you sharing one little bit of your reality, then you need a different best friend. Seriously, I'm glad you told me. Now, we've got it out in the open, and won't have to wonder what's bothering each other. *And*, maybe we can help each other come up with a solution."

"Like what?"

"What would you think about moving in together? We could split the rent."

"Well, I do have a guest room, but where would my parents stay when they come to visit this summer?"

"Maybe I could stay with someone else while they're here."

"I know! You could stay at the Hope House. It would be good for the girls to have that interaction."

"That could actually be fun."

"I'm not sure what I have to do to get a roommate added to the lease. I'll check into it. It would be nice to have some company in the evenings. Being alone at night never used to bother me, but the last couple of months...I don't know. It just feels so empty."

"I know. I go home, and I sit there at the table or on the sofa, and I do everything I can possibly think of to occupy my mind because I know once I go to bed—"

"It's just going to start all over again when you wake up."

"Exactly."

"Do you think..."

Matt waited with bated breath, wondering why his friend had stopped mid-sentence. But she didn't continue.

"Do I think what?"

"Never mind."

"No, come on. What is it?"

"I don't know how to say it. I just, sometimes I look around at all we're trying to do, and everything we're not able to maintain. I just wonder, do you think Sam would be disappointed? Do you think he would have expected us to have a different director by now? Do you think he'd be disappointed that we haven't kept everything going as well as he did?"

Everything in Matt screamed at him to stand up, lean over the wall, and say, "No. Don't ever think that again. Sam would be incredibly proud of you." But he couldn't do that. He couldn't give himself away, no matter how badly it hurt him to listen to his friend pour out the doubt she was experiencing. He waited for the other woman to say it for him, but she didn't. For a moment, her silence angered him until he realized her friend said nothing because she had the same questions.

After a long silence, the blonde woman said, "I don't think we can try to meet whatever expectations we might think Sam would have had. I think we have to do it to meet what we feel God is asking us to do. Sometimes, it's hard to discern what that is these days, but so long as we are seeking Him and His direction, He will lead us. He'll continue to protect us. Just like he did with Mr. Kerry. We just have to keep our eyes on the Lord. That's all we can do. ...Is this what was bothering you this morning?"

"I think so. I feel like a complete failure—all of the time. No matter what happens, no matter whether we have a good day or a bad day. I'm so afraid the center will fall apart around us, and all the good that could have been done won't be...because...because we couldn't handle it."

Matt's chest tightened. He had no idea his friend felt that way. She never let on in their conversations. But then why would she? Why would she ever confide such feelings in him? And why did it hurt so bad to know what she was feeling?

"I've felt the same way," the blonde woman said. "...It's a good thing God is stronger than we are, isn't it? It's going to work out. I don't know how, but God has a plan. We just have to trust him to work it out."

Another brief silence settled between them. Matt began gathering his things, sensing he might need to make a quick exit.

"I should probably run over to Hope House before I head home."

"Do you want me to go with you? Then you won't have to catch the bus from there. It's a lot further than from the office."

"That would be wonderful. It would also give us a chance to figure out how we want to set the apartment up if you move in with me."

"Good point. You know, if I move in with you, you won't have to take the bus all the time. You can just ride with me."

"True. That would be nice, although I've kind of come to enjoy riding the bus."

"Really?"

"Yeah. At first, it was a pain, but I kind of like it now. It gives me a good chance to spend a little extra time reading my Bible in the morning and praying. It's the only "no pressure" time in the day. I really like it...a lot."

Matt found himself relieved to hear this, and not just because his friend's commute provided a little extra information about the crisis center. He was relieved because, for the first time, his spying had produced a friend — a friend he didn't want to lose. He grabbed his computer bag and hurried out the side door before the women could begin gathering their things. Relief flooded over him as he sank into the front seat of his car. He'd made it without being seen. Now, he just needed to think through everything he'd heard. *That* could take a while.

CHAPTER 26

"**O**w!" A small log dropped from the basket near the fireplace, landing squarely on Matt's bare foot. "Ow! Oh, ouch!" He grabbed his foot and then the log, which he chucked into the fireplace. "Oh, that hurt," he said as he hobbled back to the sofa and sank into its soft pillows. Still massaging his toe, he scooped up his laptop, pulled a blanket over his lap, and began reading the website that had been loading as he stoked the fire.

She stood before me, small, pale, empty, and yet incredibly strong. I could see it in her eyes. She wasn't going to let this ruin her, even if it had already taken everything from her. She wasn't going to let it destroy her spirit.

"Matthew, what are you doing down here? It's one o'clock in the morning."

Matt spun in his seat. "Dad! …Man, you startled me. …Did I wake you?"

"Either that or we have a ghost howling somewhere in the house. 'Owww.' What did you do?"

"Sorry. It was just a log. On my toe."

"What are you doing down here?"

"I was just reading."

"Something for work?"

"No. When I was at the ChaiNook today the girl from the bus came in with someone else from the center. ...I know who she is now. I had a pretty good idea before, but now I know for sure. I kind of feel bad."

"Why?"

"I don't know. ...I guess...I guess today I heard more than I was supposed to hear. I heard things intended for her friend, not for me. Things she never would have said to me. I know so much about her, and yet I'm hiding things about who I really am. And I'm not sure I'm actually doing them much good in the process."

"What did you find out today?"

Matt set his laptop aside. He motioned for his father to sit, and the older man complied willingly. "I found out a lot. Both of them are still hurting. They're feeling insufficient. They feel like they're failing. They're hoping the education fund will keep one of their employees with them because they're afraid of what will happen to her if it doesn't. ...I think they're both exhausted."

"How much of that would she have told you on the bus?"

"Probably none of it unless I caught her in tears again."

"And how much of it would they have told you in an email at work?"

"Maybe the part about Sarah, but not the rest. But what can I do about it?"

"You can pray about it and be aware. When you look at their financials, you'll have perspective you never had before. You'll have an arsenal of questions to fire at them, questions that will help you get the truth out of them."

Matt shook his head. "I don't know, Dad. I don't know how long I can keep this up. It's one thing to anonymously gather information to help someone once or even twice, but this seems to be going too far. I was excited when I realized they were sitting behind me, and I could find out what's really going on at the center. But I had no right to listen in on their tears like that."

"They were crying?"

Matt could only nod.

"And you?"

"And me, what?"

"You seem pretty upset by what you heard today."

"I wish I could do more for them, for both of them and for the center. This town needs that place. The more I learn, the more I see the center is at the core of so much of the good that takes place in our community—and the heart has been ripped right out of it.

"I went through all of the charitable organization files from work, and almost all of them mention some connection with Sam Thompson. Yes, it was over several years. I'm sure he wasn't working with all of them all at the same time, but he was always aware. Always watching for needs in the lives of those around him and doing something about those needs. His absence not only rips out the heart of that ministry, but it has left those two women with their hearts pretty much ripped out as well. ...And I don't think they have anyone in their corner. Not right there. And now, they're left with the load of it all, and no one pulling for them, no one coming alongside and encouraging them. No one."

"That's not true, Matt. They have you. You can't fix everything for them, but every little bit you do is something no one else is doing for them, and it lifts a little of their load."

The white-haired man stood. He came to his son's side, taking a seat on the sofa and laying a hand on the younger man's shoulder. For a moment, he looked long and hard into the blue eyes that met his gaze. He saw there the compassion, the kindness, and the love that had always been present in his wife's eyes. He felt his chest tighten. "You're doing what you can, son."

"I want to do more, Dad, but I don't know how or what."

"Well, pray about it. In fact, we'll both pray about it. ...What were you reading when I so rudely interrupted you?"

"You mean when I so rudely woke you? I was reading the center's blog. I didn't know Kelly was the one who writes them."

"Kelly?"

"The girl from the bus."

"So, Kelly Vance is your bus friend."

"Have you met her?"

"No, but Sam always spoke highly of her. Who was her friend?"

"I'm pretty sure it was Kali Shepherd."

"Aw, Sam's right-hand man…woman. I *have* met her. She's got a good head on her shoulders. So, you were reading the blogs?"

"Yes. I thought it might help me gain some new insight into how things work there."

"Had you gotten far?"

"I read a few entries. She's an excellent writer, though I can tell a definite difference since Sam passed away. Her blogs aren't quite as sharp or focused."

"That's understandable."

"It's that fog that hangs over you after you lose someone close like that. I can almost feel her straining to see through the mist as she writes."

"I think I'd like to read some of them too. Can you send me the links?"

"Sure."

The two men sat in silence for several minutes, watching the fire, listening to the clock ticking on the mantel and the whir of the ceiling fan overhead.

"I miss Mom. If mom were here, I'd send her in there, and she'd be the mother they both need. She'd wrap her arms around them, tell them how proud she was of them, and then help them stand strong. Listening to them today reminded me of how awful those first few months were for us. Somehow, I just wanted to rescue them, but I could do nothing."

"Matt, you're doing what you can do. God will show you if there is more that needs to be done. For now, you need to go to bed. You're getting mushy and sentimental on me."

The younger man chuckled. "Thanks for talking, Dad."

"Matt, I don't say it often, but thank you. I'm always grateful you came home, and I'm grateful you stayed. You've made the last three years more than bearable, you've made them purposeful, and I needed that. Now, go on to bed. I'll take care of things down here."

"Thanks, Dad. Goodnight."

"Goodnight, son."

CHAPTER 27

"So, tell me, Mr. Owens, what led you to apply for the director's position?"

Kali sat at the head of the conference room table. Kelly sat just around the corner from her. But Mr. Owens had chosen to sit a couple seats down the table from them. He leaned back confidently, a smile twitching at the corners of his mouth.

"Well," he began, "I'd like to think it was the Lord."

The man's eyes twinkled as he spoke, but Kelly noticed it wasn't the joyful twinkle she had often seen in her bus friend's eyes, nor the kind twinkle she had seen in Sam's eyes. It was different, proud or perhaps even gloating.

"I've been praying about it ever since I heard the news about Sam," he said. "I used to volunteer here several years ago, and, even though I haven't been around much, this place has always had a special place in my heart."

"Why do you feel you are qualified for this position?"

"I've had a lot of leadership experience. As you can see from my résumé, I have worked in management for over a decade."

"Yes, I see that, but none of these places were non-profits or ministries of any type. They were all retail stores."

"True, but when you have that many employees, you learn a lot about how to keep a ship running. I've also done a lot of ministry in my church: teaching, door knocking, driving buses."

"Where is your church membership?" Kelly asked, adding her first bit to the conversation.

"Um, my membership? Well, I haven't actually joined where I'm attending right now. I'm not sure it's the right fit yet."

"How long have you been attending there?"

"Oh, about six months, I guess. Before that, I was at Shallow Brook. I listed Pastor Hanson as one of my references."

"Do you mind if I ask why you left Shallow Brook?"

The man hesitated at Kelly's question, a shadow coming into his eyes as he contemplated the woman before him. "No. I don't mind. I suppose that would be the obvious next question. I just felt the Lord was leading me elsewhere."

"Have any issues that might have arisen there been settled? We work extensively with Shallow Brook. In fact, our clothing exchange was held in their gymnasium recently."

The man cleared his throat and shifted nervously in his seat. "I don't think there were any real issues. I didn't agree with a few matters of practice, so I decided it was time for my family to move on. That's all."

Kelly opened her mouth to ask yet another question, but Kali rushed ahead, shooting a warning look in her friend's direction as she spoke.

"What did you do here when you volunteered, Mr. Owens?"

"Well, let's see. That was a few years ago. I did several different things. Once, I helped serve meals in the kitchen. Another time, I filled in when a shuttle driver had to cancel. One time, I helped around the office and helped prepare for a clothing drive. Lots of different things."

"Good. So, you've seen various aspects of what we do here."

"If someone came to you and said they were new in town and needed money for food and rent, how would you respond?" Kelly asked.

"Well, I think I would start by trying to get more information. Then I would offer help through one of the programs here based on whatever requirements the programs have in place. And if that wasn't sufficient, I would probably send them on their way. This isn't a bank."

Kelly, noticing Kali was taking extensive notes on the man's answer, pressed on. "What would you say the purpose of the crisis center is, as you understand it?"

"You are here to ask the hard questions, aren't you, Miss Vance?" The man smiled as he spoke, but his eyes betrayed a suspicion that she did not like him. He continued, "As I see it, the purpose of the crisis center, obviously, is to help people in crisis, as many as possible, with the hope of helping them see their need for Christ along the way."

Both women watched him for a moment, expecting more. When nothing came, they glanced at each other but said nothing. Kali began writing again.

"Do you have any questions for us?" she asked as she scratched her notes across her notebook. "The information sheet we gave you covers your proposed salary as it stands now. We've lost quite a bit of financial support since Sam's death. This is based on where we currently stand. We're hopeful that, as the support comes back up, we'll be able to increase your salary, but yours will come last. In order to give you this, we've had to cut our own and others' salaries by an enormous amount."

"I understand. ...I'm sure my wife will wonder what sort of hours I should expect."

A puzzled expression came over Kali's face. "Hours?"

"Yes. You do have office hours, don't you?"

"Oh, yes. We have set office hours, but that doesn't mean those are the only hours we are working. We take turns being on-call. You might be surprised how many crises happen in the middle of the night and on weekends."

"I'm...I'm sure."

"Any other questions?" Kelly asked, almost curtly.

"No. I don't think so. I might have some come to me later, though. That's the way it usually works."

"Well, if you think of anything, just drop us an email or give us a call." Kali paused, tapping her pencil on the table. She licked her lips, trying to remember if she had forgotten anything. "We'll be running a background check as a matter of course. We'll get back with you as soon as we've had a chance to process all of your information and talk it over and pray through it. Because of our situation, we may have you interview with the rest of our staff as well. We respect them too much to leave them out of the process."

"I understand completely. I would love to sit down and talk with them."

"Good. Thank you, Mr. Owens. We will be in touch."

"Thank you." The man stood, shook hands with each of them, and made his way out of the office.

When they had seen the front door close behind him, Kali turned to her friend. "Well, what do you think?" she asked with hesitation in her voice. "You certainly didn't tread lightly."

"I'm sorry. I was a bit 'queen bee,' wasn't I? He's okay. I don't know that he has the heart we need, but it's hard to know when we're just sitting at a table."

"I know. Maybe that's something we'll learn from his references."

"I hope—" Kelly stopped, straightening bolt upright in her seat, her face full of surprise, amazement, and a hint of disgust. "You have got to be kidding me!"

Kali's eyes widened at her friend's outburst. "What?"

"Look out the window! It's snowing! What happened to spring?"

CHAPTER 28

K ali fiddled with the stacks building up on her desk, straightening and reorganizing while she listened to the ringing of
the phone on the other end of the call. She'd kept up with
her work until the week of the clothing exchange. That had put her
behind, and she was beginning to wonder if she'd ever catch up.

"Hello."

The man's voice snapped the young woman back into reality.
"Pastor Hanson?"

"Yes?"

"Hi, this is Kali Shepherd. How are you this morning?"

"I'm fairly well snowed in. How about you?"

"I can't believe it! How did we end up with a foot of snow
overnight!"

"More like eighteen inches if you ask me. My wife is thrilled.
She says it's our last snow of the season, and we need to enjoy it.
Me? I'm done with snow for this season. Bring on the sunshine."

Kali joined the man's laughter. "Oh, I agree. I'm done with
shoveling and salting and slipping and sliding."

"How can I help you, Miss Shepherd?"

"Well, the snow is part of the reason I'm calling. Our maintenance
man is nearing seventy-five. This snow is heavy and deep. I wondered
if you might be able to recommend someone who would be interested
in volunteering to shovel."

"Huh."

Kali could almost hear the man lean back in his chair and run a hand across his heavily sprayed hair.

"I can't think of anyone offhand," he said, "but that doesn't mean I won't think of someone later. Let me get back to you on that one. I know that doesn't help you much, but I'm just not sure who to suggest."

"That's all right. The Lord will bring help along. ...There is one other matter. Do you have time for a few questions?"

"Sure."

"A man name Chet Owens interviewed for the director's position yesterday, and he listed you as one of his references."

"Me? Why would he use me as a reference?"

"Do you know him?"

"Sure, I know him, but I'm not going to give him a glowing reference if that's what he wants, and especially not for you."

"What do you mean?"

"Mr. Owens no longer attends our church."

"He mentioned he had been going elsewhere."

"Did he tell you he hops from one church to another only settling in one place long enough to cause strife and contention and then leaves and spreads rumors all over town about the church leadership?"

Kali's jaw dropped open. She stared across the office, too stunned to speak.

"I don't want you to think I'm speaking out of offense, Miss Shepherd. I can pretty much guarantee that if you call just about any pastor in town, they can confirm my report. And I want you to know his criticisms do not end with church leaders. They included the crisis center and Sam Thompson. Sam was the one who clued me in. He wouldn't let that man so much as step foot on the property of the crisis center."

Horror filled Kali's heart. How could they have nearly let in, not just as a volunteer but as their director, the only man Sam had ever forbidden to take part in their ministry?

"Miss Shepherd, are you still there?"

"Yes, I'm sorry. I just...I didn't know. Thank you for warning me."

"Well, I wish I could give you better news. I'm sure you're ready to have some leadership there. I know you girls have had a rough go of things the last couple of months." Hanson paused as if considering whether or not his next thought should be verbalized, but he did not consider long, which proved to be a mistake. "You know," he continued, "I always told Sam he needed to get that ministry under a church or even a group of churches. If he had done that, you girls wouldn't be in the shape you're in now. You'd have leadership from the pastors involved, and you wouldn't be scrambling for help all the time. I'm afraid if you don't get some leadership soon... Sam had the best intentions when he set that ministry up. I don't know. He was young. ...You may just have to walk away from it."

The accusation was a sharp one, one Kali normally would have borne graciously. But, on this morning with eighteen inches of snow piled up on her front walk and no one to shovel it; with their only applicant for the director's position having just been declared unfit; with a perfect understanding of Hanson's history with the center; and with her dear friend having just been accused of running the ministry in a manner that had caused their struggles over the previous weeks—it was simply too much.

"Pastor Hanson," she said, trying desperately to contain her emotions, "I have been with this ministry since its inception. I was there when Sam went to you and asked you and your church to be the umbrella for this ministry, and I was there when you said no. He went to nearly every pastor in this town, those with whom he felt he could work, and the story was the same in every situation largely due to *your* influence. It's easy to sit at your desk and criticize, but the truth is you didn't want to get your hands down in the grime where Sam spent most of his life. You wanted to keep unspotted from the world, and that is *so* much easier to do when you're not mingling with the afflicted.

"Now I understand why you had no qualms about sending Mr. Kerry to us. Don't worry about finding someone to help with our snow. We'll be just fine."

The receiver clanged down into the cradle. Tears rolled down Kali's cheeks. "I am so done with this," she fumed. "I'm done with all of it. Why can't someone just be the kind of honorable man God has called them to be and that they all claim to be? Just one man! That's all we're asking for."

CHAPTER 29

Kelly stared, eyebrows arching high over wide eyes and mouth gaping. She'd walked into Kali's office just in time to hear her friend ranting at Pastor Hanson. She'd never heard the other woman speak to anyone in that manner, let alone someone upon whom they relied so heavily for support and volunteers.

"Kali. What were you thinking?" she gasped. But as Kali turned toward her, and Kelly saw the tears on her friend's cheeks, she knew something horrible had sparked the tirade.

"Kelly, I know I shouldn't have said it, but I am so tired of the excuses and the contention and the accusations and the false piety. Don't they realize we need them to be strong and honorable and wise and humble? I'm done trying to find a director. We can do this on our own, Kelly. We're just going to do this on our own."

The color drained from Kelly's face. She sank down into a chair. "On our own?" The words barely escaped Kelly's frightened heart. Panic filled her eyes as she leaned forward and took hold of the desk. "Kali, we can't do this on our own. We can't."

"Yes, we can, and we're going to."

"I think we need to talk this through. Kali, we need help."

"Not that kind of help."

"Maybe you should tell me what happened."

"No. I'm going to shovel snow." Kali stood and walked to the hook in the corner where her coat was hanging. "How can a person say our lack of involvement with them is our biggest problem and

175

then refuse to help when we're giving them an opportunity to get involved...all in the same breath."

"He refused to help?"

"Not directly, but I know how it works with him. Every time I call and ask if they have volunteers available for a special need, he says, 'I'll have to think about who I could put you in touch with. I'll call you back.' He never calls back. Never. He knows how much pressure we've been under. He said so. And yet, instead of helping, he made it plain he feels we're reaping what we've sown."

"He said that?"

"No. He actually put the blame on Sam."

Kali wrapped her scarf about her neck and shoved her arms into her coat sleeves. Kelly watched for a moment then stood and moved toward the door. "I'll go get my coat."

By the time Kelly got outside, Kali had already cleared all of the snow that had blown in under the awning. Kelly studied the scene, considering the situation for a minute before stepping in alongside her friend. They worked without a word passing between them until Kali found she needed to stop to catch her breath.

"Kelly, thanks for being here. If you hadn't been here, I would have quit a long time ago."

"There's no way I would have left you to deal with this on your own."

"No, that's not what I mean. I mean I would have left a *long* time ago, almost three years ago."

"What?" Kelly stopped shoveling and turned to face her friend. "What are you talking about?"

"Three years ago, we were in a financial mess. We'd lost a partner who gave large donations regularly—a lot like now, I guess. But we weren't alone. The man had run into financial trouble himself and had to drop all the non-profits he'd been working with. Sam came in and told me about it one day. He said we were going to have to cut our salaries until support picked back up. That wasn't too bad, but then he told me we were going to have to let some people go."

"I remember that very well."

"I'm sure you do. You volunteered to give up your salary. ... Other things were going on at the time, and Pastor Hanson was at the center of it all. It was the same kind of thing as this morning. He was constantly on Sam to get under the umbrella of a church or group of churches. But whenever Sam gave them the opportunity Hanson declined, which generally led the other pastors in town to decline because of his influence."

"But, Kali, so many of our regular volunteers come from Shallow Brook, and they were so willing to let us use their building for the exchange. Surely our relationship with them can't be all that bad."

"Those volunteers are a result of Sam attending that church year after year after year. Those are people he touched directly. They've taken it upon themselves personally because they personally saw the need and the opportunity to serve. Pastor Hanson has never truly been interested in being involved. He's played the devil's advocate with Sam more times than I can remember—even when we were still in college, Kelly. It goes back that far. The only way he would have gotten more involved was if he had full control over the ministry. I think Sam would have willingly done that, except Pastor Hanson repeatedly told him he didn't believe the work we were doing was the right work to be doing.

"Most of the pastors in town support the work financially because they see we're doing what they can't. When Sam presented what the job would entail, they knew they couldn't handle it out of their church alone. But with Hanson, it was always different. It went far beyond that.

"Anyway, three years ago, we had faced conflict after conflict over how we were handling certain aspects of the shuttle program. It was really a simple problem of logistics, which could have been— should have been—resolved with a simple meeting to work out the kinks. But several people made a huge stink over it."

"Why don't I remember this?" Kelly interrupted.

"Because Sam kept it quiet. He couldn't stand 'infighting among the brethren' as he put it. He felt it was a terrible testimony and did his absolute best to be the one to step up and keep the peace. Sometimes it just got him further into trouble, but he tried.

"Pastor Hanson made his opinions about Sam and the ministry and the shuttle program—all of it—very clear. He was sharp and cutting in his words, especially toward Sam. I don't think he knew I was listening to the conversation, but Sam always had me listen. He said he felt it was important to have a witness, but that it should never go past the conference room."

"Wait. Were you on the phone?"

"Yes. ...Kelly, he was so awful. When the call was over, Sam and I just sat there and stared at each other. He apologized that I'd had to listen to it all and then he just went to his office and locked the door. Knowing him, he went in there to pray. Pastor Hanson did eventually apologize, but I made up my mind that night I wasn't going to put up with it anymore. I was tired of the hypocrisy and the contention and the bickering.

"The next morning, I came to work ready to turn in my notice, but I saw you sitting in the office with Sam. I headed over there to find out what was going on. I got there just in time to hear you make your offer to work for free until we were able to pay you again. Sam was shocked. I remember him asking why you would do that. You said, 'Read today's blog. You'll understand.' As far as I knew, neither of you had seen me yet, so I turned around, went to my office, and started reading.

"You laid out how much God had changed you through your first three years at the center, you mentioned individual stories of people God had helped through our work...and you mentioned me. You told how grateful you were that your best friend had invited you to work in the most amazing, life-changing place you had ever been, and if it weren't for her—for me—you wouldn't have been the person you are.

"I knew right then, I couldn't quit. I simply couldn't. The work we were doing was too important. It was bigger than me and the petty problems I was facing. I had to get over myself, let God resolve the problems and fight the battles, and do what He told me to do."

Kelly leaned on her shovel. She smiled at her friend. "I'm glad you stayed, Kali. I don't know what I would have done without you here. I probably would have left too. ...But I don't understand. If the relationship with Pastor Hanson was so bad, why did Sam maintain it? Like you said, he went to that church for years and years. Why?"

"Because of a commitment he made in college. He purposed never to leave a church because of unresolved personal conflicts or because he was disgruntled. Long before he ever started the center, he wanted Hanson's support in what he was doing, but it never came. Shortly after that incident three years ago, Pastor Croft asked Sam to help him at Trevor Street Chapel's new sister church. ...Sam always held out hope that somehow God would change Hanson's heart, even after he left Shallow Brook. But, if where we are hasn't changed Pastor Hanson's heart, I don't know if anything ever could."

Kelly studied her broken, disheartened friend for a moment before daring to ask the question she knew she must ask. "Kali, can you tell me what he actually said this morning?"

Kali shrugged and returned to her shoveling. She rehearsed the entire conversation. When she reached the end, she stepped back, examined their progress, and sighed. "When I tell it to you like that, it doesn't sound nearly as awful as it did when he was saying it to me over the phone. Maybe I overreacted, but somehow, I think he has the same agenda as Mr. Kerry and Chet Owens. He sees this as an opportunity to achieve a little more control over the ministry and a little more status for himself. And if he can't get it, then he can at least lord his opinions over us."

"He *did* do us a great service in warning you about Chet Owens."

"Yes, that's true, but he also sent Mr. Kerry. ...Do you think I'm being stubborn or irrational about the idea of just going it alone?"

Kelly's mouth twisted to one side, then she drew in a deep breath. "It's a lot. I don't know how much longer either one of us can keep up all the work we've taken on. Something's going to have to give if we don't get help soon."

"I know, but maybe it's just an issue of restructuring."

"Maybe."

"You sound pretty unconvinced."

"That's because I'm not convinced. We're both exhausted. The others are exhausted. We all need a break, not an indefinite sentence to hard labor."

Kali giggled at her friend's exaggerated description of their lives. "You don't really feel that way, do you?"

"Of course not. I'm just saying we need help. I liked the idea of you becoming the new director in the beginning. But if we do that, we need to hire more people to take some of the load off of both of us."

"Maybe I should talk to Mr. Marsh again. Maybe he could give us some ideas for restructuring, at least for a little while. Just to get us through until we find the perfect fit for our director's office. Then we can ease into it and not feel like we're making a rash decision. ...I'm sure it would take a lot of time though. I'm not sure he has that kind of time."

Kelly laughed. "Well, if he can't help us, there's always M&Ms. ...I wonder what's keeping Mac. It isn't like him to be late."

"I was just thinking the same thing. Maybe I should call him."

"Go ahead, it won't take me long to finish this up now."

"Are you sure?"

"Yep."

"Okay. I think I'll give Mr. Marsh a call as well."

Kali leaned her shovel against the building, but before going inside she came to her friend's side and wrapped her in an enormous hug. "Thank you for being my friend."

Kelly leaned back, meeting her friend's gaze, her face beaming love. "Thank you for being mine!"

Kelly watched her friend go and then went back to her shoveling. A few minutes later, she realized that, for the first time since Sam had gone to Heaven, she was humming. She smiled to herself and let her thoughts drift to Kali. She'd never imagined that Kali had ever considered leaving the crisis center. She'd always known Kali was incredibly strong. Knowing the other woman had chosen to stay, even when it was painful, strengthened that conviction.

"What song is that?" a voice broke into her thoughts, and she looked up to see her bus friend striding through the snow toward her.

"It's nothing really, just a melody I like to hum."

The man stopped in front of her, considering her task. "Do you always shovel the sidewalks?"

"No, but not only is our maintenance man running late, he's also nearly seventy-five. We figured he could use a little extra help this morning."

"We?" he said, wondering where and who the others might be.

"Oh, Kali just stepped inside for a minute."

Matt spotted the shovel leaning against the wall and went to it. He picked it up and began shoveling where Kali had left off.

"What are you doing?"

"Shoveling. What does it look like?"

"But, aren't you on your way to work or something?"

"No. I was on my way to the ChaiNook for a round of tea lattes and hot chocolates for the gang back at the office. They can wait a little longer."

"Are you sure?"

"Yep. I have no desire to sit at my desk today anyway. Not with everything glistening like this."

"The snow really is pretty, even though there's so much of it. Shoveling is pretty good stress relief too." Kelly shoved her shovel into the snow as she spoke.

Matt, on the other hand, stopped and straightened to his full height. "It's only 8:30 in the morning. Surely, it hasn't been so stressful that you're already looking for physical activity to work it off."

"Sometimes, all it takes is one phone call. But those phone calls tend to bring a little clarity, don't they? I mean, once you step back and think them through, you realize who people really are and who you should no longer depend on."

Matt didn't move. He studied his friend for a moment, concerned about what she had just alluded to, but more concerned about where it could lead her.

"I'm going to say something that might seem harsh," he began cautiously, "but please hear me out. ...Please don't let the ridiculousness of others in times like these make you skeptical of people. You...you have a kind, sweet, accepting spirit about you. Please don't let them steal it from you. It's not worth it. I know people are going to do and say some idiotic, selfish things—already have—but don't let them change who you are. Please."

Kelly stared, uncertain of how to respond.

"I'm sorry. I've been too bold, haven't I? Poked my nose in where it didn't belong. I'll shut up and shovel."

"If it had come from anyone else, then I would say, yes, you went too far."

Matt fidgeted with the shovel, waiting for her to continue, but she didn't. "But?" he pressed.

"But it *is* you, and you have experience in these things, don't you?"

To his own surprise, Matt blushed. "Unfortunately, yes. I'm afraid I do."

"Do I sound like I'm becoming skeptical?"

The man considered her question, running a gloved hand over his cold chin. "No," he said at last. "You don't sound skeptical. You sound like someone who has had their trust violated. Like someone you thought you could depend on turned out to be untrustworthy — again. That's always terrible, but it hurts a lot more when it's in the wake of losing one of the most important people in your life."

"Did you…I mean, did that happen to your family?"

Matt hesitated, once again finding himself in a situation in which he couldn't reveal too much. Still, he felt the need to be completely honest with her. A heavy shadow passed over his blue eyes.

"Yes, more than once. My father had friends and acquaintances alike who proved to be opportunists. I had friends who simply disappeared. Others appeared only when they could somehow get some kind of pleasure or fulfillment out of joining in our sorrow. It left us feeling empty and betrayed. But, it's also what led to my 'spying.'"

"Your spying?"

Matt nodded. "For a while, I just didn't want to be around anyone anymore because I didn't think I could trust them. I didn't feel they really cared. I didn't think I mattered to anyone anymore, and I couldn't understand why they all left me right then, when I needed them the most. Then something happened inside of me, and I realized I'd been walking through life without any concern for the people around me. I *thought* I cared. I was involved at church. I volunteered. I did all sorts of good things. But every single day, people walked by me, and I never gave a second thought to who they were or what struggle they might be passing through.

"I started paying more attention. Listening more closely. Eventually, as life began creeping back into my heart, I started acting on what I was hearing and seeing. But it could have gone a completely different direction. If it wasn't for God's grace in my life, I could be a very different man…a very bitter, lonely man."

Kelly considered her friend, sensing the pain he felt at some of the memories, admiring the courage he had in sharing his story and the wisdom and purpose he had gained from it all.

"I'm glad you didn't become that man," she said at last. "I'm so glad you had the courage to talk to me that morning at the bus stop. Neither of us ever could have known what was about to happen…but God knew. He knew how much I was going to need your kindness."

Matt smiled. "He knew I needed it too. I needed to have my heart stirred again and to be reminded of the depths of His love."

Kelly kicked at the shovel and then stepped toward the snow again. "Thank you for your warning," she said, "I'll try to be more aware of how I'm—" She stopped, cutting herself short with a laugh.

"What's so funny?"

"I just realized that, once again, you are God's answer to prayer."

"What do you mean?"

"The issue that got us out here! A request for volunteers to help with this snow was dismissed and turned into a rather scathing rebuke. But here you are, helping us shovel snow! Thank you!"

Matt grinned, a sparkle coming up in his eyes as he dipped his head in a shallow bow. "Glad I could be of service."

CHAPTER 30

Kelly stood in the doorway of her office and stared at Sharon's empty desk. Three days had passed since she and Kali had gathered their staff and told them of their decision to hold off on finding a new director until they had a better handle on what they were searching for. Sharon had missed every day since that meeting. The first day hadn't seemed unusual. Sharon worked part-time and set her own schedule as it best fit in around the rest of her life. But it was rare for her to be gone three days in a row. Something wasn't right.

With new determination, Kelly crossed the room to where Gil sat, engrossed in his work. "Gil, have you heard from Sharon at all?"

The accountant looked up, blinking the stare out of his eyes. "What? Sharon?"

"Yes. Have you heard from her?"

"No. I noticed she wasn't here when I stopped by yesterday, but I haven't heard anything from her. Maybe check with Brenda."

Gil's cellphone buzzed, and he glanced in its direction. His eyebrows drew together in a frown.

"Everything all right?" Kelly asked.

"It's Beth. She says she's not feeling good and might need me to come home."

"She's been sick a lot lately."

"I know. She can't seem to kick whatever this bug is. I told her if it doesn't clear up in the next couple of days, she needs to go to the doctor. She's been putting it off because of the cost, but sometimes you just have to go."

"Well, stick to your guns. There's a lot of terrible stuff going around, she could have some kind of infection or something."

"I know."

"I'll be praying for her."

"Thanks."

Kelly left Gil's desk and went to the corner where Brenda sat quietly working away at a menu for the after-school program.

"Brenda, do you have a sec?" she asked. "I don't want to break your concentration."

Brenda laughed, her green eyes smiling back at Kelly. "It's already broken, believe me. I haven't made it through my first cup of coffee yet, so there's no concentrating going on at all."

"I understand that for sure, except I'm usually in search of tea. Hey, have you heard anything from Sharon? She hasn't been here the last three days."

Brenda set her pen aside and drew in a deep breath. "I have a feeling Sharon won't be back."

"Why do you say that?"

"After the meeting the other day, I heard her mumbling at her desk. She said something like, 'I can't do this anymore. I can't watch things fall apart.' I asked her if she was okay, and she just stared at me for a long time. Then she said, "No, I'm not okay. I haven't been okay since the day Sam died. I can't do this anymore. I'm exhausted.' I tried to encourage her that it will get better eventually, but even though she didn't say anything, I could tell she didn't agree. This morning, I noticed her family pictures aren't on her desk anymore. I'm guessing she took what was hers and isn't planning on coming back. It's not the right way to leave, but I think it was the only way she knew how to do it. I don't think she could bring herself to tell you and Kali she intended to quit."

Kelly nodded, her voice choked by tears.

"I'm sorry, Kelly. I know that's going to add a tremendous amount of work to you and Kali. Maybe I can pick up some of what Sharon was doing."

"Oh, Brenda, you have your hands full. I don't know how you do what you do already. We may just have to tie up any ends she left loose and let her projects sit for a while. I don't know how else we can manage. …I'll go call her. At the very least, I want to make sure we haven't offended her."

The phone call was brief but tearful. Sharon had been a faithful friend and coworker for several years. To lose her now was devastating.

"Kelly, I know it isn't the strong thing to do," she said, "and I don't want to hurt you and Kali, but I just can't watch that ministry fall apart. I can't."

In her heart, Kelly wanted to yell, "It's going to fall apart even faster if everyone keeps giving up!" But she refrained. Instead, she said, "I understand, but we sure are going to miss you. We all love you very much. I wish you would reconsider."

But Sharon was not to be budged. She'd been thinking about the decision for weeks. The choice to remain as they were, without a director, was the deciding factor. She simply couldn't stay any longer.

So now, they were down not just one but two employees. M&Ms had emailed to say the education fund would continue to cover Sarah's tuition the following year. When her brother learned this, he had agreed to let her stay in college and to continue to attend church. He had insisted, however, that she find another job and quit working at the crisis center. They were now just two days shy of the end of her two-week notice.

Sometimes, Kelly wondered if they would ever start surfacing from the depths. It seemed like they only sank deeper and deeper. She remembered Kali's words the day she had spoken with Pastor Hanson.

"Why can't someone just be the kind of honorable man God has called him to be and that they all claim to be. Just one man! That's all we're asking for."

Just one man. How hard could that be to find? Kelly sighed. Apparently, it could be very hard.

❊ ❊ ❊

Kelly stepped through the front door of the crisis center and greeted the young volunteer who sat in the seat that had been Sarah's.

"I can't believe how beautiful the weather is," she commented. "Last week, we were shoveling out from under eighteen inches of snow. Today it's nearly seventy-five, and I'm loving it!"

The young woman behind the reception desk joined in Kelly's enthusiasm. "Me too. I've been watching the birds fly in and out under the awning all morning."

Kelly stopped her trek across the main office. "Oh. That's not good."

"Why not?"

"We have a pair of swallows that like to nest up in there. When they have young, they dive-bomb everyone who walks by. And they make a horrible mess. Can you let Mac know they're back?"

"Sure, Miss Vance. I'll do that right away."

"Thank you, Grace Anne."

"Kelly."

Kelly turned to see Kali standing just outside of her office. "Yes?"

"Can you come here for a minute? Or are you in the middle of something?"

"I just got back from Hope House, and I need to go over to the tutoring station, but I have a few minutes. What's up?"

"I need to show you something. Can you come look?"

"Sure." Kelly crossed the room and followed her friend into the office. She started to sit in the chair in front of the desk, but Kali motioned her to follow all the way around where she could better see the computer screen.

"I just got an email from Mr. Marsh," Kali said.

"Oh? What about?"

"Our phone conversation last week after my conversation with Pastor Hanson."

"What does he say?"

"You're never going to believe this. Look for yourself." Kali pulled up the email and then stood, allowing her friend to take her seat.

"Dear Miss Shepherd," Kelly read aloud as she seated herself,

"I have given much time to thought and prayer regarding the matters we discussed last week. I would like to offer what I believe will be a good starting point for restructuring. I hope you won't think me too forward in the matter. It is not my desire to overstep any bounds.

"The relationship your staff has developed with my head of accounting seems to be a good one. I know he has enjoyed becoming more acquainted with your organization and has developed a genuine concern for your wellbeing. I would like to propose him as an advisor for the crisis center. I know him well enough to know he will not make any rash decisions or disregard any concerns which you might have about proposed changes. He will listen to your concerns and will weigh them and reconsider any suggestions he has made in light of those concerns.

"Please, pray about this, and get back to me when you have reached a decision about the matter, one way or the other. I will say nothing to him about this proposal until I have heard from you. Please take all the time you need to consider this matter.

"Sincerely, McKinsey Marsh."

Kelly leaned back in her seat. "Wow. I never saw that coming. What do you think?"

"I don't know. I mean part of me says we should do it just because it would help so much. Part of me says, wait. We really don't know very much about this guy. Just because Mr. Marsh trusts him, doesn't mean we can. What if he turns out to be like these other men? Part of me just wants to close the email and never come back to it because I don't trust myself to make the right decision."

"Kali, don't second-guess yourself like that."

"Well, I certainly didn't do very well picking out Mr. Kerry and Mr. Owens."

"You didn't pick them out. They came to us."

"True. ...And now this one is coming to us."

"No," Kelly corrected emphatically, "Mr. Marsh is bringing him, offering him, to us. And he isn't trying to take the lead. He's just offering him as an advisor. In fact, M&Ms doesn't even know his services are being offered. ...But I do think we should take time to pray about it."

"Well, that's a given."

"The question is, how long?"

"That's...that's actually what I wanted to talk to you about."

"Uh oh, I don't like the sound of this."

"It's nothing bad. In fact, it's good—for me. I just don't know if you'll like the idea. ...Micah's parents have reserved tickets for me to fly out there for a week. But I don't want to go if it's going to be too much for you here."

"Kali, that's wonderful! I want you to go. You *both* need that. I know Micah has been a bit discouraged ever since his trip here. Please don't let us hold you back. We'll be fine."

"Are you sure?"

"Yes. When do you leave?"

"Saturday and I would be back the Sunday night a week later, Lord willing. The return trip is all standby, so I can't guarantee anything."

"Go. Go and have a wonderful time! And give them all my love. The only thing I don't like about the deal is that I'm not going with you. Oh, I'm so happy for you."

Kali grinned. Emotion surged within her, and she couldn't help swooping down on her friend with an enormous hug. "Thank you! Thank you so much!"

Kelly didn't respond. She couldn't form the words. She was too happy for her friend...and a little worried for the rest of them.

CHAPTER 31

Kelly sighed with relief as she stood patiently at the bus stop. They'd survived their first day without Kali—barely. Nothing had fallen apart, nothing had exploded, and no one had been hurt. Brandon had been missing, but she assumed that, like the last time, he'd had a change in schedule at the college. The only real mishap had been when the newest receptionist had accidentally told someone Kelly would meet them at the Hope House at the exact time Kelly was meeting with several of their tutors. The chaos of not being able to get back in touch with the woman had led to Gil finishing the meeting with the tutors, so Kelly could have one of the shuttle drivers rush her to the Hope House. But in the end, all had gone well.

She sighed again, feeling the stress of the day begin to melt away. It was a lovely evening, the kind that tempted her to walk home. But tonight, she was too tired. The bus rounded the corner, and her eyes brightened. A tiny hope rose in her heart. Perhaps her bus friend would be there. As the bus pulled to a stop, her eyes searched the windows, but there was no sign of him. The doors slid open, and she stepped forward.

"Kelly!" came a panicked voice.

Kelly stopped mid-step and looked down the street. A young woman with long, red hair ran toward her from the direction of the crisis center.

"Kelly! Wait!" she called. "I need to talk to you!"

"Sarah?" Kelly whispered, stepping back from the bus and waving the driver on. "I'll catch the next one," she said, addressing the man whose name she didn't know, but whose smile had now become a familiar part of her commutes for weeks on end.

The driver returned her wave, closed the door, and cautiously pulled away from the curb.

"Sarah, what are you doing here?" Kelly asked as Sarah reached her.

"Just a second," the girl wheezed, "I need to catch my breath."

Kelly's dark eyes brightened with amusement. "You were running pretty good there."

"Ugh. I tried... to catch you...before you left the office...but my last class got out late."

"What's going on?"

"Can we go to the center? ... I need to tell you something...but not here."

"Sure. Is everything all right?"

"Yes. I think you just need to know about something. ...I'll tell you when we get there. ...How are things going?"

"Pretty well. We made it today without Kali, just a few more days to go. How is your new job?"

Sarah shrugged, her rosy countenance losing some of its light. "It's okay. I'm still trying to get used to things. I miss working with all of you, especially you and Kali."

"Well, you're welcome to come by and hang out with us any time you want."

"Thanks."

The short jaunt back to the crisis center provided just enough time to do a bit more catching up, but as Kelly unlocked the door an uneasy silence fell between them. They walked through the dark main office without a word. Kelly opened the door to her office and flipped on the lights. Sarah waited, glancing around the office as if to make sure no one else was around.

"So, what's going on, Sarah?"

Sarah sat down in the chair by the door and watched as Kelly made her way around her desk to her own chair. "I don't want to be a gossip, Kelly, but I think you need to know what happened at the college today."

"At the college?"

"With Brandon."

"Brandon?" Kelly's voice cracked with surprise and confusion. "Is he okay?"

"He's fine, but he deserves whatever he gets."

Kelly jerked back at the sharp statement. "Deserves whatever he gets for what?"

"He was dismissed from the college today."

"For what?"

"For destruction of school property and public intoxication. I don't know if they're actually pressing criminal charges against him or not."

"What!"

"I think it's been going on for a while, but I can't prove it. He just finally got caught."

"But...no...It can't be. No." Kelly sank back in her chair, all of her strength draining from her body into an invisible puddle on the floor. How could this be happening? He had been such a help to them over the previous months. How could this possibly be true? "Are you sure, Sarah? Are you one hundred percent sure it was our Brandon?"

"I'm positive. I was in class with him when the president called him out, and I left class as the security guards were escorting him off the campus. It didn't take long to find out what happened after that. Too many people saw him throw a chair through the window at the Rec Center."

"Brandon! Brandon threw a chair through a window?"

"Yes."

"Why?"

"Because he was angry and drunk."

"But I've never even had the slightest inkling that he drinks. I've never had any idea of him going to parties or anything along those lines."

"Well, I think there are other things you've probably never had the slightest inkling about where Brandon is concerned."

Sarah's words stopped Kelly's racing mind. She recalled the moments when she had noticed the mistrust between the two college students. Now, she understood the caution she'd seen in Sarah's face in those moments.

"But, Sarah, if you knew this was going on, why didn't you tell us?"

"Like I said, I can't prove anything, but I've been suspicious for a while just because of the people he hangs out with at college. I don't trust them, which makes me question him. I'm sorry. Maybe I should have shared my concerns with you, but I didn't want to be spreading rumors. This, however... I was afraid if word got very far, his actions could end up damaging the center. I didn't want that to happen. We've had too many problems this year as it is."

Kelly's heart warmed at the way the girl still included herself in their number. "Thank you for that, Sarah. I just don't even know what to think. I mean, I know what I need to do, but I think I'll call Kali and Micah first. ...I think I'll go get something to eat before I make that call though. I need to think this over a little. Would you like to join me?"

"I'd love to."

❊ ❊ ❊

"So, you're not sure you're coming back at all?"

Kali and Micah sat in a quiet café with a simple plate of apple pie and vanilla ice cream on the table between them. Micah ran his spoon through the ice cream that had melted along the edge of the plate. Kali, on the other hand, had forgotten the pie altogether. She waited for his answer, chewing her bottom lip in a nervous attempt to hold back her emotions.

"I'm not sure of anything, Kali. Sometimes, I don't even know who I am anymore. Things at home, well, you've seen it. The time away was so good for Mom and Dad, but their world is still pretty upside down. I haven't even begun to sort through mine."

Kali cringed at that thought. What did that mean for her? Did she still have a place in that world? Where would she fall in all of his sorting?

"Kali, did you hear me?"

"What?"

"Did you hear my question?"

"I'm sorry, Micah. I'm having trouble processing everything. What did you ask?"

"It's okay. That's exactly what I've been struggling with."

"So, what did you ask?" Kali leaned forward, fixing her gaze on his brown eyes and hoping to see beyond the pain and uncertainty there.

"Are you tired of waiting for me?" he whispered.

"What!" Kali sat back, shocked. "Tired of waiting for you? Micah, how could you ever think that? I miss you more than I can even explain, but that just makes me realize how worth the waiting you are. No, I'm not tired of waiting for you. I want to honor you by giving you the time you need."

"But what if things don't work out? What if I never get to go back? What if my parents need me to stay here permanently? What do we do then? I don't want to hurt you, Kali, but I'm terribly afraid I will disappoint you...have already disappointed you."

"No, Micah, you haven't. I understand. Look at where I've been the last three months. We still have no director, and the only ones who have applied have turned out to be absolutely the wrong fit. Dangerous even. Micah, we're both still picking up the pieces. Neither of us knows what a day will bring, let alone the next year. ...Please, don't give up on me. I promise I won't give up on you."

Kali was surprised to see tears in his eyes. *Tears*, she thought, *of relief.*

"Please, Micah."

He managed a faint but sincere smile and whispered, "I promise."

They were silent for a moment, each scooping a lump of the smooth ice cream into their mouths and savoring it.

"This is the best ice cream I've had in ages," Kali remarked, reaching into her pocket at the same time to pull out her vibrating phone. "Oh! It's Kelly."

"Wait. Let me answer it. I want to say hello." Micah grabbed the phone from Kali, a renewed excitement coming into his face at the same moment. "Hello."

"Hello? Um. I think I may have dialed the wrong number."

"No, you didn't, Kelly. This is Micah. I can't believe you've forgotten my voice already."

"What! No! Micah, stop. I just wasn't expecting a male voice. How are you?"

"I am well. How are you?"

"Oh, I'm enjoying the last few moments of a beautiful spring evening. How are things going there?"

"Well, you know Seattle. We're sitting here watching the raindrops trickle down the windowpanes."

"How are your parents?"

"They're all right. Still struggling, of course, but beginning to function a little more...from time to time."

Kelly hesitated, then summoned the courage to say what she was thinking. "You sound tired, Micah. Are you really all right?"

"I'm okay, Kelly, really, I am. For one thing, I have your gorgeous best friend sitting across the table from me, sharing a piece of delicious pie."

Kelly gasped. "You're on a date. I am so sorry."

Micah broke out in laughter. "You're fine. We needed an interruption. The conversation had gotten too serious."

"Oh, Micah. I'm so sorry."

"You're fine. Do you want to talk to Kali?"

"Well, I did. But I don't want to interrupt. You can have her call me back. I'm pretty sure I won't be going to sleep anytime soon."

"Why do you say that?"

"You know how it goes. Your brain gets stirred up by something, and then it never wants to shut down."

"Is that 'something' why you were calling?"

"Yes. So, like I said, if I'm interrupting, she can call me back tomorrow morning."

"No, it's all right. Maybe I can help too. I miss being there to help. Here, I'll let you talk to her, and she can fill me in. Okay?"

"Sounds good. Micah, it's great to hear your voice. We miss you around here."

"I miss being there. Just a sec." He handed the phone back and whispered, "I think she's upset."

Kali frowned. "About what?"

"I don't know."

Kali's frown deepened, but then, knowing her friend would hear it through the phone, she pushed it aside and smiled. "Hey, Kelly, how's it going?"

"Kali, I am so sorry to interrupt."

"It's okay. You're not interrupting. What's going on?"

"You're never going to believe it. I don't believe it. I don't know what to do. I mean, I know what I've got to do, but I don't want to do it, but I think I have to. I wish I could wait until you get back, but I don't think I should. Oh, Kali, I just don't like this part of the job."

"What are you talking about? Don't like what part of the job?"

"Letting people go."

"What! Who?"

"Brandon."

"But why? Please start over from the beginning. Why would you let him go?"

"Brandon was expelled from the college today."

"Why?"

"For throwing a chair through a window at the Rec Center."

"He did what!"

"Oh, there's more. He was drunk at the time."

"What! Wait a minute. Are you sure?"

"Yes. Sarah came this evening. She wanted us to know because she was afraid of the effect it could have on the crisis center. After we had supper together, I called the college. To be honest, I didn't expect anyone to be in the office, and I didn't expect them to give me any answers. But as it turned out, the Dean of Students was there. He verified everything. He even shared a few things Sarah most likely hadn't heard. I know what I need to do, Kali, I just really don't want to do it."

Kali couldn't believe what she was hearing. It was too fantastical. How could sweet, diligent, fun-loving Brandon have gotten himself into such a mess?

"Kali, are you there?"

"Yes. I'm just...I'm shocked. What were the other things?"

"They suspect he has been using other substances. They couldn't prove it, but there is evidence he may be involved in drug activity as well."

"But why have we never seen any signs? I don't understand."

"I don't either. None of it makes sense. But I do know that tomorrow morning when he comes in, I'm going to have to sit down and talk with him about it."

"Don't do it alone, Kelly. Please. Have Gil go in with you. You need to have a witness on this. You need to make sure he knows it isn't because of a rumor we heard, but because our investigation of the rumor proved it to be true, and that it is in direct violation of the terms upon which he became a volunteer. You need to make sure he understands we are not singling him out. We're very grateful for everything he has done, but he, by his choices, has made it impossible for us to allow him at the center any longer. ...Oh, Kelly. I'm so sorry you have to deal with this. I am so sorry—just a minute. Micah's begging for information."

Kali put her hand over the microphone and leaned across the table, whispering, "Brandon got himself kicked out of school for breaking a window in a drunken rage. There may be drugs involved as well."

"Brandon!"

"Shh. Keep your voice down. Yes, Brandon. She's going to let him go in the morning."

Micah shook his head, disgust darkening his gaze. "Let me talk to her."

Kali handed the phone over and leaned back, curious about what he would say.

"Kelly, are you all right with this? We could set up a video conference, and Kali could be there through video."

Kelly considered the idea. It might be nice.

"I could be there too, Kelly."

That, she realized, would also be nice. "I think that's a good idea, Micah. He should be into the office by ten, would that work?"

"That would be perfect. Do you want to call us, or do you want us to call you?"

"Text me when you're ready," Kali interjected from across the table, "and we'll call you."

"We'll wait in the conference room until you call. It won't hurt him any to be in the hot seat for a few minutes. Might help a little."

"Sounds like a plan," Micah said, "I think you should still have Gil or Brenda join you. Just so you have another witness."

"All right."

"Kelly, I'm so sorry. I wish we were both there."

"So, do I, Micah, but none of us can change that. It will be all right. I'm just glad to know I won't be doing this alone."

"Why don't we pray together, the three of us?"

"I'd like that."

Micah and Kali bowed their heads, but it was some time before Micah found the composure to speak. The moment brought home, once more, how very different life was without his brother. He took a deep, shaky breath. Then a calm came over him as he felt the weight of Kali's hand on his arm.

"Lord, I want to thank You for Kali and Kelly. Thank You for their faithfulness. Thank You for protecting them and the crisis center thus far. We pray now, Lord, that You would continue to protect them. Please give us all wisdom in this situation. Lord, we all love and care about Brandon. We ask that you would be working in Brandon's heart already. Help him to see the wrong of his actions and to have a heart that is willing to turn around. Lord, we pray You would protect the center from any slander or libel that might come as a result of his actions, or any other attacks. Lord, thank You so much for loving us and for caring for us. We don't deserve it. We commit this situation into Your hands. I pray, Father, that You would help both of the girls to have a good night's rest tonight and that You would keep their hearts and minds in the peace that passes understanding. We love You, Lord. Thank You. In Jesus name, Amen."

"Thank you, Micah."

The man could hear tears in Kelly's whisper. He let out a soft sigh. "Wish we could be there, friend. We'll keep praying. Don't lose heart. Do you want to talk to Kali again?"

"No. I've interrupted long enough. Just tell her I said goodnight, and I love her."

"I will."

"Goodnight, Micah. Thank you."

"You're welcome. Have a good sleep."

"You too."

Micah disconnected the call. Pity filled his eyes. "She said to tell you goodnight, and she loves you."

Kali nodded, wiping tears from her eyes. "Thank you, Micah. I know she needed that prayer. Thank you."

CHAPTER 32

Gil sat stolidly, arms crossed over his chest. His eyes followed Kelly as she worked to set up the computer for their video call. He'd sensed an uneasiness about her as soon as he'd arrived. Then she'd locked herself in her office for almost an hour before coming out and asking him to meet with her and Brandon in the conference room. That was all she'd said, nothing more. They'd been friends for nearly 20 years. He knew her well, well enough to know something was very wrong.

"What is this all about?" he asked at last.

"Ah, Gil, it's a mess. Brandon has gotten himself into some trouble."

"How much?"

"A lot."

"Huh," he grunted, wishing he was more adept at the type of conversation he was sure was about to follow.

Kelly straightened from where she'd just plugged the computer into a wall outlet and eyed her friend. Stress marked the lines around his eyes. "Gil, is something bothering you?"

The man shrugged. "Beth is sick again."

"Again? Has she gone to the doctor yet?"

"She's going this afternoon. I was going to try to finish up here in time to go with her."

"You think it's something serious?"

"I hope not, but something is definitely not right."

"Well, hopefully, this won't take too long. Why don't you just go ahead and go when we're finished."

"I need to get the reports to Mr. Marsh's accountant."

"When does he need them?"

"He asked me to have it to him tonight, so he can finish going over ours before he has to start theirs."

"Hmm. Well, I could send him an email and let him know you've had a family emergency of sorts. Do you think you could finish it up in the morning?"

"Sure. I can even come back this evening and have it in his inbox by morning."

"I'll email him. I'm sure good ol' M&Ms will understand."

"Thanks, Kelly."

Kelly stopped what she was doing and inclined an ear toward the main office. "I think Brandon's here. Yep, there he is." She went to the doorway and called to the young man. "Brandon, when you get everything settled, can you come here please."

"Sure."

Kelly returned to the table, sat down at its head, and sent a quick text to Kali. By the time Brandon sauntered into the conference room, the video call was already ringing.

"Have a seat," Kelly told him as she accepted the call and positioned the laptop where everyone could see it.

"What's going on?" Brandon asked, surprised to see both Micah and Kali on the call.

Kelly closed the door and went to her seat, using the moment to collect her thoughts.

"Brandon, we heard some disturbing news yesterday," she began. "Would you like to tell us what's going on at the college?"

"What do you mean?"

"We heard you had a little trouble over the weekend."

Brandon squirmed in his chair while at the same time attempting to maintain a façade of composure. "Yeah, there was a bit of a misunderstanding, everything's been taken care of."

"What kind of misunderstanding?"

"Well, someone accused me of something I didn't do. A bunch of rumors were going around about it. But none of it's true."

"Are you sure about that?"

"Yeah. It's all good." The young man's eyes darted back and forth between Kelly and the silent couple on the computer screen. He glanced at Gil once, wondering why he had been included in the meeting. "Everything's fine."

"Brandon, please be honest with me. I have taken you at your word for the last three years. We all have. We've been your friends. We've been there when times were rough and when they were good. We've supported you and encouraged you, and we've been blessed by *everything* you have done for us here. ...We need the truth."

Brandon repositioned himself, glancing down at his hands. "I made a mistake. It's the first time. It won't happen again."

Kelly closed her eyes and let out a soft moan, wishing for all their sakes that he would simply be honest. "Brandon, I spoke with the Dean of Students last night. I know this was your fifth infraction. This isn't a mistake. This is a pattern—a pattern in desperate need of help."

Brandon's gaze dropped. His head sagged, but he said nothing.

"I spoke with a counselor from my church's addiction program this morning. I didn't give them your name or any other information. Don't worry, I wouldn't do that to you. But she did tell me they have a place for you in their program if you're willing to give it a try."

The young man's eyes shot up, his gaze full of anger. "Addictions program! What makes you think I need to go through an addictions program? Who has been talking to you? It was Sarah, wasn't it? I knew I couldn't trust her. She's a liar. She—"

"Brandon, that's enough. I already told you I spoke with your dean. You are the one who threw the chair through the window. No one else. You're the one who caught towels on fire in the dorm restrooms. You're the one who spray-painted a wall and then passed out so they could catch you in the act, so to speak. *You* did those things."

In times past, both Kali and Kelly would have expected the young man to drop his gaze timidly, to color with embarrassment, and to admit his wrong; but this time he bristled.

"What difference does it make what I do on my own time?"

"It makes an enormous difference. When you came to work for us, you signed an agreement that you would live a life outside of this work that exemplified the work going on inside of it. You committed to lead a life which would not bring blame to this organization, but more so, to Christ. Among the standards you committed to uphold was that of avoiding the use of intoxicating and/or illegal substances. Your actions at the college clearly violate that commitment."

"So, you're firing me? From a job I don't even get paid for!"

"No. We're asking you to take time off to go through the program. If you agree to that, then you're more than welcome to come back."

"And if not?"

Kelly sighed. Her gaze was sharp and firm, but in its depths, everyone in the room could see disappointment. "If not," she stated with conviction, "then we will have to ask you not to volunteer here anymore. It's not what we want to do, but it is what we will have to do. We want you here, but you know as well as we do that right now your actions make that impossible."

"Just like that. Based on what? On hearsay?"

"Hearsay? Twenty people saw you throw that chair through that window. I'd hardly call that hearsay. Please, Brandon. We love you. Please, let us help you."

The young man leaped to his feet, sweeping his pen and notepad from the table. "Help me? It's too late for that. You can find a dozen kids out there at the snap of your fingers to do my job. What does it matter if I'm here or not? Go find someone else to help you. I'm done."

Brandon stormed out of the room, slamming the door behind him and making as much commotion as possible as he passed through the main office.

Gil rose to go after him, but Micah stopped him.

"Don't, Gil. It'll only cause a scene. Give him a couple of days to cool down, and then we'll try again. You did fine, Kelly. None of this is your fault."

The corner of Kelly's mouth twitched in response. It wasn't a smile. It wasn't a frown. It was both a weary acknowledgment of the fact that Micah had tried to encourage her and a tacit admission that her heart found it hard to agree.

The building rattled as Brandon tore open the front door, letting in a sharp gust of wind. From her seat, Kelly could see him force a box containing his few belongings through the doorway. Then he disappeared into the morning light.

"He's gone," Kelly whispered.

They sat in silence for a moment. Kelly could feel her own emotions rising inside of her. She propped her elbow on the arm of the chair and rested her chin in her hand, turning her face away from the laptop to hide the rising tears.

"Kelly, are you okay?"

Somehow the concern in Kali's voice made the moment all the more painful for Kelly. She felt she had disappointed her friends—all of them. And somehow, they, as a group, had failed Brandon.

"Kelly?" Kali persisted.

Kelly shook her head and dared to glance at Gil and then her friends, who so patiently awaited her answer from the other side of the computer screen. Tears began to trickle down her cheeks.

"No. No, I'm not okay," she whispered, "but I will be."

With that, she left the room.

CHAPTER 33

Kelly sat in her dark living room, motionless, hovering over her laptop with finger poised over the return key. Kali's words from the day she had spoken with Pastor Hanson echoed in Kelly's mind.

"Why can't someone just be the kind of honorable man God has called them to be and that they all claim to be? Just one man. That's all we're asking for."

"Just one good man," Kelly whispered.

She stared at the words on the screen. They reflected the ache in her heart. It had been there all day, ever since Brandon had stormed out of the office. When had chivalry died? What had happened to honorable men?

"Where's the knight in shining armor when you need him?"

As she formed the words, her heart sank further still. With one click, she could send her questions out into the world of social media. It was one o'clock in the morning. Most of her friends and followers would be asleep. Chances were they would never see the two simple lines of text. But would she, in that moment of venting, be condemning those who had tried to help them? They had done the best they could, hadn't they? What about Gil? Three times a week, he came to the office and worked without complaint, without so much as a penny in return. What about Mr. Marsh and M&Ms?

They had stepped up and met every request sent in their direction. What about the man from the bus? She didn't even know his name, nor he hers, but he had done what he could to help and encourage.

"But it isn't enough." The words were empty. They seemed to fall to the floor with a hollow rattle as if God Himself were so convinced of their worthlessness that He stood unperturbed at their clamor. The silence that followed was equally empty. And yet Kelly knew that, for the depth and weight of that silence, God was listening — patiently, compassionately, tenderly. Waiting for her heart to bleed out its pain in full.

"It's all going to fall apart: the center, its programs, the community — all of it. Just because no one is willing to step up and be honorable and courageous and real." Tears coursed her cheeks. She wiped at them with the back of her hand and stared once more at the message on the screen:

"Is the world completely devoid of knights in shining armor? What has happened to chivalry, to valor, to strength in the face of adversity?"

She sighed deeply. Her shoulders sank and she bit her bottom lip. With a trembling hand, she reached out, selected the text, and hit "delete." That was it. She couldn't do it. She wouldn't. For Micah and Gil's sake and the other three men, she wouldn't do it. But her questions remained. Why was no one willing to stand up for them? Did their work mean so little? Did *they* mean so little? Why had everyone forgotten them? Why were so many showing themselves to be untrustworthy when they needed them to be at their best?

It seemed no one could answer her questions. No one dared. No one cared to fight anymore. No one bothered to stand. Someone else, they all assumed, would do it.

Her bus friend's story floated through her mind, almost as a dim candle in the dark. She wished he were there, so they could talk. He had experienced the same things. He had felt abandoned, but he had turned it into purpose. He'd let it steer him toward meeting the needs of others rather than coddling his wounded ego.

Her gaze shot up from her computer, striking the windowpane and fixing intently on the lights in the street below. Was that the crux of it all? Was her pride wounded? Wounded—yes. The unintended sense of rejection, betrayal, and abandonment cast upon them by others hurt beyond her heart. It ached in every muscle, in every joint. She felt old, incredibly old, and tired. But was it her pride that made the pain linger? Was she ungrateful? She slid down off the sofa, letting the computer drop onto its soft cushions. Why did it all have to be so confusing? Why couldn't they just go back and start over? Why did Sam ever go up on that roof?

❊ ❊ ❊

The sound of Kelly's ringing phone wriggled into her dark world. She took a deep breath, hoping the noise would go away, but it came again. She opened her eyes. Sunlight spilled in through the windows. It was morning. It was late! The phone rang again, and Kelly dove for the spot on the floor where she'd left it lying the night before. She fumbled with it, nearly dropping it twice before eventually managing to get it to her ear.

"He-hello?"

"Miss Vance?"

"Yes."

"This is Mel Zimmerman from Marsh and Line. We were supposed to receive a file from you this morning, but it hasn't come yet. I was just calling to find out if there was some kind of problem, or if the email just hasn't come through yet."

"OH! Oh, Mel, I am so sorry. Oh. What time is it?"

"It's 9:36."

"Oh, I am so sorry. I'm not even dressed yet. I…it was a long night. I…um…did you receive the email I sent yesterday about our accountant's family situation?"

The other woman hesitated. "Yes," she finally replied.

"Okay. Well, he never made it back to the office, at least not while I was there. I'm sorry. I should have emailed you last night to let you know it wouldn't be there first thing."

"Okay. Well," the woman paused, this time for longer than before. When she began again, a strange uncertainty had come into her voice. "Can you…why don't you go ahead and send whatever he had finished. We'll take care of the rest."

"I don't know how…I mean…I'm not sure what he was supposed to send. Why don't you call the office and ask Gil how he is progressing? That would probably be the best solution." Kelly repressed a sigh of relief. She was impressed with herself. Not a drop of caffeine in her system, and she was actually making sense.

"We already did. He's not at the office yet. The receptionist gave us your cell number."

Kelly rose to her feet and then sank down onto the sofa. "Oh, that's not good. That means something is wrong. Really wrong. Oh."

Her concern was met with silence. For a moment, her thoughts remained on Gil and Beth, but then she realized Mel was still waiting for instructions.

"Well," she said, "I guess there's only one other option. Tell M&Ms to send me an email detailing what we need to send to you, and I'll gather everything up."

"I'm sorry, M&Ms? What do you mean?"

"The man who has been helping us. He never signs his emails with his name, just *M.M.*, so I call him M&Ms. For all I know, it's Mr. Marsh himself."

Kelly heard a strange snorting sound on the other end of the line, but it didn't seem to be coming from Mel. The snort was followed by a slap and then the sound of shooing.

"I'm sorry about that, Miss Vance. One of the accountants thought this was a good time to pester. Seriously, I don't know how anything gets done in this office. If I weren't here to keep them all in line, this place would fall down around their ears. I will pass the message along."

"Thank you, Mel. I'll get to the office as quick as I can. Thank you so much for all of your help. All of you."

"No, problem. Just doing my job. Now to get these other guys to do theirs. Have a good day, Miss Vance."

"You too, Mel."

The call ended before Kelly could even look at the phone and comprehend what was on the screen. She groaned. It was going to be a long day.

She headed for the kitchen, hoping to scrounge up a quick breakfast before beginning her rush out the door. As she went, she found Gil's name in her contacts list and called his cellphone. It rang several times, but just before it went to voicemail, he answered.

"Hey, Kelly. I'm sorry I haven't touched base yet."

"No problem, Gil. I just woke up. I haven't even been to the office yet. I only knew you weren't there because I got a call from Marsh and Line."

"No. Oh. I'm sorry."

"It's not a problem. We're working things out. I just wanted to make sure you guys were okay."

"We're at the hospital. They wanted Beth back for tests first thing this morning. I'm just sitting in the waiting room."

"Is she feeling any better?"

"Not really. I have a bad feeling about all of this, Kel. I just don't know. Pray. Please pray."

"I will. We all will."

"I'll be into the office once I get her home and settled in."

"Don't worry about it. You just do what needs to be done. If Beth needs you at home, then stay home. Aren't you supposed to be at your real job today anyway?"

"They told me the same thing you told me. But, really, I don't mind swinging by to help you get that information sent off. Everything is in a folder on my desktop. It won't take me long to pull it together and send it."

"No. Don't come by just for that. I've already got a plan worked out with M&Ms' assistant. I'll probably have it all done before you guys even leave the hospital."

"You're sure?"

"Yep. Go take care of your wife, and don't worry about us. We'll be praying."

"Thanks, Kelly."

"You bet. Keep us posted."

"I will."

Kelly disconnected the call and laid the phone down on the counter. She opened the refrigerator and stared at its nearly empty shelves. Why was she always out of eggs when she was starving?

CHAPTER 34

Matt stood in line at the ChaiNook, glancing around at the room's many occupants. It had been a while since he'd just sat and listened and observed. This evening seemed like a good time for it. In fact, it seemed like a good evening to do his spying on the patio. The air was warm, and it would give him a chance to convince himself the trees were beginning to bud out.

He turned his attention back to the line. Two other customers still stood in front of him. He sighed and looked out the large front windows toward the street and the park that stretched out beyond it. Two children biked by from one direction, and a woman was passing from the other direction. There was something familiar about the woman's long, brown hair and casual gait. He squinted, leaning forward slightly as if the slight change in posture would help him see better. He saw her reach for her shoulder and swing a red leather bag from one arm to the other.

"It's her!" he said under his breath. "What is she doing over here this time of day?" He watched as his bus friend, whom he now knew to be Kelly Vance, stopped, glanced in the direction of the teahouse and then turned into the park. "Well," he whispered, "we'll just have to find out what she's doing here, won't we?"

"Are you ready to order, sir?"

Matt spun around, realizing he'd been staring out the window much longer than he'd intended.

"Yes," he stuttered, "Um…sorry. I got distracted. I'll have a large London Fog…make that two."

"Sweetened?"

Matt studied the young girl behind the counter in confusion, knowing full well that a London Fog should be sufficiently sweet without any additional sweetener. "Nothing extra if that's what you mean. I'll just grab some sweetener on my way out in case we need it."

"Okay. Would you like anything to eat with that?"

"No, thank you. That will be all." Matt laid his payment down on the counter and waited for the girl to process it.

"Here you go," she said, handing him a receipt. "Your order will be ready in just a minute."

"Thanks." He stepped aside and waited for someone to hand out the two cups of steaming milk and tea. He glanced across the street. Kelly had found a seat on a bench near the pond. That was good. He wouldn't have to waste time finding her.

"Here you are, sir."

"Thank you." He scooped up the drinks and a wad of sweetener and then hurried out the door and across the road. As he approached the bench, he hesitated, noticing his friend had just pulled out her Bible. Maybe he shouldn't interrupt her, but then, what would he do with two London Fogs? He plucked up his courage and stepped out in front of her.

"Hello." He grinned from ear to ear, his blue eyes shining.

"Wow!" she said, eagerly returning his smile. "Where did you come from?"

"I was just across the street, ordering tea when I saw you. I recognized your bag. If you ever get rid of that bag, our friendship is over. …I brought you a London Fog. Hope that's okay."

"Oh, that's one of my favorites. Thank you."

"I'm not guaranteeing it will be any good. The girl behind the counter didn't seem to know what it was. …Do you mind if I sit for a minute? I don't want to interrupt."

"Please. That would be nice. I was just getting ready to do a little reading, that's all."

He nodded toward her Bible. "Looks like pretty important reading to me."

She nodded. "Seems hard to get any extra in these days."

"I know what you mean." Matt handed her the cup of tea and sat down beside her. He settled himself, crossing one ankle over the other knee and shoving his free hand into his jacket pocket. He sighed contentedly. "I'm glad the workday is done. How about you?"

"Yes. Today, I have to agree."

"Rough day?"

"Rough start. The day got better, but I am so tired. Sometimes, I feel like I've aged twenty years in the past couple of months."

Matt nodded, but then he laughed. "Sometimes, I feel like I age a century overnight!"

"True. Very true."

Silence settled between them as they blew on their scalding beverages.

"Got them a little too hot today, didn't they?" Matt said to break the silence.

"Sure seems like it. That's okay. It'll just make it last longer."

"Do you want any sweetener? I didn't know what you might use, so I grabbed a little of everything." The man produced a handful of multi-colored packets of sugar, artificial sweetener, and sugar alternatives.

Kelly giggled. "Why did you take so many? It's a wonder they didn't charge you with theft."

"They know me in there. They know I can never pick which sweetener is the best. I would have gotten some honey too, but I was afraid it would break in my pocket. You know how honey is. It just goes everywhere."

"Even if it's just one tiny drop."

"Exactly."

"I'll take two raw sugars, just in case."

Matt managed to pry the two sugars out of his fist without spilling the whole mess onto the ground. He handed them to his friend and then shoved the rest back into his pocket.

"So…do you guys have any major events coming up at the center?"

"Yes, actually, we do."

"What is it?"

"Mother's Day."

Matt's chest tightened. He felt the tension spread to his neck and across his shoulders. His stomach knotted. He preoccupied himself with the stirring of his tea and then flicked his stirring stick into a nearby trashcan.

"Isn't that kind of a national holiday?" he said, barely managing to mask his emotions in a nonchalant, teasing tone. "What makes it so special for the center?"

"Oh, it's huge for the center. We work with a lot of single moms—a *lot* of single moms."

Matt's mouth rose in a shrugging motion. "I suppose you do. Guess I hadn't really thought of that. So, what do you do that makes it so big?"

"Well, we usually have an all-day event on Saturday. We have several hairdressers and nail salon owners who volunteer their time. Sometimes, the beauty school actually allows us to use their facility. We start the day off with classes at a church, usually Shallow Brook, but I don't see that happening this year. We usually have at least one or two practical classes on finances or parenting or cooking in the morning. We try to make them fun, so everyone has a good time while they're learning. Then we do the whole hair and nails thing. Sometimes, we have a special outing planned. Then we have a special dinner catered by a local restaurant. All the while, childcare is provided by some of our volunteers—also usually at Shallow Brook. We're going to have to work on that part."

"Wow. That's big. Why don't you think you'll be able to have it at Shallow Brook?"

"Well...remember that day you caught me shoveling?"

"Yes."

"That's where the stress had come from. I didn't know until then that the relationship had been strained for several years. I guess Sam did a lot to keep it smoothed over. With him gone...well, there's just not much to keep things in check."

"Oh." Matt's eyes widened with understanding. "I guess that could be a little awkward."

"Just a little."

"Man, you guys need somebody in there who can really stand up for that place, don't you? Somebody these guys aren't going to try to bully."

Kelly laughed. "Well, I've never thought of it that way, but I suppose we do. ...Got any suggestions?"

"Ha! Uh...no. But I'll let you know if anyone comes to mind." His laughter faded as his mind went back to the event they'd been discussing. He took a deep breath and let it out slowly through the tiny hole in the lid of his cup. He dared to test the hot liquid, found it bearable, and took a long drink. He stared out across the still dormant grass. He hadn't realized Mother's Day was already drawing so close. Of all the holidays, it was his next to least favorite, after Christmas. It was the primary reason he wanted to skip spring and go straight to summer.

"Is something wrong?"

Kelly's gentle voice pushed the tightness in Matt's chest into a strange trembling. He shook his head and swallowed hard.

"You're not telling the truth."

He spun in his seat, ready to defend himself, but one look into her sincere gaze drove the urge away. He sat back. "Mother's Day isn't something I do well these days. I didn't realize how close it was."

Kelly bit her lip and studied her friend compassionately. "I'm sorry," she said, "I hadn't thought about that, but I should have."

"No. It's all right. I think maybe I haven't done it well because I'm doing it wrong."

"What do you mean?"

"I mean... It's hard, it's really hard because I—"

"Because you miss her so much."

"Yeah. But maybe it's time I started doing it differently. Maybe it's time I started focusing on other moms, moms who need what you're giving them."

Kelly blinked back her surprise. "Wait. You mean...you want to help?"

"I don't know. I want to think about it, but maybe. In fact...do you still have my email address?"

"Yes."

"Can you send me an email detailing what you need in a venue? I'd love to work on that for you."

"Really?"

"Yes. I can do that much."

Kelly was ecstatic. She didn't know whether to jump up and down with joy or throw her arms around his neck in an enormous hug. In the end, she grabbed hold of his sleeve and shook it with excitement. "Thank you, thank you, thank you!"

Matt laughed heartily, leaning forward in his seat and holding his cup out over the grass to make sure she didn't spill the hot liquid in his lap. "Wow! If I'd known that's all it takes to get you excited, I would have offered sooner."

"Sorry. That was probably a bit much, but you have no idea how much pressure that will take off of us. Really."

He smiled and leaned back, happy to have made her so. "Make sure to send me the dates and how much time you need to set up and how many you intend to have there. All of that good stuff."

"Oh, I will! Don't worry. You'll get everything! Oh, thank you—" She cut herself off, disappointment replacing the excitement.

"What?"

"I don't even know your name."

The corner of Matt's mouth lifted with pleasure and a hint of teasing. "You will. When the time is right, you'll know."

Kelly twisted her mouth to one side. "Hmm. Well, you're going to know my name as soon as you get my email because it's right there in the address."

"That's okay. I already know your name."

"What!"

"It's not that hard to figure out. I went onto the center's website to find out more about what you guys do. The staff page doesn't have pictures, but it has names. You talk about Kali all the time, so I knew you weren't Kali. You've told me enough about what you do that it didn't take me long to figure it out from there."

A dissatisfied scowl crossed Kelly's face. "But I know almost nothing about you. I know you live near where I live, or at least I assume you do, and you work near where I work. I know you work in accounting or finance of some kind. I know you like to help people. But that's it."

"That's plenty."

"Why don't you want me to know? Are you hiding something?"

Matt considered her question for a moment, then he shrugged. "Nothing bad. It's just that, well, when I started riding the bus and sitting in coffee shops and other such things to find ways to help my 'neighbors,' I never intended to let it be known who was helping them. You are the only person I've ever actually developed a friendship with."

"Other than Gordy, you mean."

Matt chuckled. "Well, I guess you got me there. I'm just not sure. I mean…I try not to make a big deal about what I do. I just want to do it quietly. I just want to bless others. …That's one of the reasons I didn't come inside at the clothing exchange though. I knew someone I've helped could be inside, and I didn't want to be discovered in that setting. That was the first time I ever realized that, while my 'spying' opens many doors, it also brings limitations."

Kelly considered her friend, wondering how many people he had helped over the years since his mom had died, wondering how many lives he had quietly changed probably never to know the full impact of his gifts. She wondered how such a simple, seemingly normal man could possess such a big, giving heart. But another question tugged at her.

"What if God wants you to step through those limitations to something bigger?"

"Bigger?"

"Maybe broader is a better word. Maybe He wants you to take what you've already begun to do and expand it."

Matt took a long sip of his tea. "Maybe. What did you have in mind?"

Kelly chuckled. "I don't know. I just wonder if the limitations you see indicate that you need to do things differently."

"Hmm," Matt contemplated the thought a moment, then broke into soft laughter. "You just want to know my name."

"No! That's not true." She gave him a little shove, feigning irritation, but he could hear the laughter in her voice.

"Maybe you're right," he said. "I'll pray about it."

Kelly's eyes brightened. She leaned back against the bench and surveyed the park. A great sense of contentment settled over her. She had a sudden urge to loop her arm through his and cuddle against him, but she refrained. "Thank you for the tea. It's delicious. ...Even if it isn't actually a London Fog."

Matt laughed again. "You're right. I don't think that girl knew what I was ordering. ...I should get going and let you get back to your reading. I don't want to steal that away from you." He stood and stretched, drawing in a deep breath, which quickly turned to a yawn. "Whew, I'm beat. I'll be watching for your email tomorrow. Have a good night. ...Don't stay here too long. It'll be dark soon."

"I won't. I promise. Have a good night."

"Thanks—*Kelly*."

CHAPTER 35

"Hey, Boss! What are you working on?" Mel traipsed across the office to Matt's desk. "It's almost six. Can I help you so you can get out of here?"

"Thanks, Mel, but this is something I want to do myself."

"Oh? What is it?"

"It's something for the crisis center."

"The crisis center? You sure have been doing a lot for them lately."

"They need a lot of help lately."

"You know you almost gave yourself away yesterday, don't you?"

"What do you mean?"

"That snort right in the middle of the phone call. Miss Vance heard you. ...Why does it all have to be such a big secret anyway?"

Matt studied her for a moment, wondering how much he should divulge. "It's a long story."

Mel's shoulders bounced in a carefree shrug. "I've got time. My cat is the only one waiting for me."

"What happened to your roommate?"

"She moved out. She decided if she was going to get married, she should probably live with her husband."

"That's usually a good idea," Matt said with a roll of his eyes.

"Yeah. ...So, what's the story?"

Matt leaned back in his seat, lacing his fingers behind his head. "You're not going to let this go, are you?"

"Well, I *am* the one who has to intercept their calls."

"True. Okay. So, a couple of months ago, I met this girl on a bus. We had a conversation and went our separate ways. That night when I got on the bus, she was there again, and she was crying. She told me her friend had died, and she'd just found out about it. We talked all the way to our stop and then some. I found out later her friend was Sam Thompson."

"The director of the crisis center?"

"Yes. We ran into each other a few other times and developed a friendship, but I made sure I stayed anonymous."

"Why?"

Matt tilted his head to one side as if it were a perfectly reasonable thing to go around making friends with people but never telling them your name. "It's just something I do," he said.

Mel raised an eyebrow. "Something you do? And it doesn't strike you as a little bit odd, even just a tiny bit?"

"I just try to help people. It's something I started doing after Mom died. I meet people, learn about their needs, and, if I can, I help. I try to do it quietly. There's never been a need to give anyone my name. I never wanted anyone to have it. I wasn't doing it for recognition. So…when the blue folder arrived on my desk, I asked that I be allowed to carry it out without giving my name. By that point, Miss Vance knew I was an accountant. I'd actually offered to help. Doing things this way allowed me to help without her knowing it was me."

"Wait. So, it was Miss Vance you met on the bus?"

"Yep."

"And now she calls you M&Ms."

Amusement broke out across Matt's face. "I guess so."

"So, what are you working on tonight?"

"She actually knows I'm working on this one. I'll probably get myself in over my head, but… They need a new venue for their Mother's Day event. I figured that was something I could do."

"I've been to that event."

"You have?"

"Yeah. As a volunteer. I only did it once. I've wanted to do it again, but it never seems to work out. It's pretty cool. If you need any help just let me know. …And by the way, your secret is safe with me. I won't tell. I think it's pretty cool what you do. A little like Batman or Spiderman…in a less violent, more practical sort of way."

Matt burst out laughing. His eyes lit up with sincere relief, "Thanks, Mel."

"Well, I'm gonna head out, boss. I'll see you in the morning. … You haven't forgotten it's Wednesday, have you?"

"What! Oh! I did forget. I'd better go, or I'll be late for church. Thank you for the reminder." Matt shot out of his chair as he spoke. He gathered the files he'd strewn across his desk, shoved them into his bag, and hit the sleep button on his computer. "Why am I always running late?"

Mel chuckled. "Because you work here, that's why. We're all always running late…or maybe we're just always running."

"This is true. Can you do me a favor?"'

"Sure."

"Can you call my dad and ask him to bring some dinner to—" The ringing of Matt's cell phone cut him off. He dug frantically in his pocket, trying to free the gadget from the folds of fabric. Finally, he got hold of it and pulled it out where he could see it.

"Dad?" he said with a look of puzzlement on his face. "Why is he calling? Guess you won't need to call him, Mel. Have a good night. …Hey, Dad, what's up?"

"Hey, Matt, I'm parked out front. Want to get something to eat on the way to church?"

"Ha! I was just going to have Mel call you and ask you to pick something up. I'll be right out."

Matt finished shutting down his office and hurried through the building. Even before he got to the car, he could see his father grinning at his rushed pace. He laughed at himself, feeling as though he were eight all over again, and his father had come to pick him up from school. How blessed he was to have such a father.

He yanked the door open, tossed his bag inside, and squished into the passenger's seat. "Whoa, who sat here last? My knees are in the jockey box."

"Oh, it's more of a question of who sat in the back seat last. I had lunch with a few clients and investors this afternoon, and one of them was an absolute giant."

"Oh, who was that?"

"Neil Anderson."

Matt jerked around in his seat, staring at his dad. "The owner of Wymont Steel? The company that pulled their support from the crisis center?"

"Surprised?"

"Yes! How? Why...why were you meeting with him?"

"Well, it was business, but I made sure to get a little time with him alone to talk about the center and reassure him it would be a good 'investment' to pick back up next quarter."

"And?"

"He says he won't do it until they have a new director, and he knows the man's goals and plans for the center."

"Oh... Well, thanks for trying."

The older man popped the car into gear and eased into traffic. "Don't let it discourage you, Matt. It was a good conversation. I'm confident once they've got the right person in there, he will be back on board."

"But in the meantime, Kelly and Kali are suffering big time."

"What do you mean? Is there something you haven't told me?"

"They're both falling short on rent."

"Kelly told you this?"

"No. I overheard it. I've been trying to figure out what to do ever since."

"By how much?"

"I don't know. But it's enough that Kali is considering moving in with Kelly when her lease is up because she doesn't think she can keep up the payments. They cut their salaries by way too much, Dad. I don't know why they did it, but they're feeling it. Kelly said something to me that night of the clothing exchange about the suggestions hurting some of the staff with families, so they had made adjustments. That was before I saw what they had actually done, so I didn't think much of it. It concerned me, but she said it in such a way... I had no clue they cut things that much. I think those two took all of that hurt themselves. I know why they did it, but it was too much."

The older man was quiet for a while. He let his mind mull the situation over as he turned into the drive-thru lane of a favorite burger joint.

"Can you get their addresses for me?"

"I've got them right here in my bag. Why?"

"I think this is one *I* should do something about."

They pulled up to the speaker and were instantly greeted by a crackly voice. "Hi, take your time and order when you're ready."

"Hey there, Flo. We'll have our Wednesday usual."

"Well, if it isn't my favorite father-son duo. How are you boys tonight?"

"We're just fine. How are you?"

"I'm great! So that'll be a number four and a number six, right?"

"Yep."

"Drinks?"

"Whatever lands in the cup—so long as it isn't diet."

"Coke it is then."

"Sounds good."

They pulled forward and waited behind a rumbling diesel pickup.

"Looks like you brought a lot home tonight," the older man observed. "Working on something for the center again?"

"Yeah. I told Kelly I would help her find a venue for—" Apprehension cut him off. He hadn't considered his dad's feelings about his involvement in the project. He swallowed hard.

"A venue for what?"

"For their Mother's Day event."

"Oh, that's one of their biggest events of the year. You've got your work cut out for you."

"You don't mind?"

"Why would I mind?"

"Well...you know...it's Mother's Day."

The man glanced sideways at his son as he pulled the car up to the drive-thru window. He paid Flo, commenting on her friendly service and ever-present smile. He took the bag she handed out through the window and passed it to Matt. As he drove away, he glanced at his son once more.

"Your mother would be honored to know that you've found a way to give that day new meaning and purpose. It's haunted you long enough. If she were here, she'd be right in there with you."

"But what about you?"

"What about me?"

"Does it bother you?"

"Not in the least. I think it's great. I can't think of a better way for you to approach that particular day."

"Okay." Matt reached into the bag and began fishing out their sandwiches, but something about the whole situation bothered him. He turned his attention back to his father, dropping the sandwiches back into the bag. "Do you think it's dangerous for me to get this involved?"

"Dangerous? What do you mean?"

"Well, here I've been going around trying to do things in secret, and the more I get involved with the center, the more difficult it becomes. I don't know. I feel like I'm about to jeopardize everything."

"What do you mean by everything?"

"The whole community spy thing. My anonymity. My ability to help you help others...like with the rent."

"How do you stand to lose it?"

"Kelly." Matt's voice was matter of fact as if the answer should have been obvious to anyone. There was no malice or regret, in fact, there was little emotion in his voice at all. "She already knows more about me than anyone I've ever helped before. I don't think she'll tell anyone, but if I start helping with projects here and there, I'm going to get caught eventually. Someone will recognize me and start putting two and two together."

"Well, I suppose you just have to decide what's more important: being anonymous or helping your friend. ...Seems pretty obvious to me."

Matt sat silently, contemplating his father's words. He was right. Matt took a deep breath and forged on, "What can you tell me about Sam Thompson?"

"What do you mean?"

"How did he get his start? What made him so passionate about what he did?"

"Good questions. I knew Sam for close to twenty years. Sam had a deep passion for doing what was right—fighting for it even. Have you ever read his obituary?"

"No."

"You should. It tells a lot about him, and, if I remember right, Kelly wrote it. ...But you need to be cautious about something."

"What's that?"

"You can learn from Sam's example, but you can't be Sam. No one will ever be just like Sam Thompson. Never. Don't try to make up what they've lost in him, just help in the way God leads you— *Matt*—to help."

The younger man nodded. It made sense. No one ever could have replaced his mother any more than he could fill Sam's shoes, even in part. But that wasn't why he had asked.

"You're right, Dad, but what I want to know is what made Sam different?"

"I think we've had this conversation before, Matt. If you want the answer to that question, you're going to have to start looking in other places. Start with the obituary. That's all I can tell you to do."

CHAPTER 36

Kali yawned, rubbed her eyes, and grabbed hold of her carry-on bag's long handle. She stumbled wearily as she trudged toward the baggage claim.

"Never again. I'm never flying standby again," she mumbled to herself as she stepped up to the conveyor in the baggage claim.

"Bad experience?"

Kali moaned and turned toward the businessman next to her. "It could have been worse but making a two-hour trip in sixteen isn't something I'd like to repeat anytime soon."

The man chuckled. "I don't blame you. Where you coming from?"

"Seattle."

"It took you sixteen hours to get here from Seattle!" The man whistled, swinging his head back and forth. "No wonder you don't want to fly standby again. You could have driven here faster than that. ...Oh, here's my bag. Can you hold this for me?"

The man shoved a newspaper in her direction and headed for the trail of suitcases slithering around the carousel. He heaved a massive black duffle bag off of the belt and onto his shoulder. Then he spun around, grinned broadly, and waved at Kali as he raced by her. "Hope the rest of your day goes better than it has so far."

Kali watched him go and then turned back to the carousel in time to see her purple suitcase passing. She rushed forward, managing to catch the handle before it was out of reach. She tugged until the heavy bag lurched and rolled onto the floor.

"Well," she mumbled, "at least I don't have to pick it up."

With bag in tow, the woman made her way toward the long-term parking and her little, blue Corsica. She shoved her carry-on and suitcase into the trunk and dropped into the driver's seat, glancing at the newspaper the other traveler had thrown at her as she set it aside. A photograph grabbed her attention. She snatched the paper up again and flipped it over to read the headline. In that moment, her day went from bad to worse.

❀ ❀ ❀

Kelly had come to work early. She wasn't sure why, but she had. Part of her felt she would get more done that way. Part of her was hoping Kali would be there. Part of her just liked the memory of coming to work early and hearing Sam humming away in his office. Even though the humming was absent, somehow the quiet was soothing. Little by little, the others had trickled in. Brenda. Mac. Gil. The new receptionist. Everyone seemed tired from the weekend. No one said much. Fingers clicked on keyboards, coffee and tea were slurped, the phone rang once or twice, but the calls were short, and soon, the silence of the early spring morning returned.

It was nearly eleven when the front door burst open. The loud clattering of a rolling suitcase reverberated through the office as the bag rumbled across the threshold. Kelly looked up from her desk to see Kali marching through the office, newspaper and coffee in one hand, carry-on dragging behind the other. Her friend did not greet their officemates. Instead, she walked by them as if they were not there. She stopped briefly outside her own office to deposit her carry-on bag, slamming the handle down into place as she did so. Then her march continued right around the room to the door of Kelly's office. She stepped inside, slammed the door, and stared at her friend, nostrils flaring.

"I-s something wrong?" Kelly dared enquire.

"Have you seen this morning's paper?"

"N-no. That's not something I usually do in the morning."

"Well, you'd better." Kali stepped forward and slapped the paper down on the desk. Then she stepped back and took a long, frustrated drink of coffee.

Kelly picked up the paper and unfolded it. "Eight-month operation breaks up drug ring. Six arrested," she read softly.

"Look at the arrest photos."

Kelly glanced down the page and then gasped. "Brandon!"

"Exactly. How did we not know what he was doing?" Kali paced the floor. "How did we not know what kind of man he was? How did Sam not know? How did he work his way in here? Has he been using us for a front?"

"What! Wait. You think that's possible?"

"I don't know. But from the article, it sounds like he was the go-between, the courier. You know how many people we have in and out of this place. Do you think he was here just to have better access in the community? Oh, Kelly, please tell me that's not true!" Kali sank into the chair beside the door and buried her face in her hands. "When will this nightmare end!"

Kelly got up from her desk, but instead of going to her friend, she went to the window that looked out into the main office and closed the blinds. Then she knelt on the floor beside her friend, taking her into her arms, and letting her cry.

"I'm sorry, Kelly. I'm so sorry."

"For what?"

"For losing it like this."

"Kali, you've been up all night and got hit with a huge blow as soon as you got home. There's no need to apologize. I understand completely. I was in exactly the same spot last Tuesday after the conversation we had with him. He deceived us all, Kali. You have every right to feel betrayed and even used. ...For all his good, he sure turned out to be a miserable character."

"What should we do?"

"I don't know if there's anything we can do. Does the article mention that he worked here?"

"No. Not at this point, but I'm afraid some reporter will start digging and find out about it and make accusations."

"That's borrowing trouble, Kali. *'Sufficient unto the day is the evil thereof.'* Let's just deal with where we are, and if something more comes up, we'll let the Lord show us how to handle it. You know what I think? I think you should go home and get some sleep. We can handle things around here until you get back...all day if need be."

"Are you sure?"

"Yes. But I think you should sit here with me for a while first, so it won't be so obvious to everyone else that you've been crying."

Kali wiped her eyes, nodding her agreement. "Thank you."

Kelly stood and went to her desk. She sat down on its edge. "How was your trip?"

A new light crept into Kali's tear-reddened eyes. "It was wonderful. Micah's parents are wonderful. The coast was wonderful. Everything was wonderful."

Kelly couldn't help but smile with pleasure at her friend's response. She knew how very much Kali had needed the break, and it had obviously hit the mark.

"How's Micah's mom?"

"She's starting to do a little better. Still kind of in a fog at times, still breaks down in tears often. But Micah said it was good I went out there because she actually started cooking again. He and his dad have done all of the cooking and cleaning since Sam died. Micah's dad is tired. He needs a break, but I don't know when he'll get one. Maybe never. It might just be one of those things you have to survive until it slowly resolves itself. I'm not sure he's really had a chance to grieve. My heart breaks for him. He's such a kind man."

A knot formed in Kelly's stomach as she listened. She'd first met Micah's parents when they'd come for Sam's graduation from college. The years that had passed had taught her to love them just as she loved Kali's parents. They were like extended family. She hated to think of them hurting and broken. She cleared her throat, hoping to squelch the emotion rising in it.

"How's Micah?"

"Good. That night you called about Brandon, we had been talking about our relationship. He was afraid I was tired of waiting. I think he was going to tell me I didn't need to stick around if I didn't want to, but we worked that out. We're just going to take things one step at a time. We saw some amazing sights together. I so enjoyed being with him and his family, but part of me wished you were there too. I wish you could have seen so many things. Maybe you could come by on your way home for a bit of supper and to see my pictures from the trip."

"I'd love that," Kelly said. She had greatly missed her friend, even though it had only been a week.

"Let me know when you're headed my way, and I'll have supper ready." Kali pulled herself to the edge of the seat. "I should go. I'm going to fall asleep right here in this chair if I don't get a move on."

"Should you be driving? Abby is here getting ready to pick someone up for a job interview. She probably wouldn't mind dropping you off along the way."

"I'll be okay. It's not far. I'm not that close to sleep…yet." Kali stood and came to her friend's side. She wrapped her arms around her in a tight hug. "Thank you so much for being here. Micah says the same. He worried about you being here alone last week. I think he felt like he was being selfish or something." Kali stepped back and looked her friend squarely in the eyes. "He's hoping to be back here soon—to stay. Then my two best friends will be back in the same place, and I won't have to leave either of you."

Kali's kind words brought tears to Kelly's eyes, but she managed to keep them in check. "That will be wonderful, Kali. Now, go get some rest."

"Thanks, Kelly."

❊ ❊ ❊

Kali dropped into her favorite armchair and sank contentedly into its soft cushions. "I got a strange letter in the mail today," she commented.

"Oh, what kind of letter?" Kelly leaned further into the corner of the sofa, pulling her feet up under her and running a hand through her messy brown hair.

"It was from my apartment manager."

Kelly grinned. "Was it good news?"

How did you know?"

"Because I got one too. I couldn't believe it."

"Me either! I even called the manager to make sure there hadn't been some kind of mistake."

"What did they say?"

"That my rent had been covered for the next six months. There was no mistake."

"Did they say who covered it?"

"No. They wouldn't tell me anything. No description, no name, not even an approximate age. Who could have possibly known we needed that help?"

"The Lord."

Kali laughed. "Well, of course, the Lord knew, but I mean who else could've possibly known."

"I'm not sure. Gil maybe, but he doesn't have that kind of money."

"Maybe he told someone?"

"I doubt it. He's pretty careful about what he says."

"True. Maybe the Lord just put it on someone's heart."

"Whoever it was, I'm very grateful. I liked the idea of living with you, but I really didn't like the idea of moving."

Kelly tossed her head back in laughter. "I know what you mean. I hate moving!"

Their laughter subsided, and they sat in silence for a few moments, each sipping at a cup of rich hot chocolate infused with the light flavor of lavender. Finally, Kali sighed with deep contentment and resolution.

"I've come to a decision," she said.

"About what?"

"I think we should accept Mr. Marsh's proposal."

"To have M&Ms be our advisor?"

"Yes. ...But you may have to stop calling him that."

Kelly was laughing again. "Yeah. Probably. ...But honestly, after this thing with Brandon, I completely agree. I almost brought it up this morning, but I didn't want to pressure you."

"Thank you for that. I've been thinking about it all day, and I think it's time. I definitely think it's time."

CHAPTER 37

"Samuel Judson Thompson, 41, went home to be with his Lord Saturday after an accident that occurred while making repairs to his home."

Matt stared at the website. When he had first looked at the crisis center's website, he had seen many photos but had never spotted anyone he thought would be their director. Now, as he studied the picture of Sam Thompson on the Daily Chronicle's obit page, he realized Sam had been in many of the center's images. He had just blended in with everyone else. No pretensions, no flaunting himself, just part of the action—all of the action.

Matt sighed, feeling a certain heaviness begin to creep over him as he read further.

"Born to Gloria and Andrew Thompson of the Seattle area, Sam grew up with a love for family and friends, baseball, and anything that would get him outdoors. Sam graduated from High School as Valedictorian and went on to business school where he also excelled.

"During his final year of business school, Sam traveled with a church group to a war-torn region of Africa. The trip was a

short two weeks, but his interaction with one man changed his life forever.

"Sam always said the final quarter of his education was the hardest, not because of the workload or the subject matter but because his heart was somewhere else. During these months, he spent his free time helping at food banks, driving families to doctor's appointments, and making sure families facing layoffs still had a special meal for their tables on Easter. All because of a new determination to fight for what was worth fighting for…"

The obituary went on to discuss how Sam's ministry had grown until he could no longer handle everything on his own and, one small step at a time, it grew into the Trevor Street Crisis Center.

"A small handmade plaque sits on Sam's desk," the piece concluded, *"the words read, 'Fight the good fight. Finish the course. Keep the faith.' Sam made the plaque in his father's wood shop the week after he finished business school—he lived it every day for the rest of his life."*

❊ ❊ ❊

Kelly slipped into a pew and breathed a sigh of relief. For once, she wasn't late. She picked up the hymnal in the rack in front of her and began flipping through its pages, stopping on a song that had haunted the corners of her mind for days. She hummed softly to herself, letting the words penetrate the hollowness that was so often present in her heart these days,

O Love, that will not let me go,
I rest my weary soul in thee;
I give thee back the life I owe,
That in thine ocean depths its flow
May richer, fuller be.

O Light, that followest all my way,
I yield my flickering torch to Thee;
My heart restores its borrowed ray,
That in Thy sunshine's blaze its day
May brighter, fairer be.

O Joy, that followest me through pain,
I cannot close my heart to Thee;
I trace the rainbow through the rain,
And feel the promise is not vain,
That morn shall tearless be.

O Cross, that liftest up my head,
I dare not ask to fly from thee;
I lay in dust life's glory dead,
And from the ground there blossoms red
Life that shall endless be.

"I've heard a very heart-touching story goes along with that song."

Kelly hadn't noticed the man who'd slipped into the seat beside her until his kind voice drifted into her thoughts. She turned toward him, surprised to realize her eyes were misty.

"It's beautiful — You!"

The man, who happened to be her bus friend, couldn't help tossing his head back and letting loose a full out belly laugh.

"What are you doing here?" she exclaimed.

"Well, it is Sunday, and this is a church." He replied, still laughing.

"I know that, but what are *you* doing at *my* church."

"Do you want the truth?"

"Of course I do!"

"Hoping to find you. I wasn't sure if this was where you attended, but there are only so many to choose from. You don't go to my church, and I'm pretty sure you don't go to Shallow Brook. So, I thought I'd give this one a try."

Kelly stared, her gaze searching his dancing, twinkling blue eyes. "Why?"

"Why what?"

"Why were you looking for me?"

The man shrugged. "I wanted to talk to you, and I didn't want to wait until the next time we meet up on a bus."

"You have my email address...which you haven't used yet, incidentally."

"Well, that's part of what I wanted to talk to you about. Have you ever thought of having your Mother's Day event here? I think it would work wonderfully."

Kelly tipped her head to one side. "No, I guess I haven't, but it would have some good potential, wouldn't it?"

"Do you think your pastor would be open to it?"

"Maybe."

The instruments began playing softly, prompting Kelly to turn toward the front of the auditorium.

"Do you have plans after church?" Matt whispered.

"No," she whispered back.

"May I take you to lunch so we can talk?"

"Sure...but only if you promise to tell me the story."

A puzzled look crossed the man's face. "What story?"

"The story behind the song."

The man's eyes lit up once more with genuine excitement. "I'd love to!" He covered his mouth, realizing he'd said it a little louder than he'd intended to.

Kelly stifled a snort. "I hope you weren't planning on staying incognito here because you've just managed to attract a whole lot of attention."

He snickered. "We'll just have to make a quick getaway."

CHAPTER 38

Since meeting Sam and Micah Thompson, Kelly, who had grown up in a home with hamburger and hot dog taste buds, had not only grown accustomed to Chinese food but had actually come to like it. Her bus friend, she was about to discover, practically lived on it.

"Oh, hello! And how are you today?" A kind, smiling man greeted them as they stepped into the busy restaurant. "You have friend with you today. You want the usual, or we bring you menu?"

Matt turned to Kelly, "Do you want the menu, or do you trust me to order something you'll like?"

Kelly bit her bottom lip for a moment, but then her uncertainty disappeared. "Well, you did pretty good with the tea the other day," she said. "I'll put you to the test."

"Oh! It's a test, is it? ...Mike, we'll have two orders of the usual."

"Very good! We'll bring right out. You find seat wherever you want. We'll know how to find you. Everyone know you."

The pair smiled and waved their gratitude as they turned toward the establishment's seating area.

"His name is Mike?" Kelly whispered out of the side of her mouth.

"That's what everyone calls him. I don't know his real name."

"Oh! Sort of like I don't know yours."

Matt tilted his head in mock apology and shrugged. "You missed your chance on that one."

"What do you mean?"

"Well, you could have said the only way you'd come here was if I told you my name, but instead you requested a story. So, you get the story and no name."

"You are cruel."

He smiled, pleased with himself. "I know. Hey, how about that table? There in the corner. It has a nice view of all the activity on the street. Proves to be rather entertaining from time to time."

"Sure."

As they settled into the booth, Kelly realized for the first time that her friend had brought his Bible in with him. He set it down on the table and slid it toward the wall.

"Did you mean to bring that in, or just forgot you had it?"

He chuckled. "I meant to. I've learned that in conversations like this, sometimes it comes in handy."

"What? You don't have a Bible app on your phone that you can whip out and pull up any verse or topic you want?"

"Of course I do! But there's just something about handling the real thing that makes it…well, real."

"I agree. …So, what are we having for lunch?"

"Nope," he said, shaking his head, "not telling. It's a surprise."

"All right, then it's story time. What is the story behind that song?"

"First, tell me why you were so fascinated by it."

She shrugged. "It's been running through my head the past few days. Something happened at work last week that left me feeling pretty empty. Ever since then, this song has been tugging at my heart, but I haven't had a chance to look it up. This morning, I got to church a little early. I didn't have a class to teach, so I took the opportunity to look it up."

Matt studied her with concern. "Have things worked themselves out?"

"Things?"

"With whatever happened at work."

"No. I mean…well, things actually got worse, but so far we haven't had any of the fallout we thought we might have. I just hope that continues to be the case. That kind of publicity would destroy the center I'm afraid."

"Wow, sounds serious."

Kelly nodded, realizing a waitress was approaching with a tray containing two cups, a teapot, and two servings of Wonton soup. They waited as the young woman quietly placed the items on the table.

"The rest of your meal will be ready in just a few minutes. Can I get you anything else?"

"No, I think we're fine. Thank you." Matt said, his voice full of genuine kindness.

The waitress nodded and turned away into another part of the restaurant.

"Is it something I can help with?"

"What?"

"The issue at the center."

"I don't think so. We're actually trying to keep it kind of quiet. This probably isn't the place to talk about it."

He nodded. "I understand. So. The song. A man named George Matheson wrote it. The story goes that his eyesight was very poor, and his sister learned Hebrew, Greek, and Latin so he could become a preacher. On the day of his sister's wedding, something happened, which hurt him very deeply. In one account, he says it was something only he knew. But other accounts say he had shared with his fiancé that his eyesight was growing worse and he would soon be blind. At that news, she left him."

"On his sister's wedding day!"

"Perhaps," he said with hands held out in uncertainty.

"Oh, how awful! Well, she didn't deserve him anyway because she obviously didn't have a heart."

Matt laughed. "That's pretty swift and severe judgment."

"You know what I mean. How could she do something like that?"

"What would you do?"

"I don't know, but I wouldn't leave him on his sister's wedding day. That's cruel."

Matt rolled his eyes. "Anyway," he said, drawing the word out in mock exasperation, "he went back to the manse and in his pain wrote the words to that song—in five minutes."

"Really?"

"Yes. From the testimony he gave, he believed it was the Holy Spirit working upon his heart. He never corrected it. We sing what he wrote in those five minutes."

"Wow. It's such a beautiful song. I love the third verse best. 'O Joy, that followest me through pain, I cannot close my heart to Thee; I trace the rainbow through the rain, and feel the promise is not vain that morn shall tearless be.' I'm ready for tearless mornings. I'm about out of strength. I just," she paused. "I feel empty. Like I have given everything my heart can possibly give. My hands and my feet and my head are still going, but my heart has run out of gas."

Matt reached for his Bible and began flipping through its pages, hoping once more that he wasn't overstepping his bounds.

"One morning, I was reading in Psalms, and I came to Psalm twenty-nine. Are you familiar with it?" he asked.

"Is that the one that starts, *'Give unto the Lord, O ye mighty, give unto the Lord glory and strength'*?"

"That's the one. I read that, and I thought, 'I have absolutely no strength to give you, Lord. How can you ask for more?'"

"That's the way I've felt at times too."

"But you have to keep reading the Psalm to find out the answer to the question."

"You do?"

"Yes! It's right there in the psalm. In the very last verse."

"It is?"

"Yes! Look." Matt slid the Bible toward her and pointed out the verse, reading it aloud. *"The Lord will give strength unto his people, the Lord will bless his people with peace.'"*

They both stared at the words on the page before them, Matt with excitement, Kelly with tears. A moment passed before the man realized how deeply the words had touched her. But, when a tear splashed on the table, and she reached to wipe moisture from her cheek, he knew she'd needed the verse. He dropped his voice to a whisper as he cautiously slid a napkin toward her.

"You don't have to do it alone, Kelly. You've used up all your strength, now let the Lord fill you with His."

She smiled at him, blinking back tears unsuccessfully and biting nervously at her bottom lip. "Thank you... again."

"Sometimes, it's okay to be weak, Kelly, because His strength is made perfect in our weakness. When we are weak, then are we strong."

She nodded, wiping her eyes on the napkin and leaving black mascara smudges across her cheeks. "Why don't you pray over our food while I pull myself together."

Compassion pulled a smile across his face. "I'd love to."

When they opened their eyes, the young waitress stood next to the table. "I would ask if everything is all right," she said, "but you haven't even tasted it yet."

"Sorry, Suzy, we'll get down to business now."

"What did you say to make her cry?"

Surprise raced across Matt's face. He stuttered and stumbled about for an answer but came up with nothing.

"It's all right, Suzy. They are tears of relief. He was being a good friend."

"He'd better be. We like to have him around here, but not if he makes the ladies cry. I'll be back with your food in just a minute."

Kelly watched the waitress go and then turned back to her friend. "You know everyone here, don't you?"

"Pretty much. So, how's the soup?"

Kelly dipped her spoon in the less than piping liquid and sipped experimentally. "Wow! That's the best Wonton soup I've ever had."

"I know, right! I love this place."

They sat in silence for several minutes, slurping soup, gazing out the window, shooting nervous glances at each other when they thought the other wasn't looking. Both realizing this friendship was a part of their lives they never wanted to lose, and both trying to convince themselves it was just that—a friendship and nothing more. Just as Matt pushed his empty bowl back, Suzy arrived with their main dish. She set a large plate of steaming, delicious smelling food in front of each of them.

"Mm…Pineapple chicken," Kelly said with genuine excitement. "Oh, this smells wonderful."

"So, you like my choice?"

"Well, I haven't tasted it yet, but if it's half as good as the soup, I'm in love already."

Suzy beamed at the obvious compliment to the restaurant. "I'll tell the cooks. Enjoy!"

"Taste it," Matt urged as Suzy walked away.

Kelly obeyed, but she couldn't stop at just one bite. It wasn't until after the third forkful that she finally said, "This is amazing."

Matt didn't respond, but the grin that beamed down on his plate as he finally tasted the meal for himself told her he was very pleased.

Kelly leaned back in her seat, contemplating the man for a moment. "Why did you want to come here?" she asked. "You've been very kind. You told me the story, you let me cry, and you encouraged me, but that's not why you invited me here. What did you want to talk about?"

Matt gulped down his mouthful of chicken and rice and then washed it down with tea. He wiped his mouth and leaned back, wondering how to broach the subject, especially since he'd already sent her into tears once.

"Is something wrong?" she pressed, noticing his hesitation.

"No, no. Nothing's wrong. I just...I've been wondering about something, and I think you're the only one I know who can answer my questions."

"About what?"

He studied her for a moment, then determination crept into the set of his jaw and he took a deep breath. "About Sam."

"Sam? Sam Thompson?"

"Yes. I know that probably seems strange, and you don't have to answer if you don't want to, I just," the words tumbled out in a nervous flood, tripping and spilling over each other. "Well, I just, I didn't know him, and there are things I would like to know, and—"

"Slow down! I can't understand half of what you're saying. Why are you so nervous all of a sudden?"

He took a deep breath, hoping to regain his composure. "Because I don't want to upset you, but I'm afraid I will."

"You, of all people, should know that won't upset me. Do you know how often I wish people would talk about him, but they won't because they don't want to bring it up or upset me? You like to talk about your mother, don't you?"

"Yes."

"Then why do you think I wouldn't want to talk about Sam?"

She wasn't angry. He could see that. But incredulous might be another story.

"You're right. I'm sorry. I just didn't want to ask for more information than maybe I should."

"If you're asking for too much, I'll tell you."

"Okay."

"So, what do you want to know about Sam?"

"A lot, but for starters, how did you meet him?"

"We were all in college at the same time. A big group of us, me, Kali, Gil, Sam and Micah, our friends Ben and Jordy. Kali and Sam went to church together, and eventually, they went on a missions trip together. Oddly enough, it was through my church. Anyway, they both came back from the trip changed. Before the trip, Sam had pretty much planned on living a normal, picket fence kind of life with most of his energies tied up in business and as much family and fun time as possible. After the trip, he started looking for ways to help others. He'd always done that anyway, more than anyone I know. But after that trip, it became a passion for him. He was always dragging Kali and his brother Micah into it. Well, all of our group really. No one got out of it. No one wanted out of it either."

"Wait. Micah? Micah Thompson is his brother?"

"Yes. Do you know him?"

"Yeah! Well...I mean...if it's the same Micah Thompson. We went on a trip together several years ago, a missions trip. We hit it off right away because, even though I was living out of state at the time, we were both from here. We kept in touch for a while, but then I lost his contact info. I had hoped to catch up with him after I moved back here, but I never ran into him. Is he still here?"

"No. He's in Seattle...or near Seattle, helping his parents. His mom took Sam's death pretty hard. Very hard, actually. You should have come into the clothing exchange. He was there. He'd come back to help and take care of some things at Sam's house."

"Wow. I wish I'd known. I'll bet it's been six years since I've seen him. I don't know why I didn't put two and two together before now...I remember seeing in the obituary that Sam had two brothers, but I still didn't put it together."

"The obituary didn't actually have Micah's name in it. We only listed his parents' names. Where were you? On the missions trip, where did you go?"

"Singapore."

Kelly's eyes brightened, and a wide grin spread across her face. "It has to be the same Micah Thompson. I've heard him tell about that trip so many times. He talks about his team leader, who was always getting them lost and losing things."

Matt's cheeks colored. He squirmed in his seat. "That was me."

Kelly laughed. "You? You don't seem like the getting lost and losing things kind of guy."

"I didn't speak the language! Surely, that counts for something! ...Wow." Matt shook his head, still trying to digest the news. He'd been fond of Micah. They were nearly the same age, had a lot of similar interests and had found a common love for the Scriptures, which had sealed their friendship. "I wish I had made the connection sooner."

"Do you want his contact info? I've got his number and email address right here on my phone."

"Sure. Maybe I'll give him a call later this week." Matt waited as Kelly found the information and scribbled it on a napkin. "Thanks. He still has a local number? Is he planning to come back?"

"He wants to. Between you and me, I think there's someone here he'd like to marry."

"Really? Who?"

Kelly shook her head. "Nope. I'll let him tell you that part."

"Now who's cruel? ...Wow. That would be great if he came back! That would be awesome—I'm sorry. I completely interrupted what you were saying about Sam. What *were* you saying?"

Kelly laughed. "I don't remember. Something about how he was always pulling the rest of us into his schemes to help others, I think."

"Yes. That's it exactly."

"We were always close. I volunteered at the center for a long time, and then six years ago, they asked me to come on board as their communications director. I've been there ever since."

"Something in Sam's obituary stood out to me. It said when he went on that missions trip, he met a man who changed his life. What happened?"

Kelly took a long sip of tea, wondering where to begin. She set the cup down, watching a drop of tea slide down its side and smiling as memories of Sam flooded her mind.

"I didn't get to go on that trip, but Sam talked about that man a lot. If you stop by the office, we have a picture of him…of them. He was an older man, too old to join the war, but every day he got up and walked three miles to a refugee camp. It wasn't a camp the UN or the local government had started. He had started it. He housed the wives and children of men who had died fighting or been killed by the corrupt military leaders of the equally corrupt government. 'God told us we are to love our enemies,' he told Sam, 'In my mind, this means I should treat them as I would treat my friend. If I would care for my friends' children when they died, then I should care for my enemies' children.' And so he did, day after day, month after month for years.

"Sam asked him once why he did it, why he put out so much effort for people who would never be able to repay him, never prosper him in any way, and possibly never even return his love. His answer was, 'In life, some things are worth fighting for, and some are not. Once you find the things worth fighting for you should always fight for them till the end of your course because that is what God would have us to do. People and God's work are always worth fighting for no matter how they love you, or how they repay you, or how they prosper you. They are always worth fighting for. God will work out the rest, even if all my reward is on the other side, I know He will not forget.' Those were the words that changed Sam's life. I doubt they would've had much effect if they hadn't been backed up by such an amazing, sacrificial life. That man lived his convictions."

"Is he still alive?"

Kelly shook her head slowly. "He was killed about a year after Sam came home. I think that just made Sam all the more determined to fight his own fight."

"What about his work? Did others continue it?"

"Yes. His son, but his son was also killed. Now his wife and daughter do their best to maintain it. Sam supported them as often as he could. I think that was one of the most difficult calls Micah had to make after Sam died. The country is still volatile. Now they mostly work with the women who are still struggling to rebuild their lives. ...Why did that interest you so much?"

Matt shrugged. "The more time I've been around you and heard about Sam and the center, the more I've realized he was an unusual man—in a good way. I've just wanted to know what made the difference."

Kelly smiled. "It was God working through a little old man named Moses."

Matt's eyes brightened. "God seems to have a habit of doing that."

"Yes, He does."

CHAPTER 39

Matt stepped off the elevator and into the yellow world that was the accounting department. He groaned at the thought of the scheduling that waited on his desk. He'd managed to avoid it all morning, but it would have to be done by the day's end, which was quickly approaching.

"How was lunch?" Mel asked as he walked by her desk.

"Delicious. Best burger I've had in months. They have the best sauce at that place."

"What place?"

"Red's."

"Oh! I love their western BBQ."

"I'll have to try that next time. ...Did Pastor Meeks call back about the Mother's Day event while I was out?"

"No, but Mr. Marsh called while you were gone."

"Oh?"

"He wants you to call him. Said it was important and not to do anything else until you'd talked with him."

Matt raised an eyebrow. "Sounds serious. Did I do something wrong?"

"I don't think so. He didn't seem upset, but he did seem concerned about something."

"Hmm. Kind of odd, don't you think?"

"I'm just the assistant. I don't try to figure out what's going on."

Matt laughed, grateful, not for the first time, for the carefree, nonchalant attitude of his faithful assistant. "That's probably wise in this place. Guess I'd better go find out what's going on. Thanks, Mel."

Matt picked up his pace. He unlocked his office and made his way to his desk, punching the speakerphone and the line for Mr. Marsh's receptionist as he dropped into his chair.

"McKinsey Marsh's office."

"Hey, Phyllis, this is Matt. How are you today?"

"It's Monday. Need I say more? Just a minute, he's expecting your call."

"Thanks." Matt waited, his curiosity growing with every chord of the music that played over the line.

"Hey, Matt."

"Hey, I hear you've been looking for me."

"I have. How was your lunch?"

"Delicious. And yours?"

"I haven't eaten yet. I ordered in, but it hasn't arrived yet. Listen, I've got a meeting in just a couple of minutes, so I need to make this quick. Something has come up at the crisis center."

"Oh?"

"It started a couple of weeks ago. They've kept it quiet so far, but they got a call from a reporter this morning."

Matt leaned forward, resting his forearms on the desk. Intense curiosity filled his eyes. "A reporter?"

"Did you see the headline last week, something about a drug ring?"

"Yes. It was a pretty big deal."

"Well, one of the men arrested worked for the crisis center."

"What!" Matt grabbed up the receiver, glancing toward Mel's desk. She didn't seem to have heard. "Are you serious?"

"Yes. A young man named Brandon Shaw."

"You've got to be kidding me. Hang on." Matt laid the receiver aside and went to close his office door. "No wonder Kelly didn't want to talk at the restaurant," he muttered as he walked back to the desk. He picked up the phone, not bothering to sit back down. "Okay. Go ahead."

"What was that all about?"

"I just wanted to shut the door. So, what's going on?"

"Well, apparently they had already dismissed him the previous week. He'd gotten into trouble at college. They tried to get him into a counseling program. When he refused, they had to ask him to leave. They didn't know about the drugs at the time. I guess it happened while Miss Shepherd was out of town."

"So, who dealt with it?"

"Miss Vance and their accountant."

"No wonder." Matt sank into his chair. He leaned forward, rubbing his forehead and then resting his forearm across his knee.

"No wonder what?"

"It's a long story, and you're short on time. It just...it explains a conversation I had with Kelly yesterday after church. ...How can I help?"

"Well, that's exactly what I want to talk to you about. Before she went on her trip, Miss Shepherd and I had talked about some other things. They need an advisor, Matt. I suggested you."

The color drained from Matt's face. "Wait," he stammered, shaking his head in disbelief. "What did you say?"

"I know. You have so much on your plate as it is, but I'm willing to hire extra help if we can give them the support they need. Miss Shepherd called me last week to say they'd like to accept my offer. I spent the whole week working on the details. After she called this morning, I finalized and emailed a proposal to you. I wanted to go over it in person, but I didn't know if you'd get back before my meeting. I know you haven't wanted them to know who was helping them, and I'm willing to help you maintain that anonymity... somehow...but they need help. And, I think you're the one to do it. Just look at the proposal, think about it, and let me know by tomorrow."

"Tomorrow?"

"Morning, if possible. ...Hey, I've got to run. My lunch and my appointment are both here. Talk to you later."

Matt heard the phone click down on the other end. His own phone dangled from his hand for a moment before dropping slowly into its cradle. "This can't be happening," he whispered. "How did this happen?"

He turned to the computer, his mind spinning as he searched numbly for the email. He heard a soft knock at the door.

"Not right now, Mel," he said, not bothering to look up. The knock came again. "Give me a couple minutes."

His intercom beeped. "That isn't me knocking, Matt. It's Phyllis."

Matt's gaze jerked up to see the woman standing at the door, peering through the glass wall, file box gripped tightly in her hands. He jumped up and rushed to open the door. "I'm so sorry. Here let me take that for you." Matt took the box, surprised at how heavy it was. "What is this anyway?"

"I'm not sure. Mr. Marsh had one of the file clerks bring it up to his office and sent it down here with me. He said you'd be needing it. I don't think he realized how heavy it would be. That's the last time I'll be making that trip with a box like that."

Phyllis Rush, a kind woman in her mid-fifties, had always been a genteel sort of woman. Lugging thirty-pound boxes down three floors, even if it was on an elevator, had never been her cup of tea.

"You should've called me. I would've come up and gotten it."

"Ah, well. It got me away from my desk. Have fun."

The woman turned, waved sweetly to Mel, and disappeared into the elevator. Matt carried the heavy box into his office and sat down, dropping the box on the floor between his feet.

"Everything okay?"

Matt's gaze came up, surprised to hear his assistant's voice at the door.

"You look awful, boss. I haven't seen you look so overwhelmed since—," she cut herself off.

"Since when?"

"A long time ago. What's wrong?"

"The crisis center, for lack of a better way of putting it, is in crisis. He wants me to become their advisor."

"Aren't you already their advisor?"

"I've just been giving them suggestions about how to handle their finances. That's different."

Matt turned his attention to the list of emails he'd abandoned, immediately spotting the one he was looking for. He clicked it open and began scanning through the introductory material, the summary of the center's situation, and finally the proposal.

"You have got to be kidding me," he breathed. His eyes darted away from the screen and down to the box at his feet. With both dread and suspicion, he flipped the box lid back, sending it whirling onto the floor. Just as he'd suspected, every file bore the name of a local charity. "You've got to be kidding me!"

"What is it?" Mel had moved closer, but her boss' frantic state still held her at a considerable distance.

"He wants me to take on a new title altogether."

"What? You mean you wouldn't be in legal and accounting anymore?"

"No, I would be, but I'd also be Head of Charitable Operations. And this..." he grunted as he lifted the box and let it drop noisily onto his desk, "this would be my new realm of responsibility: some type of involvement with every charity we support or have volunteered with in the past. All of them."

Mel stared, dumbfounded. "But...but, boss, how...how would we ever manage that? I mean, if Mr. Raska didn't filter the issues from legal before they get to you, we'd be drowning."

"He said he'd hire extra help, but this is a ridiculous amount of work to add to this department. What in the world could have possessed him to come up with such a scheme?"

Mel opened her mouth to agree, but then she stopped. Her lips scrunched up to one side, and her eyes rolled slightly toward the ceiling as she considered his question.

"What?" Matt's suspicion had returned. Somehow, he knew she was going to nail him with something he'd done, something that had led to all this.

"Well...there was the other day?"

"What are you talking about?"

"The Mother's Day project. You were all over that, and no one even asked you to do it."

"So?"

"Well, don't you think that expresses a fair amount of personal interest in what happens to the crisis center?"

Matt shrugged off the statement but couldn't find much in the way of defense.

"Did Mr. Marsh know you were working on that?"

"He knows everything I do. Of course, he knew."

"So, he knew you were interested in helping them get through this. Maybe you should do it…just until they have someone of their own to fight for them."

Matt felt his heart skip a beat, he was sure of it. What had Kelly said just the day before about that man Moses and the philosophy behind the work he did? About fighting for what was worth fighting for?

"The crisis center, yes," he argued, his brain kicking back in and speaking over his heart. "But what about all the rest of these. I don't even know what the Head of Charitable Operations does. I didn't even know we had one. I've never seen it on any paperwork, never met them."

"Maybe he's creating a new position—just for you. Maybe he wants you to have a purpose beyond numbers and legal documents… the one that's already in your heart. You're not a paper pusher, Matt. You never have been. You're a problem solver with the biggest heart of any problem solver I've ever met. Go out and fight for them—for all of them. We'll back you up."

Matt stared at the tall, pretty young woman for a moment, then, half to himself, he whispered, "People and God's work are always worth fighting for, always."

She smiled. "But I get to be a part of the hiring process. If I have to work with them, I want to help choose them."

Matt shook his head in amusement. "If I agree to this proposal, then, yes, you can be part of the hiring process."

The phone rang, breaking off their conversation. Mel headed to her desk as Matt picked up the receiver.

"This is Matt."

"Hi, Matt. This is Pastor Meeks. I got your message a little while ago, and I've already spoken with our deacons. We would *love* to host the Mother's Day event."

"Really! That's wonderful!"

"We think so too. You know, I've wanted to get involved at the crisis center for a while, but I have trouble working new things into my schedule. I always heard the other pastors talking about what they were doing there, so I guess I kind of figured all the bases were covered."

"Well, I think a lot of them were. Things were running pretty smoothly, but a lot changed after Sam Thompson died. Both supporters and churches have pulled back until they find a new director."

"Really?" the man's voice rose with surprise. "Seems to me, this is when we should have pulled in around them. ...That explains a lot."

"What do you mean?"

"Well, you know both Miss Shepherd and Miss Vance attend my church. I've noticed both of them looking very tired and more than a little frayed from time to time over the past few weeks. ...Do you think there's more we could do? More than just the Mother's Day event?"

"I'm sure there is, but I think *they* are the best people to tell you what that is."

"Well, why don't you talk with them and find out if there's a morning this week when they could meet with my wife and me. I'm sure she'll want to join us. We can discuss the Mother's Day event and any other ways we might be able to help them. I can't guarantee it will be much, but we'll do what we can."

"I will do that. I'm sure that will be a tremendous blessing to them. Thank you so much."

"You bet. I'll be waiting to hear from either you or them regarding a time."

"Sounds good. Have a great day, Pastor, and —"

"Wait, Matt, there's one more thing."

"What's that?"

"My wife and I were offered a week-long getaway at a timeshare in North Idaho, but we can't go. It includes the airline tickets and the rental car. My wife was in the room when I got your message earlier, and she's been listening in on our conversation as well. I think we're both in agreement. We'd like to give that getaway to the ladies, to Kali and Kelly. I have a feeling they need it a lot more than we do. If you'll present it to them as an anonymous gift at the Mother's Day event, we'll take care of getting it put into their names instead of ours. We might need your help to get some info. Could you do that for us?"

"Wow," Matt leaned back in his seat, "wow, Pastor, that would be amazing. I'm not even them, and I don't know what to say. Wow, that's just…wow. Thank you. I will do whatever I can to help. Those two women are exhausted. I can't even begin to tell you what a blessing that will be to them. Thank you."

"Well, you're welcome, but it's the Lord's doing. We're just passing on the blessing someone else passed on to us. I've got to run. Have a good afternoon, Matt."

"Thank you. You too. Thank you for everything."

Matt hung up the phone, his eyes dancing at the thought of the respite awaiting Kelly and Kali. But as his gaze drifted from the phone to the email to the box of files, his smile faded to an expression of concern. "Man, I've got a lot of thinking to do."

❊ ❊ ❊

Kelly looked up at the sound of her inbox pulling in yet another email. They seemed endless today, and most of them were mere distractions: advertisements, blogs, letters pushing some issue or product. This one, however, caught her attention. "ComSpy," read the address.

"ComSpy?" she mused aloud as she reached for her mouse. "Well, that's got to be junk if there ever was junk mail." She was just about to delete the letter when she caught sight of the subject line. "Mother's Day," it read. She gasped, realizing she'd seen the address before—it was from him. She picked up her phone and pressed the button for Kali's line.

"Yes?" her friend answered, a distinct tone of distraction echoing in her voice.

"Get in here. He emailed."

"Who emailed?"

"My friend from the bus. He emailed about Mother's Day."

"Really? I'll be right there."

Kelly wasn't sure she'd seen Kali move that fast in four months. The thought stopped her. Four months. Had it really been that long?

"What's it say?" Kali said with beaming eyes as she rushed through the door.

"Let's find out." Kelly clicked on the email and waited for it to open. Then she read aloud:

"Kelly, I left a message for your pastor this morning about Mother's Day. He just called me back. They would love to host the event, but he would also like to meet with you and Kali to discuss other ways the church might get more involved at the center! He said any morning this week would work for him, so if the two of you want to discuss it and then get back with him, that would be great.

"Please, let me know what comes of the meeting, and if there is anything else I can do to help. Your Friend...Matt."

Kelly momentarily forgot everything she had read before the salutation.

"Matt," she whispered. "His name is Matt."

Kali laughed at her starry-eyed friend. "Snap out of it."

Kelly blushed. "I didn't expect him to tell me. He was so tight-lipped about it yesterday."

"Well, we have a lot to thank him for, and just in time too. This is amazing. I never really thought Pastor Meeks was interested in helping."

"I never gave it two thoughts. I figured Sam must have talked to him about it at some point and nothing came from it."

"I don't know if Sam had talked to him. Pastor Meeks had only been there a year before Sam died."

"I'm not sure it was even that long. ...Wow...so his name is Matt."

CHAPTER 40

Matt slid his chair back from the kitchen table, wincing as it scraped across the stone tiles. He carried his dishes to the sink and began washing them.

"We found a place for the Mother's Day event," he said, glancing over his shoulder to the table where his father was still finishing the last few bites of his meal.

"Oh, really?" the other man asked with interest, "Where?"

"Trevor Street Chapel. Pastor Meeks and I talked about it this afternoon. He wants to do more as well."

"That's wonderful. What more is he interested in doing?"

"I'm not sure exactly. The girls were supposed to set up a meeting with him for later this week."

"Still trying to keep out of it as much as possible?"

Matt shrugged. "That seems further and further out of reach. I don't think it will be at all possible if I become their advisor. I can only go by my initials for so long—or M&Ms as Kelly calls me." He chuckled at the thought, almost letting it derail his attention completely. "I told her my name today...just my first name, but my name."

"Why did you do that?"

"I don't know. It was just time."

"Well, maybe it's time to tell them all."

"I don't know about that."

"What do you think about the advisor idea as a whole?"

Matt watched a pile of suds slide down the clean surface of his plate and into the sink. Then he sighed. "It seems like a lot of work on top of a lot of work. You know I'm not afraid of work, and I'm never opposed to working hard. But, I'm not sure I can handle that whole box of charities and everything else I'm already responsible for even if I have two more people on my staff."

"Have you thought it out yet, though? I mean, have you thought about what involvement you would actually have with each of the other organizations? Would it be as much involvement as you have with the crisis center?"

"No. I haven't gone over things that closely yet. I was going to do that tonight. Things got a little crazy at the office this afternoon. That's why I brought everything home. Thanks for the ride, by the way. I already carried most of those files by bus once, and I don't care to do it again." As he spoke, Matt dried his hands and then went to the front door where he'd left his bag and the box of charity files.

"At least I'm somewhat familiar with them from when I was researching the education fund," he said as he returned with the items and set the box down on the table. "Mostly we just send a monthly or quarterly donation and, in some instances, attend board and planning meetings. We haven't really been involved in the daily operations of any of them."

"So you add a few meetings to your schedule, so what? That's not asking a whole lot, is it?"

"But, don't you think Marsh and Line should be more involved with them? I mean, look how little help the crisis center has had. What if the others are in the same boat? Remember, some of the others found out what I was doing for the center and wanted to be next in line."

The older man chuckled, his eyes lighting up at the thought. "I do remember that. So, you're actually afraid that, even if all you have to do is go to a few meetings, you won't be able to keep yourself from getting sucked in and involved in other ways."

"Well, that's putting it rather bluntly, but yes."

"Just pray about it, son. The Lord will show you what He wants you to do."

Matt pulled his laptop out of his bag and set it on the table next to the box. He opened the computer and, waiting for it to start up, looked up at his father with serious eyes. "I think He's already shown me what I should do. I think there's really only one right thing to do. I'm just not sure about the how yet."

"Well, He will show you that too. I have every confidence you can do it, son, not a single doubt in my mind; but you have to know it's what the Lord wants you to do and not what anyone else wants."

Matt nodded and slid into the chair in front of the computer.

"I'll let you get to your work," his father concluded. "If you need anything, I'll be in the den catching up on the news."

"All right. Enjoy."

"Ha! Since when is the news enjoyable?"

"True. Don't let it push your blood pressure up too high."

"I'll try."

Matt chuckled to himself as his father left the room. He pushed the computer aside and pulled a handful of scrap paper out of his briefcase. He was big on scrap paper. He never saw any sense in throwing away paper that had only been printed on one side. It drove Mel crazy, but he didn't care. He kept it around for projects just like this, and it always came in handy.

One file at a time, he began diagraming what his new responsibilities might entail and how to work them into a manageable system. Before he realized it, the clock in the dining room was striking eleven-thirty, and his father was shuffling and yawning his way into the kitchen.

"Still at it, are you?"

"I'm just about done. Here take a look at this and see what you think." Matt handed the stack of pages to his father.

"Just a minute. I'll have to get my glasses." The man laid the papers down on the end of the breakfast bar and left the room.

As he waited for his father to return, Matt scrolled through the emails he'd heard come in an hour earlier. Most were advertisements that had come to his personal mailbox, but a few had come into his work account. Normally, he would have let them go until morning, but, since he was still working, he decided it wouldn't hurt to check them out. One email in particular caught his attention. It had come from the crisis center. The subject line read, "Important." He opened the file and began to read,

"Dear M.M.

"I hope this finds you well. I am writing to thank you for the help you have given over the last couple of months regarding our financial difficulties. With everything that has come our way, it would have been a struggle for me to keep up with it without your help.

"I have an enormous favor to ask of you. I believe Kelly may have told you my family has been facing some health issues. By necessity, tomorrow will be my last day with the crisis center. I would like to tell them they can count on you for help in this area, but I understand if it is too much. I have one other person in mind to suggest to them if you are unable to assist, but I value your skill and advice to a much greater level. Please, pray about it and let me know as soon as possible."

Matt's breath caught in his chest as he read the details of the ordeal the other man was facing. He stared at the computer, completely aghast. How could this be happening?

"What's wrong?"

Matt gasped and spun around to face his father.

"Sorry," the older man said, "I didn't mean to startle you. Is something wrong?"

"I—I." He glanced at the computer, dumbfounded. Somehow, the words tumbled over his clumsy tongue. "I just found an email. I—Oh, Dad, it's awful. Read it."

Matt stood and motioned for his father to take his seat.

The older man obeyed and was soon caught up in the short note. When he had finished, he let out a heavy sigh, leaned back in the chair, and stared at his son for a moment.

"Brings back memories, doesn't it?"

"Keenly."

"What are you going to do?"

"You have to ask?"

"Not really. Just checking. We need to pray about how we can help the family as well, not just the center."

Matt nodded. "I'll email him tonight, let him know I'll do it, and ask him to come by my office when he's finished at the center. I'll have him bring everything I need to manage things from there."

"*Can* you manage it all from there?"

Matt cocked his head to one side and raised a shoulder in a shrug of surrender, "We'll have to until we can work something else out. At least we use the same software as the center. That helps."

"Let me see those papers."

Matt scooped the papers up from the countertop and handed them to his father. "Guess I'll be adding a little more to them, won't I?"

His father did not respond. He glanced through the stack, occasionally pausing to grab up Matt's pen and make a note of some sort or another. After several minutes, he looked up at his son with a tired but satisfied expression on his face.

"This is very good. It looks manageable to me."

"We'll have to hire three more employees to pull it off."

"I noticed that, but you showed clearly why you'd have to do it and where the money would come from. I truly doubt you'll have any trouble getting approval with a plan as well laid out as this—especially since it wasn't your idea to begin with."

Matt let out a soft laugh. "I hope not because I'm not going to have much of a chance to set out any other plan. I'm going to have to hit the ground running."

"You're doing a good job, son. Keep it up. I'll let you get back to work, so you're not up all night. See you in the morning."

The man stood and headed for the kitchen door, but as he reached it, he stopped and looked back. "We need to help that family somehow." Then he was lost in the darkness of the hallway.

Neither of them would be getting much sleep.

CHAPTER 41

Two and a half hours later, Matt still sat at the kitchen table. He had reworked the proposal, adding in the extra work he estimated would come with the full responsibilities of the center's finances. He knew Gil only volunteered part-time, but from what he had seen, he was pretty sure Gil had been taking work home with him — often. Matt had typed everything up, formatted it, and added in a couple of charts and graphs in case someone needed to see a visual of the ideas.

Now, he sat motionless, eyes wide with the craze of exhausted determination. He read back over every page, critiquing the material as meticulously as his tired mind would allow. Finally, convinced he could do no more good than damage at such a late hour, he composed a short email, attached the file, and sent it off to a handful of his unsuspecting coworkers at Marsh and Line.

He leaned back in the chair, rubbing his bleary eyes, and moaned. "I'd bet just about anything Amber in HR will be calling by seven. This will throw her day into a whirlwind."

Amber was a very competent, caring, responsible woman, but she was known for being methodical to the extreme. A curve like this would give new meaning to the word frantic. Mr. Marsh along with Bill Raska and Jim Chalmers, his assistant directors of the legal and accounting departments, were the others to whom he had sent the email. They, of course, were already in the loop and would take the suggestions in stride. Both Raska and Chalmers had already expressed both their concerns and their support for the idea. So now, it seemed they would just need to hash out the details.

Matt contemplated the whole process. It felt too easy. Sure, it had thrown his entire day off, and he was still up at a quarter to two in the morning, but it just didn't seem right. Worse yet, his heart told him it wasn't right. It was a good, quick, viable solution to everyone's problems, but it wouldn't last. It gave Marsh and Line a whole new realm of influence for good. It would give their employees opportunities to get involved in the community. Raska and Chalmers had been most supportive on that point. Raska, in particular, had been excited. He'd even sat down at the small conference table in Matt's office and thumbed through the list of charities, commenting on how they could get various departments involved in each one. That had, in turn, excited Matt. Even so, Matt knew he was taking the easy way out.

He picked up his laptop and went upstairs to his bedroom. Along the way, he'd convinced himself he could sleep on it, but as the door closed behind him, he knew that wasn't going to be the case. He set the laptop down next to his Bible on the small desk nestled in the corner of his room. He started to sit down but then decided he'd had enough of hard, straight-backed chairs for one 24-hour period. He picked up the Bible and computer and made his way to the soft armchair on the far side of the room. He flipped on the lamp that stood on the table beside the chair.

"Lord," he prayed aloud, "I'm not going to make this decision without knowing for sure I have your direction in it. I can't. It's too big of a change. It's not something I have ever…" His voice trailed off. Of course this wasn't something he'd ever planned on, but wasn't that usually the way God worked? He opened his Bible to the passage he'd read that morning in his quiet time.

The first two verses of Romans twelve were verses he had memorized as a teenager. He'd tried to keep them at the forefront of his mind for years and always tried to live by them—although he was pretty sure he'd failed in that endeavor more than once.

"I beseech you therefore, brethren, by the mercies of God, that ye present your bodies a living sacrifice, holy, acceptable unto God,

which is your reasonable service. And be not conformed to this world: but be ye transformed by the renewing of your mind, that ye may prove what is that good, and acceptable and perfect, will of God."

As he read back over the verses, Matt couldn't help but be amazed at how appropriate they were for his situation. Little had he dreamed when he'd read them in the morning that by bedtime he would so desperately need discernment for that good, acceptable, and perfect will of God. Even so, it wasn't the opening verses that nagged most at his heart. Instead, it was the principles of the passage that drew him back into the chapter: Don't think higher of yourself than you ought to; each of us have gifts, which are to be used for God's glory and the edification of others with no thought of self but rather of the body of Christ. Perhaps more than any other, verse fifteen seemed to bore holes in his heart.

"Rejoice with them that do rejoice," it said, *"and weep with them that weep."*

His mother's unexpected death had taught him it was easy to rejoice with those who rejoiced — unless you were passing through a time of sorrow yourself. But it also taught him that people who would enter into another's pain were few and difficult to find. His community spying had allowed him to do just that. He had entered the sorrows of many, done what he could to help, and continued on. The idea of working with the crisis center potentially made that opportunity bigger. In fact, it made it possible not only to step into a family's sorrow and difficulty but also to actually walk through it with them.

He poured over the Scripture passage, not for five minutes or even ten, but for an hour. He followed cross-references, read all the notes, looked up words in the Greek. The passage seemed to overflow with all the direction he ever could have needed, not just for this decision but beyond. It laid out an entire philosophy of ministry, which he had never seen before. It overwhelmed him so that, in the end, all he could do was lean back in his seat and draw in a deep, settling breath.

"Lord," he whispered, "this is amazing! Even if I never ever help the center again, I want this in my life. I want You to have the control of me that is needed to live this way; to put others first and to use the gifts You have given me in the way You desire them to be used. Please, Father, guide me. Show me what You want me to do, and how You want me to do it. You know my heart. You know I want to help the center, to help Kelly and Kali, but I'm not sure to what extent I should take it. Please, show me."

Matt leaned over his Bible and laptop once more. Not sure what else to do, he began reading again, this time picking up in chapter thirteen and purposing to read on until he sensed the Lord stopping him. He paused once or twice to follow up on a cross-reference or to read a footnote, but for the most part, the next half hour was spent simply resting in the presence of the Lord and the comfort of His Word. He had just about decided it was time to sneak in an hour or two of sleep before morning when something caught his attention.

"We then that are strong ought to bear the infirmities of the weak, and not to please ourselves."

He knew the verse spoke of those whose faith was small. It was about those who, for whatever reason, doubted the liberties given by Christ and still clung to the mandates of the law. He knew that, while the law might not have been the hang-up for many of those with whom the center worked, they were certainly in need of a strong hand of faith to pull them toward the Savior. Once again, he thought of Sam and Moses.

"People and God's work are always worth fighting for, always," Moses had said.

No other place in the community offered that opportunity better than the Trevor Street Crisis Center, and Matt knew it.

"Fight the fight. Finish the course. Keep the faith."

Sam's motto marched across Matt's mind, drumming out a beat he could not ignore. His heart echoed the rhythm. He flipped to the passage in Second Timothy from which he knew the motto had come. It was nearly word for word. Sam had merely changed it to the imperative. For a moment, Matt wondered how the world would be different if everyone changed that verse to the imperative in their lives. Would more people stand for what was right? Would fewer families be broken? He glanced at a note scribbled in the margin of his Bible next to the verse. It read simply, *"Jude 3."*

Matt flipped to the passage, accidentally bypassing the tiny book three times before his tired fingers found the single spread bearing the entirety of the book. Near the end of the verse, five words were underlined in bright, red ink:

"Earnestly contend for the faith."

That was all he needed to see. His mind was made up with new conviction. He just needed to do one more thing. He closed the Bible and slipped a napkin out from under its front cover. He just needed to make one phone call.

CHAPTER 42

Micah Thompson sat silently in the low, sway-backed armchair which his parents' guest room offered. A single, low wattage bulb spread a circle of light out from under the crimson shade of the floor lamp beside him. His feet rested comfortably on the corner of a desk as his finger followed the lines of text in the Bible spread open across his lap. The house was quiet with only the occasional pop or creak accompanying its adjustments to the night air.

"It's settling," his mom always said about those sounds.

Funny, he thought, *how unsettling its settling can be.*

He yawned and rubbed his eyes, considering for a moment the idea of crawling back under his warm blankets and sleeping until noon. He snorted at the thought. He hadn't slept more than two hours put together for a week. Why would this time be any different?

A soft, buzzing sound caught his attention, and he leaned over the side of the chair to see his phone lit up and vibrating on the floor. His eyebrows drew together in confusion. He grabbed the phone and looked at the screen, wondering who could be calling at such a ridiculous hour. He would have ignored the call from the unfamiliar number if it hadn't been for the area code. It was from home, which told him it could have something to do with the crisis center, which meant it could have something to do with Kali. *That* couldn't be ignored.

"Hello," he said in a hushed voice, not wanting to wake his parents or his nephew who had spent the night and slept in the room next to his.

"Micah?"

Again, Micah's brow furrowed. There was something familiar about the man's voice, but he couldn't quite put his finger on it. It seemed strained, tired.

"Hello?" came the voice again.

"Yes, this is Micah."

"Hey, this is Matt."

"Matt?" his eyebrows tightened once more and then sprang up in utter surprise, "Matt from Singapore!"

The strain on the other end of the call dissolved into musical laughter. "Well, not exactly *from* Singapore, but, yes, that Matt."

"Hey! How are you?" Micah's feet dropped from the desk, and he leaned forward with excitement. "Kelly texted me yesterday and said she'd given someone my number, but I wasn't sure if it was you or someone else. I'm glad you called. It's been ages, man."

"I know. I had no idea you were here for that clothing exchange or I would've gone in. I've been hoping I'd bump into you around town for three years. I never even knew that all the time my dad and your brother were acquainted. If I had known...if I had known — Man, I'm so sorry about Sam. If I had known, I would've been there. I would have done whatever I could have done for your family."

"Thank you, Matt, but it sounds like you've already been doing a lot for us and didn't even know it."

Matt, hesitated, puzzling over the statement. "What do you mean?"

"Kelly told me you've been a pretty amazing friend the past few months. Thank you. Kelly doesn't have many friends or much of a life outside of the center right now. Her family all moved to Arizona a few years ago, but she chose to stay behind. She knew God wanted her at the center, and she chose a pretty lonely path in the process. Sam asked me a long time ago to watch out for her and Kali if anything ever happened to him. He felt responsible for them. They both helped him so much in the ministry. I feel like I've failed both of them. I've been worried about Kelly. ...Thank you for being there for her, Matt."

Matt did not respond. He was again puzzling over Micah's comments. He thought he'd gathered so much information about his bus friend over the previous months, but this he'd never known.

"Are you still there, Matt?"

"Yeah. Sorry. I just didn't realize moving with her parents had ever been an option. She seems so matter of fact about them being there. Does she have any other family in the area?"

"No. The last few years, she has spent every holiday with Sam and Kali and me and a few other single friends."

"Doesn't Kali have family in the area?"

"No. She moved there for college and just stayed. She goes home more often than Kelly, though. I think her family is in a better position to help her with the travel expenses. They're closer too. That makes a big difference. ...So, what are you up to, and why are you calling me at four-thirty in the morning?"

"Four-thirty! What? Oh, Micah, I'm sorry. I've been up all night, and I didn't even think to look at the clock, let alone remember the time difference. I am so sorry."

Micah laughed and then covered his mouth, remembering the others sleeping in the house. "No worries. I've been up most of the night too. Couldn't sleep. What's your excuse?"

Matt let out a loud, frustrated sigh. "I've got a lot on my mind—about the crisis center. I didn't know you were Sam's brother until Sunday. Dumb, I know, but I just didn't put the pieces together. If I had known, I would have called you sooner."

"That's okay. What's on your mind?"

"Everything."

Micah chuckled. "That's a pretty big topic to cover this time of day."

"I know. I'm sorry. Here's the thing. I've been asked, through my job, to become an advisor for the center, but no one at the center knows that. They don't know I've already been helping them with the budgeting and the like. I've just kept it quiet. I wanted to be able to help them, but I didn't want them knowing it was coming from me."

"Wait. *You're* M&Ms?"

Matt snorted. "Yes. I'm M&Ms. I can't believe I'm saying that."

"So, you're the one Mr. Marsh had offered as a possible advisor before Kali came out here?"

"Yes. Although, I didn't know he'd done that at the time."

"Man, if I'd known that, I would've called Marsh and Line for Kali and told her to accept."

"You would?"

"Yes! Of course I would. Matt, if I had known you were in the area, you would have had to deal with me at your doorstep every other day. I was so bummed when we lost contact. What happened?"

Matt groaned. "I had a job that pretty much took over my life. For a year, the only people who even still knew I was alive were my coworkers and parents. Then my computer crashed and wiped out all of my contacts."

"Didn't you have anything backed up?"

"No. That was a huge lesson for me, an expensive one too. But, it got me back on track. It was like God said, 'I've put all these wonderful people in your life, and you've wasted the time you could have had with them. So, now you'll have to start over.' You were the one person I couldn't find that I wanted to find the most."

"Why didn't you ask your dad? He and my brother were together a couple times a month."

"I didn't know that. Or if I did—I guess, with the way things were, I just forgot."

"With the way things were? What brought you home?"

"My mom." Matt hesitated, finding he had to choke back unexpected hurt and emotion at the question. "She got really sick about three years ago, so I came back to help my dad. I was only home a week before she died. Dad took it pretty hard. We both did, I guess. My sister was here for a week or two, but she had to go back to her family. I stayed on to help for a while and just never left. It's been good. Except for not having Mom around, I wouldn't change things. I'm glad I came back."

Micah could hear the pain in his friend's voice. He knew that pain well. "Sorry about your mom, Matt. She was a very special lady. Sam and I were in Seattle for the holidays, or we would have been at the funeral. I should have asked your dad how to get in touch with you. I didn't realize you had moved back. I'm sorry. I remember you talking about your mom all the time on our trip. I know you two were close."

"It's okay, Micah. You didn't know. And yes, she was a special lady. But that isn't why I called."

"Why *did* you call? I'm getting more curious by the minute."

"Well, I guess I just wanted your perspective on the center, on the various programs, on how involved I should get as an advisor. ...I guess part of me also wanted your blessing to go ahead with it. I know how much the center meant to your brother and, I think, to you as well. I'd like to know I have your backing if I go through with this."

"Matt, it's been a long time since we've seen each other. People change over the years, especially when you go through something like what we've been through. Just the same, if you're still the guy I knew in Singapore, and the guy I corresponded with for those two years after Singapore, I'd back just about any idea you had. I'd recommend you for far more than an advisor."

"You would?"

"Well, for starters, I'd put a bug or two in Kelly's ear that she needs to catch you and marry you while she has the chance. I don't know how many times I've thought that—long before you two ever met. You'd be a great—"

"You're getting way off subject there, bud."

Micah laughed. "Don't tell me you haven't thought about it. I know you both better than that. For this friendship to have gone on this long in the way it has, there's way more to it on both sides than either of you are saying."

"You think so?" Matt wasn't sure whether to be pleased or appalled. "Do you think I've led her on?"

"No. You'd have to be uninterested to be leading her on, and I don't think that's the case at all. I think both of you are too preoccupied with other things to see what's happening. ...You love her, don't you?"

Matt didn't answer. His mind was spinning, overwhelmed by the sudden shift in the conversation and the absolute truth of what his friend was saying.

"Matt?"

"Do you really think I'd have a chance with her? ...What am I saying? Quit sidetracking me! I've got to get ready for work in a little bit."

Micah burst out laughing, no longer caring who heard him. "And there you go with the avoidance," he said. "Come on, Matt, admit it."

"I'm not admitting anything. Look, here's the deal. I really think the Lord wants me to do this, I just need some feedback from you on a couple of areas, so I know whether or not it's really something I can handle."

"Okay. I'm sorry. I will answer any questions you have to the best of my knowledge. ...But there's something I should tell you. If you really want to know whether or not you can handle it, the answer is no. No one can handle it, Matt. I couldn't handle it. Kali and Kelly can't handle it. Sam couldn't handle it. It has to be the Lord. If you really feel the Lord wants you to go ahead with things, then just do it. I will support you. I'll be there to answer any questions you have. In fact, I haven't told Kali this yet, but I'm actually hoping to be back there permanently in about two weeks. I can't take the separation anymore. I'm done. I need to get back to work and back to life and...well, back to Kali."

"So, it's Kali! Kelly said there was someone she thought you wanted to marry. It's Kali Shepherd, isn't it?"

"Well, we're not engaged or anything, but...yes. I can definitely say yes to that question. Now *you're* the one off topic. ...Look, if you think God wants you to step in there and fill that position, do it. We will stand behind you."

"Even the girls?"

"I'm pretty sure when they find out who M&Ms is they will not only support you but they'll also be incredibly relieved. Kelly trusts you. She respects you. The only men I've heard her speak about with as much respect as she has for you are her dad and Sam. That's saying a lot. And if Kali knows I trust you, she'll be confident in any guidance you give them."

"You're really planning on being back in two weeks? Are you planning to step into Sam's place at the center?"

"Well, two weeks might be pushing it. I don't know if I can get there that fast. It might be three weeks. As for the center, no. I'm not taking over. I think a lot of people thought I would. I wish I were the right person for the job, but I'm not. I don't have the right temperament or skill set. You, on the other hand, you would fill the position very well."

Again, Matt was silent. This call had been far more positive than he'd expected. He'd expected his old friend to grill him about why he hadn't told Kelly his name and why he hadn't been more of a help to them and why he hadn't done more for Gil. This response was the complete opposite of all that.

"Matt, just do it. Whatever God is telling you to do, do it. ... Now, we have about four years of catching up to do, so unless you're going to get specific about the center, I want to know what you've been up to."

CHAPTER 43

Gil Paulman dropped the receiver back into its cradle and glanced around the office. Sharon's desk was empty. Brandon's desk abandoned. Three different girls had found a place at Sarah's desk over the past couple of weeks, and today a fourth was scheduled to fill the empty seat. His eyes drifted to the office in the far corner of the room; dark as it was most mornings, belongings still present and unmoved in four months. Tears climbed in his eyes at the thought of the pain that had begun for all of them the day that desk had emptied. His chest tightened. Sam had been his lifeline at one of the worst times of his life. Now, he was gone, just when Gil needed him once more.

The big accountant tapped the desk with his pen. He was about to do something he'd never imagined himself doing. He sighed and let his gaze travel down the long wall of offices to the window beside the door to Kali's office. Kelly and Kali were both there. Setting up a plan for the day, he imagined, a plan he was about to ruin. He took a deep breath and moaned as he got to his feet. If only it were a nightmare, then at least there would be the hope that what he woke up to would be better than all of this.

He stepped up to the open office door and knocked softly.

"Come in," Kali responded, but neither she nor Kelly looked away from the computer screen that had gripped their attention for the previous ten minutes.

Gil entered but said nothing. He waited, standing just inside their peripheral vision.

"Here, we can move this driver to Wednesday, and let Abby fill in the slot. She said Tuesday would work. Let's—" Kelly stopped, finally realizing Gil was still waiting. As if on cue, the two women faced their friend.

"Gil," Kali began, her voice full of concern, "Is something wrong?"

Gil nodded, feeling the tears return to his eyes. He turned to close the door even though the only other person in the office was Brenda. She could hear what he had to say. He didn't mind. But he needed the moment to swallow the lump in his throat. He turned back to them and tried to speak, but the ache in his heart prevented it. He saw both women blanch. Somehow, they knew what was coming. He took a shaky breath and pushed out the words, "Beth has cancer."

The women gasped, and, though he wasn't sure how, he saw their tears through his own.

"It's very aggressive," he said, "there's nothing they can do. I don't want to leave you in a mess, but I—"

"Gil, oh, Gil, please don't worry about us. God will take care of us—and you," Kali said. "You just worry about taking care of your wife and children."

"Thank you." He wiped his eyes and gathered his emotions into some semblance of order. "I emailed Mr. Marsh's accountant last night. I didn't expect him to get it until this morning because I sent it so late, but he must have gotten it then because I had a phone message waiting from Mr. Marsh when I got here. I just got off of the phone with him. His accountant is willing to take over all of the bookkeeping and accounting until we find someone else to do it. I'm supposed to take everything over to their offices when I've finished things here. He said it might take M&Ms a little time to get things set up and running, but he'll get on it as quickly as possible. …Mr. Marsh also said to have you call him as soon as you can. He said he has an answer for you on 'the other issue you discussed.' I guess that's it. I'll pack up everything he needs and my belongings and then get going."

"Thank you for making those arrangements, Gil. You didn't have to do that." Kali paused. She studied the man intently, her gaze breaking down every line of his face. "How is Beth?" she asked at last.

He shrugged, once more feeling his heart would burst within him. "It's hard to tell. On the outside, she seems to be taking it better than I am. I'm not sure how deep that goes. I'm not sure it has sunk in yet...and on the other hand, I wonder if she already knew."

"Can we do anything to help?"

Kelly's eyes revealed the sincerity Gil knew to be so true to her character. He knew she and Kali would do anything to help them, but he also knew how very much they had on them already.

"Thanks, Kelly. I'll let you know. Right now, I just need to focus on getting my family through these first few days. We haven't told the kids yet. We're going to wait until we've had a chance to talk to their teachers this afternoon. We'll probably keep them home the rest of the week, so we can be together."

Suddenly the big man felt weak in the knees. He stepped forward and seated himself in the chair across from the two women. "I don't know how I'm going to tell them. How do you tell a seven-year-old his mommy is going to Heaven and never coming back?"

Kelly bit her lip and turned away, trying not to break down into a fountain of sobs. Kali, on the other hand, looked the man straight on. "You'll do fine, Gil. God will give you the words. Does your pastor know what's going on?"

Gil shook his head. "I've been looking for a new church ever since things went down the way they did with Pastor Hanson. I just couldn't keep going there, knowing what I know. The only reason we've stayed all these years was for Sam's sake. I've talked with Pastor Meeks about attending Trevor Street Chapel, but I've only been there twice because Beth has been sick. I think it was while you were in Seattle and Kelly was teaching a children's class or something because I never saw either of you."

Kali nodded her understanding and pressed on in the line of reasoning she had begun. "Why don't I call Pastor Meeks and fill him in. I'm sure if you wanted him to, he and his wife would be willing to be there when you tell the children. I would be willing to be there if you wanted the extra support, but I think it would be good to have a pastor at your side, not just today but the whole way through."

"Thank you, Kali. I'd appreciate that. Just give him my number. He may already have it. I can't remember if I gave it to him or not. I'd like for him to be there. ...We'll have other arrangements to make as well."

Neither of the women had expected this. Their eyes widened as the importance of what he'd just said settled over them.

"So..." Kali began, "you don't think it will be long."

Emotion rushed over the man. He tried to contain the tears, but they were ever so much stronger than all his efforts. He shook his head emphatically. "No. They've given her six to eight weeks, but that is the best prognosis. Worst-case scenario, maybe a month. A month! How can we only have a month left together?" Gil could hold back no longer. Sobs overtook him, shaking his body and tightening the muscles in his chest and stomach. He leaned forward, burying his face in his hands. "I just don't understand. I don't understand."

He felt the two women come to his side and wrap their arms around him. He heard one of them begin to pray, but he could not focus on the words. His heart had been torn from him, and he could only wonder if it would ever be healed.

CHAPTER 44

Kali drummed her fingers on the desk. Something wasn't right at Marsh and Line. Mr. Marsh had said he wanted to talk with her, but every time she had called, he'd been on another line or out of the office. No one had returned her calls, and now no one was even answering.

"Marsh and Line. Accounting. How may I direct your call?"

"Mel?"

"Yes, this is Mel."

"Oh, Mel. I'm so glad to finally get a hold of someone. Is everything okay there?"

"This place is a zoo today. Really. I don't know what's going on. Something came up overnight. I'm not sure what it was."

"Oh." Kali felt her cheeks blush as she spoke. "I hope it wasn't us."

"You? Who is this?"

"Kali Shepherd from the Trevor Street Crisis Center."

"Oh. It might have been you. Your poor accountant had to wait an hour before anyone could help him."

"Well, what do you think I should do? Mr. Marsh asked me to call him today, but I haven't been able to get through to him."

"I'm sure he'll want to talk to you. He doesn't just randomly ask people to call him. Let me put you through to his assistant. If no one answers, it should go to voicemail. Make sure you leave a message. You might even want to mark it as urgent."

"Thank you, Mel."

"You bet."

Kali waited. The phone began to ring, and she began formulating her message, but the message wasn't needed.

"McKinsey Marsh's office. This is Phyllis."

"Phyllis! I'm so glad to finally get a hold of you. I've been trying all day."

"This is Kali Shepherd, isn't it? I'm so sorry, Miss Shepherd. We just finished up with a huge meeting. I know Mr. Marsh wants to talk with you, but I'm not sure if he's ready. Can you hold for just one minute?"

"Sure."

Kali used the time to straighten a few piles on her desk and to choose which would receive her attention next.

"Miss Shepherd."

"Yes."

"Mr. Marsh is still in a meeting. He said he'll call you in about five minutes. He asked that Miss Vance be there if at all possible."

"We can do that. Does he need us to have anything else ready?"

"I don't think so. I think he just wants to talk."

"All right. We'll be ready."

"Thank you so much for your patience, Miss Shepherd."

"Thank you for your help, Phyllis."

Kali hung up the phone and rose from the desk. She walked to Kelly's door and poked her head around the corner. "Mr. Marsh is going to call in a few minutes. He'd like you to be there."

"Okay. I'll be right in."

"I'm going to grab a soda from the break room. Want anything?"

"Water would be nice."

"One water coming up."

Kelly beat Kali back to her office. She was already seated in the chair across from the desk as Kali entered and closed the door behind her.

"Your water, m' lady."

"Thank you. I'm parched."

"How has your corner been this afternoon, Kelly? You seem tired."

"I am. My heart is just broken for Gil and Beth. I keep wondering how things are going for them."

Kali glanced at the clock above her office door. "Pastor Meeks was planning to be over there by three-thirty. It's almost four."

Kali paused to open her soda and take a drink. She set the can down and studied her friend for a long moment. "I want to do something for them, Kel. I just don't know what. I have a feeling Gil isn't going to tell us anything because he doesn't want to be a burden."

"Gil and Beth are family. We can't let them go through this alone."

"I know. I think we should give it a couple days. Let them be together and to find some balance, and then I think the two of us should go over there. We can peek our noses in their refrigerator and see if they need help with any housework. We can take the kids out if they need us to. Whatever the need is."

Kelly nodded but didn't respond.

The reaction concerned her friend, but she knew this wasn't the time to pry. Mr. Marsh would be calling any second, and it wouldn't be good for the two of them to be in tears when he did. So, instead, she decided to keep her friend's mind occupied. "What have you been working on?"

Kelly sighed. "I've been staring at a flashing cursor all afternoon. Kali, I have needed to write our monthly update for two months now. I just, I don't know what to say anymore. It's like there's a huge blank. We don't know the future, we can't share much of the present, and we don't want to dwell on the past. Where does that leave us?"

"I know. I don't envy you that job. I'll be praying you know what to write. Maybe you just need to do a basic program update. No stories this month, just facts."

Kelly shrugged. "Maybe."

The friends fell silent. The darkness that had surrounded them so often over the previous weeks was looming again, and they both knew it. Gil's absence would bring their staff down to the lowest point it had been in years. Neither of them was sure the center could survive that.

They heard the phone ring in the main office. Each sipped once more on her drink. The phone on the desk chirped and then began ringing. Kali instantly tapped the speakerphone.

"Kali Shepherd speaking."

"Hello, Miss Shepherd. This is McKinsey Marsh. Is Miss Vance with you?"

"Yes, she's here."

"Hello, Mr. Marsh."

"Hello, Miss Vance. Listen, before we start, I want to apologize. I know you have been trying to get in touch with me all day, just like I asked you to, and I have been unavailable. I'm so sorry. I want you to know, however, that your waiting has not been in vain. I want to talk to you about the ideas we discussed before your trip, but a second possibility has also come up, which may be a better, much more permanent solution."

"Oh, really?" Kali's curiosity was clearly peaked at this news. She smiled encouragingly at Kelly but saw little hope in her friend's shrugged response.

"Let's start with the first proposal. Remember, I promised not to mention any of this to my head of accounting until after I had heard from you?"

"Yes. I remember that."

"Well, I presented the idea to him yesterday, but not just as your advisor. I proposed that he become our new Head of Charitable Operations. We would actually create a new position in our company for this. It would allow us to be more involved with all of the charities we support. In talking with some of the other department heads, he has discovered there would be ample volunteers for many different types of services and events."

"That's wonderful, Mr. Marsh."

Kali's enthusiasm was genuine. It pulled Kelly out of her weary world and into the conversation. "Would his involvement still include helping with the bookkeeping here?" Kelly asked.

"Yes. Yes, of course. He was very adamant about that. He spent quite a long time with Mr. Paulman this morning going over everything. So, regardless of what we decide, that will be covered."

"Thank you so much, Mr. Marsh." Kelly couldn't hide her relief. She was on the verge of tears, and they all knew it.

"You're very welcome. Now, the second option. This came as a bit of a surprise to me, and I want you to know that, to the best of my knowledge, I did nothing to influence it. At least not intentionally. At first, I wasn't sure how to handle it. I mean, it wasn't what we were supposed to be talking about today at all, but...someone has applied to the board for the director's position."

"What?" both women gasped.

"Yes. That was my initial response, as well. I think this person would be a good fit, but because of our relationship I wasn't sure... well, I just wasn't sure how to present him to you. Since he contacted me first, I got in touch with Mitch Oberlander. He felt we should move ahead immediately. He called an emergency meeting of the board, so while you were making your many phone calls to my office, I was meeting with the board. We discussed the matter. They interviewed the candidate and unanimously agreed to give him a chance—*if*, and only if, you ladies feel this is the right course of action after you've met with him."

Kelly and Kali sat stunned. How could this be happening so fast? Their eyes shot questions and concerns back and forth across the desk, but neither spoke.

"Are you there, Miss Shepherd? Did we lose our connection?"

"No, no," Kali jumped in. "We're still here, but I think we're both in shock."

"I know. It's sudden, isn't it? And I know it probably seems like we've rushed into this and left you behind, but we haven't. Most of the men on the board know this man, if not personally, then by reputation. He's a good man, and he really cares about what happens not just to the center but also to the two of you. He made that very plain. He's concerned for both of you, especially when he heard about what was happening with the Paulmans."

"But we haven't had a chance to even meet him let alone interview him or do reference or background checks."

"I know, Miss Vance, but you will. Nothing is final. You can take all the time you need to do whatever needs to be done. Please, don't suppose, however, that he is like these other men who have tried to take advantage of the situation. He is not. He truly cares. He's not perfect, but he is a diligent, hard-working, big-hearted fellow whom I would trust with my very life."

"That is a very high recommendation, Mr. Marsh," Kali said.

"It is, and I mean every word of it. There *is* one catch. He is also in my employ, and I know you will not be able to pay him well, at least not until you're able to recover some of the support you lost earlier in the year."

"That is true. Kelly and I have nearly cut our own salaries in half."

"I've been meaning to talk to you about that. That needs to be corrected as soon as possible. ...Now, back to what I was saying. For this man to be able to survive, I would like to keep him in my employ as the Head of our Charitable Operations."

"The position you were going to give M&—" Kelly stopped herself. "I mean, to your accountant?"

"Yes. He would have no other responsibilities here, and it would only be a part-time position, but it would make up for what he is able to make working there until things have balanced out there a little. It will also allow him to properly develop that position and train someone to take it over when he moves on to work with you full-time.

"So, what I'm trying to say is that, either way, whether we go with the advisory position or whether you choose to accept this applicant it may take us some time here to readjust. We may have to make it a slow transition, but my staff is fully committed to helping make either transition as smooth and quick as possible."

The man paused, but neither of the women spoke, so he pressed on. "I was hoping it might work for us to come down there and meet with you tomorrow morning. I don't want to force important things out of your schedules, but I do think this is important enough to keep on top of it, so as not to lose our momentum."

"I agree completely." Kali pulled up the calendar on her computer as she spoke. "What time did you have in mind?"

"Would ten o'clock work? That will give us time to pull together any last-minute information and then get across town to your office."

Kali glanced at Kelly, who nodded in response.

"Yes. That will work. How many should we expect, so we can set the conference room up accordingly? Will your Head of Accounting be coming with you?"

"Yes, he'll be coming. I'm not sure how many there will be. No more than four of us, I'm sure."

"We'll be ready."

Kelly leaned forward, somewhat awkwardly, "Mr. Marsh, I'm sorry to interrupt, but there's something you still haven't told us."

"Oh, Miss Vance, you're not interrupting at all. I wanted you to be a part of this conversation. Your input is essential. What have I forgotten?"

"You haven't told us who the candidate is."

"Oh." The man cleared his throat and coughed nervously. "Well, ...he's my son."

CHAPTER 45

Matt sat at the bus stop watching the corner at the intersection a half block away. His right heel pumped up and down, up and down, faster than a skilled typist can delete a row of text. He was thoroughly exhausted, but he couldn't let the day end without seeing Kelly. He needed to be sure she was okay. He'd been waiting at the stop since five-fifteen. Gordy had laughed at him more times than he could count over the past two hours. He'd finished his supper, a chicken wrap from the deli just around the corner from Marsh and Line, and was about to drain the last two swallows of soda from his extra-large plastic cup. The bus rounded the corner. He hoped, for her sake as much as for his own, to see Kelly run around the corner in pursuit, but there was no sign of her.

Gordy laughed once more, but his bus was full, and he couldn't risk angering his riders by stopping for a conversation. Instead, he shook his head with a look of pity in his eyes, closed the doors, and drove on.

Matt pulled out his cell phone. He and Micah had been texting back and forth all day, mostly about the two proposals for the center. Matt had wanted to handle things correctly, and he knew Micah could help him through that process. But, as the details for the meeting the next day had fallen into place, their conversation had shifted to Kelly. At first, it had bugged him that Micah wouldn't leave things alone, but then he realized what really bugged him was the truth in it all. Kelly had become much more than just a friend. He thought about her every moment of every day.

He realized the line between his love for the center and his love for her was extremely thin. The two loves had grown up together, and Matt knew he was willing to take the risks he'd been taking for one as much as for the other. He realized it wasn't just fear of losing a friendship that had him sitting so anxiously at this bus stop. It was fear of losing the only friend he could never live without. He had to talk to her before tomorrow's meeting. Not doing so was not an option. He had to speak to her.

As he glanced back through the text conversation that had led him to this point, another text came in from Micah.

"Don't hate me," it said, *"but I did a little digging. Brenda helped me. I'm sending you the number for Kelly's dad. You and I both know you should do this, so do it the right way. His name is Terry, but if I were you, I'd call him Mr. Vance."*

Matt chuckled. *"Way to make me even more nervous while I'm waiting for her to show up at the bus stop,"* he replied.

"Glad to help!"

Matt rolled his eyes at the text and shook his head. He looked at the time and then put his phone away. He could wait through two more buses. If she hadn't come by the third, he'd have to take it, especially if he was going to call Mr. Vance when he got home. That was one call he *wouldn't* be making at a bus stop.

Another ten minutes passed. Soon the bus had turned the corner and was once more lumbering toward him. The bus slowed and pulled to the curb with its meager load of two passengers. The doors opened and Gordy stared at his friend for a moment.

"Come on, man," he said at last, "go home. You look like death warmed over. Can't you talk to her in the morning?"

Matt shook his head. "No. I want to see her tonight. Thanks, though."

"You're going to wear yourself out, Matt. Do you ever take a break?"

Matt laughed. "Far more often than I should most likely. Just wait until the ground dries up a bit and hiking season is in full swing. You'll be hard put to find me anywhere near all this cement."

Gordy grinned. "Well, now, I might just have to tag along with you sometime. I'll see you next time around."

Matt waved and watched the man pull away. The bus had barely disappeared from sight when he turned in the other direction and saw Kelly coming down the sidewalk with her big, red bag swung over her shoulder and two large cups in her hands. Matt stood and smiled as she approached.

"You just missed it," he said.

"Apparently, so did you. I knew I was going to miss it. I saw you sitting here waiting the last time the bus came. When you didn't get on, I figured you were waiting for me. So, I went over to the coffee shop and got us both something to drink. But it seems you've already had enough to float you down the river."

Matt glanced down at his large cup and laughed. He tossed the empty container into a nearby trash can. "I've had my share of soda this afternoon, but right now I welcome caffeine in any form."

"Oh...that's too bad. This is decaffeinated."

Matt stared in complete disbelief. "You drink that stuff?"

The young woman broke out in sidesplitting laughter. "No. I was teasing. It's strong. Very strong." She handed him a cup, and he took a moment to smell the aromatic steam sifting out of the hole in the lid.

"This isn't coffee."

"Nope. But it's the only tea I've ever had that actually keeps me awake at night. The blend is imported from a Russian company, but I'm not sure where the tea originated."

"It smells good." He took another whiff of the hot liquid and then turned his attention back to his friend. "How did you see me? I never saw you, and I was watching for you."

"I had been out with one of our drivers. We were stopped at the corner at the light. I saw you sitting there, and when the bus came you stayed behind."

"Oh, that explains it. I wasn't looking in cars. ...Do you want to walk? We can probably make it at least two stops before the next bus catches up with us."

She considered him for a moment. "Maybe," she said hesitantly, "the question is, do you? You look awful, are you feeling all right?"

He waved the comment away. "I'm fine. I was just up all night, and then it was a pretty crazy day at work."

"Why were you up all night?"

"Had a lot on my mind." He motioned for her to start walking and then scooped up his bag from the bench and fell in stride beside her. "You were right," he said.

"About what?"

"I *was* waiting for you. I had a feeling you might have had a rough day, and I wanted to make sure you were ok."

"That is kind of you...*Matt.*"

He smiled down at her. He liked the way his name sounded when she said it.

She blushed a little under his gaze and looked away. "You have good intuition. It was a rough day. Until I saw you sitting there, I planned to get on the bus, stare out the window, and hope no one recognized me. ...I'm glad it didn't work out that way."

"Me too."

They walked on in silence, reaching and passing the next bus stop.

"We found out some bad news today," she resumed as they followed a jog in the sidewalk and ducked under the low branches of a young aspen. "Our volunteer accountant has worked with us since the center started. He has been the biggest help of anyone on our staff since Sam died. So consistent. Faithful. He found out yesterday that his wife has cancer, and they can do nothing for her. He was so broken, and I don't blame him. ...I just keep thinking of their children. They have four children. The youngest is seven. The oldest is twelve."

"How are they taking it?"

"I don't know. He hadn't talked to them about it yet when he was in the office this morning. Pastor Meeks was supposed to go over to the house this afternoon just to be there with them when they told the kids. I don't envy him that job."

Matt shook his head. "Not at all."

"We're going to do whatever we can to help. ...But we can't do what they want the most, and that's the hardest part. Situations like this make me feel so helpless, hopeless even."

"Aw, Kelly, no. There's always hope. Don't lose sight of that. There's always hope."

She turned away as if to look at something on the other side of the street, but Matt could see she was fighting tears. He caught hold of her forearm and squeezed it gently.

"Kelly." He waited until she had turned to face him. "There's always hope. So long as we have fixed our eyes on Christ, there is always hope."

"I know," she forced the words out past the tears escaping down her cheeks. She wiped at them in embarrassment, but Matt stopped her.

"Hey," he soothed, "don't be ashamed of your tears. You love that family, and you are allowed to grieve with them. The Bible says, '*Rejoice with them that do rejoice, and weep with them that weep.*' I just read it this morning. Not only is it perfectly normal for you to grieve with them but it's also what God wants us to do. It's okay."

She bit her lip and blinked another tear onto her cheek. She smiled at him feebly. "Thank you. ...Look, you were right. We're almost to the second bus stop. Two more and we'll be home."

"Yes, but the next two are much further apart. Do you want to keep going?"

"I'm fine if you are."

He nodded. "It's nice to be moving."

The two were silent again. Matt knew he needed to tell her something, something to prepare her for the meeting in the morning. He didn't want her to be shocked when he walked into their conference room. He didn't want her to think he'd befriended her so he could get information for Marsh and Line.

"The board has an applicant for the director's position. We're scheduled to interview him tomorrow morning," Kelly announced.

Matt cringed inwardly. This wasn't the direction he'd planned on taking the conversation, not this quickly at least. He wasn't sure what to do with it now that it was in front of him.

"I'm afraid we're moving too fast," she continued. "We know nothing about him. He's our board member's son. If there's one thing I don't like, it's nepotism. I've never seen Mr. Marsh as that kind of man, and he said he didn't have anything to do with the decision, but just the same, it makes me nervous."

"Do you trust Mr. Marsh?"

Kelly nodded without the slightest hesitation. "He's a good man. I've never actually met him, but I've seen him at work, so to speak. He has a good heart, a good business head, and he loves the Lord. Those are all important for this process. Very important."

Matt said nothing. Instead, he nodded his agreement and walked on.

"I'm nervous," she said at last. "I want us to have a new director, and I want him to be the right person. At the same time, I can't stand the thought of anyone else sitting in Sam's office. I wish Micah could take his place. I really do."

Again, Matt said nothing. They walked on to the third bus stop and were surprised that they had yet to see any sign of the bus.

"Should we keep going?" Kelly asked.

"Might as well, we've gone this far already."

But Kelly stopped him, laying her hand on his arm to make sure she had his full attention. "What if I mess everything up, Matt?"

"What do you mean?"

"What if I say the wrong thing, ask the wrong questions, and scare this guy away?"

"If he scares away that easily, you don't want him anyway."

She laughed. "I guess you're right there. I just. ...I don't know. I feel like Mr. Kerry was my fault. And, I should have seen what was coming with Brandon, but I didn't. I don't want to mess this up too and get us further stuck in this situation."

Matt started to speak but then realized if he answered her the way he'd planned, he would reveal his hand. She had never told him the name of the man who had caused her so much pain. He'd overheard it at the ChaiNook. She'd never said anything about Brandon either. That information had come across his path at work, and she didn't know that yet.

His hesitation prompted something inside of her. "Oh, you have no clue what I'm talking about, do you?" she said apologetically. "Mr. Kerry is the man who was so awful at the clothing exchange. I was the one who suggested he help us until Micah arrived."

"Mr. Kerry wasn't your fault, Kelly. The guilt for that one, plain and simple, lies on Kerry himself. I don't know what you mean about Brandon, but I'm pretty sure that wasn't your fault either. You won't mess things up. I'm sure of it. If that man knows God has called him to the center, he'll be ready to answer any question you put out in front of him. And if he isn't, well, like I said, you don't want him there anyway."

The silence returned. By now, their tea had cooled sufficiently to drink. They sipped at the strong, butter rum flavored drink as they walked.

"This is good," Matt said with a lick of his lips. "Someday, you'll have to show me where you buy it."

"Sure. I'd love to."

They walked on, neither speaking, Kelly beginning to sense something was troubling her friend. She scolded herself inwardly for not noticing sooner. He was clearly exhausted and had admitted to being up all night. There must be a reason behind it all.

"You're pretty quiet tonight," she ventured, "everything okay?"

He shrugged as they reached the sidewalk, which he knew from previous bus rides would lead her off toward her home.

"I've got a lot on my mind, that's all."

"Work-related?"

"Yes. I actually…I wanted to talk to you about that. There's something I need to tell you. Something important. I haven't told you before because, well, it never seemed relevant. But as of today, it has become very relevant, and I don't think it's right for me to keep it from you."

Matt saw fear and confusion fill his friend's eyes as he spoke. His chest tightened. He'd done it. He'd gone and messed everything up, and now he was about to destroy any chance he might have had with her, not to mention any chance of further helping the crisis center.

"What is it?" she pressed.

He let out a deep breath as if about to confess a great crime. "Kelly, ...I work for Marsh and Line."

"But you're—"

"An accountant. Yes. But I work for Marsh and Line."

"So, you know..."

"I know everything that happened today. I know about Gil Paulman. I know about the two plans Mr. Marsh has come up with. I know about it all."

"But you just let me say all those things, all my worries and concerns about Mr. Marsh and his son. ...Do you know his son?"

"Yes."

Suddenly, the uneasiness she had felt at the thought of her earlier venting melted into the hope that her friend could offer her some insight.

"What is he like? Do you think he would be a good fit?"

Matt pursed his lips tight, not sure what he should say about any of the situation.

"Please, Matt, don't leave me wondering and in the dark. Is he a good man?"

"I don't think it's my place to offer an opinion of what sort of man he is...except to say he is a man you can trust. He cares very much about what happens to the center. He may not know exactly how to handle things at first because he's never done something like this before, but he'll catch on quickly if you give him a chance."

"Did Mr. Marsh tell you to say all that?"

"No."

"Does Mr. Marsh know we're friends."

"Yes, actually, he does."

"Did you tell him about our conversations."

"The only person I've ever said anything to about our conversations is my father. You and he are the only people I really talk in depth with these days. Kelly, I wanted to tell you this now because I didn't want you thinking I've been gathering information for Marsh and Line. I haven't. I truly have been here as your friend, simply because I believe God wants me to be available to those who need a friend, and...because...well because I care about you. You're the first real friend I've had since my mom died, and I feel blessed to have you. I don't want to lose our friendship. It means far too much to me."

Kelly blushed again. She'd been on the verge of accusing him of some terrible things, but she knew they weren't true. Micah had told her in their text conversation that if this was the guy he'd met in Singapore, then she couldn't ask for a better friend. Matt had proven that over the months, and she'd been willing to throw it all away over something small.

"I guess it really shouldn't surprise me," she said at last. "I know you weren't trying to hide things from me. You were just trying to protect your identity so you could go on anonymously helping people—something you do very well, I might add. I agree. I don't want something so small to ruin our friendship. I don't want *anything* to ruin our friendship. But, maybe it's time we sat down and found out who the other really is. I know you want to be anonymous, and I'm willing to help you be that person, but I would really like to know the real Matt."

He smiled, relieved by her gracious words. "I agree. How about lunch tomorrow after your meeting with Mr. Marsh? I could text you, say around 12:30?"

"Will that give us enough time?"

"Lunch? Ha! My life isn't that interesting. Believe me. It will be plenty of time."

CHAPTER 46

Kelly rushed into the conference room, shoving a set of keys into her jacket pocket and at the same time struggling to remove the garment. "Am I late?"

Kali, the room's sole occupant, glanced up from where she was trying to connect her laptop to a stubborn electrical outlet and laughed. "Does it look like you're late?"

"I'm sorry. I did my best to get here as fast as I could. Do you need me to help with anything?"

"Just catch your breath. I think we're all set in here. You might want to grab your laptop, just in case you need to pull up a file or something. Abby was very kind to bring refreshments. We're certainly not going to starve over the next couple of hours."

"Is Abby sitting in on the meeting?"

Kali laughed again. "No. Calm down so you can think, girl. I'm guessing Abby sensed our nervousness about it all last night and decided this might ease the tension."

"That was sweet of her."

"I thought so too. Mr. Marsh's assistant called a little while ago and said some of the board members will be attending as well. So, I think there will be eight of us: The four Mr. Marsh mentioned last night, the two board members, and us."

"Ok. I'll go put my jacket away, grab my stuff, and be right back."

"Take your time, Kelly. They aren't supposed to be here for another ten minutes."

292

"I'm guessing Mr. Marsh is the sort of man who shows up early just to make sure he isn't late."

"You have a point there. You might want to stop by a mirror somewhere. You've got a little grease on your face."

Kelly groaned. "Of course I do. You know me, can't let the mechanic handle it all, just have to get my fingers in there."

"Just like your dad taught you. What did Rick say about the shuttle van?"

"He said it's not fatal. Should have it back up and running in a day or two." Kelly paused to take a deep breath. "Okay. I'll go pull myself together."

As promised, Kelly was quick about gathering her things. She stopped by the ladies' room to redo her hair and eliminate the grease from her cheek and then headed back to the conference room with a sigh of resignation. Her make-up was shot, but there was nothing unusual about that, nor could she fix it. It would have to wait until she got home, at which time it would be pointless to do anything about it anyway.

She was in the process of setting bottles of water around at each seat when she heard a commotion. She peered through the door to see four men laughing their way through the narrow entrance and into the main office. Kali, who'd gone to her office to retrieve a file, stepped out to meet them. The smiling woman walked straight up to a white-haired gentleman with her hand extended in greeting.

"Mr. Marsh, it's so good to see you. Please, come in. We're all set up in the conference room."

Kelly noticed that Mr. Marsh wasn't a big man. He was of medium build and about as tall as — Matt! Matt was with them! He glanced up at her from behind the older man, his blue eyes sending a quick, nervous smile in her direction before he looked away to respond to one of the other men. She could see in his movements that he felt uncomfortable, and she purposed to make those feelings disappear.

Kali led the men into the room and motioned for them to find a place at the table. Instead, they stood awkwardly about the room.

"Mr. Marsh, gentleman, I don't know if all of you have met Miss Vance," Kali said, waving gracefully toward her friend. "Kelly is our acting Assistant Director. She has done a wonderful job. In fact, I'm pretty sure she's done a better job of it than I ever did."

"That's not true," Kelly responded, her cheeks coloring with embarrassment. "Mr. Marsh, it's a pleasure to finally meet you in person."

The two stretched across the table and shook hands. When Marsh stepped back, he paused to examine the table.

"Miss Shepherd, are you expecting someone else?"

"Phyllis called and said some of the board members were coming?"

"Well, yes, but I'm afraid it's just these two." He motioned to the other two men whom Kelly had never met before. "You remember Mr. Truman and Mr. Oberlander, don't you?"

"Yes, of course," Kali responded. "I guess I misunderstood. Was anyone else from your office coming?"

"No. This is it. We're all here."

"So, this must be?" Kali's voice rose in pitch as she awkwardly indicated the younger man at Mr. Marsh's side.

"My son. Matt."

Kelly stared at her bus friend who shook hands with Kali and then turned toward her, his cheeks red with embarrassment and nerves. Their eyes met, and she knew. She knew what he'd been trying to tell her the night before.

"It was you," she whispered. "You're M&Ms. Matt Marsh. But that means...that means you—"

Tears cut her off as she realized how very much her friend had come to care not only for the center but for her as well. He was willing to give up life as he knew it to come to their rescue. He was willing to risk personal loss to make sure they survived. *He* was their knight in shining armor.

Her thoughts whirled. Her hand came to her mouth to cover an involuntary gasp. Part of her wanted to collapse into a chair in a heap of tears. Part of her wanted to rush across the room and throw her arms around his neck. But in the end, she could only stand and stare with tears slipping down her cheeks.

"Thank you," she said at last in a voice so low only those looking directly at her knew she had spoken at all.

The blush drained from Matt's face, and a smile climbed in his eyes. He said nothing, but he didn't have to. She knew those eyes well by now. She could see he was pleased and relieved and happy all at once.

Mr. Marsh cleared his voice. "Miss Vance, I have never met you before today, but I truly feel I have known you for a very long time. I feel almost as if you are a part of the family. I hope you won't hold it against Matt for not revealing his full identity before now."

Kelly shook her head but still said nothing.

Kali, on the other hand, was full of questions. "Kelly, what's wrong? Why are you crying? Is this...is this your bus friend?"

Kelly's tear-laden laugh lingered on her face as a smile. "Yes! Finally, you get to meet him. Matt, this is my best friend—and boss—Kali Shepherd. Kali, meet M&Ms."

"Wait. What? *You* are M&Ms?"

Matt nodded, grinning and dipping his head in a slight bow. "At your service."

Kali gasped. "I...I don't know what to say...I mean. Thank you. Thank you for all of your help."

"Forgive me," Oberlander interrupted, "but poor Truman and I are completely out of the loop on this one. Who, or what, is M&Ms, and what does that have to do with all this?"

Kali patted the man on the arm. "It's a long story, Mr. Oberlander. Why don't you all have a seat, and we'll explain...or maybe I should say Matt will explain since he seems to be the only one who knows *all* sides of this story."

Kelly heard little of the first ten minutes of the conversation. She was too busy watching Matt, his interaction with his father, his responses to Kali and the board members—everything about him was the same and yet somehow new. She had known he was a good man from the moment she'd met him. Experience had deepened that conviction, and Micah had confirmed it. But today, he'd stood up and shown just how good a man he was. She was smitten. There were no two ways around it. Matthew Marsh—M&Ms—had captured her heart.

CHAPTER 47

"**L**et's get down to business," Marsh said, raising his voice slightly to be sure he had everyone's attention. "We have a couple of options on the table, so we need to consider which of them would best fit the needs of the center. As you now know, Matt has been helping with the center's budgeting. He has already talked with Mr. Paulman about completely taking over that area of responsibility. When Miss Shepherd called me about the situation with Pastor Hanson and...what was his name?"

"Chet Owens," Kali replied.

"Yes. Mr. Owens. After that call, I suggested we have Matt serve as advisor until a director could be found. Miss Shepherd asked to be allowed to pray about the idea while she was away. In the meantime, I got to thinking. Marsh and Line is associated with several charities, but we have no one overseeing our involvement with them. They are sort of just programmed into our books. So, when Miss Shepherd called to let us know she would like to accept our offer, I took a few days to pull together a plan and proposed that, in addition to his current position, Matt become the Head of Charitable Operations at Marsh and Line."

"In addition to everything else you do?" Kelly's eyes were wide, and her voice cracked with the question.

Matt nodded.

"But I've seen how much you do. I've seen the huge amount you're already taking home. How could you possibly do that?"

For a moment, an expression of puzzlement crossed Matt's face, but then he grinned. "You're talking about that night on the bus when I had so much 'homework.' That was the research for the education fund Kali had asked me to do. You have no idea how many questions I had running through my mind that night. Or how absolutely terrified I was that I would give myself away."

Kelly laughed. "Serves you right."

"I know," he said shamefully. "I guess if you really think about it, I've already been taking work home for the center for quite a while. So, it wouldn't be anything new."

"But you're talking about adding on several charities," she argued.

"Not to the same extent." Marsh hurried to correct. "The center would receive special attention. I intended to have him keep us up to date with the other organizations, so we could share the needs with others, be aware of special projects, and do whatever we could to help. It was Matt's idea to take it beyond that and open up volunteer opportunities to the various departments."

Matt smiled with both excitement and pleasure. He spun the cell phone that lay on the table in front of him, giving himself a moment to contain the energy building inside of him. Finally he said, "The two men who report directly to me from the legal and accounting departments are both excited about the idea. They kept texting me all day Monday asking if we had a plan yet."

"So," Marsh said, "no matter what the outcome of today's meeting, we're planning on going through with the development of that position."

Kali leaned forward, resting her forearms on the table. "So, how did this go from Matt taking on a new department at Marsh and Line to Matt applying to become the director of the crisis center? That seems like a pretty big jump."

"Well, I suppose that's a case of limited vision on my part," McKinsey said. "But then, we never know what's going on in someone else's heart—even when we think we do. I could see Matt's heart was in this place far more than it was in the legal and accounting departments. I just didn't realize to what extent. As to how he came to that point, he'll have to explain that."

All eyes turned to Matt and, for the first time since Kelly had realized who he was, a nervous expression came across his face.

Matt fidgeted with his phone, surprised to find tears threatening. He swallowed hard and let his gaze come up to Kelly's. She smiled, giving him the courage to press on. His eyes swept across the other faces in the room as he began.

"Four months ago, I knew nothing about the crisis center. Sure, I authorized a check for it every month, but I knew nothing about it. Then one morning, I met this girl at the bus stop. We chatted about her broken car and went our separate ways. That night, when I went home, she was on the bus again, but this time she was crying. I sat down next to her, and she told me about how her friend had died. She told me about this amazing man and how she'd watched him literally give someone the shirt off his back. What she told me shamed me. The more I heard about Sam Thompson, the more I knew my life needed to change. The more opportunity I had to help, the more I learned about the limits I had put on myself—the boundaries. I was only willing to go so far, but Sam…Sam went all the way.

"Then, Miss Shepherd, you asked for the information on the education fund. The further I dug, the more I realized how vast the influence of this one little ministry really was. Every time this place took a hit, all I could think about was the effect it would have on this community if the center was gone. When that man Kerry did what he did…" his voice trailed off for a moment and his cheeks colored with embarrassment. He turned his gaze on Kelly and Kali. "I've never wanted to hit someone so bad in my whole life. I saw you both struggling. I knew where you were with your salaries, I…I even knew where you were with your rent."

"What!" Kali exclaimed, nearly coming out of her seat as she did so. "How could you have known?"

"I overheard you talking at the ChaiNook. I was there on the other side of the wall behind your table. I didn't mean to be there, but…then I sort of took advantage of the situation. I figured it was the only chance I'd have to find out what was really going on. And then I felt terrible for listening. I heard everything you said. I knew how exhausted you both were. The more I learned, the more I wanted to help. I wanted to step up and fight for you, but all I could see was how lacking I was — I am — compared to Sam.

"I couldn't figure out how to go about it. I knew I couldn't take on much more than I already had on my plate. I didn't want to give up my ability to go about helping others anonymously, but then my dad said something that made me reexamine everything, and I realized my anonymity was nothing in comparison with helping a friend. I knew it was far more important to help you out than it was to keep my secret.

"Then Kelly told me the story of Moses, the man Sam met in Africa. I think I knew the answer to the situation then, but I wasn't ready to commit. The next afternoon, I came back to the office after lunch and found Dad's proposal regarding the new position. I wrestled with it all day. I stayed up until well after one in the morning, working out a plan and then reworking it after I received the email from Gil Paulman. But as I was heading for bed, I knew I was taking the easy road. I spent the rest of the night praying and searching the Scriptures and praying some more. And it all came down to the very thing that had been in my heart all along: It's time for me to contend for the faith. Just like Moses said, 'People and God's work are always worth fighting for, always.'

"I called Micah Thompson before I left for the office — "

"You called Micah?" Kelly leaned forward, surprise evident in every line of her face. She'd given Matt the number, but with everything going on and his love for secrecy, she'd doubted he would ever call him. On the other hand, that did explain a strange text she'd gotten from Micah the night before.

Matt nodded. "I didn't want to make any move without getting his perspective. I wanted to know if he thought I could do it. He told me I couldn't, but the Lord could do it through me and, therefore, I should just go for it. At that point, he didn't know the extent to which I was willing to go, but the longer we talked, the more definite he became. That was the last little bit of confirmation I needed to at least summon the courage to make the suggestion to Dad. He took things from there.

"I'm not perfect by any means, and I'm no Sam Thompson, but if you'll let me, I'm willing to fight tooth and nail for this place for as long as God lets me."

Kelly had tears in her eyes again. Kali, on the other hand, eyed him cautiously. She knew he had already given them a tremendous amount of help. She knew Kelly had found him to be a true friend... but they knew so little about him.

"Do you mind if we call Micah now?" she asked.

The suggestion was met with surprise all around the table, but Matt recovered quickly. He shrugged and smiled. "It's fine with me."

Kali pulled her phone out, dialed the number, and laid the device in the middle of the table so everyone could hear. "Micah said he'd try to be around in case we needed his input. ...I suppose that means he knew more about this meeting than I did, doesn't it?" She might have backed away from the call at that thought, but the phone was already ringing.

CHAPTER 48

"**H**ello."

"Hey, Micah, this is Kali. I'm here with Kelly, Mr. Truman, Mr. Oberlander, Mr. Marsh, and his son... whom you apparently already know."

"Oh, so you're still in your meeting then?" he surmised, completely and wisely, dodging the implications of her last statement.

"Yes. We wanted to talk with you about something in particular."

"Okay. Shoot."

Kali hesitated, knowing her question was going to sound dumb. She knew the answer. Everyone in the room knew the answer, but something compelled her to ask anyway.

"Did you talk with Matt Marsh earlier this week about him serving as an advisor for the center?"

"Yes. Well, I think that's what he called about initially. But, by the time we were done, I think he was pretty convinced he should do more than that."

"What do you mean?"

"I think he was considering applying for the director's position."

"What were your thoughts on the matter?"

"I told him to go for it, Kali. I told him there is no one I would rather have step into my brother's shoes. I've known him for a long time. Haven't seen him for a while, but I've known him for a long time. He's a good man, Kali. I trust him."

"So, if we were going to consider him for the position you would recommend it?"

"Absolutely. If I had a vote, which I don't, but if I did—he would get it."

"It isn't just because you're friends, is it?"

"No. Matt was my team leader when we were in Singapore. I don't think he knows it, but he's got what it takes to do the work you're doing at the center. He has the heart for it too, and...he's in love."

Micah paused, knowing the statement would set his friend to squirming. He wished for all he was worth that he could see the blush creeping up the other man's neck.

"He's in love with the work," Micah said at last, pausing again to see if he could hear his friend's sigh of relief. When he had, he continued. "You'll be hard put to find someone who's already in love with that job. Most people will want to make it their own—as you've already discovered. Matt doesn't want to do that. He wants to take what is there, build it back up, and grow it from there, however God leads. Just like Sam did."

Kali stared at the phone, chewing pensively on her bottom lip. She hadn't expected to find that Matt was lying, not really, but neither had she expected Micah to be so sure of Matt. It meant a lot that he would say Matt was the best choice to fill his brother's shoes. It meant a whole lot.

"Are you still there?"

"Yes. I was just thinking about what you said. ...Does anyone else have any questions for Micah?"

Most at the table shook their heads, but Truman leaned in toward the phone. "Micah, if we send you a reference form, would you be willing to fill it out?"

"Sure! I'll have it back to you the same day."

Truman looked at Kali, and she nodded to confirm that she would get it out before the day was done.

"Anyone else?" she asked.

"Micah," Kelly began, "I know this isn't what we're here about, but how are your parents?"

"They're doing okay. And by the way, Mr. Marsh, thank you. Thank you so much for sending them to that retreat center and helping me get back there for the clothing exchange. It meant a lot to all of us. I think it helped my mom more than I realized at first. She keeps talking about how quiet it was and how it was the first place she could think. So, thank you."

Matt's eyes flashed questions at his father. He'd known nothing about his father's involvement in getting Micah to the clothing exchange, and certainly nothing about the retreat center.

Marsh shrugged, waving his son's questions away, "It was the Lord's doing, Micah."

"Somehow, I'm not surprised to hear you say that."

The conversation lulled. People began casting those awkward sidelong glances around the table that are so often cast when the conversation is done, but no one wants to say so. Then a soft ripple of laughter went through the room at the sound of Micah attempting to shoo his parent's dog away discreetly.

Kali realized the conversation was about to get out of hand and leaned forward toward the phone once more. "Well," she said, "if that's all the questions, I guess we'll let you go, Micah, so we can finish up here."

"All right. Sounds good. Hey, Kelly, did you get the text message I sent you last night?"

Kelly's gaze instantly jerked to the phone, her face went red, and she barely managed to say, in a rather terse tone, "Yes. I did."

"Okay. I didn't hear back, so I just wanted to check."

Kelly rolled her eyes, wishing she could toss something at her friend through the phone. "You know perfectly well why you didn't hear back from me."

"Yeah. I thought so. Okay, well, I hope the rest of your meeting goes well. Enjoy the hot seat, Matt."

Matt chuckled. "Thanks, man."

"Yep. Anytime. Kali, can you call me tonight, or even when you guys are done there. I need to talk to you about something."

"Sure. I'll call as soon as I get a chance."

"Sounds great. Have a nice day."

"You too." Kali reached for the phone and disconnected the call.

For a moment, everyone glanced around at one another with uncertainty, not knowing where to go from that point. Finally, Truman stepped in. "As the board suggested yesterday, I think we should take Matt through the same process we would take anyone else through. A thorough background check, reference checks, drug test if need be, and then the decision will be up to the two of you, Miss Vance and Miss Shepherd, and your staff. The board has agreed to accept his application. Most of us know Matt, or we know his reputation. We know his diligence. We know his heart. We know he went to bat for you when no one else would, even though you didn't know he was doing it.

"I think if you're still not sure, even after we have done all of the checks, etc., then it would be appropriate to give him a trial period, say three months. That would take us through the summer. If at any point anyone, including Matt, feels it isn't going to work, then we can prayerfully take the next step."

Kali nodded. The idea made sense. "I think that sounds like a good plan, Mr. Truman," she said, "but I would like to confer with Kelly for a moment. Would you excuse us, gentlemen?"

"Of course," all four men said, each starting to rise, but Kali stopped them.

"No, no. That's okay. We can just step out."

Marsh waved her back into her seat. "Allow us to be gentlemen, Miss Shepherd. The world is lacking that commodity."

Kali smiled and sat back down. "Thank you, Mr. Marsh."

The two women watched as the men stepped out into the office and closed the conference room door.

"Is something wrong?" Kelly asked immediately.

"No. I'm just…I'm overwhelmed. Do you really think this is a good idea? Do you think he could do it?"

Kelly nodded as tears climbed in her eyes once more.

"Last night, Matt was waiting for me at the bus stop. We walked all the way home. …Well, to where our paths split. At the very end of our conversation, after I had ranted and raved about all sorts of things, including 'Mr. Marsh's son' and my disdain for nepotism, even after all that he told me he worked for Marsh and Line as an accountant. He told me he knew what was going on."

"But he didn't tell you *who* he was."

"No. He didn't. But I'm glad he didn't."

"Why?"

"Because this way, I saw how much he has come to care. It didn't start that way, Kali. God has put this place in his heart, and I don't think there will be any getting it out."

"So, you trust him, even after all the secrecy? Don't you feel, even a little bit, like he deceived you—and the rest of us too?"

"Think about it, Kal. He's the son of one of the most successful businessmen in town. If people knew who he was and what he's been doing to help those in need, the word would spread and instead of being able to do what he has been doing he would be swamped with people wanting him to do more. People would take advantage of him, or at least try to take advantage.

"But with him, I think it goes deeper still. He's not doing what he's been doing for the praise of others. He just wants to help, and he didn't want any attention for himself. I completely understand why he would want to hide his identity from the general public."

"And from you? Why did he hide it from you?"

"He was afraid the people he'd helped would recognize him as the man from the bus or the coffee shop or from wherever he met them. At the same time, he was afraid some of our volunteers would recognize him as McKinsey Marsh's son. Then his secret would be out. It's as simple as that. The clothing exchange scared him half to death. Now I understand why he was so adamant about not coming in that night. ...But don't you see, Kali? He's willing to give all of that up, and an excellent job, because he's realized how much more good he can do here, helping us."

"So, you're with Micah?

Kelly hesitated, her eyebrows rising in a look of concern and confusion. "I guess so. ...Are we taking sides?"

Kali laughed. "No. I didn't mean it that way. I was just surprised to hear him be so positive about it. He has absolutely no reservations."

Again, Kelly hesitated. She knew what she was about to say could upset Kali, but if she didn't say it, her friend would feel deceived by the omission every bit as much as she felt Matt had deceived them.

"Kali, there's something I should tell you. ...When you suggested calling Micah, I knew he would be in favor of Matt. I had talked with Micah about Matt after Matt asked for his contact information on Sunday. At that point, Matt just wanted to reconnect. The rest of this hadn't come up yet. Anyway, I texted back and forth with Micah about my friendship with Matt for close to an hour. When Matt finally told me his name, I texted him again, and he confirmed that his team leader's name had been Matt. But he respected Matt's anonymity and didn't tell me his last name. Still, he was very positive…maybe even a little more forthright about some things than he should have been."

"Like what?"

Kelly picked up her phone. "Here," she said, scrolling through her text messages, "read the strange text I got from him last night."

Kali took the phone and read the text,

"I've been thinking, Kelly. …You should catch Matt while you can and marry him."

Kali burst out laughing. "Is he serious?"

"Yes."

The laughing started again, but this time Kali had to grab her side to contain herself. "This is the text he was talking about on the phone call, isn't it? Oh, Kelly. I'm sorry. I shouldn't laugh. I'm sorry. He shouldn't have said that. I'm sorry."

Kelly didn't laugh. Instead, she stared at her friend with one disapproving eyebrow raised.

"I'm sorry," Kali said again, finally getting herself under control. She leaned in toward her friend and whispered, "But you know what, if Micah was serious about that, then I think we can trust Matt with just about anything around here. Micah has a lot of respect for you, Kelly. He values you every bit as much as Sam did. I think he's always seen you as the little sister he never had. He's been worried about you. He would never make a suggestion like that unless he had the utmost respect for the man in question. I mean it."

Kelly's eyes were reddening again. "He really feels that way about me?"

"Yes. …Kelly, he and Sam have always both loved you, far more than I think you realize. He feels like he abandoned both of us. The whole time I was out there, he was afraid we'd left you with too much, especially after Brandon pulled his little stunt. Kelly, I'm glad you showed me that text because that pretty much settles it in my mind. If Micah trusts Matt that much, then I think we should give him a chance."

Kelly smiled. "I agree."

"But, Kelly, be honest with me, how *do* you feel about Matt? I mean, is Micah on target? Do you love him?"

Kelly blushed and looked away sheepishly. "I don't think this is the time for that conversation."

Kali let out a soft squeal and threw her arms around her friend. "Oh, Kelly! I'm so happy for you. So happy." She sat back and took in her embarrassed friend. "I'm so grateful for you, Kelly, and now I'm so happy for you. ...But I suppose we should get back to business, shouldn't we?"

"With all the giggles and squealing, they probably think we're a couple of schoolgirls in here crooning over some guy...Kali." The accusation behind Kali's name couldn't be missed, but the woman waved it off.

"Oh, don't be that way. I doubt they heard a thing."

"How could they not? They're standing right outside the door."

"I'm sorry if I embarrassed you, but, Kelly, I really am happy for you. So very, very happy."

They called the men back into the room and waited for them to settle back into their seats. Then Kali began in her most professional voice.

"We've reached a decision. Matt, we've decided to give you a chance. Mr. Truman's plan seems like a good one, and it will provide an opportunity to ease into the new situation. I don't foresee any problems, but I want you to feel that you can be entirely open and honest with us about anything. If you think things aren't working, please tell us. And understand that we will do the same.

"Now, I know Mr. Marsh plans to keep you on to some extent at least for a while. Do you already have a plan for how that will work, or is that something we need to hash out?"

"We have a suggested plan for you," Marsh began, "but it is certainly open for change. Here, I have it in my briefcase."

As the man dug for the document in his bag, Kelly's eyes drifted to her bus friend in the seat next to him. Matt smiled at her and then looked down at the phone in his hands. She saw him type something into it but was surprised to feel her own phone vibrate in her lap a moment later. She picked it up and read the text on the screen.

"Are we still on for lunch?"

She smiled at him from across the table and responded with a simple, *"Yes."*

CHAPTER 49

Matt's face lit up as his friend walked through the door of the airy sandwich shop. He watched as she glanced around the bright room and waved when she finally looked in his direction. Her eyes smiled at the sight of him, and she picked up her pace, allowing her heavy, ever-present bag to drop from her shoulder as she made her way across the room.

"Have you been waiting long?" She asked as she slid into the booth.

"No. I've only been here about five minutes."

"Oh, good. I was afraid I'd kept you waiting much longer than that. Today has certainly been the day of the unexpected."

Matt grinned, but she waved away his assumption that she was referring to the events surrounding the meeting. "Oh, I'm not just talking about that. Did you know I started the day with a broken shuttle car, a tow truck, and a volunteer mechanic?"

Surprise crossed Matt's face. "No. I didn't know that."

"And did you further know that after the meeting, I chased a guinea pig around the office, squeezed a house load of stuff into a hatchback, and fished a shirt out of a toilet?"

"What!" Matt couldn't contain the snort that escaped him. His head swung back and forth as he considered the strange life of the kind, brave brunette across from him. She possessed a beauty few women could boast. It wasn't in the rose of her cheeks or in her soft, brown eyes. It came up from her heart and shone out of those eyes like a beacon of hope.

"How in the world did you manage all of that in the last forty-five minutes?"

"It's a long story. But perhaps not so long as the one I came to hear. You lied to me last night."

Matt sobered instantly at those words. His blue eyes filled with sad disappointment, not in her but in himself. He had tried to fix things, tried to help her see that he hadn't meant to hide things that would hurt her or the center. Now, it appeared he had failed.

She leaned forward, resting her arms on the table and squaring her gaze up to his. A smile lifted the corners of her mouth and slipped up into her eyes. "You told me your life isn't interesting, but I don't think that's true at all."

Matt let out an enormous, pent up sigh of relief.

Kelly sat back, laughing as the color came back into her friend's face.

"You scared me for a minute there," he admitted.

"You deserve it. I don't know how you kept all that up for so long."

"I don't know how you didn't figure me out. I was so afraid I was going to 'blow my cover' so to speak and end up either ruining our friendship or completely destroying my ability to do what I'd been doing before I met you."

"See, that right there. How can you go around playing community spy and helping who knows how many people and still insist your life is uninteresting? Tell me about all that. How does it work?"

"Don't you think we should order our food first?"

Kelly's mouth scrunched up to one side. "I suppose, but don't think you're going to get out of telling that easily. We had an agreement. We're here to find out the truth about each other, and you, in particular, have been hiding a great deal."

"Oh, no. You're not going to get away with that," Matt blurted out indignantly.

"With what?"

"It so happens that when I talked to one Micah Thompson, he told me some things you've been keeping to yourself."

"What! Like what? I haven't been hiding anything."

"Well," Matt paused, looking down at the table and straightening the paper placemat in front of him. A moment later, he looked back, determination filling his eyes as their gazes met. "When was the last time you saw your family?"

Kelly's shoulders drooped instantly. Her smile slid away, and she bit her lip. "A while ago."

"How long?"

"Almost two years."

"Kelly, why?"

She shrugged. "Finances mostly. Mom and Dad usually come up here in the summer, but last year they couldn't come."

"Are they coming this summer?"

"I don't know."

"Have you told them what's been going on here?"

"Yes. ...Well, some of it. I haven't told them everything. I mean...I haven't told them a lot of things. I didn't want them to worry."

"So, who have you talked to over the last few months when things have been so rough? Do you and Kali talk things through? Do you have friends at church? Who do you talk to?"

Tears pooled in Kelly's eyes, but she held them in check. For a moment, only their gaze and the soft music in the shop hung between them. Then she whispered, "You, Matt. I talk to you."

Matt stared. He hadn't expected that response.

"Don't you see, Matt?"

"See what?"

"Remember that morning we met?"

"Yes."

"Do you remember our conversation? I know you do because you said something about it in the meeting today."

"I remember."

"Do you remember telling me that your mother used to say inconveniences, like my car breaking down, may very well be God's mercies; that He might just be protecting us from something much worse?

"Yes, I remember that."

"You were right. If I had driven to work that day, or any other day since, I would have missed one of the greatest, truest friendships

I have ever had and during the most difficult time of my life to boot. God's mercy was allowing my car to break down so I would meet you—so I wouldn't have to go through this alone. I know He sent you into my life. It wasn't an accident. You were ready and willing for God to use you, and He did."

Again, Matt stared.

"I don't think I've been a good friend in return, Matt. I've let you carry the load. I want you to know that's going to change. You have chosen to stick your neck out and fight for us, and I'm going to do everything I can to help make it a success. Please, if there's anything I can do to help, let me know. ...I hope I haven't embarrassed you."

"No. I just...I didn't expect you to say that, any of it. Micah told me you didn't have many friends outside of the center, and I know that not only has the staff dwindled but your responsibilities have also increased. I was afraid you had no time and no one to talk to. ...I didn't expect..." his voice trailed off and his gaze dropped to the table. The idea that God would use him that way in her life humbled him.

"That's what has made your friendship so meaningful, Matt. You didn't see yourself as anyone special. You just...you loved the way a friend should love, even though you didn't know me."

He met her gaze with new passion. "And you trusted the way a friend should trust, even though you didn't know me. Thank you."

Kelly patted his hand and then slid to the edge of her seat. "Come on. Let's get our food before they throw us out of here."

"Wait." Matt reached across the table, his hand coming to rest on her arm. "We need to finish the topic we started."

"What do you mean?"

"About you seeing your family. Are you going home anytime soon?"

Kelly smiled at Matt's concern, but a hint of patient forbearance had come into her eyes. "Matt, I *am* home. This is where I live. It's where I grew up."

"But are you going to see your parents anytime soon?"

Kelly had known what he meant. Now, that became evident in the shadows that crept into her eyes. "Probably not. They usually come up around the fourth of July."

"And you're not sure they're going to make it this year?"

"I guess we haven't really talked about it yet. Last year, they couldn't come because Dad broke his foot and had to have surgery. I'm sure they're probably planning on coming. At least I hope so."

"Why don't you invite them to come up for Mother's Day?"

"For Mother's Day?" Kelly's voice cracked. Where had this idea come from?

"Yeah. In fact, why not have them come up for Mother's Day and stay through the summer?"

"That would be wonderful, but I don't think it would work."

"Do you have room for them to stay with you? If not, I'm sure we could work something out somewhere else."

"I have an extra room, so that's not a problem. I guess that just seems like something you hope for, but that never actually happens."

"Does your dad still work, or is he retired?"

"He still works, but he's a teacher, so he's fairly free in the summer."

"What about your mom?"

"She works from home." Kelly chuckled at the thought of her mother. "She usually brings half of her office with her."

"When does school get out for your dad?"

"I don't know for sure. Probably not until the first week of June."

Matt frowned. He leaned back, pulling his hand away from her and drumming his fingers on the table.

"It's okay, Matt. I really will survive until July. I appreciate your concern, but you're letting it get to you too much."

"No, there's something else," he said, trying to assume a relaxed appearance, but Kelly saw through it.

"What aren't you telling me?" She questioned suspiciously.

For a moment, Matt considered rushing to the counter to order their food so he could force the conversation to an end. But one glance into her sincere eyes drove that thought away.

"Kelly, you were right. I'm going to need your help to get my feet under me over the next few months."

"But what does that have to do with me seeing my parents?"

"I was just hoping you'd be willing to stick around and help me for more than a few months."

"What? I'm not planning on going anywhere, Matt. If anything, Mom and Dad will come here. And I'm certainly not planning to work anywhere else. I love the work at the center."

"I know you do, and that's why ...that's why I was hoping we could...I mean...that you'd stick around permanently."

An expression of utter confusion covered Kelly's face. She leaned back in exasperation. "I don't understand. I am permanent. I've never been a temporary or even a part-time employee at the center. ...Are you planning to let people go? Who would you let go? There's hardly anyone left!"

"No! Not at all. No. This has nothing to do with the center or anyone but you and me—us." He groaned and gnawed at the corner of his mouth. His cheeks reddened, and he looked down, running his hands through his hair and muttering to himself, "I am *so bad* at this."

At that, Kelly's eyes widened. "Matthew Marsh," she gasped, the words catching in her throat, "is this a proposal?"

Matt's head jerked up, his blue eyes now wider than hers. "NO. No...I mean...No. It's the hope that someday soon there might be a proposal, and that in the meantime I might get to know you a little better and you might get to know me a little better, and I might get to know your family...and that you won't go away. That's all."

By the time he had finished, Kelly's eyes had filled with tears. Her bottom lip caught in her teeth. He laid his hand on her arm again, this time leaning forward ever so slightly and whispering, "Will you let me do that, Kelly?"

She smiled a faint, girlish smile, the movement pushing a single tear down her cheek.

"Yes."

He sighed deeply, and Kelly couldn't help but laugh.

"I talked to your dad last night," he said cautiously. "Micah sent the number. He seems to have a plan, that guy. Anyway, I told your dad everything. I told him about the bus and about being M&Ms and about our conversations and how close we've become and how much I admire your courage and tender spirit. And...I told him I love you. I asked for permission to actually date you, and he granted it. Kelly, I really do love you. I've gone for thirty-six years without even considering marriage. I didn't date or look for relationships. I just did what was in front of me. But you have changed all of that. …I love you."

"I've been longing to hear those words for weeks, but I don't think I fully realized it until this morning. …I love you, too." She smiled, wiped her eyes, and stood, holding a hand out to him. "We'd better get our lunch ordered if we have any intention of getting back to work today."

Matt chuckled and followed her example, taking her hand and moving toward the counter. As they stepped into line, he stopped her.

"What if it had been a proposal?" he whispered. "What would you have said?"

Kelly considered him for a moment, noticing for the first time a tiny scar under his right eye. Where had it come from? There was so much she still didn't know about him, and yet, in her heart, she knew the one most important thing.

"I would have said yes."

His eyes lit up. "I don't have a ring."

"Why would I need a ring if I have you?"

He contemplated the idea. He could see in her eyes that she had no doubts. They had both waited a very long time for the right person, and they both knew they'd found what they'd been waiting for. He took a deep breath, smiled, and opened his mouth to ask that all important question. Then, just before it slipped from his tongue, he stopped himself. He clapped his mouth shut and shook his head emphatically.

"No. I'm not going to ask yet. I love you too much to rush into it. I'm going to do this the right way. I promised your dad I would, and I intend to keep that promise. But we need to get them up here as soon as possible."

Kelly laughed. "That will win major points with my dad, Matthew Marsh. Whether you ask now or four months from now, with decisions like that one, he'll have us married by the end of the year."

Matt's eyes twinkled. "That's definitely what I'm hoping for."

They turned back to the line in front of them, her hand still gripped in his. Matt struggled to turn his thoughts to the menu board. He'd been so nervous during the meeting that he hadn't touched any of the food they'd provided. Now, he was starving, but his brain was so excited for the future he could hardly focus on what was written on the board.

"I think I could eat everything on the menu," he commented.

"I noticed you didn't seem interested in the food at the meeting."

"I was too nervous."

"You didn't seem nervous. ...Well, maybe a couple times. But mostly, you seemed completely convinced you were doing what you were supposed to be doing. In fact, you seemed confident."

"I was confident about almost everything. I spent hours praying about it. And Micah—that guy had me so convinced I was doing the right thing. It was all I could do to keep myself from walking in there and saying, 'Let's do this!' I know this is the direction the Lord is leading. I know it's not going to be easy. My whole life is about to change. But I know it's right."

"So, what weren't you sure about?"

Matt shoved his free hand into his pocket, the nervousness returning. "How you and Kali would respond. Kelly, I have to say this. I never meant anything but good for you and the center. I never meant to do anything more than meet the need set in front of me. And that's what I did, but then all of a sudden *this* was in front of me, and I knew. I knew I couldn't take the easy way out and let you and Kali keep fighting alone. I couldn't do it. God wouldn't let me. My own heart wouldn't let me. I hope you both know I never meant anything but good. And I certainly never wanted to deceive you. That's why I was so eager to talk to you last night."

"I know, Matt, and I'm pretty sure Micah and I have Kali convinced of that by now too. You're okay. None of us hold anything against you."

He smiled his gratitude and turned toward the young man waiting behind the counter.

Kelly thought about what Matt had said as he stepped up to place his order. She wasn't sure what he'd ordered, but she ordered the same. As they waited for their food to come out, they stepped aside and leaned quietly against the condiment station. Neither said anything until they had returned to the table with their food. Matt prayed over their meal, and then Kelly watched as he dove into his sandwich. She wondered if he'd already forgotten what they'd been talking about. Still, she felt the need to reassure him.

"Can I tell you something?" she ventured.

"Sure," he said, licking mayonnaise from his fingers.

"The day I had to ask Brandon to leave just about did me in. I went home, changed into some comfy clothes, lay down on the sofa, and cried for an hour. Then I sat in the dark with my laptop and just scrolled. I didn't even really know what I was looking at. I just scrolled through screen after screen of social media posts. Then I realized I was hungry, so I did the only thing you can do in such a moment: I ate chocolate."

Matt laughed, but he was too involved with his food and too interested in the rest of the story to say anything.

She continued, "Then I sat down with a cup of tea and started writing. I wrote about chivalry, about how it seems to be lost, about how just as it seems to be showing its head it turns out to be a mere shadow, the appearance but not the real thing. I was sure the world was completely devoid of knights in shining armor. No one, from my point of view, was willing to fight for anyone or anything unless it was for their own advancement. Chivalry, it seemed, had just become a cloak for opportunism and self-serving—and that's not chivalry at all.

"When we had lunch together on Sunday, I was reminded that Moses had been a man of chivalry, and Sam had learned it from him. It encouraged me to hope that perhaps there was still just one man out there who would be willing to fight. I dared to hope someone would follow in their steps, just like they had followed Jesus—and then you walked into our conference room."

She paused and began searching the depths of her enormous red bag. "I brought you something. I made it for you Monday, but I didn't quite have it finished until last night. I'm glad I didn't because I think it's more appropriate now."

Matt watched her with curiosity. She pulled out a square object wrapped in white tissue paper and passed it to him. He wiped his hands on a napkin. Without a word, he unfolded the paper, uncovering the back side of a picture frame. He turned the frame over, revealing a picture of two men. One of them, he quickly recognized as Sam.

The other, who stood with an arm draped across Sam's shoulders and an enormous grin lighting up his face, he assumed was Moses. Beneath the picture were the words,

"Fight the fight. Finish the course. Keep the faith."

He looked up at her, amazed.

She smiled a misty smile back at him. "I showed it to Kali before I came here. We both agreed it was the right time to give it to you. Sort of like passing the torch. I don't think either of us have any doubts. You're the one God has prepared for the center. You're the real deal, Matt. There are no shadows of chivalry with you. To be honest, if Sam could have chosen his own replacement...I think it would have been you. And I know he would have chosen you for me, just like his brother."

Matt couldn't seem to absorb all she was saying. It was far more than he had expected. He studied the photo, tracing the outline of the two men with his finger.

"You know," he said at last, "in a way, even though he didn't choose me, it was Sam who got me to this place. His life challenged me so much. I couldn't stop until I had found out what was different about him, what had motivated him."

"What did you find?"

Matt popped a pickle slice into his mouth. Then he shrugged as if the answer was simple and obvious.

"He understood that love looks like the life Christ led and laid down. He cared more about the lives around him than his own. He was willing to fight for them, willing to fight for every soul that crossed his path, just like his friend, Moses. He did it wisely, and sometimes that meant setting up boundaries and limitations, but he was always willing to fight for those who couldn't fight for themselves. As you said, Sam was chivalrous."

Kelly smiled. "I know you don't see it, Matt, but you already had what it took. God and Sam just polished your armor up a bit."

Matt laughed. He'd never really thought of himself as a knight, but now he realized he was willing to take up the challenge. Not in his own strength, but in the strength He knew the Lord would provide. He smiled at Kelly, for the first time allowing himself to truly bask in the love that had grown between them. A new gratitude for broken down cars and faithful city buses overwhelmed him. He reached across the table and took her hand once more.

"And then there was you," he said softly, "my damsel in distress. The girl who taught me the meaning of love and grace and courage. I know this is the fight God has called me to, and I'm so grateful—so amazed—that I get to go into the battle *with you.*"

AUTHOR'S NOTE

Shadows of Chivalry was an unplanned book. My best friend had encouraged me to take part in National Novel Writing Month (NaNoWriMo), a writing challenge in which writers attempt to complete a 50,000-word novel in the 30 days of November. Crazy, right? I wanted to join her, but I had no plan.

Three days into the month, a thought flitted through my head while I was washing dishes. In that moment, the characters and story were born. By the end of the month, I had those 50,000 words and a few more. But it has taken years to get the book to the point of publishing. Some delays were caused by the rewriting and editing process, others were because of unexpected life events, and sometimes it was because of my own misgivings. But this is a book about courage, so it couldn't stay hidden away.

Shadows of Chivalry is fiction. Plain and simple. But the conflicts in the story ring true to life. Having grown up in ministry as a child and worked in it as an adult for more than 25 years, I have seen these types of conflicts firsthand—around the globe. They are not unique to any one place, any one setting, any one circumstance, or any one people. And yet, as Paul said to the Corinthians, I believe there is "a more excellent way."

My prayer is that this book will reveal that, while shadows abound in both pulpit and pew, chivalry is present there too. I hope it will inspire us to put on the armor God has provided. I hope that, whether preacher or Sunday School teacher, musician or janitor, in

321

the trenches or behind the lines on our knees, our hearts will seek to do the right thing, to fight the good fight, to finish our course, and to keep the faith. I pray that we will each choose to follow the more excellent way God has set before us — because people and God's work are always worth fighting for.

SCRIPTURE USED IN
SHADOWS OF CHIVALRY

Chapters 1, 4, 5 and 49
"In every thing give thanks: for this is the will of God in Christ Jesus concerning you." 1 Thessalonians 5:18

Chapter 36
"Take therefore no thought for the morrow: for the morrow shall take thought for the things of itself. Sufficient unto the day is the evil thereof." Matthew 6:34

Chapter 38
"Give unto the LORD, o ye mighty, give unto the LORD glory and strength." Psalm 29:1
"The LORD will give strength unto His people; the LORD will bless His people with peace." Psalm 29:11

Chapter 41
"I beseech you therefore, brethren, by the mercies of God, that ye present your bodies a living sacrifice, holy, acceptable unto God, which is your reasonable service. And be not conformed to this world: but be ye transformed by the renewing of your mind, that ye may prove what is that good, and acceptable, and perfect, will of God." Romans 12:1-2

"Rejoice with them that do rejoice, and weep with them that weep." Romans 12:15

"We then that are strong ought to bear the infirmities of the weak, and not to please ourselves." Romans 15:1

"I have fought a good fight, I have finished my course, I have kept the faith." 2 Timothy 4:7

"Beloved, when I gave all diligence to write unto you for the common salvation, it was needful for me to write unto you, and exhort you that ye should *earnestly contend for the faith* which was once delivered unto the saints." Jude 3

OH, LOVE THAT WILL NOT LET ME GO

By George Matheson

O Love, that will not let me go,
I rest my weary soul in thee;
I give thee back the life I owe,
That in thine ocean depths its flow
May richer, fuller be.

O Light, that followest all my way,
I yield my flickering torch to Thee;
My heart restores its borrowed ray,
That in Thy sunshine's blaze its day
May brighter, fairer be.

O Joy, that followest me through pain,
I cannot close my heart to Thee;
I trace the rainbow through the rain,
And feel the promise is not vain,
That morn shall tearless be.

O Cross, that liftest up my head,
I dare not ask to fly from thee;
I lay in dust life's glory dead,
And from the ground there blossoms red
Life that shall endless be.

As noted in the scene between Matt and Kelly at the restaurant, various versions of the story surrounding this hymn exist. Some make no mention of Matheson's fiancé. Many imply that she left him on or shortly before his sister's wedding day. Still others say that the jilting took place twenty years earlier and was merely brought to mind on that raw day when his sister, the woman who had cared for him and made it possible for him to stay in the ministry though losing his sight, married.

Whatever the exact details, we know this: Matheson wrote this hymn in a moment of deep turmoil—in a mere five minutes. He never edited it. In that moment of darkness, he took hold of the Love that had taken hold of him long before. He clung to it as a man dangling over a great precipice clings to a rope. And there, he found joy and peace. So too may we cling to that Love—the Love that will not let us go.

For more information visit:

www.hymnal.net

https://www.thegospelcoalition.org/blogs/justin-taylo
r/o-love-that-will-not-let-me-go

https://www.umcdiscipleship.org/resources/
history-of-hymns-o-love-that-will-not-let-me-go

www.hymnary.org

ABOUT THE AUTHOR

Rachel Miller is an author, speaker, and coach who helps individuals, groups, and churches uncover the joy of living with courageous faith, compassion, and the love of Christ; discovering the power not only of doing the right thing but also of doing the thing right in front of us.

At nineteen, filled with fear and excitement, Rachel stepped onto Russian soil for the first time. How could she, a homeschooled girl from Montana, make a difference in that former Soviet land? Did God really expect her—the wallflower—to be bold? Ten years later, she returned to the States, a testament to the transforming power of a life surrendered to God and a walk of faith.

Rachel has been involved in ministry for more than two decades. She has had the joy of serving both in her hometown and in various countries around the world. She is also the founder of Forbid Them

Not Ministries, which works with orphans, single moms, and those walking alongside them.

Rachel is the proud aunt of 10 nieces and nephews. When not writing or involved in ministry, you can find her working in her lavender garden, adventuring around her home state, or enjoying a cup of tea!

Connect with Rachel, her books, and ministry at the links below:

To inquire about speaking or consulting:
Please write to: rmiller@rachelmillerwriter.com

Books and Blogs:
Facebook:
Autor Page - https://www.facebook.com/rmillerwriter/
Shadows of Chivalry Group –
https://www.facebook.com/groups/462858440812091/
Instagram: @rachelmillerwriter
Author Blog: http://www.rachelmillerwriter.com/
ChaiNook Online: https://chainook.rachelmillerwriter.com/

Forbid Them Not Ministries:
Website: http://www.forbidthemnot.com/
Facebook: https://www.facebook.com/forbidthemnot/
Twitter: @forbidthemnot

MEET ME AT THE CHAINOOK

While we can't join Matt and Kelly at the ChaiNook, you're invited to the next best thing—the ChaiNook online!

At the ChaiNook, you'll discover:

- Encouraging resources focused on Chivalry, Courage, and Compassion,
- Inspiration as you and others share real stories of courage and chivalry,
- A passionate community, pursuing chivalry and courageous faith,
- The specialty tea and book shop, which gives a portion of every purchase to organizations working with at-risk youth and those walking alongside them,
- Learning opportunities through the ChaiNook Academy.

Let's walk courageously and change lives together! Join the community today!
https://chainook.rachelmillerwriter.com

LEAVING THE SHADOWS

A Companion Study Guide To
Shadows of Chivalry

You've longed for a life of meaning, but where do you start?

In *Leaving the Shadows*, you'll discover how to begin a journey of courage and compassion. Rachel Miller walks you through the lessons of her own falling apart moments. She shares the questions, struggles, and soul-searching she faced while writing Matt and Kelly's story in *Shadows of Chivalry*. More importantly, Rachel shares the answers she found to those quandaries.

This companion study challenges you to apply what you're learning through simple, life-changing exercises. The topics covered in this study include:

- Understanding what chivalry is and why we need it today,
- The components of chivalry,
- Choosing the right battles in the face of need,
- Finding simple solutions to the needs around you,
- A Simple approach to building chivalry into everyday life.

Perfect for individuals and small groups! If you long to make a difference, to live with hope, faith, and courage, *Leaving the Shadows* is the place to begin.

OTHER BOOKS
BY RACHEL MILLER

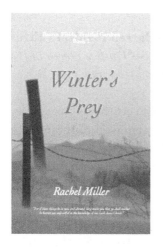

Winter's Prey (Barren Fields, Fruitful Gardens, Book 1) - When the cruel elements of the Montana Territory inflict tragedy on the Bennett family, life is forever changed. Jess is certain the answer to her pain lies in starting over. Her brother Marc is determined to stay true to what he has always known.

Amidst the constant battle for survival and the conflict in their hearts, both siblings stand at the threshold of surrender to God. What will they choose?

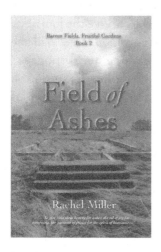

Field of Ashes (Barren Fields, Fruitful Gardens, Book 2) - After losing her fiancé to the wild elements of the Montana Territory, Jessica Bennett is sure the key to her happiness is in leaving Twin Pines. But from the moment she steps foot in the untamed, cowtown of Grassdale, Jess discovers a whole new world of challenges: An unruly superintendent, a ramshackle school, drunken cowboys, and a letter from home that changes everything. When the hidden wounds of her heart are discovered, will one man's secret past hold the key to her healing?

Easy has never been the path Marcus Bennett sought, but as summer unfolds, he comes face to face with the one struggle he has avoided for years. When life takes an unexpected turn, he finds himself torn between his responsibilities, his love for his family, and the promptings of his heart. Would God really ask him to abandon his home and family?

This sequel to *Winter's Prey* explores the beauty of God's amazing grace and astounding love, the freedom of surrender, and the hope of experience, though faith be tried by fire.

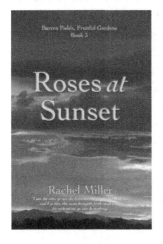

Roses at Sunset (Barren Fields, Fruitful Gardens, Book 3) - *"Faith is proven in the storm not in the calm."* — Anna Close, Roses at Sunset

Jessica Bennett returns to Grassdale, finding joy in her renewed faith and life at the Crescent Creek Ranch. Clues begin to surface in the mystery of the wildfire that destroyed the school, putting Scotch Jorgenson in the middle of it all. When Wesley Close announces a trip across the wilderness during winter's coldest months, new questions and fears arise. Has Wes discovered something new about the fire? Will he survive the journey? The true depth of Jessica's surrender faces an enormous test. Will she choose to trust? And what about the man watching her responses?

When Marcus Bennett chooses to step out in the direction the Lord is leading, he expects to see God provide. But the days of waiting prove longer than anticipated. As Papa's health declines and the family's needs grow, will Marc keep his eyes on the Lord? Or will he disappear into the storm raging in his heart?

This sequel to Field of Ashes explores the peace found in Christ, the consolation of the God who never leaves us comfortless, and the fruit of a heart well-tended.

NEW! (Barren Fields, Fruitful Gardens: The Story Begins, 3-in-1 Bundle) – *Get the first three BFFG books in one! Available only on Kindle.*

The King's Daughter: A Story of Redemption (Bible Study) –

Abandoned. Left to die. Rescued. Redeemed. ...Adoption. Betrayal. Unfailing love.

The King's Daughter: A Story of Redemption traces one of the most beautiful love stories of all time. This collection of short Bible studies searches out the life of the King's Daughter, a familiar figure of Psalm 45.

Though often lifted up as an example to Christian women, her full story is rarely told. Has she always been the most beautiful ornament in the King's throne room? Will she remain so? Will she turn her back on the One who loved her more than any other, or will she let Him be as a bundle of myrrh about her neck? From a field to a palace, from disgrace to glory, from shame to restoration: her story reveals not only the magnitude of our redemption but also the chastening hand of a loving Father and the beauty of His everlasting covenant.

In All Thy Ways (Devotional Journal) - Some journals will feed you, find verses for you, and even pray for you—What's left for you to do? God wants us to dig into His Word for ourselves. *"In All Thy Ways"* offers eight weeks of journaling pages, each designed to help you dig deeper into Scripture. It asks simple questions that bring depth to your daily Bible reading and application to life. It also provides room for word studies, prayer, praise, and for recording God's working in and through you. Don't let someone else chew your food for you. Dig in and dig deep!

In All Thy Ways: Walking in His Promises (Devotional Journal) - Has your world spun out of control? Are you looking for something to grab onto—something that never moves, never changes? Are you looking for hope as you seek direction, or the strength simply to survive?

God's promises offer unfading light in the darkness. The *Walking in His Promises Journal* presents the opportunity to step out of the storm and into the safety of His presence. Like its predecessor, the journal provides eight weeks of journaling pages—56 verses of promise and assurance. Enter the world into which those promises were spoken through contextual readings, cross-referencing, prayer, praise, and simple questions designed to bring depth to your study and application to your life. Don't remain unanchored in a world spinning out of control. Take hold of His promises and rejoice as you record His unfolding plans for you.

Made in the USA
Middletown, DE
28 September 2021